# FRAGMENTS

Sarah Foot grew up in North London. She was a prize winner of the *Vogue* talent contest and then worked at *Vogue*, before moving to the *Daily Telegraph* and subsequently editing Irish *Tatler* in Dublin. She now lives in Suffolk.

# SARAH FOOT

# FRAGMENTS

Quercus

First published in Great Britain in 2015 by Quercus Publishing Ltd
This paperback edition published in 2016 by

Quercus Publishing Ltd
Carmelite House
50 Victoria Embankment
London EC4Y 0DZ

An Hachette UK company

A CIP catalogue record for this book is available
from the British Library

PB ISBN 978 1 84866 501 9
EBOOK ISBN 978 1 78429 461 8

10 9 8 7 6 5 4 3 2 1

Typeset by Jouve (UK) Milton Keynes

Printed and bound in Great Britain by Clays Ltd, St Ives plc

Gather up the fragments that remain, that nothing be lost.

John, chapter 6, verse 12

# Prologue

All night it had been snowing and for one lovely hour the graveyard was quite transfigured. But now a muddy thaw had set in. Piles of icy slush melted over the gravel path and, having raided the church's kitchen, the curate was hurling handfuls of table salt before the feet of the elegant mourners slithering past the tombstones.

Passers-by heading off to work in the London rush hour paused a moment to watch at the wrought-iron gates as the gilded and the gifted stepped out of taxis in their sombre suits. These were men and women in touch with life at its most rich and delicious. Yet today they hesitated, flicking at the snow on the yew hedge, not knowing what to say, exchanging platitudes.

'What a loss.'

'So sudden.'

'Far too young.'

'And just before Christmas.'

'God knows what the family are feeling.'

But they did not linger. The weather was too cold, the sky too ominous. They hugged themselves and one another. Then, as the harsh wind whipped their faces, they hurried inside while a lone seagull screeched and wheeled round the bell tower, its cries intermingling with the strains of the Brahms Requiem from the organ loft.

'May I sit here?'

'Is there room?'

'Would you mind . . .?'

People shifted themselves, moved over, tried not to stumble on sodden, freezing feet. Normally, at this time, these mourners were on their way to boardrooms and courtrooms, to artists' studios and newspaper offices, certainly not in church at this ungodly hour. But it had been the only slot available. The vicar had made special arrangements to fit the funeral in first thing on December 23rd. Otherwise the family would have had to wait until the New Year, which everyone agreed would be dreadful. A few strings had been pulled, though nobody would be unkind enough to say so. Indeed, almost every one of those now taking their places on the Georgian pews would have done the same. This was a congregation who prided themselves on having the strength and intelligence to transform circumstance, the ability to take control. Not that they had all been born to this life. Far from it. Most had known the good and the bad. But what distinguished them was that they were, by and large, unconquered.

But their courage and brilliance were useless now. And for this moment, at least, they remembered it. No power on earth could alter the reality of that coffin standing starkly before the altar.

'I can't believe it.'

'What a tragedy.'

'Always so good.'

'So good' seemed to echo around the stone pillars because, in an irony not lost on any of those reading through the service sheet, they all knew that if it had not been for an act of goodness by their 'dearly departed' friend they would not be sitting here. There would have been no untimely death.

The place was filling up quickly, though few were regular churchgoers. The scent of damp flowers had, to some, the odour of self-righteousness. The colossal Christmas tree, laden with trumpeting angels, seemed a Sunday School banality. If there was light in the darkness from this death, they did not expect to find it today.

Nonetheless, here they were, with red and puffy eyes, sitting under the gaze of Christ, his bleeding arms nailed apart at the altar, and the ritual of death was on its way. The organ music climbed to a crescendo and everyone stood as the vicar, step by slow step, made his way up the aisle to the coffin covered in creamy white narcissi.

In his deep, educated voice, he began: '*I am the resurrection and the life, saith the Lord. He that believeth in me, though he were dead, yet shall he live . . .'*

Such beautiful, hopeful words.

*'And whosoever liveth and believeth in me shall never die . . .'*

Even this collection of sceptics could not be unmoved. But it was not so much death that frightened them – at least, not only that. At four in the morning, stumbling through shadows, their fear was of failure, of work unfinished. Very few here had really known what it was not to succeed. But the idea that all your efforts would, in the end, prove pointless, that was what was truly terrifying. And now in this fashionable and famous church they were being asked to meekly kneel and pray.

There was somewhat too much fidgeting among a congregation unused to surrendering their ego to anyone, even God. Not sure whether to bend right down on the kneelers or simply lean forward, a few balanced half-on, half-off the pew as the vicar led the prayer.

*'Grant us, Lord, the wisdom and the grace to use aright the time that is left to us on earth.'*

Certainly, among the bowed heads, many had used their time aright to become 'good' lawyers, 'good' architects, 'good' doctors, 'good' artists, 'good' journalists. But good husbands and wives? Good mothers and fathers? Good men and women? Whatever that was supposed to mean.

Most of the time they could persuade themselves they were as good as the next man. Actually, a fair number suspected they might be rather better. They were a crowd who passionately defended the rights of others, knew inside out the arguments over self-fulfilment versus self-sacrifice and could be all too articulate on the subject. But under the chill regard of the marble effigies, their self-belief faltered.

*'Lead us to repent of our sins, the evil we have done and the good we have not done . . . And lead us to the fullness of eternal life, through Jesus Christ our Lord.'*

Yet few here wanted to wait for eternal life. They wanted life here and now. And as soon as the funeral ended most would return to it, heading straight off to their desks, soon to have lunch, engage in the pleasure and effort of work and competition, race to Christmas parties, return home loving and hating their families, then begin again the next day. They would move on, trying to put the thought of the good they had not done to one side, and most of the time succeeding.

But not all.

A stifled sob rose from the front pew where the bereaved family were sitting, and everyone's heads dropped yet lower. For the family it would be another story. As the next of kin knew only too well, staring face down into the embroidered kneeler, reading the cross stitch as if it was a judgement: '*For whatsoever a man soweth, that shall he also reap.*'

If I had acted differently, acted better, if my love had been more kind, more patient, would I be in such hell? Is this intolerable loss also my own fault?

And here, where there was no place to hide among the unresisting walls, the answer seemed to be a resounding yes! Yes! And in the anarchy of grief and guilt it felt as if everyone was rising to their feet in condemnation. Even the organ seemed to be striking up in agreement, though it was only to herald the first hymn.

'The Lord is my shepherd, I shall not want . . .'

With graceful, lucid voices the choir led the way.

Oblivious to their beauty, and standing near the back of the church, was another in the congregation who had also loved the 'dearly departed' both body and soul. With face white and jaw set hard, trying to hide the pain within, this mourner could hear nothing but echoes of the vicar's injunction 'to repent of our sins' with full biblical force. On almost every spare slab of stone were elaborately carved epitaphs hammering home reminders of trembling sinners, redeemed sinners, sinners who had risen. But what was sin? There had been sin in the last days of this life they were here today to mourn. Because it was a sin – wasn't it? – to betray one's marriage vows. The joy of life was found in keeping your word, in doing your duty, in acceptance. Wasn't it?

But what if your sin has also proved to be your saving grace? What then? Because there was also the sin of negating your better self, the sin of wasting – through laziness, cowardice and blindness to the truth – all the gifts of God. Like the gift of this wonderful human being now lying lifeless in that dreadful box. Not so many days ago that glorious, glorious body had been so warm and tender, so supple and strong, rising and falling in loving arms. But now . . .

'Surely goodness and mercy shall follow me all the days of my life . . .'

Surely? The vicar's full, rounded tenor rang out with confidence as if he was saying, yes, as a matter of indubitable fact, goodness and mercy will follow you, most surely.

But among the mourners, there were those who only heard that 'surely' as a terrible, unresolved question. Because how, in the space of just four short weeks, could goodness and mercy have brought them here?

## I

It was a mild evening in late November and Julia Snowe steered her new car through the more prosperous districts of North London to her daughters' school. Julia was a good driver. She handled the powerful Cabriolet – as she had everything in her forty-five years – with authority and nerve. A cyclist swerved in front of her, a bus almost clipped her gleaming wing mirror. But Julia braked calmly and waited, tapping her long, slender fingers on the steering wheel.

These smart, tree-lined avenues were less than five miles from the ugly, overcrowded estate where Julia had grown up, in a tenth-floor flat around the corner from the bus station – still there, as far as she knew. Julia had not set foot near her childhood home in decades and had absolutely no intention of doing so. The less she saw of tower blocks and urine-soaked underpasses the better. The past, she recognized, may have made her, but her home now was this moneyed, self-confident world. And she adored it. She put her foot down and swung up the gravel drive to St Catherine's Girls' School, where her younger daughter, fifteen-year-old Rose, was performing a cello solo in the traditional Advent concert.

Julia was that rare thing – a true atheist – but she had worked hard to ensure her two girls were accepted by an exceptionally expensive school that made a point of nurturing the High Anglican beliefs of its early feminist founder. Julia had long rejected what she saw as her own mother's sentimental and self-denying brand of Methodism, but she maintained it was important for children to grow up with what she called a 'mythic structure'.

Looking for somewhere to park along the avenue of plane trees, she passed her husband Phillip's car. Since he had sold his advertising agency he had become zealous about his paternal duties and, she guessed, had probably been here for half an hour, making sure they had seats at the front of the hall, chatting to the teachers and other parents. But Julia was in no hurry. She found a space over by the music block, switched off the engine and eased back into the leather seat. She had left the office early after giving an interview to a new current affairs magazine on her work as a lawyer in the London practice of a leading American firm. Julia was used to trotting out quotable opinions about combining work and motherhood, glass ceilings and so on. But, almost as an afterthought, the young pretty journalist had asked her how happy she was on a scale of one to twenty.

Without a moment's hesitation, Julia had replied, 'Twenty . . . twenty out of twenty.' And it's the truth, she thought, checking her iPad. Twenty out of twenty.

Admittedly she wished that she had more time with Phillip who, despite no longer having a business to run, was working every bit as hard for whichever charity came knocking at his door, chairing the governors at a nearby state school, Hartley High, sitting on a prison board . . . Julia was losing track of all the good causes he was adopting, though he was also making a real effort to spend more time with their daughters. It was true, too, that Julia would also like to see more of the girls, though she could do without the constant battles she was having with Rose.

Julia grimaced. Rose's cello recital, she was in no doubt, was going to be excruciating. Last night Julia had insisted on hearing her perform the piece and would, if she still swore, have described her daughter's playing as 'bloody awful'. The trouble was, Rose was too bone idle to practise. There was no getting away from it. Julia, who had never been idle in her life, had, to her dismay and incomprehension, produced the most slothful creature she had ever encountered. But Rose was only fifteen. Her daughter's laziness was certainly not a real problem as Julia had once known real problems. She pressed her strong hands together. Twenty out of twenty, she repeated to herself, suddenly in love with life – or rather, *her* life and all that she had made of it.

She swung round to retrieve the half-dozen Fortnum & Mason

cakes she had sent her assistant to buy – parents had been asked to provide 'seasonal fare' to sell in the interval to raise funds for yet another
extension to the science block. Then she climbed out of the car.

'Julia!'

A slight, fair woman with a daughter in Rose's class came rushing
towards her, clutching a biscuit tin in her arms.

'Alex, how are you?' smiled Julia, knowing Alex would say she
was exhausted.

'Exhausted,' panted Alex.

'Oh dear,' said Julia. 'But you look well.'

'Really? I don't feel it. I just flew out of work. I thought I was
going to be so late.'

'No, we're in good time.'

'Yes, thank God,' said Alex with a deep sigh, as if it was the first
time all day she had had a moment to breathe. 'I'd hoped to leave
early to start on the Christmas shopping . . . but I've got so much
on . . . and to get my husband to do a thing . . .' She wiped her brow.
'Well, you know.'

Julia didn't, actually. One Sunday afternoon in October she and
Phillip had sat in front of the computer ordering off the Internet.
And that was the Christmas presents solved. But to Alex she just
said, 'I don't have as many presents to buy as you.'

Alex had four children and another on the way. Why Alex produced so many when she was perpetually exhausted was an utter
mystery to Julia. She could understand the one. You produce the
first child, and then think, blow this for a lark. But to keep on having
them when all you did was moan about how shattered you were
was, to Julia, downright stupid. Though Alex was far from stupid
and earned a fortune as a consultant obstetrician at a private fertility
clinic.

'But don't you have all the family extensions?' asked Alex. 'I seem
to have so many nieces and nephews and –'

'Alex!' interrupted another blonde, also out of breath, running up
to join them. At St Catherine's Julia always felt as if she had stumbled into a convention of white rabbits.

'Hi, Eleanor.'

'Oh God, I was so worried I was going to be late,' said Eleanor, looking at her watch. 'This stupid fool of a judge just went on and on. I thought he'd never finish his summing up. And I was late for the concert last year.'

'Me too,' said Alex, rolling her eyes. 'I came barging through right in the middle of the madrigal.'

'But Eleanor, have you met Julia Snowe?'

Julia would have shaken Eleanor's hand – if one hadn't been holding a briefcase and the other a baking tray.

'Julia, this is Eleanor Lennox whose twins are both here.'

There were a disproportionate number of twins at St Catherine's and, with a curiosity that rattled her, Julia would find herself wondering how many of them owed their existence to Alex's obstetric interventions.

'I see you've both brought your "seasonal fare",' groaned Eleanor. 'Though with the fees they charge, you wouldn't think we'd have to stump up food as well.'

Julia thought this the first sensible thing she had heard from either woman and laughed.

But Eleanor then asked, 'What did you make?'

Julia looked at her blankly as Alex replied, 'Christmas cake.'

'You made it yourself?' queried Julia.

'Yes,' Alex grimaced.

'But why?' asked Julia, genuinely interested to know why Alex had spent precious hours making something she could easily have picked up in two minutes from a shop.

'I think it's right, you know, to make the effort.'

'But when you've got so much on, you shouldn't bother,' said Julia. From an early age Julia had trained herself to look for solutions to problems, but in so doing had failed to appreciate the desire in others to moan. In the office, rather than listen to complaints, she would launch in with remedies and demolish most problems in five minutes. 'You should have just bought one.'

Alex pursed her lips in a way that Julia recognized from her work colleagues, as Eleanor asked, 'Did you remember to include a list of ingredients?'

'Oh God, no!' said Alex. 'And the note specifically told us to.'

Julia, normally impervious to mood swings, was suddenly depressed. She could not conceive of a safer world than the one she had provided for her own children. Yet in these over-anxious times it could be made to feel every bit as dangerous as the Hartley Estate where she had grown up.

'I presume there's a list of ingredients on these,' she said, looking at her Fortnum's cakes for the first time.

'Perhaps I should have just gone to Marks,' Eleanor went on. 'As it was, I was up till one making wretched gingerbread men, by which time I was so desperate to get to bed that I took them out ten minutes early, so they're horribly soft.'

'Then at least you won't be sued for breaking our teeth,' smiled Julia.

Eleanor heard her in earnest. 'You're right, seriously, there was a case the other day . . .'

But Julia was already hurrying on ahead into the school's eco-neutral, solar-heated theatre, not wanting to hear about the damage a biscuit could do.

# 2

As Julia had expected, Phillip, her husband, was positioned right at the front, standing head and shoulders above a circle of women with hair just the right shade of blonde. He had always weighed too little for his height yet, noticed Julia, seeing him afresh among this crowd of strangers, he had filled out since giving up his business. And it suited him. Among the pasty, pre-skiing holiday faces, he was glowing.

Her steady good humour restored itself. Even after more than twenty years, she could still feel a delight and pride in her husband. They had met when she was in her fourth week at Cambridge, reading Law, and Phillip was in his final year of Theology.

Theology had immediately put her off.

She could count among her childhood neighbours on the Hartley Estate more than twenty different religious practices and this had introduced her to so much inconsistency, hypocrisy and violence, it hadn't taken her mother's stoic insistence that Jesus would look after her – in Julia's view, He had most decidedly not looked after her mother – to make her want nothing to do with God.

She had asked formally, 'Are you going into the Church?'

He shook his head. 'They wouldn't have me. You see, I don't believe in God, not that that's always a problem in the C of E these days, though I made the mistake of admitting it.'

'So why Theology?' She assumed he had to be a stupid public school boy and that only an unpopular department like Theology would take him.

'Because the English department wouldn't have me either. I wasn't clever enough.'

Julia could never have admitted to such weakness. She was so anxious to prove her cleverness, it was all she could do not to let people know that she had won a scholarship. But then he laughed with the ease and authority she was convinced that everyone at Cambridge possessed, and she wondered if he was making fun of her.

She had been terrified that at Cambridge she would spend her time feeling undermined by people whose experience was as remote from hers as the lunar mountains. But, to her surprise, she soon came to realize that Phillip, for all his advantages, was actually far more uncertain in the world than she was. And this had given her confidence. She could look after herself. If the Hartley Estate had taught her anything, it was basic survival skills. She was in control of her destiny, whereas Phillip regarded his place in life as the result of a series of lucky accidents.

She learned later that he had chosen Theology partly because he had a vicar for a father, so he had what he called a 'head start' on the basics, but also because he was fascinated by what he saw as the beliefs people create to make their lives worth living, and he would spend hours writing long essays on Tolstoy and the quest for a moral life. Julia herself had never needed any philosophy either to get her through the day or give her life meaning. What she believed in, pure and simple, was the strength of the human mind. She had total faith in its ability to bring about happiness and peace, and she had only to look at her own life to confirm her views. Her intelligence had conquered the tedium and drudgery of her childhood. Her intelligence had given her an exciting, lucrative job. Her intelligence had brought her here, to this incredibly equipped theatre where her husband, handsome and bright, was waiting for her. And she was happy.

She deposited her cakes, then made her way over to Phillip. With a vanity she was not proud of, Julia revelled in walking into parties and restaurants with her husband. Physical opposites, they made a striking couple. His hair was as fair as hers was dark, his skin as golden as hers was pale. Even his tweed jacket had been crumpled as carefully as her tailor-made grey dress had been pressed.

As he stood engrossed in a discussion about the impossibilities of parking while dropping off the children at school, she slipped her arm through his.

'Julia!' he exclaimed. 'Darling.'

She held up her face and he kissed her lightly on the cheek.

'How are you?' she murmured.

'Fine, fine. Now let me introduce Fiona Bliss, Amy Gibbons . . .'

He ran through the names of the women and Julia smiled and said hello, wondering how he knew who all these women were. From, she supposed, the school run – a chore he had taken over this last year from the au pair.

'Fiona and Amy,' he explained, 'have written to the Council and to the local residents about the possibility of introducing a voluntary one-way system during the school run.'

'You see, the neighbours are being pretty stroppy about all the congestion,' said Amy, 'and, quite frankly, the only solution is a one-way system.'

Or making the girls walk or catch the bus, thought Julia, but keeping, as she so often did, her thoughts to herself.

When she was eleven, Julia had won a coveted free place at one of London's leading independent schools and had had to make an hour-long bus journey every morning and afternoon. Many of the girls had been driven to school but a good minority came from poorer families like hers, without a car. At St Catherine's such division between the pupils' backgrounds was unthinkable. Almost every one of the girls was the progeny of extremely rich parents – or with very wealthy grandparents – who could either afford not to work or could employ someone to chauffeur their children door to door.

'You see, if the cars ran clockwise, up from Beech Road along Lime Avenue,' Amy was explaining, when she stopped in her tracks. 'Laura!' she cried.

'Laura!' repeated Phillip and Fiona in unison.

And Julia glanced at her husband, wondering who Laura was.

# 3

Julia followed her husband's gaze to a wind-blown woman, with light brown curls pulled up into a knot on her head and wearing an old sheepskin coat and high-heeled green suede shoes with scuffed toes. In this room full of mothers so buffed and polished they positively gleamed, Julia would normally have overlooked her. If Laura stood out at all, it was because she appeared to have made absolutely no effort, except when it came to baking an enormous chocolate cake which she held before her like a crown on a cushion.

'Oh Laura, that's amazing!' cried Amy.

'Amazing!' echoed Fiona and Phillip.

As cakes went, it was indeed amazing, and Julia felt duty-bound to add to the chorus. 'Amazing!'

'It's a work of art,' gushed Fiona. 'Really!'

At which, Julia noticed, Laura gave them all the quickest glance as if to ask, are you being kind or are you patronizing me? It wasn't a defensive or aggressive look, merely curious. But a moment later there was nothing but an innocuous smile as Phillip was saying, 'Laura, let me introduce Julia, my wife.'

Julia beamed most warmly upon Laura's tired face, aware of the advantage she felt over women not as attractive as herself. With her high cheek bones and long-legged grace, she knew what it was to be the most beautiful woman in a room.

'How nice to meet you,' she said, as Laura's coat began sliding off her shoulders, revealing a knitted dress stretched in a way that suggested Laura was the only woman here who was a stranger to the gym.

'And you,' smiled Laura in turn. 'But let me get shot of this cake,' she said, as Amy took hold of her arm.

'Just a minute, Laura,' said Amy, 'now tell me, how did the meeting go?'

'Badly, they didn't like them,' said Laura.

'But why? Laura is the most wonderful artist,' Amy explained to all within earshot, 'and does the most wonderful drawings of flowers. Simply wonderful. And I set up this meeting for her with a greetings cards company.'

'It was just the usual platitudes,' said Laura. 'You know, "Lovely, but not right for us." But this damned cake's heavy, let me –'

'But your pictures are wonderful,' repeated Amy. 'Don't be so modest.'

'She's right,' said Phillip. 'They are extraordinary.'

Laura looked at him in surprise.

'I hope you don't mind,' Amy bellowed on. 'But I showed them to Phillip.'

Julia caught the irritation on Laura's face.

But Phillip, with his unfailing politeness, was saying, 'They made me think of those Dutch masters. The detail . . . they're exquisite.'

'Thank you,' Laura said, equally politely.

'See? Listen to Phillip,' said Amy. 'And me. Those people you saw this morning were idiots. Opinions are like arseholes – everyone's got one. So ignore theirs. That's what my husband says. They should have snapped you up, Laura, especially with your father, and what you have to do . . .'

But what Laura had to do would have to wait as a bell rang to encourage everyone to take to their seats because the performance was about to begin.

'That Amy woman,' murmured Julia. 'Does she always lord it about?'

'Tries to,' grinned Phillip, leading the way to the seats he had secured at the front of the hall.

Julia hesitated. 'Do you think this is a good idea? Sitting in such a prominent place? Let's face it, our daughter is hardly going to be the star of the show. Quite the opposite.'

'Don't be so hard on her,' said Phillip, settling himself down and stretching out his legs.

'I'm not.'

'She'll do her best.'

'Her best on no practice.'

'But the cello's very difficult, and Rose is very young.'

Not that young, thought Julia, who believed it absurd that Rose should have cello lessons. Julia regarded this as yet another money-making ploy on the part of the school, and had said as much at the time. But now she said nothing. Although she spent all day at work arguing, believing it vital to fight for her point of view, at home what she wanted more than anything else was peace and harmony. She changed the subject to neutral territory.

'That woman, Laura, with the chocolate cake. Who's the father that awful Amy was going on about?'

'Patrick Cusack.'

Cusack was one of the country's foremost portrait painters. He had managed the Herculean task of being both a darling of the art world and the artist of choice for those whose public face was always airbrushed to perfection but in a 'Cusack' were prepared to be depicted in all their grim humanity.

'But is Laura's work really any good? Or were you just being polite?'

'No, no, it's good.'

'Not as good as the father's?'

'Well, I've only seen a few and . . . I suppose not. At least, as far as I can tell. It's completely different, certainly.'

'Does she want your help?' In Phillip's saving-the-world mode, it would not have surprised her if he had decided to use his old advertising contacts to see if he could find Laura some business.

'God, no. She barely says a word to me. Not that she talks much to anyone. Though she couldn't avoid Amy, who's like a bloody tank. But it's a shame she didn't get that work. I mean, I think she's terribly hard up.'

'Phillip!' protested Julia, forgetting her desire for peace and harmony. 'If she's got Patrick Cusack for a father, and can afford to send a child here –'

'Two children,' interrupted Phillip. 'She's got twins.'

'Then clearly the one thing she's not is terribly hard up.'

'Bringing up twins on your own is not easy,' he said, glancing round to check that Laura was not nearby, but she was at the back on her own, stifling a yawn. 'And the children's father has never been around – no one knows who he is.'

'She must have some help. Or how else is she here?'

'I imagine the parents pay the school fees.'

Julia restricted herself to saying, 'Oh.'

She sighed. There was in her still, after all these years, a class chippiness. She despised herself for it. Yet to hear Phillip telling her that Laura was hard up irked her. He was normally far too level-headed for that sort of sentiment about a woman with healthy children and generous parents.

One of the many things that had drawn her to him was his gift for making you recognize all that was good in your life. The first time she had gone back to his room at Cambridge she had been bowled over, not just by the way he had divested her of her prejudice that the rich and privileged would prove lacklustre in bed, but because he had persuaded her that all the disadvantages in her life could be turned to good account. Her hunger and fear would take her far, make her stand out from the crowd. It was certainly not an original line, but on Julia there was none better. Most importantly, it changed her.

Until Phillip, she was used to viewing men with a sort of anthropological curiosity. She quite liked having sex with them but she had not, if she was honest, been particularly nice to them. Far from it, in fact.

But Phillip had made her realize that a man could be a support, that you could have a partnership and work as a team where you could be greater than the sum of the two parts. It was not a particularly difficult lesson, but having watched her own mother give up on men and deride them as useless beings, for Julia it was a revelation.

She went to take Phillip's hand as the lights dimmed for the start of the show but he had crossed his arms, his eyes concentrating on the scene unfolding before them as the curtain rose. A dozen little girls dressed as flower fairies came belting on to the stage and Julia steeled herself to endure.

## 4

The perfectly drilled flower fairies danced in time; a group of seven-year-olds in Tudor costumes sang 'Greensleeves' in almost perfect harmony; the eight-year-olds performed the lullaby '*Suo Gân*' in Welsh (a translation was provided in the programme); the nine-year-olds followed with the French carol '*Il est né*' (it was assumed no translation of this was needed).

Julia sat through it with mounting tension. Her daughter was about to make a fool of herself. Not, thought Julia, that a little humiliation would do Rose any harm. But she was surprised that the school would expose itself in such a way. So far, the standard had been exemplary, hammering home a comforting message to the parents: your money is being well spent; we are turning your daughters into intelligent, accomplished young women. But Rose was going to let the school down.

Rose's year was putting on a performance of the Annunciation scene in Latin, and soon enough the curtain rose upon the Arch-angel Gabriel, resplendent in a rainbow-coloured robe and matching wings, about to give the message to Mary. Behind them was a magnificent tableau depicting a wild and beautiful world of mountains and rivers. St Catherine's certainly had a great art teacher. And adding to the beauty of the scene in no small measure was Rose, with her golden head bowed over her cello.

Julia looked at Phillip but his eyes were fixed before him, waiting for the performance to begin.

But nothing happened.

Julia glanced again at Phillip when suddenly a teacher's voice hissed, 'Rose.'

Still, nothing happened.

'Rose,' the voice insisted, even louder.

Rose had missed her cue.

'*Rose!*'

Slowly, Rose lifted her face to the audience. Even allowing for maternal indulgence, Julia knew her daughter to be beautiful, but today, under the spotlight, she was exceptional, gazing around the room, as if in some deep and private search. She should be playing Mary, the lovely young woman, sitting alone, unsupported, over-awed by the great task before her, thought Julia, as she became aware of a shift in the audience's mood. Until now, the parents had watched with polite patience, their attention really only focused when their own darlings were performing. But now, for the first time that evening, they were joining together, all held spellbound by this one young woman with her cello.

At last Rose raised her bow and Julia braced herself for the racket ahead. But Rose, gorgeous as the first spring day, forced them to wait yet longer.

'She's loving it,' Julia muttered to Phillip. From her seat in the front row Julia could see her daughter's clear green eyes brightening, her full pink lips resisting the temptation to smile.

Phillip looked at his wife uncomprehendingly.

'The control,' Julia whispered, watching the bow hover.

Then Rose quivered, and dropped the bow with a great clatter.

A collective sigh rose up from the audience, as Rose ran her hands through her golden hair, her breast heaving as if overcome with stage fright and the enormity of the occasion. Great torrents of sympathy gushed towards her. This thing of beauty was suffering and humiliated, and people wanted to make it better.

Julia was moved differently. 'For God's sake,' she whispered to Phillip, her arms firmly crossed, as the audience began applauding. 'What the hell are they clapping for? Don't they get it?'

'What? Oh my darling Rose –'

'Phillip!' Julia had to say firmly as the applause grew even louder and louder.

'What?' repeated Phillip, his eyes only on Rose.

'This is a performance.'

'A what?' he asked, desperately smiling at his daughter.

'A stunt. You know. She's planned all this. Look at her.'

'Julia, she's crying!'

And very good at it she is too, thought Julia, as the tears flowing down Rose's cheeks enhanced the beautiful picture she was presenting to her audience. Julia was appalled. She was not sure who to be most angry with – the audience, her husband for being taken in by Rose, or Rose herself for lapping up the attention and manipulating them all. She wanted to take Phillip to task, but the applause was dying down at last. The Archangel Gabriel was having her say, in iambic pentameters, and Julia had to wait until the interval for hers.

But as the curtain went down, Phillip spoke first.

'For pity's sake,' he muttered, while everyone was clapping, 'how can you possibly think she did that deliberately? She'll be devastated.'

'No, she won't. She got the biggest applause of the night for doing absolutely nothing but looking sweet.'

'Sweet?' He shook his head. 'She's more than sweet, and you know it.'

'That's not the point. It's just that if she thinks you can swan through life –'

He interrupted her. 'You're not jealous, are you?'

Julia gulped the air hard. She forced herself to speak calmly.

'No, Phillip, I am not jealous of our daughter. Even though she is so stunning –'

'I don't mean her beauty – at least, not just that. I mean, that she can get what she wants without working, and we always worked so hard. And the way,' said Phillip, groping for the words as if he had just seen his daughter in a new light, '. . . the way everyone loves her and she doesn't have to do anything to earn it.'

'But is this what she wants?' Julia demanded. 'A love based on pity because she's incapable?'

'This isn't pity,' he said. 'It's . . . I don't know . . . she gave people something, made everyone feel good about themselves, at least for a moment.'

Only because everyone here is so damned competitive and their own daughters all did so much better, Julia would have retorted if Fiona Bliss had not joined them.

Phillip rearranged his face into a smile and Julia forced herself to do the same as he said to Fiona, 'Your daughter sang beautifully.'

'Yes, quite beautifully,' said Julia, not having a clue who the daughter was. She wanted to finish talking to Phillip. But that was impossible now with Fiona here, going on.

'You know how I do the advertising for one of the big beauty companies,' Fiona was saying. Julia didn't, but Phillip nodded. 'Well, Rose is quite exceptional. She really is, and I wondered whether she had ever thought of doing any modelling?'

'No,' pounced Julia. 'She hasn't. And won't.'

'Oh, it's just,' Fiona went on lightly, smiling at Julia, 'there is an interesting quality about her look, something very special. Obviously, it's hard to tell without taking photos. But given what she pulled off up on that stage, people warm to her, and I know the girls all copy her.'

Julia glanced at Phillip. Copy her at what? she wondered. Not her work, that was for sure.

'And there's a new range of anti-ageing creams being launched soon. I know, yet another lot of magic potions,' Fiona smiled, seeing Julia's expression, 'but we're looking for a new face. And Rose has an interesting quality.'

'Rose is too young,' said Julia.

'Well, actually,' continued Fiona, 'you mightn't believe it, but many of the models for beauty products are that young.'

Julia did believe it.

'Their skin is so perfect, you see. Perhaps Rose would like –' she went on, spotting Rose in the doorway, surrounded by a group of her friends, all wearing identical long silk ribbons in their hair.

'No, please don't,' interrupted Julia in a polite and stony voice. 'Don't mention this to her. I really do not want her even thinking of modelling.'

'Of course,' said Fiona, 'of course. But they all do think of it, you know. At least, the pretty ones do. Anyway, here, take one of these.' And she handed them her card. 'In case you change your mind. Now I'm off to have some of that cake of Laura's.'

'Phillip,' began Julia the moment Fiona had gone. 'Rose is not –'

'Sweetheart,' he said calmly, 'it's all right. I agree. She's not doing any modelling. She's much too young.'

But she is not too young, thought Julia. At fifteen, Rose had long put away childish things. But Rose's vanity was fuelled enough and she already had far too many excuses for not doing her school work. 'Thank you,' she said, taking his arm, 'I thought perhaps you might think it was a good opportunity for her.'

'For heaven's sake, no. I don't want her modelling and not eating and all that nonsense. Now come on, let's go and find our daughter,' he said, and they walked into the foyer where the food was laid out.

It was the policy at St Catherine's to have a long interval where pupils and parents mingled, so that from a young age the girls acquired the assurance to shake hands, look people in the eye and, as they got older, enjoy opportunities to set up work experience in the sort of professions their parents either practised or approved of. Indeed, Julia and Phillip's eighteen-year-old daughter, Anna, who had a place at Cambridge to read Maths next autumn, was an intern at the magazine her friend Phoebe's mother edited.

Julia cast around for her younger daughter.

'Where's she disappeared to?' began Phillip, when Julia felt a tap on her shoulder.

'Mum,' said a little voice behind her, 'I'm so sorry, I really, really am, I don't know what happened, but . . .'

Julia turned and looked straight at Rose, who was staring down at her shoes.

From an early age, Rose had learned the power of saying sorry. After the slightest misdemeanour she would start apologizing to pre-empt being told off. Julia could never understand how Rose managed it. When, as a child, Julia had been made to say sorry, she would almost choke over the word, putting herself through agonies before she could endure the humiliation of being in the wrong. Even now, she thought there was much to be said for 'don't apologize, don't explain'. But Rose, putting her arms around Phillip, couldn't care less.

'Sorry,' she was saying, 'I'm so sorry, Dad.'

'Are you all right, sweetheart?'

Rose gave a murmur of assent.

'It wasn't your finest moment, my darling.'

'No.' She shook her head. 'I missed my cue,' she mumbled into her father's shoulder, 'and that's what threw me.'

'Your cue was a whopping great curtain going up,' snapped Julia. 'How on earth could you miss that?'

'I know, it was so stupid of me . . . . I'm just so stupid.'

'If you were stupid, I would understand.'

'But I'm sorry . . .'

'For God's sake, you're not a bit sorry. And what will your teachers say?'

'Nothing I can't handle –'

'Now enough,' interrupted Phillip. 'We're not having this argument here. Or later, even. I'm not sure what you were up to on that stage, Rose, but it's over. And it won't happen again.'

'No, Dad.'

'Too right,' said Julia.

'And it's just a school concert,' Phillip said pointedly to Julia. 'It's not the end of the world. Now, I'm hungry.'

'Me too,' said Rose. And, knowing exactly how to divert her father, she added, 'I missed lunch.'

'Oh Rose, you need to eat properly. How many times do you have to be told? Now let's get something and forget about it.'

But Julia wasn't going to, not just yet. She caught her daughter's hand.

'Rose,' she said, as Phillip moved away. 'I'm not paying for cello lessons any more. That's it.'

'You'll have to pay for next term as you have to give a term's notice.'

'Fair enough,' said Julia, ignoring Rose's triumphant tone. 'But I'm not paying for you to make a fool of yourself like that again.'

There was a shift in Rose's eyes. Suddenly she looked older – too clever by half, as Julia's own mother would have said.

'I did not make a fool of myself,' said Rose in a collected voice. 'And the thing is, Mum, you know it. Because what will people remember from tonight? That awful madrigal stuff? The interminable Latin? No. They'll remember me. If I'd been brilliant, they'd have just felt envy and competition. But they loved me. The girl who dropped her bow with stage fright. Know your market. Isn't that what Dad would say? I fooled everyone.'

'Not me, Rose.'

'Oh Mum, please. Just lighten up,' she said, taking Julia's hand. 'See the funny side. Think how much worse it would have been if I had actually played something.'

Julia did not smile. 'It's such a waste,' she said, 'you could do so much.'

'And I will.'

'I'm serious. It's not enough just to be pretty and get people to feel sorry for you.'

Rose slipped her arm through her mother's and planted a kiss on her cheek. 'That might have been true for you when you were my age. But not these days. Not that you're not pretty. All my friends say so, and wish they could borrow your clothes. Mum, please, this coat you're in,' she said, fingering the collar. 'It's gorgeous. The way it falls . . .'

'No, you can't borrow it,' smiled Julia.

Rose just laughed. 'I guessed not. But don't be angry any more. I hate it when you're angry.'

Julia hesitated. Because of her work she saw little enough of Rose as it was, and it always seemed such a waste to spend those precious moments carping and criticizing.

'Mum, please.' Rose squeezed her arm. 'Mum?'

So Julia let herself be won over. Gently kissing the top of Rose's head, her hair plaited with a long scarlet ribbon, she changed the subject and asked, 'Is this some new craze? Lots of you seem to have these ribbons in your hair.'

'Do you like it?'

'Not really. It's a bit fey.'

Rose smiled. 'That's the sort of thing you would say. I'll do something different next term.'

'Did you start this fashion?'

'Yes.'

So this is what they copied from her daughter.

'Last term it was those bracelets. Do you remember?'

Julia nodded, but she didn't.

'Now I've got to find Rose B.'

'I wish you wouldn't call her Rose B,' said Julia. Rose B was a new girl in Rose's class. 'It makes her sound second best.'

'She doesn't mind, and anyway she's much cleverer than me. But her mum's desperate for her to speak to this woman Laura Cusack, to see if she can get some work experience with her father who's some famous painter.'

'I can't think for one minute a busy man like Patrick Cusack would agree to that. Or that his daughter will want to be asked.'

'That's what I said. But Rose B says her mother is amazing when it comes to getting what she wants from people, because what she can do is flatter you and make you feel you're her new best friend as she listens so terribly nicely – like she really cares. Rose B says it's awful watching people being taken in by her.'

'You make her sound like a witch.'

'No, she's a journalist – brilliant at interviews – and Rose B says I've got to see her in action. And I must, because I really want to be able to do that too. Rose B just gets mortified with embarrassment when her mum's on her mission as there's no stopping her, and she's clutched at this business of Rose B being good at art because she's so hopeless at everything else.'

'But you said she was much cleverer than you.'

'Oh, she is. But she's masses and masses better than everyone at art. She's done some really beautiful pictures of me – everyone says so.'

'Rose, it's not just about you.'

'I know, but they really are good and Miss Thompson says Rose B is the only girl she's taught in twenty years who has a jot of real talent.'

'I thought teachers now had to say everyone was brilliant at everything.'

'Not Miss Thompson. She's like you. Not like . . . oh, there she is, Rose B's mum.'

Julia watched a delicately pretty woman with pale blonde hair head deftly across the room.

'But which one's Laura Cusack?'

'There,' said Julia, looking round, 'in that sheepskin coat, by the wall.'

'The one on her own?'

'Yes.'

'In that falling-apart coat? I'm never going to let myself go like that. It makes her look shattered. And she's not even that old.'

'For goodness' sake, Rose, it's not just about how you look.'

'Whatever. But it's still an awful coat.'

And yet, thought Julia, looking across at Laura, her hair piled up on top of her head, slipping slowly down her neck, undoing itself in soft disorder, curl by curl. And yet . . .

'Anyway,' Rose was saying, 'now I must go and learn something useful, which is more than I've done all week.'

And with that Rose was gone. And Julia was left feeling uneasy.

Rose's problem, Julia had always thought, was pure laziness, but now Rose was displaying a shrewdness Julia had never seen before. She wondered where it was taking her. Rose was moving out of her reach and that was inevitable, of course. Julia could never forget the desperation to get out of her own mother's reach. But I am not, thought Julia, like my own mother. And I have worked so hard to make sure my children see nothing of what I endured. And need never see.

## 5

'Mum, please,' begged Laura Cusack's twins as they walked out to the car after the school concert. 'Do we have to go straight home? Can't we have an adventure?'

'No,' said Laura, getting them into the car. 'You need to go to bed.'

'But we're not tired.'

'Just a small adventure? Please. We're allowed to go in late to school tomorrow.'

Laura hesitated. Like her daughters, she too did not want to go home. She had not enjoyed the evening. Yet what was there not to enjoy? Eliza and Alice had danced in time – albeit rather heavily. The other parents had been perfectly pleasant, even though most just wanted to talk to her about her father. But she was used to that.

'Why can't we go to your old school again?' asked Eliza. 'And climb in over the wall?'

'No, no,' said Laura.

'But that was the best night ever,' said Alice.

'No.'

'Can't we break in somewhere else, then?'

'We didn't break in.'

'We did,' said Alice.

'We did not break in,' said Laura once more, rather loudly. 'Do not say that.'

'Then why were you worried about being caught?'

'Because . . .' said Laura. 'Look, we just climbed over the wall.'

'We trespassed,' said Alice.

'Didn't we? "Trespassers will be prosecuted". That's what the sign said.'

One evening last summer her daughters were in bed, supposedly going to sleep, and Laura had sat with them describing her beautiful school. Laura had had a privileged upbringing, she knew full well – and had never been allowed to forget – and had spent her teenage years at a school housed in the glorious grounds of what had once been the eighteenth-century home of a duke who made a fortune in sugar.

She had told the girls about the rose garden, the pagoda covered in wisteria, the great long avenues of horse chestnut trees, the bench by the Cupid statue where she used to sit and where – though she did not tell this to her daughters – not for a moment had she thought she would one day be thirty-four with seven-year-old twins to bring up on her own.

And that June evening, one of those fleeting midsummer nights, all caressing warmth and rose-scented air, it seemed sacrilege to be making such a small bargain with life that you only watch from a bedroom window. So Laura put the girls in the car and drove out to the school. The gates were locked, of course, but they had clambered in over a stone wall.

'It was wonderful,' pleaded Alice from the back of the car.

'Really wonderful,' echoed Eliza.

And it was, the gardens transfigured by summer moonlight.

'It was one of the very best evenings of my whole life,' said Eliza portentously, knowing the power of this argument on her mother. 'The absolute best.'

Laura laughed.

'And it's so boring just to go home,' added Alice.

It is boring, thought Laura. They are right. And she had boring work to do. Laundry, ironing, along with laying out a brochure for a children's charity her mother worked for.

'Mummy, please, you know you want to.'

Laura did. She was annoyed with herself for finding a school concert such an effort, but as the evening wore on her awareness of her own failings had heightened. Her looks were ordinary, her conversation stilted. Even before Laura had children, her idea of a good time had always been to stay at home and paint. She had put this down to immaturity. It was naive, she told herself, to think that just because people gave the appearance of having everything perfectly arranged, their inner and outer lives actually matched. Wearing gorgeous clothes and having a fabulous job did not mean you could not be an outcast to your own heart.

'Or what if we go to Brighton?' pleaded Eliza.

'No, no, that's miles away.'

'But it's fun doing that in the middle of the night. Can't we do that again?'

'No, no,' muttered Laura, thinking that the good things in life could seem so rare it was wrong not to make the most of them. And if the afternoon had not been much fun, neither had the morning, being patronized by some greetings cards company. Or rather, she had been given about ten minutes as her portfolio was examined with smiling condescension. She was a fool. She should have known her work was not suitable, that she would have been better off at home, painting. At least she would have enjoyed herself, and now she suddenly felt desperate to do something to redeem the day rather than let domestic duties swarm over her.

'Please . . . I love your old school.'

'But,' said Laura, 'there's been all this rain, and it'll be so wet now.'

'So? We can slosh around in the mud.'

'And it was summer then,' said Laura, 'so it was warm.'

'It's starry tonight, though.'

Laura wound down the car window. 'It's not,' she said, looking out into the damp darkness.

'But please . . . It will be joyful.'

'Joyful?' echoed Laura. 'That's a nice word,' she said as Alice put her soft arms about her neck.

Oh, don't, thought Laura, let my daughters ever feel they are making a bad bargain with life. It is too short and too precious. Don't break their zestful hearts.

'You're the best mummy, you give us the best adventures, so please . . .'

With that Laura swung the car round. 'All right, then,' she said, 'we'll go. But don't tell anyone.'

And she smiled.

If she had smiled such a smile earlier, no one would have thought of overlooking her.

# 6

Laura glanced at the clock. It was almost eleven. It had taken that long for the girls to fall asleep. And this was not simply because of the school concert and getting overexcited as they climbed into Laura's old school grounds. This late night was all too typical. Her daughters were unlike other children – and certainly unlike Laura – in that it seemed they barely needed sleep. Laura gazed at their closed eyes in relief. They still insisted on sleeping together in the same bed, their sturdy arms entwined and their rose-pink faces turned to one another.

'Mummy,' muttered Eliza, stirring as Laura untangled her hot little arm, 'read to me.'

'No, no, hush now.'

'Please . . .'

'Back to sleep . . .'

And Eliza's eyes drifted, her breathing slowed.

Laura never loved her daughters more than when they were asleep. Although, she thought, to love them most when they were semi-conscious surely defeated the point of having children. But hers would be wide awake again by half past six the next morning, and not tired. *Not tired*. Laura yawned.

They had been like that from the start. Other parents would ask, 'When do they have their nap?' and she, who had always been regarded as so organized, would mutter bleary-eyed, 'Well, it varies, they don't actually sleep that much in the day.' Not that much at night either.

And people would assume it was because she had twins that she was so exhausted. Because she was a single mother. Because she was always letting herself get roped in to doing favours – for her neighbours, for her mother's endless good causes. Because she agreed to do unpaid jobs – the priest at the Catholic church she had attended as a child had persuaded her to help with the accounts.

But it wasn't that. The twins simply had more energy than most people, their constant presence a vortex which sometimes seemed to drain all that was good in her and leave her fighting to disguise how miserable she was.

But now they were at school and she had more time. Now I should not be so tired, Laura told herself, putting away their Tudor costumes in their pale green wardrobe painted all over – by Laura – with cornflowers and poppies to look, she had told them, like a meadow. A beautiful room, Laura believed, could be like welcoming arms. And the home Laura had created was beautiful.

She replaced the Beatrix Potter the girls had been reading to each other on the neatly ordered bookshelf. She had been very fortunate, she kept reminding herself. Her daughters were wonderful, and yet sometimes she wished they would just hurry and grow up so she might have an adult conversation in her own home.

Laura had been the first among her contemporaries to have children. At the time, her friends had been very kind and provided the twins with such gorgeous clothes that Laura had had to stop herself screaming when told it was really easy to hand-wash the lace or the cashmere. But pretty soon, the friends had, not surprisingly in Laura's eyes, drifted back into their own worlds of careers and romance away from the drudgery of two babies who found life too interesting to spend it asleep.

But I am still relatively young, thought Laura, pulling the covers over Alice's outstretched leg. At least, I am young in comparison with most of those St Catherine's parents who had all delayed having children until they were well ahead in their careers.

Before she found herself a single mother of two, Laura had had only three affairs, each one shorter and more unhappy than the last. And at twenty-seven, as her friends seemed to be falling in and out of love with ease and joy, she was convinced that there was something wrong with her. She was odd, men did not like her, and experience had provided no reason why they would ever think differently.

Then one spring night she met a man who changed her future for ever.

At the time she was working as an assistant to a fashion photographer and was spending four days in Scotland shooting a catalogue for a cashmere company. One evening, as the team were all about to sit down to dinner in their Edinburgh hotel, a friend of her boss joined them.

Duncan MacDougall owned a large estate in Perthshire, along with a lucrative chain of coffee shops which paid for all the unkempt acres and turbulent salmon rivers he loved to stride across. Tall, with dark curly hair, broad shoulders and well-kept hands, he could, thought Laura, have been modelling in the cashmere catalogue if he had not been quite so wrinkled. But after five minutes of sitting next to him, she was bewitched by those wrinkles, particularly those at the corners of his eyes that deepened as he laughed. And Duncan MacDougall loved to laugh. More to the point, he was a genius at making women laugh, and during dinner he turned the full force of that genius upon Laura.

To a man like Duncan, Laura was as easy to read as *Peter Rabbit* and once dinner was over and they were sitting cosily in the firelit bar, he stopped plying her with laughter and changed tack. He began to ask her question after question about her work, her friends, her home, her childhood. And Laura, flattered, answered.

She carried on talking as the others went up to bed, and when she and Duncan were left alone on the sofa she told him that, if she was honest – and with Duncan MacDougall and the whisky and the warm fire honesty, for her, came easily – people became photographers only because they were not good enough at art. If she had had real talent she would have been like her father. Then she confided that she painted long into the night, and at weekends, and that what she loved to paint were flowers – and this was not simply because she needed to do something completely different from Patrick.

Duncan took her hand at this point and said he, too, knew how difficult it was having a parent who was so brilliant and revered. His own father was a top cardiologist, and he had always wanted to study medicine himself but hadn't because he knew he would never be as good as his father – though at least that had spared the world another ego the size of Jupiter.

Then, with the fire getting hotter, and Laura all too aware of how close their thighs were on the sofa, when Duncan had pressed to know what she was currently painting, she told him about snowdrops, about their scalloped petals, the soft green stripes, and how she would paint them again and again because she was never satisfied with what she had done. She had always loved those painstaking, botanical drawings, she explained, because the more she learned about the science of the flowers, the easier it was to capture their poetry. And she had told him about the difficulty of painting white on white, and with Duncan now stroking the inside of her wrist she was foolish enough to believe that she was understood.

It was all so predictable and Laura was not a stupid woman. But she was a very lonely one. He chose that moment to look at her closely with his ardent green eyes and tell her she was beautiful, and when she laughed he simply told her again how very beautiful she was and that she should take him upstairs to her bed.

And she did.

Until 5 a.m. on the dot – when the alarm on his phone rang – Duncan MacDougall behaved as if finding Laura was like stumbling upon a treasure chest that opened up a great bounty of riches. But at five o'clock, when she had been nestling her head on his shoulder, he had leaped up. He had to catch the first flight to London and he could not miss it. He rushed into the bathroom – taking his phone with him – locked the door, then rushed out. He gave her a peck on the cheek, said a quick, 'I'll call you,' and then the door shut and he was gone with such speed she half-expected to see a puff of smoke.

Once he left, the double-glazed, air-conditioned room became eerily still, as if a big storm had just blown itself out. Moments earlier, Laura had been giddy with the feeling that her life was about to alter irrevocably. Now she lay inert and subdued. I have been here before, she thought, as she curled up in what now felt like a very empty bed. She moved over to the side where he had lain to hold on to his warmth, huddled in a ball of apprehension, as the outlines of the very ordinary hotel room emerged in the dim, dawn light.

At six her alarm went off as she, too, had to make an early start. So she got up as normal and went down to breakfast. Her boss was already there, demolishing a 'full Scottish'. He waved at her to join him.

'Good night?'

'Yes, thanks,' she said blandly, ordering tea.

'Don't take this amiss,' he went on, wolfing down black pudding, 'and I know Duncan is great fun and I'm ever so fond of him . . . God, this black pudding is delicious. Do you want some?'

Laura shook her head.

'But watch out with him. His wife is literally about to have a baby. At least, they hope so – or it'll have to be induced next week.'

Laura said nothing. She just looked at the breakfast before her and almost retched, a feeling she would get used to over the coming weeks.

Surprisingly, Duncan did call. He was coming down to London, he explained, and wondered if she would like to meet.

'No, thank you,' she said, as politely as she could.

To which he replied, 'All right, sweetheart, look after yourself.'

Then he hung up, and that was the last she heard of him. Ever.

He's not even that bothered, Laura thought to herself at the time, he's probably relieved – fun had been had, obligations fulfilled with the courtesy of a phone call. But by then she was getting very bothered.

Whether it was her orthodox Catholic upbringing or – as Laura suspected some of her friends said – because her parents were prepared to foot the bill for the unplanned pregnancy of a woman living on the salary of a photographer's assistant, or perhaps it was because she was so desperate for something to love, but she did not once question whether or not to have the baby. Or what, soon enough, she discovered was two babies.

The day she learned she was having twins, she left the hospital and went straight into the pub opposite and ordered a brandy she did not touch while her tears fell for all that she was about to relinquish and everything she was going to have to face for the rest of her life.

But after that one display of emotion, her powers of organization had kicked in, as did – Laura would be the first to acknowledge this – her parents' money. They bought her a garden flat near a large, green heath, and now, just over seven years on, here they were paying the fees for St Catherine's, where the head liked the idea of the renowned painter Patrick Cusack adorning school events with his artistic presence.

Not, thought Laura, as she picked up her daughters' dirty clothes, that her father was ever likely to give up his time to anything other than art, his great calling being all too demanding to find time to watch his granddaughters thumping around a stage in Tudor dress. Though somehow she had let one of the mothers at St Catherine's talk her into asking her father if her daughter might meet him. She should just have said no, there and then, rather than subject the girl to her father's brutally honest scrutiny. But Laura had pitied the woman, who had been so persistent and anxious about her shy, plain daughter.

That was the problem with pity, thought Laura, heading downstairs with armfuls of washing. Sometimes it did more harm than good.

## 7

Laura had been brought up to put other people first – albeit having a father who thought of no one but himself. As children, she and her brothers were never allowed to forget how incredibly fortunate they were. Thanks to their father's talent for painting the sort of portraits for which the rich will happily part with vast sums of money, they led extremely comfortable lives. It was therefore only right, their mother, Venetia, told them, that they should help those less well-off than themselves. Only fair.

As if, thought Laura, the allotment of human happiness and grief had anything to do with fairness. But Laura was not immune to the argument. Once she had put on the wash, heaved out the rubbish, decided not to bother ironing, she sat at the computer to work on the brochure for her mother. Five minutes later, the phone rang.

Only Laura's mother called at this late hour.

'Darling,' began Venetia, 'I'm so sorry I missed the girls' show this evening, but you know how important those forums of mine are.'

Laura said she did, but she had no idea what this particular forum was about. Venetia, a barrister whose main work was in the family courts, also had numerous other projects on the go, generally to do with the welfare of disadvantaged children, and they made her so busy she was always asking Laura for favours.

'For lunch on Sunday, you couldn't make one of those chocolate cakes of yours, could you? You know how your father loves them.'

'Yes, sure,' replied Laura, who was always being asked to make the pudding when going to lunch at her parents' house. When making the cake for St Catherine's, she had made a second at the same time.

'And you will make sure the chocolate's organic, won't you?'

'Yes,' lied Laura. Throughout her life her mother had had strange diet fads, once drinking vast quantities of vinegar to change her body's pH. Now she confined herself to eating only food that was certifiably organic.

'And a large cake if you wouldn't mind, darling, as there will be at least eight of us with Mark and Jane there.' Mark was Laura's elder brother and Jane his new wife whom Laura was struggling to like, and who was about to have a baby boy. 'And maybe Robert too.'

Laura was sandwiched between her two brothers and, in her bleaker moments, she wondered whether their three lives had been defined by reacting against their father's artistic brilliance. Mark had read Maths at university – refusing even to do art at school though, of the three of them, Laura thought he had by far the most talent – then gone into banking and was making the sort of money that meant he could actually afford his father's paintings (though he preferred Vettriano).

Robert, at thirty-one, was earning a living decorating, splashing paint over very rich people's walls and, from what Laura could gather, seducing his female clients.

'Both Mark and Robert? Oh, wonderful,' said Laura, who adored her brothers.

'Hopefully, but Robert says he might have to work. Though what's so urgent about decorating on a Sunday is beyond me.'

'Maybe he promised to have it done by then,' said Laura, heading for the kitchen.

'You always defend him. Everybody knows builders do just as they please. Our bathroom on the top floor would have been done by now if the builder didn't have a dying mother.'

'Maybe she really is dying.'

'No, because he used the very same excuse when he did Sally Smythe's kitchen.'

'You wouldn't want Robert to say you were dying,' said Laura, starting to unload the dishwasher.

'No, of course not, but that's not the point. Darling, I can't hear you with all those plates clattering. There's something I need to talk to you about. You'll be interested.'

Laura stopped still. Whenever her mother had a particularly large favour to ask, she invariably prefaced it with 'you'll be interested' to imply that she was the one giving the favour.

'Mother, I'm busy enough.'

'Really, but with the girls at school now? And I thought you were going to get them to do some of those, you know, after-school-club things. So you'd have more time.'

More time to paint, thought Laura, bracing herself. She knew what was coming.

'Sweetheart, please, just hear me out. It's Hartley High.'

Venetia had recently stood down from being chair of the governors at Hartley High.

'I thought you'd stopped working for them.'

'I have, but the new chair has just rung me because he needs another governor and he wondered whether I might come back. But that's impossible.'

'Why?'

'Because . . . because I've got so much other work. And so I said you would do it.'

'But at a school like that,' began Laura. Hartley High was a state secondary school and although only five miles away was as removed from St Catherine's as the North Pole. 'The problems are immense. To do it properly there'd be so much work!' *Unpaid* work, she said to herself. 'You always went on about how much time it took.'

'I know, but it's in a good cause. They need someone like you.' This was not just flattery, though Venetia would have resorted to it without a qualm. 'Laura, please. Many of the parents –'

'And,' interrupted Laura, 'they won't want a governor who sends her own children to private school.'

'They don't. But they're desperate.'

Laura let this pass. She had long ago learned to ignore her mother's bluntness.

'And as I was about to say,' continued Venetia, 'many of the parents at the school would love to do it, but the paperwork would defeat them. Their English is worse than their children's. You could make a difference.'

Laura sighed. She knew herself. She was efficient. She could be relied upon to do the hard graft of reading papers, writing letters, attending meetings.

'But you always went on,' said Laura, 'about how useless the rest of the governors were.'

'That's all the more reason for them needing you. And what might make it easier to get stuck in is that you know the new chair, Phillip Snowe. He has a daughter at St Catherine's, and another one has just left.'

'Him? I can't stand him. And I don't know him at all.'

'How on earth can you not stand someone you say you don't know?'

'Oh, you know those smooth advertising types,' she said.

'Don't be so facile.'

Laura had watched Phillip in the playground at St Catherine's, the other mothers enjoying his self-deprecating, flirtatious humour. He had sought her out once, asked about her painting – put up to it by Amy, she rightly suspected – and that easy charm had grated on her.

'I'm sure you'd like him once you do know him,' went on Venetia. 'He made a mint when he sold up his business and is now sort of semi-retired and, you know, trying to put something back. All that. But he's terribly bright, hard-working and really dedicated. Ever so nice, actually.'

Laura winced. 'Ever so nice' was an expression Venetia applied to handsome men. Laura sometimes feared that one of the reasons her mother threw herself into her charity work was so she might surround herself with 'ever so nice' men in a way which gave Laura doubts about her parents' marriage that she would rather not have.

'Seriously,' continued Venetia, 'he's brilliant. I just thank God he's taken over.' This was high praise from her mother. 'And he'd be fun to work with, I'm sure. But *I'm* too busy,' she repeated.

'Yes, but . . .' But why, thought Laura, suddenly recalling the sable gloss of Julia's hair, the glint of diamonds on her manicured hands, can't his wife do it?

'They need a fresh eye,' persisted Venetia.

Laura was close to defeat. She began doodling on a notepad, tulips with tattered petals.

'And what else are you going to do with your time that's as worthwhile?'

'Okay, okay. I'll call him.'

'Well, ring him now, dear. Actually, I said you would.'

## 8

'Will you be long?' asked Julia, standing in the doorway of Phillip's study a couple of nights later.

'Half an hour or so,' he said, without glancing up from his papers.

'What's so important?' she asked, trying to keep her voice light, but her car was booked for 6.15 the next morning. And she was tired.

'Hartley High.'

'Oh?'

'We have to fire a teacher,' he said, quashing his suspicion that Julia's, 'Oh?' was filled with patronizing sympathy. Hartley High was on the estate where she had grown up and whenever he mentioned the place he always felt oddly uncomfortable, that he was intruding on territory she wished he would not go to.

'I thought it was almost impossible to sack teachers,' she said.

'That's why I'm up so late.'

'Can't it wait till morning?'

He resisted pointing out that if it could wait, he would not be doing it now. He just took off his glasses and, as she yawned pointedly, said, 'Sorry, darling. I won't wake you.' Though he was always being woken by her checking her phone for calls from New York.

'Okay,' she sighed, and kissed him. 'Well, good night.'

Phillip watched her lovely, long, straight back retreat down the hall, and it seemed to him that this was all he ever saw of his wife now. Her back as she walked out of the door, her back as she sat at her desk, her back as she lay asleep. And he missed her.

We used to make each other supremely happy, he thought. But now they both worked so hard.

For almost ten years Julia had been a partner in the London branch of a leading New York law firm. The position suited her perfectly. It spared her contending with the stultifying old boys' network in Britain's legal profession. Instead, the fact that she had pulled herself up out of nowhere appealed to the Americans, who were prepared to reward her handsomely for her guts and drive. And Julia delivered. One of the youngest to make partner, she was soon one of the most successful. But Julia also gave her time to mentoring younger female lawyers. Such encouragement and care of more youthful women was not always so freely given to those who might become future rivals. But Julia refused to insult her own intelligence, or that of the women she helped, by stinting on her expertise and experience. Phillip, of course, loved her for this generosity but wished sometimes such consideration might also be directed at him.

But tonight he could not think about wanting his wife, especially as he seemed to have every bit as much work now as when he had been running the advertising agency.

Now, of course, it was different. Different in that he had never before really enjoyed his work, or actually thought it important. And extremely different in that now he was not earning a penny. Beforehand, he had made ludicrous sums of money. He had earned it too, put in the hours, missed weekends, cut short holidays, dipped into – and more often out of – his children's lives as they grew up. But some early mornings, as he drove into work, he would look at the exhausted faces on the last of the night buses, watch the bowed backs of those scuttling down into the Underground, see shopkeepers opening up in the cold, grey dawn, and his own working life appeared to him as one long bonanza of scoffing on cake. And it sat heavily on him.

For as long as he could remember his father, who was still the vicar of a small village in Yorkshire, had hammered home from the pulpit and, with his mother's help, from the end of the kitchen table, the front seat of the car, by the edge of the bed, the message that we are all bound together in one body by the communion of saints, that we all share in the one source of life. This meant that if somewhere a child was slaving in appalling conditions for pennies, he was diminished; if an old woman in a dirty hospital bed was facing a painful death with courage, he was uplifted. We are all connected, his parents' faith taught him. And although he had lost his parents' sense of the nearness of God, he was convinced that what he did, and how he chose to use his gifts, mattered not just to him, but to all of mankind.

Soon after he had graduated, not with a first like Julia – though, to give him credit, on a fraction of the effort – the father of a friend asked him to help out on a six-month project in his advertising agency. It was not the sort of work he had ever considered. As a student he had been too intent on saving the world, and too busy going on marches and delivering speeches in support of some oppressed minority, to find himself a job. So when one had fallen into his lap he took it, thinking it would tide him over while deciding what he really wanted to do.

He had proved remarkably good at the work. He had a fine eye for the creative side but his real brilliance lay in selling the ideas. Just as he had won over Julia by convincing her of how incredibly strong and talented she was, he had the open manner and passion that persuaded clients that he understood what they wanted and no one could deliver it as well. People liked him, trusted him and respected his judgement, and within six years he had set up an agency on his own.

Knowing where his own weaknesses lay, he built up a great team who made him more money than he could ever have dreamed of. Success, as it so often does, bred more success, and his final stroke of luck was selling the business at the right time, for the sort of sum that meant he need never be gainfully employed again.

If he had wanted to, he could have gone off to the South of France or taken up motor racing or bought himself a yacht. But Phillip did want to work.

All the zeal that he had felt as a student and lost in the waterfall of money that flooded his way had, by his early forties, begun to resurrect itself. While still running his agency, he agreed to promote an organization for helping bright but physically disabled children, and it proved one of the most successful charity campaigns ever. He could name schools built with money he had raised, and it was years since he had felt such exhilaration. It gave him a glimpse of what life on earth was supposed to be, of the heaven his parents had talked of and which he had rejected so easily as a young man.

So here he was running, for no fee, advertising campaigns for three national charities, as well as fund-raising for the local hospice, setting up a maths and literacy programme for homeless people in London, along with being chair of the governors at Hartley High secondary school. Never, at his desk, had he been happier.

It was grim having to sack someone. But the woman had not been up to what must be one of the hardest jobs in teaching. Few were, what with pupils being turfed out of high-rise tower blocks into street culture that saw no point in education.

But the school was changing, Phillip told himself as he finished his thirteenth letter, and it was changing for the better. Thanks to him there was funding for a new science laboratory and money for two new classrooms. New cloakrooms were being built free of graffiti, with drains that did not stink, with lockers that could not be broken into.

He rested his head in his hands a moment. Just getting the drains fixed had meant interminable bureaucracy of the sort he had never experienced in the commercial world. But if he was to achieve anything he had to spend his considerable talents battling inertia, prejudice, vested interests and the clunking hand of the local Council. And he could, he told himself. He had the concentrated will to penetrate meaningless jargon; he had the charm and quick wit to change opinion. And he would work his damnedest.

But then, as he responded to an email from the head, for one uneasy moment, he saw himself as a do-gooding prig, trying to ease his conscience over all the money he had made so easily. A few years ago he would have been the first to describe himself in those terms, and he wondered whether that was how Julia saw him now.

He shifted his thoughts to what he had to do the next day. Most of the morning would be spent cajoling and bullying the Council to speed up the plans for a drop-in computer training centre near the homeless shelter he was working with. And after that he was meeting the new governor, Laura Cusack, at Hartley High to show her the school. He read over his notes for the meeting. After she had rung, he had taken the time to ask around about Laura, to work out who he was dealing with and how to get the best from her.

Laura intrigued him. He had seen a couple of her pictures and he was left wondering what sort of person paints with such incredible intricacy, spends hours faithfully rendering the exact shape and texture of a single rose. With his business, he was used to dealing with artists whose work hits you bang between the eyes and the wallet. But Laura's work, he guessed, required a long, slow gaze. Its beauty took a while to reveal itself and he had sought her out the other day to talk, but she had quite obviously avoided him. It had piqued him a little. He was a natural diplomat, used to being liked. So he had done his research, chatting idly in the playground, talking with Venetia, and he had picked up on her patience – you'd need it, to paint the way she did – and her unstinting kindness. Now he knew just how he would manage her.

He glanced at the time – gone midnight – and was tempted to continue working. He could go on for hours. Both he and Julia had a phenomenal capacity for hard work. Each knew what it was to operate on five hours' sleep.

He could hear his elder daughter, Anna, moving around in her room above him now, as if pacing to and fro. Something must be troubling her. But he had no idea what, and there was no way she would tell him.

Anna had always been his favourite – though he could never admit this, least of all to himself. Rose was so stunning, with such an easy manner, that his gentle soul had reached out to his diffident, plain first-born. On his desk he had a picture of her on her sixth birthday with a Rubik's cube she had been given. And she had solved it. Even now he found Anna's brilliance a source of wonder. Julia was the first to say that Anna was cleverer than she, and Philip had often wondered – though never voiced the thought – whether his daughter would have been happier with less of her mother's brains and more of her beauty. He picked up the photograph of the freckled little girl with missing teeth, staring solemnly out at him. Shortly after the picture was taken she had fallen over and had to be taken to hospital for stitches in her knee. As if to counter-balance her mental agility she had always been clumsy.

He remembered holding her in his lap in the hospital as she sat without crying, just quietly observing the blood as it ran over her dress and on to the floor. He had kept asking if she was all right and she had kept saying she was fine – and she was, he supposed, and always had been. But her quietness and her cleverness had disconcerted him. He had thought that one day, perhaps as she got older, he might be able to reach her, but he hadn't. For a while they had played chess together – until he began to suspect that she was just humouring him and letting him win.

And day had followed day, and the years went by, and here she was at eighteen with a place at Cambridge. Soon he would lose her altogether.

The thought of his darling Anna leaving home at last made him turn off the computer and hurry upstairs, his bare feet on the warm, smooth floorboards. He knocked on her door and heard a rapid movement, a sudden rustling as though Anna was trying to hide something.

'Anna?' What on earth was she up to? 'Anna?'

'Just a minute,' she called out. 'Just a . . . . okay, come in.'

## 9

'Are you all right?' asked Phillip, opening Anna's bedroom door. Anna was sitting at her desk, surrounded by papers, her computer screen blank, giving away no sign of what she had been doing.

'Sure, what is it, Dad?'

'Just checking how you are.'

'I'm fine.'

He nodded and smiled. Her legs were contorted under her. She looked tired and uncomfortable. 'What are you . . . er . . . working on?' he asked, trying not to seem too curious.

'Nothing.'

Phillip stopped himself contradicting her. She appeared extremely busy.

'How's work?' he went on.

She shrugged. 'Okay.'

This placement she had on a glossy women's magazine, through her friend Phoebe's mother, puzzled him. Fashion was the last thing he saw Anna, who wore nothing but dingy black, involved in. But he suspected that Anna was deemed a good influence on Phoebe, who had only ever expressed one goal in life – and that was to be famous.

'What do you do exactly?' he asked, trying to make conversation.

'Oh Dad,' she sighed. 'You know. Stuff.'

'All right, all right.' He cast about for something else to say. 'Do you read all the magazines?' he asked, gesturing at a pile on her desk.

'You have to,' she said.

'Do you enjoy them?' He picked one up and began flicking through it. 'I mean, is it fun, the work you do?'

'It's a job. It's to look good on my CV.'

'Yes but –' he began, when he caught sight of a brand-new shocking-pink leather coat hanging from the picture rail.

'Wow,' he said. 'You'll get noticed in that.'

'It's not mine,' she said hurriedly. 'I'm just looking after it for Phoebe.'

'Looking after it? Why? Good God,' he said, spotting the price tag. 'How can she afford it? Not on what you're being paid.' Anna was earning barely enough to cover her travel expenses.

'Phoebe gets money, you know that.'

'Yes, but –'

'Dad,' interrupted Anna, 'do I have to go to Grandma and Grandpa's for Christmas? Couldn't I stay here? I've got work to do.'

'Oh sweetheart, no.'

'But why?'

Did he really have to spell this out to his clever daughter? 'Because it's Christmas. Because we're a family. Because they love you.'

'No, they don't.'

'Don't be daft.'

'But they don't,' she said matter-of-factly. 'They think Rose and I are shallow and spoilt.'

'But –'

'They only love poor people. Or sick ones. Preferably both.'

'Anna,' he protested, but he knew she was right.

They were going to spend Christmas together, in the icy Queen Anne house which had been in Phillip's family for two hundred years, and already his daughters' vociferous protests, and Julia's equally powerful but unvoiced objection, had started. Couldn't they all, thought Phillip, just endure in silence for three nights? He had had eighteen years there, accepting that frost formed on the inside of his bedroom windows, that his mother sat at her desk saving the poorer parts of Leeds with a woolly hat on her head, that draughts and mice wreaked havoc through the gaps in the parquet flooring. But his own children were made of different stuff.

'Mum says she thinks they make that house of theirs so

uncomfortable as a penance for having inherited such a gorgeous home.'

'Just pack an extra jumper.'

'And that they run around helping people all the time as an act of contrition for being so comfortably off.'

'Well, is that so bad?' he said, rising to their defence. 'Wanting to help people?'

'They could still put the heating on.'

'It's only three nights, and they would be so hurt if they had the slightest idea you thought about them like that.'

'Them being hurt doesn't make it less true.'

'But they do love you, and they're old and . . .'

'So? They've got opinions and aren't slow to voice them. I'm not going to wash up at that homeless shelter of theirs again and put up with Grandma going on at me –'

'You don't have to,' he interrupted. Though as a teenager he would have. His parents were exhausting. Even now, in their seventies, they shared a missionary zeal that had them setting up shelters for homeless people in Leeds.

'Just watch their disapproval when they hear about me working on a posh frocks mag,' Anna was saying. 'They'll get all snooty with me because I'm not saving Africa.'

'Don't be glib.'

'Sometimes I think hell is actually full of do-gooders who are all being punished for being so smug and self-important.'

Phillip ignored this. 'They have immense respect for you and know full well how very clever you are.'

But Anna wasn't listening.

'You know what?' she said, her intelligent eyes lighting up for a moment. 'I'll tell them what I'm paid.'

'So they can perceive you as a downtrodden worker and then they'll like you?'

She gave him a contemptuous look.

'No, Dad. Because I can tell them that after all the years of social engineering and so-called equality of opportunity now only the children of the rich like me can afford to have nice jobs.'

Phillip hardly ever had anything approaching a political discussion with his daughter. She never looked at a newspaper, except to do the Sudoku. Nor did any of her friends, as far as he could tell. And it worried him. He rather expected it of Phoebe but not of his own brilliant daughter.

'Go on,' he said, genuinely wanting to talk.

'You know what it's like. I mean, Phoebe's brother got a first from LSE but he's still living at home doing "work experience" in a bank because they can get away with paying him nothing as he's got wealthy parents with a swanky house in London who'll support him. God help the poor ones offered jobs where they're lucky if they get travel expenses. Anyway, Dad, I'm too busy to talk about this any more.'

'Sweetheart, what is all this work you have to do?'

'Just stuff,' she said.

'Have you already got work from Cambridge?'

'God, no.'

'For the magazine?'

'Sort of,' she said, turning back to her computer.

'You look tired,' he persisted, still trying to talk to his beloved daughter.

She shrugged her thin shoulders. 'I'm fine.'

He supposed she was. She had always looked wan and fragile. Yet she seemed more than capable of looking after herself.

'Dad, please, I really have so much to do.'

'Good night, then.'

'Good night,' she muttered in reply.

'Don't be too late, darling.'

She shook her head, and Phillip closed the door behind him regretfully.

# 10

Laura raced home after dropping the twins at school. At half past one she was meeting Phillip Snowe at Hartley High to be shown around the school. But before then she had three whole uninterrupted hours to herself.

She had set aside the morning deliberately. On the kitchen table, which she used as a desk, was a vase of anemones and now, in all their velvety lushness, they were perfect, exactly as she wanted for painting. And nothing, she told herself, closing the front door behind her, will prevent me. She ignored the colossal pile of ironing and was about to start when the phone rang. Laura stopped herself answering it and listened to the message from her neighbour, asking if Laura could look after her four-year-old as she had 'a crisis meeting' – as usual – and the nanny was off sick. When the twins were home, Laura would often take in this child. But not today, she told herself. If she didn't work now, then another day would go by. And tomorrow it was the weekend, and in the following week she had a meeting about the school auction, and she had been roped in to chauffeur a group of elderly parishioners to a special healing service. Not that she should say 'roped in'. But soon it would be the school holidays, and it would be January before she could have a thought to herself. And she had been longing for this moment.

She unplugged the phone.

Laura had always painted flowers, partly because her father did not. But, over the last few years, she had become yet more absorbed by them. To be engrossed in their simplicity of being soothed her. Flowers had nothing to do but exist, and concentrating on their loveliness could break the hold time had on her. And that morning, even though she was interrupted – first someone coming to read the electricity meter, then later being asked to sign for a delivery of wine to her neighbours – she forgot the demands of her two young daughters, of her mother, of the coming Christmas. She forgot her loneliness. She forgot her anxieties about her future. For three hours she was still, and life was beautiful. It was the blood-red and purple mourning of the petals, the bristling heart, the intricacy of feathery leaves.

So all morning she painted, and it was with a jolt that she realized it was almost one o'clock. She was going to be late for her meeting at the school.

Laura sprang up and phoned Phillip Snowe. There was no reply. Great start, she thought, leaving a message apologizing that she had been delayed. She grabbed a banana and wolfed it down. She was still ravenous. And in the mirror she looked utterly washed out, her tiredness accentuated by her cheap cardigan. But there was no time to change. She slapped on some lipstick – too pink – and was about to make a run for the door when she caught sight again of what she had been painting and saw it afresh.

While she had been intent on capturing the density of colour and all the delicacy of texture in those gorgeous flowers, she had thought she was touching upon the vigour and beauty of a pulsing life. But now, waves of frustration rocked her as she ran out to the car, for her painting was nowhere near as good as she thought it was when she had been engaged in it.

And I should have learned that by now, she thought. I am never going to be able to paint as I want. And I have to accept it. But what was the right thing do with her life now the girls were at school and she at last had some time? She supposed she could teach art. But that would only hammer home her own failings, and the thought of looking after thirty children all day long – her own two were hard enough – made her heart sink and her head throb.

Driving away from her own beautiful home down busier, uglier streets towards Hartley High, Laura began counting her assets. Her organizing abilities, her reliability, her excellent cooking . . . She hesitated. Her father frequently asked her for her opinion of his work – a great honour, as absolutely no one else was admitted to this privilege – because he thought she had a good eye. And she did, she knew it. But what did that really equip her for? She cast around for something and thought of the girls she had been at school with, who all seemed to be doctors and bankers and lawyers. Rather like Phillip Snowe's wife, she thought, retreating into her old sheepskin, irritated with Phillip, with her mother and most of all herself, because she didn't want this meeting now.

She surveyed the roads getting greyer, the buildings grimmer. A young woman of about sixteen – possibly younger – was dragging along a screaming toddler, and the sight of the overburdened girl and the little boy's unhappiness roused in Laura a basic instinct. I ought to want to be a governor, she admonished herself. Instead of sitting back in impotent compassion, I ought to contribute something to this school and not just long for the silence and time to paint mediocre pictures.

She pressed her uncared-for hands together to try and give herself some resolution of purpose. She forced herself to focus on the meeting ahead, and by the time she drew up at Hartley High she managed to march briskly away from the car and through the gates to the head's office.

Inside, Phillip was immaculate in suit and tie. The head, too, was just as smart, as if to say to his students, this is what you are aspiring to, this is what you can become. Laura wished now that she was better dressed. She feared her shabbiness made her appear too arrogant to bother taking the trouble.

But she extended her arm confidently and shook hands, trying to hide the paint on her fingertips.

'I'm so sorry I'm late.'

'That's quite all right –' began Phillip.

'I'm afraid I only have a couple of minutes left,' glowered the head, Alan Lovell, as they were introduced. 'I've another meeting at two.'

He has already labelled me, thought Laura – rich, and careless with other people's time.

'You know the sort of school we are, the difficulties we face. We have some very vulnerable kids here. Phillip is going to show you around, but what we really want you to do –'

'That is, if you're willing,' interrupted Phillip.

He gave Laura his splendid smile, and the head a warning glance.

'We would love it,' he continued, 'if you would take over fund-raising for the school.'

Fund-raising? In a school like this that could be a full-time job, if she wanted. No wonder he needed to charm her.

'And we need some extra help with the accounts. Your mother used to do them,' he said.

My mother's accountant used to do them, thought Laura, as a favour. And the favour had clearly come to an end.

'But for that you need a proper, trained accountant,' she said.

'Of course,' said Phillip, 'and we do have one. But he needs someone to help out with a bit of the basic stuff, and I understand you do the accounts for your church.'

'Yes, I do,' said Laura. But I hate doing them, she thought.

'And if you were able to help . . .'

'Of course,' said the head, making for the door, 'we have very different problems from a rich Catholic parish.'

'Of course we have very different problems,' echoed Phillip. 'Though I suspect in your parish there are some birds in gilded cages who have their fair share of troubles too,' and he gave Laura a quick smile of complicity.

Divide and rule, thought Laura, though she was not untouched. She found herself nodding in agreement.

But her own troubles would be added to if she took on this work. It was all right for him. He had forged his career, earned his fortune and was now presuming that she, too, had time on her hands. I know his type, she thought. He was like her mother. Incredibly thoughtful in an utterly thoughtless way.

She said, 'A school is completely different.'

'The principles are the same,' countered Phillip.

'But we're talking different budgets, funding,' she went on,

*Sarah Foot*

bridling because she had so little time and he was just casually help-ing himself to some. And if she was not careful she, like a fool, would let him.

'I have a friend,' explained Phillip, 'who says she will help you to begin with.'

So why not get the friend to do it? was Laura's instinctive response. But Phillip, as if reading her thoughts, was already pouring on the oil of flattery.

'I'm afraid she's not as generous with her time as you,' he said, 'so she will not do them for us.' And he made the attractive appeal of a man laying all his cards on the table. 'Laura, we need you. I know it's a great deal to ask and that, with children of your own – and twins too – you have a lot on your plate.' He leaned towards her in his chair, met her gaze and held it. 'But please, Laura, please.'

She wanted to say no. Phillip, with his healthy good looks, his prosperity and ease in the world, represented all the men who were and always had been out of Laura's reach, and for a brief moment she was conscious of the sour taste of self-pity. She recalled her own reflection in the mirror at home. Today she felt she looked every one of her thirty-four years and more, with what she saw as shrewish lines deepening around her mouth. She had missed out somewhere. To this smooth operator – as she had already typecast him – she was a middle-aged matron upon whom he could dump the donkey work.

'To know that a big job like this is taken care of by you,' he said, with the air of a man who thinks you are the most wonderful being in the world, 'would mean we can concentrate on other priorities. Because it's all too true,' he persisted. 'We have more than our fair share of very needy children, and protecting them . . .'

She noticed him glance up from under long lashes, as if to remind the head that this was a cue. And indeed, he responded to Phillip's bidding.

'Please,' he said, now gracious, 'we would really appreciate your input. And I'm sorry I have to run, but we can meet properly at the next governors' meeting, which is . . . When is it again, Phillip?'

'Monday at six.'

So I'll have to get a babysitter, Laura groaned inwardly, calculating how much that would set her back.

'We're not just talking low expectations here,' Phillip was explaining. 'We're talking poverty in every area. And if one of those children is actually talented at something, heaven help them.'

This man's job was in advertising, she reminded herself. He was selling her a message. He knew how to get his own way, and part of her was annoyed by the assurance with which he was winning her round, that he had homed in so quickly on her weak spot.

Pity . . . could you never be free of it? Free to spend an afternoon painting the beauty of roses when there are children, just miles from your own front door, being neglected? Free to splash out on a fabulous new coat when children had no choice but to go to a school where, as Phillip was now telling her, 'Most come from broken homes, have parents – if they even know them – without jobs. There's nothing to aspire to, no role models . . .'

Laura thought of her daughters' sunny, fulfilled world.

'. . . or at least keep them out of prison –' he was going on.

But it was enough. Laura could take no more.

'I'll do it,' she said, interrupting Phillip in full flow.

'Thank you,' he beamed. 'Now, let me show you what we're doing with the science labs,' he said, getting up and holding the door open for her. 'It's just what the school needs.'

What motivates you? she wondered, following Phillip, who was striding down the corridor as if he owned the place. Boredom? Guilt? A need to feel good about yourself?

'I don't suppose,' he was saying, 'you know of anyone who would be prepared to listen to the kids read. Some of them come to us at eleven still not reading. But I thought at your church, there might be some . . . well, retired people. Perhaps you could ask.'

'Of course,' she murmured.

'It's been very successful, actually, getting volunteers to come and help. We've got one taking an after-school club in Japanese, though I'm not sure how much – if anything – is actually being learned. But it's a start.'

He's too pleased with himself, she thought, as they went bounding up the stairs. Then, conscious of her ill-will and despising herself for it, she forced herself to sound admiring of all the interminable detail he was throwing at her. But what was really irritating her, she realized, as he relayed the successes of the zero tolerance policy towards violence and vandalism, what she truly resented was his glib assumption that he was making so much progress and sorting things out, as if doing good was just an act of will. And an hour later, she had every reason to tell him so.

## II

As Laura approached her car she saw a lanky, hooded figure in a Hartley High sweatshirt crashing a lump of cement through her windscreen. Maliciously, violently, she thought in fury as she yelled out to him. He ran off, though as she stood alone on the empty street, she realized how stupid she had been. She should have let him continue bashing away and yanking out the satnav – or whatever – in case he had picked up the cement, now sitting on her front seat, and hurled it at her.

For an uncharitable moment she wished Phillip was the one whose windscreen was in smithereens. That cement, she was in no doubt, had been lugged from the site where he had boasted two new classrooms were being built. And, she thought, while she was calling the windscreen repairers, unsure whether she was shaking with fear or rage, Phillip could afford the expense, whereas she . . .

She glanced round as a colossal black car drove past. Phillip was at the wheel, eyes focused straight ahead. He's going to pretend he hasn't seen me, she thought. For all his do-gooding he's going to cruise on by. But she was wrong. Phillip swung his car round, parking behind her, then came rushing over.

'Are you all right?' he cried.

'Yes, yes.'

'But what the devil? It wasn't one of the Hartley High kids? Hell, yes,' he said, answering his own question. 'He must have got that from the building site. We should have thought – fenced the place off better – with all that cement lying around like cannon balls. But, damn them, does it have to be a prison? We want to treat those kids like adults but they let us down at every turn. If they act like bloody convicts –'

'Hang on,' said Laura, taken aback by his distress. Instead of

telling him his students had as much understanding of zero tolerance of vandalism as nuclear physics, she found herself saying, 'It's
okay. It's just a windscreen.'

'Is it? I wish. I go round the school, showing it off, but I see this
and what's the bloody point?' The unhappiness in his voice was
palpable.

'I think,' she said, 'that it's a bit early to be talking about failure.'

'Really?' He looked her directly in the eye and something about
him unnerved her, as if he was genuinely asking her for an honest
answer. But he gave her no time to reply as, changing his tone, he
said, 'Your daughters . . . don't you need to pick them up from
school? Let me drive you, or I'll go and get them and bring them
back here for you.'

'No, it's fine. I mean, thank you.' Perhaps I have misjudged him,
she wondered. He remembered the girls, that I actually have things
to do. Perhaps he is not so thoughtless. 'I rang my brother – he'll
collect them for me.'

'So, well, let me pay for this windscreen.'

'Absolutely not.'

'But you see,' he hesitated, 'I feel responsible, that you wouldn't
be here if it wasn't for me, that I've dragged you into this school
business.'

'Of course you haven't.'

'Really?' he asked in that same perturbing way again, as if insisting on a true response. 'I worried,' he said suddenly, 'that you'd
been dragooned into it by your mother, whom I certainly find a
force to be reckoned with.'

And their eyes met for a moment in a united pact, until she
reminded herself of his instinctive ability to win you round.

'But seriously,' he was saying, 'at least let me wait with you till
they come to sort the windscreen. You'll freeze out here.'

'Honestly, I'm fine.'

'But I've –' Phillip glanced at his watch.

'You're busy,' she said.

'No, no, not till tonight.'

'Please, I'm fine,' she said. 'And you looked as if you were hurrying off to something.'

'It's a habit. Looking busy. I was supposed to collect my daughter from school but she's just texted to say she's going to a friend's. So I'm not needed.' He gave a forced laugh. 'I could do with a cup of tea. Actually, more than that. I'm ravenous. Have you had any lunch?'

'Well . . .'

'No, I guessed not. Look, there's a café round the corner. They do terrific bacon sandwiches, loads of butter, fat, grease, you know. May I get you one? Or two?' he asked, giving her a lightly teasing look.

Was that what irritated her? His certainty of how very pleasing he could be? That he was so effortlessly attractive?

'You can sit in my car. Stay in the warm and keep an eye on yours?' he suggested with a raise of his eyebrow.

Oh, why not? she thought. Just sit back in his luxurious car. 'Well . . .'

He opened the door for her. She climbed in.

Sinking into the leather, she watched him inspect her shattered windscreen again and saw the strain return to his face. What is his problem? she wondered, as he strode off. He would have the sense not to expect miracles, to know that he is not going to sort that school out overnight.

If ever.

'It seems greedy,' he said, returning armed with supplies, 'but I bought four rounds and four teas. I missed breakfast as well.'

With such lean lines Laura thought he probably missed plenty of meals. Or perhaps not. There was an energy about him that would need more fuel than a couple of bacon sandwiches.

For a while they sat and chewed, Laura glancing at him from the corner of her eye. He was clearly ravenous but once he had demolished the first round he began, quite visibly, to relax.

Resting his head back, he turned to her and said, 'You know, when I was in advertising I ate out a lot, at nice places – well, very nice, in fact. Certainly with very nice prices. But nothing quite hits the spot like this.'

He offered her another sandwich. She shook her head.

'Look,' he said, starting on his second, 'sorry I sounded off earlier. I'd hate you to think you were wasting your time, helping at the school like this.'

She found herself answering his questioning glance with a raise of her eyebrow – I'm mirroring his technique, she thought. But if only it was a waste of time. Then she would not bother. She would be at home, painting.

'Seriously,' he said, 'you don't think it's all pointless, do you?'

'No.' He looked at her, then down into his lap, and he looked so dejected, consciousness of her earlier ill-will forced her to greater effort. 'I don't think either of us is wasting our time.'

'I hope you're right,' he said, looking away.

'And that windscreen,' she said, following his eyes, 'is just one small failure. Nothing more. Not an indictment of all your work. You know,' she went on, 'when my mother was chair of the governors I always got the impression – though she would never actually admit it – that she felt she was fighting a lone battle, that in the end her one and only achievement was persuading you to take over. She was thrilled someone as experienced as you had come on board.'

'Really? Well, thank you. I'm truly glad to hear that.' And he raised his polystyrene cup as if in celebration.

She was surprised. There was no irony there. Surely he didn't need her mother's approbation?

'But . . .' he began, then gave up.

'But what?'

'So much of what I do is just so damned mundane. I mean, getting the drains fixed, you'd think I was trying to build St Mark's, the amount of mindless bureaucracy.'

'It's easy to do all the glamorous charity fund-raising,' she said carefully, wary of sounding too earnest. 'But to do what you do . . . the dull paperwork. That's real generosity, not the escapism and drama of – I don't know – paying a flying visit to an orphanage in Africa, attending a gorgeous party at some fabulous restaurant.'

'Do you really think so?' he asked, with that same scrutinizing look again.

'If your drains weren't working, wouldn't you be profoundly grateful to whoever fixed them?'

He smiled. 'Well, yes, I would.'

'There you are, then,' she said, oddly pleased she had turned his mood around. 'But what about the other governors,' she ventured, 'what do they think? My mother was pretty cagey about them. Except I know she couldn't stand the deputy –' She stopped short. That was too confiding, and there was now a quite different smile on his face. A dangerous one, she noticed, her sharp eyes reading the glint in his. He probably has every governor sussed, she thought.

He looked at her over his tea.

He's assessing how far he can trust me, thought Laura.

'Did your mother,' he began, 'ever tell you about Quentin, the councillor, who's forever trying to rearrange the date of the next meeting, going on about how busy he is, though he never has time to contribute anything?'

Laura shook her head.

'Or Annabel, with her PR agency, gushing over everyone to show how lovely and caring *she* is?'

Laura smiled. 'But the deputy?' she encouraged him. Her mother would never permit herself these indiscretions.

'The deputy,' he said, clearly starting to enjoy himself, 'makes a point of never staying at a meeting later than seven-fifteen so she doesn't miss *EastEnders*.'

Laura looked at him incredulously. 'But why doesn't she – I don't know – record it?'

'She says it's not the same as seeing it "live".'

' "Live"?' echoed Laura, seeing the amusement on his face. 'But she can't really think they're acting it out in front of the nation, can she?'

'God knows.' He burst out laughing. 'You know, at the first

meeting I thought I'd stumbled into a Dickens novel. All those . . .' he trailed off.

'Characters?'

'That's a polite way of putting it,' he said. Then his face wilted. 'It would be funny if those poor kids' futures weren't at stake. But they are. And there's me, in charge of them all. God help them.'

'People used to pay a fortune for your advice.'

He shrugged. 'That was different. I was good at what I used to do. Not through any special merit on my part. I was just born with the knack for it. But all this, I wonder – without sounding arrogant, which I know I do – is this really the best use of my . . . I don't know, skills, talents?' he said with scornful emphasis, staring out of the window as if embarrassed at this confidence.

'Maybe,' said Laura, 'you're setting yourself too high standards. Not that that's always bad, but in this case . . . trying to save this place, I think you're trying to be a saint . . .' She paused, but he was listening intently. 'And if the world only depended on saints, nothing would ever get done. So the odd drop of goodness from one person here and there is about as much as we can hope for. And if something you do at this school helps just one person, maybe in ways you can't ever imagine, then for at least that one person, that's wonderful.'

She cut short her sermon, oddly disorientated that she had moved on to such personal territory. She did not know what to say any more. Nor, clearly, did he.

They sat in a stuffy silence, the windows misting up, until he said, 'Drink up! The windscreen repairer's here.' And, downing the dregs of his tea, he got out of the car to meet him.

## 12

At ten o'clock on the following Sunday morning, Rose Snowe was rushing to finish her essay on disguise in *Twelfth Night*. That she was up at that time on a Sunday was unusual, but that she was at her desk was unheard of. How her mother endured her interminable slog as a lawyer she had no idea, but she would not end up like her mother. That was for sure. But she had an absolutely massive favour to ask of her parents. And the only way she had the slightest chance of them agreeing was to have all her homework completely done without any of the drama she normally enjoyed.

She did a word count. Too short. She turned back to the text and Viola saying:

> *She sat like Patience on a monument,*
> *Smiling at grief. Was not this love, indeed?*

No, it was pathetic, decided Rose. You would never find her smiling at grief, stoically pretending that all was well. She didn't believe in self-sacrifice. And she certainly didn't believe in sitting around patiently enduring. Instead, *she* would make things happen. *She* would take control. (In this, at least, she was her mother's daughter.) Adrenaline pulsed through her. Because she had made things happen. A whole new world was opening up. Excitement awaited her, as long as . . . as long as she could persuade her parents.

Rose turned back to her essay because once she was done she would embark on her campaign to convince Julia and Phillip that they should allow her to go on a reality television show. Put like that, thought Rose, casting around for some sort of conclusion about Viola who was quite clearly going to end up horribly unhappy with the appalling Orsino, the task did sound hopeless. But she was prepared. She had spent hours marshalling her arguments with all the dedication of her mother.

Two months ago Rose had seen an advertisement from a television company asking for families to take part in a reality television show about out-of-control teenagers. Called *Tough Love, Tough Luck*, the first series had run earlier in the year and Rose and her friends had been riveted. Appallingly behaved adolescents were wrested out of their home environments and placed with families thousands of miles away who held very different views on parenting from their own. After a fortnight in this alien culture teenagers were dramatically changed. On the show at least, they came home apologetic, compliant and respectful.

But what drew Rose's attention was that one of the teenagers from the first series had gone on to be a co-presenter on a teen music show and was about to front a new boy band. News of the advertisement raced around St Catherine's, fuelling the ambitions of all those who saw television as the Holy Grail, and Rose, along with the others in her illustrious set, had applied.

Rose was desperate to be chosen. She could see herself in the Maldives – where one especially difficult boy had been placed in the previous series – dressed in a tastefully revealing sundress as she slowly but dramatically realized the error of her ways. The sun would set behind her and one dewy tear would roll down her cheek as she apologized to her parents and yearned to make amends. It would make great television, she knew it. And so much could follow – stories in the tabloids, appearances on chat shows, a media career.

So, displaying a creativity and eloquence almost non-existent in her school work, Rose had invented a tale of her own dreadful behaviour, along with what she thought was a most moving *cri de coeur*, supposedly by her parents, bewailing their despair at their inability to handle their beautiful but terrible teenager.

She had also, with a forethought she was most proud of, bought a new mobile phone and given that number as her mother's. So if the researchers rang – as, indeed, they did – to discuss the application,

Rose was able to pretend she was her mother and assure them that she desperately wanted her daughter to take part as she was unable to cope.

Rose had surpassed herself. She had written and acted with such conviction that she was now on a shortlist – the only one from her school to make it this far – and the producer, along with a well-known presenter, wished to come to the house and interview the family. Now she would have to tell her parents.

*Now*, she told herself, sitting at her desk – otherwise she would have got up early to write this wretched essay for nothing. She ran over her notes again for her 'pitch' to her parents. She had discussed it long and hard with Rose B, whose mother was so good at getting her own way, and Rose B had told her to use the 'fish-slapping' technique. As soon as she had explained what she wanted, she had to shoot down her parents' arguments against her going on the show before they had time to voice them.

Rose had expected to find her parents on the large kitchen sofa reading the Sunday papers. Both were at home this weekend – her mother wasn't flying to Boston until that evening, and since her father had given up his job he never spent a night away. But when Rose walked into the large airy kitchen, the newspapers were untouched. Her mother was concentrating on stirring a stalk of fresh mint around in her favourite mug. And her father, dressed as if he was on his way out, was hunting for his car keys. They both turned to her in surprise. For a moment she wondered whether they had been arguing. Except they never really rowed.

There was an odd, uneasy silence.

Her father broke it. 'You're up early, sweetheart.'

Rose replied with her brightest smile. 'Yes, but where are you going?' she asked, taking her father's hand as he kissed the top of her head. If she was to get her own way she needed him there. She wouldn't have a hope with her mother on her own.

'Church,' he said.

'Again?' He had gone last Sunday as well.

He nodded. 'Want to come?'

Rose rolled her eyes. 'You're not getting like Grandpa, are you? Going to church all the time.'

She caught her mother's quick grey eyes turning to Phillip.

But he just laughed and said, 'I heard you up hours ago.'

At this her mother looked at her properly. 'Are you all right, Rose?'

'Sure, yes, I'm really . . . I'm really . . .'

Rose hesitated. Her plan was to speak to them now. But her mother seemed distracted, and if her father was going out then she would not have time to make her case properly. Perhaps this was not the moment. But her mother was on to her.

'What is it, Rose? You look as if you want something.'

Rose braced herself. This was as good an opportunity as she was ever going to get. She launched in. 'I've had some really, really good news. And it's the most amazing thing that has ever happened to me.'

Already there was a smile on her father's face. This was how she had planned it. Her mother was inscrutable, but she had expected that too.

'I'm just so excited. You see . . .' she paused for what she considered dramatic effect, 'I've been asked to go on a television show.'

This was not strictly true. She had not been asked yet, but no matter.

'And the opportunity for me will be so great as it's a really big prime-time show.' She had rehearsed this line, and the next. 'And I know you'll be worried about how much time it'll take, especially as the workload at school is increasing, but that won't be a problem. Because you're absolutely right, Mum, when I put my mind to it, I can do it well and quickly. I've already done all this weekend's homework, and I've started the physics project for the holiday. Because going on this show will make me organize my time better . . .' Rose hesitated.

Her mother was looking at her as if she was in the witness box. Perhaps she was overdoing the fish-slapping. And the hardest bit

was yet to come, as her parents loathed reality shows and were ludicrously obsessive about their privacy. Rose made herself come to
the point.

'The thing is, if you would just say I'm a difficult teenager – and
I know at times I am – but if you would just exaggerate a little . . .
well, a lot . . . then I promise . . . I promise . . . I promise I will
always, always be good. All my homework will be done. And on
time. I will not stay out late, I will work hard – really hard. I will
never, ever get drunk . . . I will . . .'

A smile was playing about her father's lips, but her mother had
returned to stirring her stalk of mint. 'I will be as good as you could
ever want. And you need never worry about me again, ever.'

She beamed broadly as if to ask, how could you resist? She
watched her father put his hand to his mouth, and give an odd
cough. She almost had him, she was sure. But her mother had on
that really irritating Mona Lisa face of hers.

'Mum,' continued Rose, using a line Rose B had taught her, 'this
is a "win-win" situation. You get the perfect teenager and I get a
whole brilliant career opening up. Because I've thought it all
through. Seriously, this is what I want to do with my life – be a presenter. And I know I'm good on television, because we've done
television work at school.'

This took her mother's attention off her mint stalk, for she actually stopped stirring a moment.

'We had to do a talk,' explained Rose, 'and they filmed us and I
heard Miss Hunt tell Miss Sinclair that I was a natural, and I was. All
my class said so too. And by the time the show actually comes out
I'll be sixteen, and then I'll be able to get work in television. And I
can be a presenter . . .'

And I can be famous, and I can be rich, sang Rose's glossy hopes.
And I will be adored and wear beautiful clothes and people will pine
for me like Patience on a monument and there will be no more
essays and no more doing what other people tell me.

'. . . but I need to be . . . I need to be . . .'

She couldn't say to her mother that she needed to be discovered. Even to Rose's ears this sounded a cliché, and she knew the derision with which her mother would greet it.

But she was sick of wasting her time at school being ordered around by people who were neither clever nor pretty. She was sick of being kept down by her mother – who was clever and pretty, but was as negotiable as a fox with wings.

'. . . I need,' she said, 'to be seen.'

Her parents greeted this with silence. Rose B had warned they might try and trap her with silence. She must not blunder into it and keep on talking and tying herself up in knots.

But she could not bear it, so she said, 'What do you think? Dad?'

'Let me get this straight,' he replied. 'What you want is for us to tell this television company that you are really, really bad. And in return you will be really, really good. For ever. Is that right?'

Rose wasn't sure whether her father was laughing at her or whether he was happy for her or whether he was simply trying to make up his mind. She nodded.

'So what,' he asked, 'do you want us to say you do that's so bad?'

'Well, I've . . .' Rose gulped and stopped herself from playing with her hair. She must not show how nervous she felt. 'Actually,' she said, 'I've already done that.'

'You have?'

'Well, yes, because . . .' Rose's heart was beating fast. She knew her parents were scrupulously honest. She doubted her mother had even put a lunch with a friend on expenses. So she had to present the lies on her application form – 'lies' was the only word for it – as one big, clever joke.

'. . . because I . . . I exaggerated a bit about how I don't always do my homework and how you get angry if I spend too long messing about on the computer. And . . .' She trailed off.

'And?' he asked.

'Well, I made some things up about borrowing your clothes, Mum – but I said you had great style, which is true. And that I'd used your credit cards and that when you're away I have parties here and break your things and drink all your drink, that I go out with unsuitable men – which, of course, is all complete nonsense – but they believed it. But now the producer needs to meet you, and if you would just go along with what I've said.' Her eyes sparkled. Glory awaited her. 'Then I can be on television.'

'Just explain to me,' Julia spoke at last, 'exactly what you hope to gain from this.'

There was no mistaking her mother's withering tone. And Rose knew she must not rise to it. If she got angry with her mother, there was no doubt who would lose the argument.

Articulating carefully, Rose repeated, 'I can be on television.'

Julia's silence made it clear to Rose that her mother still failed to grasp the significance of this.

She spelled it out. 'Television is what everyone wants to do, and all my friends think I could be famous. And Mrs Green is always saying to me, "When you're famous, Rose . . ."'

'I suspect you'll find,' said Julia, 'she's being sarcastic.'

Rose caught the glare Phillip directed at Julia, as if to say, 'Don't be sarcastic yourself,' then he said, 'Look, sweetheart, your obsession . . . your entire generation's obsession with being on telly, with celebrities, with living the dream and all that, it's so vacuous, so shallow, so . . . so . . .'

'Dad,' said Rose carefully. She was prepared for this argument. 'For most people it is. But not for me. I tell you, I've thought it through. I don't just want fifteen seconds of fame.'

'Minutes,' corrected Julia and Phillip in unison. 'The quote is fifteen minutes of fame.'

'Whatever, but for lots of people it is only fifteen seconds. That's all you get because, Dad, you're right in that for most of those poor suckers on talent shows the fame doesn't last. But I'm not interested in that. I don't want some quick fix. I want a proper career, and this show would be the start. I'd make sure of it.'

'But you can't . . . sweetheart, you can't make sure of something like that.'

'But I'm good,' said Rose, taking her father's hand again and looking at him, to impress on him that although she was his little girl, she was totally grown-up. 'Truly. I know it. I can hold an audience. Look at me at the concert the other night. I mean, if it was physics I was good at you'd be encouraging me. Why not this? And it's not some flaky thing, if that's what you're thinking,' she went on, returning to her fish-slapping. 'I mean, do you have any idea what sort of lives people lead, being famous? What they earn? Going to premieres, getting tables at restaurants like The Ivy, The Caprice –'

'I prefer the food in the pub at the end of the road,' interrupted Phillip.

'It's not about the food. It's about being seen. It's what everyone dreams of.'

'Not everyone,' murmured Phillip. 'I don't think it's once crossed your sister's mind or your friend Rose B's.'

'Trust me,' Rose said, 'Rose B would love to go on TL2.'

'On what?'

'That's the show – *Tough Love, Tough Luck*. Or TL2. It's actually a really good programme with really high ratings. Honestly, you must be the only people who haven't heard of it.'

'Sweetheart,' said Phillip, 'if I'd known you take these stupid shows so seriously . . .'

'You never watch them,' muttered Rose. 'And if you did, you'd realize they're not all bad.'

'So,' said Julia, ignoring this, 'your big dream . . . your great ambition . . . the one goal of your life is to be on television. Is that right?'

Rose nodded. How many times would she have to hammer it home?

'And to achieve this goal of yours,' continued Julia, 'it has not occurred to you that you might actually need to work hard.'

'But I have,' protested Rose. 'I wrote the application and that was really hard work. And it was good, otherwise they wouldn't have chosen me. Even Jane in my class, who's supposed to be so great at English and whose Dad's a novelist – though I've always thought he helps her with her coursework, and now I'm certain he does – didn't get a look in. But mine did, it was so brilliant.'

'So to realize this dream,' persisted Julia, 'you have lied. Rose? Isn't that right?'

'I don't know if I'd say "lied" exactly.'

'What would you say, then?'

'I don't know. Okay, all right, yes, I lied.'

'And you have cheated, and you have no doubt misrepresented me, and your father.'

'All right, all right. I've done those terrible things, but it'll mean I can be on television. And the producers really want me.'

'I bet they do,' said Julia. 'The posh family with problems. Honestly, Rose, I can't believe you thought for one minute that we'd agree to go on record – on television – saying we can't control our own daughter. Surely you know us better than that.'

'But you don't have to. I told you. I've thought it through,' cried Rose triumphantly. She had anticipated this. 'You could be anonymous. I asked them – arranged it so you could appear in shadow and they'd use actors' voices. The producer thought this was a great idea, and it was all mine.'

'Don't be ridiculous,' said Julia. 'Of course we'd be identified, because everyone would recognize you. And you say the whole point of this exercise is for you to get known.'

Rose hesitated a moment under her mother's merciless gaze. Then, she saw an opportunity. 'Who are you worried about seeing it, Mum? Surely not your friends? They're far too snooty for this sort of telly – too busy watching *Newsnight*,' she went on facetiously.

But that was a mistake. She adopted the role of loving, sensible daughter.

'Mum, look at that model who got a first from Cambridge. It's possible to be both shallow – as you see it – and deep. And this show would be like doing A-levels in the opportunities it would give me – better, actually, a million times so.'

'Get your A-levels,' said Julia, 'and we'll think again.'

'But what's the point of someone like me doing A-levels?' cried Rose. 'No one asks what A-levels Diamond Dee has.'

Julia looked at her blankly, and Phillip asked, 'Who's Diamond Dee?'

'Oh, for God's –' Rose steadied herself, then answered calmly. 'She's the judge on that new Saturday-night talent show, she's released the fastest-selling single ever, she's on the cover of the latest *Hello!*, she's –'

'How you could possibly have thought we would say yes to this, I've no idea,' interrupted Julia. 'It sounds complete rubbish. Really, Rose.' Julia finished her tea as if to say the discussion was over. 'Don't be so naive.'

'Mum, you're the one who's naive. Why do MPs, who one minute promise to solve all our problems, go on reality shows and do things like sit in crates of insects, or pretend to be cats licking saucers of milk?'

Julia did not answer this but said, 'Even one of those modelling shows would not be as bad as this.'

'I thought about that,' said Rose seriously, 'but I can't make it on my looks alone. I need more, and I'd have thought you'd be the first to say that, Mum. And on a show like this I can show my personality.'

'Humiliate yourself, you mean.'

'That's the world we're in, and you know it. I mean, the number of times, Mum, that you whinge on about how there's nothing on telly but watching people humiliate themselves. And that,' Rose assumed her mother's clear voice and mimicked her all too well, ' "we live in a humiliation society, except in schools, where some humiliation might actually do some good".'

One look at her mother made her realize she had blown it.

'Sweetheart . . .'

Rose caught the smile in her father's voice.

'. . . I'm sorry, but your mother and I are in complete agreement on this.'

'But you can't do this to me,' cried Rose. Suddenly the tears were falling fast and she could not stop them, and she could not bear it when she cried for real. 'You can't, and if you do –'

'Trust us,' said Phillip. 'This won't do you any good.' He held out his arms to his daughter.

Rose stayed put. Of course they could stop her doing this show.

But in return she would . . . What would she do? She watched her mother open the dishwasher, realize it was full of clean crockery, put her dirty mug in the sink and then turn to her.

'Would you empty the dishwasher please, Rose,' said Julia, turning her attention to her iPad. 'Now I must go and pack.'

Rose's eyes burned, aware of the hidden menace in that bland tone. If her mother thought getting her to empty the dishwasher was a way of showing who was in control, then she had another think coming.

'You know,' said Rose, grasping at one last argument, 'it's so easy for teenagers to go off the rails. Eating disorders, drugs, drink, debts, sex . . . and all because their parents don't understand them, their needs.' Rose hadn't intended whining and threatening, but she saw no other way. 'There's a girl in the year above me who, when her parents stopped her seeing her boyfriend, went off to live with him, gave up school, got pregnant.'

But Julia, in her silk embroidered dressing gown, was already out of the door.

Rose contemplated screaming after her. Both her parents hated 'scenes' and it occurred to her, seeing the way her father's mouth had hardened as Julia left the room, that he was angry Julia had just waltzed out, leaving him to deal with their daughter on his own. Perhaps she could capitalize on this.

'Sweetheart, don't blackmail us. It won't work.'

'Won't it?'

'No,' said Phillip, handing her two mugs to put away in the cupboard.

## 13

Julia went straight upstairs and began equipping herself for her trip to Boston. So used to travelling for business, she was packed in ten minutes. She was often invited to lecture at international forums for other lawyers, and this time she was taking a seminar at Harvard Law School on the flaws in new European legislation, as well as meeting a publisher of legal textbooks.

She flicked through her papers, checking that she had all she needed, yet her brain was flitting back and forth. How could Rose think nothing of humiliating herself so publicly? How could she have been so deceitful? What's more, seen nothing wrong in deliberately lying?

Rose had not only been fraudulent, she hoped to realize her shallow dreams by getting away with as little effort as possible. The one tenet Julia had imbibed of her mother's devout Methodism was the unrelenting work ethic. Not that she believed her conscientiousness justified a seat in heaven. Instead, the pledge she had made was to arm herself with the knowledge and expertise to fight the deadening drabness of life. And in so doing, she believed she was setting an excellent example and protecting her own beloved daughters. So what had gone wrong?

In the office, Julia had young women falling over themselves for her advice on their careers. And she enjoyed helping them guide the trajectory of their professional lives. But, she thought, as she put out the cashmere sweater she always liked to fly in, I would love, most of all, to help my own daughter.

For a moment Julia floundered. She was livid – and she was hardly ever angry, because it was such a waste of energy. But now, rage, like poison, surged through her. She sank on to her vast white bed as if she had been punched. She had trained herself not to think too much about her own past but her thoughts jerked away from the calculated beauty of her own bedroom to the cramped, ugly flat where she and her elder sister, Angela, had been brought up. She could picture their exhausted mother, burdened with no education and the need to bring up two daughters on her own after their father swiftly fled the drudgery of paternity and wage-earning. But against all the odds, both sisters had triumphed over adversity – Angela, Julia readily acknowledged, even more so than her.

Now a consultant in geriatrics at a big London teaching hospital, Angela had had the tougher ride. She was the one who helped their mother as arthritis took hold of her body and her life. Julia, seeing the strain this put upon her big sister, had quickly learned to adopt the role of the younger daughter who was too much of a child for such duties – though, outside the home, there were few areas of adult experience she had not soon tried or seen. And when the arthritis finally rampaged out of control, leaving their mother incarcerated in their dingy flat, it was Angela who put her medical studies on hold for three whole years to face the oppression and distress of caring for someone so chronically disabled and in pain.

How Angela had stood it all – the boredom, the imprisonment, the smell – was beyond Julia. But Angela was her mother's daughter and believed joy was to be found in living hourly, daily, yearly for others – in laying your life at the feet of God. The old and sick were her children; God was the focus of her passions. How else could you explain her decision to specialize in geriatrics, the most unfashionable and least rewarded branch of medicine? Also, in a typically Angela-like spirit of self-sacrifice, six months ago she had adopted a four-year-old girl from Romania, Mirela, a child deemed 'unadoptable' by the agency because she was too old and too damaged. Julia knew, rightly, that the label 'unadoptable' had proved irresistible to her sister.

Yet for all their differences and her lack of understanding of her sister, Julia had immense respect for Angela, and she knew the sentiment was returned. We worked hard and we escaped, thought Julia, from that grim childhood. But Rose's enviably gilded life had produced a spoilt –

Julia stopped right there. Anna, she reminded herself. Think of Anna, her brilliant elder daughter, with her Cambridge place, her internship on a magazine, her diligence and good sense.

Everything in Julia's nature revolted at the idea that suffering could be redemptive. She had only to recall her mother's neighbours on that Hartley Estate, or spend half an hour in the criminal courts, to know exactly where deprivation could lead. As a mother her overriding goal had been to spare her daughters her own experience. And she had succeeded beyond even her wildest expectations. All the wonderful things she had given Rose rushed in on her: the beautiful home; the books and music; a large bedroom she did not have to share; delicious food in a full fridge; holidays three times a year; theatre trips in the best seats; lovely birthday parties. Yet what had such easy affluence done to her daughter?

Julia was used to people talking about their terribly poor childhoods, though she soon learned that those who liked to flaunt their working-class origins did not always, on closer inspection, truly have them. She was utterly private about her background, giving no excuses, no justifications. It was simply assumed she was from a comfortable middle-class family. Among her family, friends and business associates, only her sister and Phillip – and not even he was privy to all the details – knew about her past. She did not want to remember it, and she certainly had no sentiment about it. For her, poverty was not an intellectual exercise. It was the grotty flat on the rough council estate, playing in parks littered with broken glass, learning at the age of four not to touch the empty syringes, free school meals, the humiliation of not being able to go on school trips.

She reached for her favourite orange-blossom cream in its pretty golden jar and massaged it hard into her soft hands. A memory of chapped wrists in a damp, unheated bathroom darted through her mind. If she could have had a different childhood she would have snatched at it. She had had to get away, and if it had taken a degree of selfishness, then what choice did she have? If she had stayed, she would have drowned.

Yet even her darling Anna affected a faux-working-class poverty with her grungy black clothes and the roll-ups she smoked on the quiet. Couldn't Anna, thought Julia, straightening her perfume bottles on the top of her gleaming rosewood dressing table, realize how patronizing and ignorant that was? That she was playing Marie Antoinette? That poverty was a real nightmare you did not romanticize, and Julia's greatest unspoken fear was that it was still all too close, that it would take very little – a wrong turn here, a lack of concentration there – for her to be pulled back into that hell?

At this Julia's robust spirit rose to the fore. She could not admit these terrors. She sprang up, fetched the yellow notepad and pen she kept by her bed, and she began to write. At once, her ideas started to flow with their customary speed. If she could define a problem, put a barrier of words around it, she could control it. Just as she did when taking on a new case, she committed her thoughts on Rose to paper.

Julia was so engrossed she did not hear Phillip come into the room.

'You might have stayed and talked to her,' he said, keeping his voice low.

Julia looked up from her neatly numbered ideas and, ignoring the implied criticism, gave him a big smile because she had already worked out what they needed to do. It would be all right. She could deal with Rose.

'Sweetheart,' she said, 'you're better with her when she's like that. You really are. But look, I've been thinking, and we need to reconsider that school. Really,' she added, as a frown appeared on Phillip's face, 'that's where the problem is. It's obviously wrong. The way they let her get away with that fiasco on the cello, that even the teachers are telling her how she'd be good on television. She's not got enough to do and isn't being challenged –'

'Stop a minute. You can't just go rushing in blaming the school. Anna always did brilliantly there.'

'Anna's a completely different character. Ten times as clever. And

she's sensible. Now I've made a list, because I think we should seriously consider boarding schools. Rose is the sort of girl who needs
to be kept busy. Not staring at a screen or at her own reflection all
day. At a boarding school they'd have to structure their time properly, there'd be activities.'

'How do you know what the devil they do at boarding school?'

'Because it's obvious they'll be organized. And Kate's daughter is
at boarding school.' Kate was Julia's personal assistant. 'And she
does masses of debating and drama and . . . and all that stuff.'

'Kate's daughter once told me her favourite thing at school was
watching *Sleeping Beauty* or *Cinderella* – one of those Disney things –
with all her friends, as they know all the songs and they sit together
in their bedroom and sing along. Be grateful Rose isn't lying around
singing for a prince.'

'Phillip, please, you know what I mean. At boarding school she
couldn't just mess around.'

'But I don't want her to go away,' said Phillip, putting his arm
around Julia. 'I didn't sell the business so I could see less of my
daughters.'

Nor my wife, hung unspoken in the air.

At breakfast, before Rose had announced her news, Julia had said
that, instead of returning on Tuesday morning, she would not be
back until Wednesday as she needed to meet some new bright
whizz-kid at Harvard. Uncharacteristically, Phillip had objected.
While he was running his own company they had each accepted the
other's professional preoccupations and catered to them without
question. But now he wanted his wife, and he wanted her alone –
just the two of them. He wanted to talk to her, not just to exchange
timetables and discuss the girls. He wanted to tell her that he was
worried about the commitments he had taken on, that he feared
failure.

When Phillip had been in advertising, results had been tangible
and not just in his bank balance. But at Hartley High he could easily
be out of his depth. Of course, with his skills he knew exactly how

to make it look as though he was achieving wonders at the school. Managing the idiocies of the education system was like knowing how to seduce a client, realizing what boxes needed to be ticked. But although he might fool the bureaucrats, he was too honest to fool himself. He wanted to explain this to Julia, to be listened to and understood. It occurred to him that he had said more to the new governor, Laura, about his thoughts than he had to his wife in the past year.

'I want,' he said, 'my family around me.'

Julia trod carefully. 'Darling, I know you want to see more of her. So do I . . .' She hesitated.

She and Rose used to have lovely times together, seeing an exhibition, having lunch, going shopping – an activity Julia normally loathed. But they had had fun, doing the sort of things that Julia had longed to be able to do with her own mother. Of late, however, Julia had not had time. But I will make time, she told herself. Quite when, she did not know. She was never in the office later than seven-thirty every morning, and to be home by nine was an unusually early night. And she could see no respite. Her biggest case – representing a leading technology company, Clifford James, in a dispute with an oil company and an offshore trust – had been dragging on for what felt like decades. The sums involved were the largest she had ever dealt with, and for the last few weeks articles had been appearing in the papers – not that morning, thankfully, so she did not have to deal with that right this minute. Plus a new CEO had been appointed last week, which only added to Julia's worries. But I will manage, she told herself. I will. She had faced problems every bit as bad as this before. And sorted them, both to her and her client's advantage.

But to Phillip she said, 'It's not about what we want, but what's best for Rose. And we could get a new school sorted over the next couple of months, so she could start somewhere in the summer term. I'll get Kate on to it tomorrow, getting prospectuses. But we don't want one of those smart finishing-school types where they all end up doing history of art. She's bright enough to be –'

'For heaven's sake, Julia. She's fifteen. Here,' said Phillip, taking her notepad from her, 'what's this?'

'Things to do in the meantime. Ration her television watching.'

'Okay, though I'm not sure what good that'll do.' And, he found himself thinking, you won't be the one policing her, as you'll be at work.

'Well, we can't do nothing. I mean, you don't think it's good, do you, that she wants to go on this stupid show and that her head is filled with all that celebrity nonsense?'

'Of course I don't! I hate it as much as you do. But boarding school is an overreaction.'

Julia kept quiet. She had grown up hearing couples screaming, shouting and worse through thin walls but she had never had a full-scale row with her own husband. And she would keep it that way. In their twenty years of being together, if they disagreed, she had learned to sow the seed of an idea in Phillip's mind and let him mull it over till he came round to her way of thinking.

'What's she doing now?' she asked.

'Washing her hair.'

'Again?'

'Yes. And she said she might go into town later this afternoon.'

'That's another thing,' said Julia in an even tone, 'the way it takes her a whole day just to arrange to see her friends has got to stop. At boarding school she'd actually have to learn to make a commitment. And keep it.'

'She won't if she's unhappy.'

'Why should she be?'

Because, thought Phillip, she will construe boarding school as a punishment and she has the sort of stubborn nature that could easily determine on being unhappy just to hurt us in return. He put down Julia's notepad. He had always loved and admired the way his wife could solve problems. She was a fixer, and in the days before they could afford to pay someone else to do such chores, she could follow instructions to install a new computer, make up a flat-pack wardrobe, change a wheel. He was used to Julia treating life as if it was a performing seal that she could simply train to balance a ball upon its nose. But he would not have her dealing with Rose in the same way. Rose would not go to boarding school. He gritted his teeth. Julia had suddenly come up with this idea as though their daughter, too, was a quick fix. His annoyance possessed the sharp edge of anger. He moved away from her to the window, arms crossed.

But Julia did not notice.

'I'd have loved to have gone to boarding school,' she sighed. 'I used to beg my mother – particularly in the sixth form. If I could get a scholarship and then I could just get away, and not have to . . .'

She trailed off. On the very rare occasions she alluded to her childhood Phillip had to listen carefully. For her to reveal any sadness was as rare as an eclipse. His anger subsided as quickly as it had flared. His instinct to protect Julia was fierce. It always had been, though she had never recognized it. When he first met her – so brilliant and unhappy at university – he wanted to show her that sometimes good things happen – not because you have worked hard, not because you deserve them, but simply for no reason at all. The problems he had had in life – at a push, he might say he wished his parents had been a little less distracted, but that was about it – were about as serious and long-lasting as a midge bite. But Julia's ran deep, affecting every ounce of her being and her vision.

He left the window. He saw her gorgeous strength now, her beautiful body.

'Julia,' he said, taking her hands. 'It was different for you. You can't compare yourselves.'

'Yes, but . . .'

When he turned the full force of his tenderness upon her, Julia could not say no. And it had been a long time. Too long. She felt the hairs on the back of her neck prickle. His arms were around her.

'Promise you'll think about it,' she said.

'I promise. But please, turn that off,' he said, nodding at her phone. 'Just for a few minutes, please.'

She did as he asked. But then, seconds later – or so it seemed to Phillip – their home phone rang.

'Ignore it,' he said. 'One of the girls will get it.'

They lay still. The ringing stopped. Then, next minute, Anna was stomping up the stairs.

'Mum! It's David.' David was one of Julia's associates. 'He needs to speak to you.'

Julia raised herself up. 'Sorry, sorry,' she said to Phillip.

'Mum!' called Anna. 'He says it's urgent.'

Julia got up, pulling her dressing gown tight. Phillip lay back on the pillow, his hands clasped behind his head. David saw everything as urgent. Julia opened their bedroom door.

'Thank you, darling,' she said to Anna, taking the phone.

She sat on the bed and picked up her notepad again. Phillip took a deep breath, watching her concentrate. Utterly unbidden came the question, when had she last concentrated on him like that?

When Phillip had been running his company, both he and Julia were used to going away separately, staying late at the office, cancelling a trip to the theatre at the last minute. A night when neither brought work home was a treat. Lolling about, or going for a walk because they just happened to feel like it, was almost unheard of.

And it was not a problem. But today, Phillip felt a weight in his chest. It seemed to him that Julia's job was taking all the oxygen out of their room, their home, their life.

'Let me ring you back in ten minutes,' she was saying. 'I'll get the papers.' She put down the phone and slipped her arms back around Phillip. 'I've got to sort this.'

'How long will it take?'

'Couple of hours.'

He nodded.

'Sorry. What'll you do?'

'I told you. Go to church.'

'Oh, of course.'

This was what they had been discussing when Rose surprised them in the kitchen.

'You always used to go on about the evil religion does,' she said, it crossing her mind that going to church was another cause he was adopting. 'All the wars and intolerance and so on.'

'Take a beautiful idea,' he said carefully, 'and give it to human beings, and what do you expect?' And he kissed her on the lips.

She kissed him back, absently, and then got on with her work.

## 14

Laura was peeling parsnips in her parents' kitchen. Her mother was 'running late' with the Sunday lunch for the whole family so had phoned to see if Laura would come over early and help. In return Laura hoped she might secure a favour.

'I know you've never babysat the girls before,' Laura explained, 'but they're so much easier now they're older –'

'Don't tell your father the parsnips are organic,' interrupted Venetia.

'No, I won't –'

'You know what a waste of money he says organic is.'

'Yes . . . but, Mum, I can't get a babysitter at such short notice for the governors' meeting tomorrow night, and I wondered . . .'

'Darling, I'd love to, but I can't,' said Venetia, taking eight linen napkins from the drawer. 'Ring up an agency.'

Laura chopped through a parsnip. Her mother had no idea what an agency cost. Nor how difficult it was getting out of the house if the twins were left with somebody they didn't know. 'But they're hopeless settling with anyone new.'

'It's about time they learned. You and your brothers were perfectly happy being left with strangers.'

No, we weren't, said Laura to herself – particularly Mark, who would refuse to speak to babysitters he disliked – and even Robert, who normally got on with everyone, made himself so unbearable on two occasions that the babysitters refused to come back. But her mother had selective blind spots which, over thirty-four years, Laura had learned to accept. So she just asked, out loud, whether Venetia had done the potatoes.

'No, I was going to but . . . now, how about asking Robert if he'll babysit? The girls adore him. And you'd better do lots of potatoes, as you know how Robert loves them.'

'He's probably busy,' said Laura, knowing full well that her younger brother was going to Paris for the night with one of the women he was decorating for.

'Well, ask him,' said Venetia, hearing the front door open. 'That's probably him now, as Mark said that he and Jane would be late. They've got some pre-natal yoga class.'

'Mark does pre-natal yoga too?'

'Apparently. The class is for pregnant people.'

For one brief and all too rare moment Laura and her mother enjoyed a common thought. 'Yes, darling, do try not to laugh. You know how seriously he takes everything.'

'I think it's Jane who's so serious,' began Laura, when Robert came bounding into the kitchen.

'Did I hear correctly? Jane's making Mark do pre-natal yoga?' he said, throwing his arms around his mother. 'Good God, Mum, you're not on one of your mad diets, are you? You're nothing but bones.'

'I'm fine,' said Venetia, disengaging herself. 'And don't tease your brother, please, he won't see the funny side of it.'

'Jane won't, is what you really mean,' he said, kissing Laura. 'Hello, big sister, you look exhausted. Is that because of those nieces of mine, or has Mum been slave-driving you?'

'Robert, don't be ridiculous,' protested Venetia. 'It's because of you she's having to do all these vegetables. If you didn't eat so much . . .'

'Yes, Mother,' he said, and his gentle voice broke into laughter. Robert was tall and slim, with a strong body that vaulted up scaffolding and sweated in the sun. 'So, Mother, how are you?'

'Well, your father,' began Venetia, 'is terribly busy, right in the middle of some new picture –'

'Don't tell me how Dad is. He's always terribly busy. I asked about you, and you look –'

'I'm fine and very grateful to Laura for taking on that work at the school.'

'You landed Laura with it? Mum!'

'I wanted to do it,' said Laura, her voice almost inaudible as she ran water into a large saucepan for the potatoes. But she gave Robert the sort of look that begged, 'Be quiet!' and he acquiesced and just talked to his mother about her work until the phone rang and Venetia left the kitchen to answer it.

'Is she all right?' he asked, watching his mother depart.

'I think so, why?'

'She's so thin and, I don't know, there's something about her . . . oh, nothing. But for God's sake, Laura, why on earth did you agree to be a school governor? You've got enough to do as it is.'

'Because . . .' She felt her brother's sharp eyes on her. There was little he missed when he could be bothered to look. She felt a not unfamiliar sadness. Robert was one of the enrichers of life, so why was he wasting his big heart and talent redecorating houses that were pretty much perfect in the first place, while seducing their lonely, bored and expensively groomed chatelaines? 'Because I feel I should,' she snapped, suddenly irritable.

'What you should be doing is starting to look after yourself. And you hate sitting in meetings, paperwork . . . all that stuff you do for the church. You'd rather be painting.'

'So?'

'So, don't do it. You don't have to be generous. You don't think all Mum's do-gooding stems from generosity?'

Laura shrugged.

'Of course it doesn't. It's just that it's a nightmare living with Dad's damned genius, and domesticity bores her rigid – as it does you, if you were honest.'

'It doesn't bore me. Well, whatever . . . anyway, what's it matter why I do things? Of course I'm not generous. That's why we're given consciences, so we dredge up the energy to act as if we were,' she said, trying to split a rock-like cabbage in half with a cleaver, 'to make a difference.'

'Want me to do that?'

'No.'

'Well, careful with that axe thing,' he warned, getting up to go to the pantry and take out a packet of cashew nuts. He returned to his seat, poured himself a huge handful and began crunching loudly. The speed at which he ate, and the quantities he managed to consume while remaining as lean as a hungry lion, always amazed Laura. When he had finished – seconds later – he asked, 'Make a difference to whom? To you? Laura? I am, believe it or not, thinking of you.'

'But it was all so easy for me, I ought to give something back.'

'Pretty,' he yawned. 'Very pretty.'

'And true.'

'Come off it, you had twins on your own.'

'For God's sake, Robert, what's it to you?' she said with a violence that enabled her to cut through the cabbage. 'I need to do this, can't you accept that?' She was angry. Angry with Robert for getting at her and angry because the twins had woken her so early, angry because she was fed up with preparing vegetables and angry because for days now some free-floating rage had been gnawing at her insides. So she took it out on her kind-hearted brother. 'Haven't you got any sort of conscience?'

If she had intended to hurt Robert, she failed completely. Instead, his face flooded with concern and contrition.

'Oh, Laura, I'm so sorry. I didn't mean to upset you. Here, let me do that.' He took the cleaver from her.

'No, I'm sorry,' said Laura, ashamed. What was she lashing out at him for?

'And you're right,' went on Robert, 'it was easy for you. Very easy.' He gave her his big smile. 'Because it was a million times easier having twins on your own than being poor Mark and married to Jane with all her rules and regulations about how she is going to run this baby – and Mark, no doubt.'

Laura could not help herself. She smiled back.

'Jane's all right . . . probably,' she said, following his change of subject. 'But I keep thinking, what if they have one like my two? That'll teach them,' she added, reining in her not infrequent desire to see Jane with an out-of-control monster on her hands.

'Yours are gorgeous,' insisted Robert. 'They were hiding under the table when I came in, cuddling up saying they were lost otter pups.'

'Really?' Laura's heart expanded. When her daughters had woken her at half past five that morning, tearing each other's hair out – quite literally – her beautiful home on that dark winter's morning had seemed utterly grim and lonely. But on the occasions her children transported themselves to some imaginary world together, they could make her happier than she had ever believed possible.

'And anyway,' continued Robert, 'if they don't get a clockwork baby, it won't be Mark dealing with it. Or Jane. She's like Mum. Her greatest skill is delegation. The maternity nurse is all booked, the night nurse and God knows what else. Jane's most difficult job will be to choose its clothes.'

'Stop!' laughed Laura. 'I'm jealous, I can't help it.'

'Don't be.'

'But . . .'

A sudden longing for what she and her daughters would never share stabbed her. For a moment she could see herself in her own home with someone – some imaginary man – with his warm arm around her and the room filled with soft light from the fire and the accumulation of all the memories and strains and safety of shared family life.

'But what?' pressed Robert.

'This child will have a family. Mark and Jane and this child – and they'll no doubt have a second – will go on family holidays, have days out together, go to the park, just watch the telly together.'

'Good luck to it,' grimaced Robert. 'Think of some of our family holidays. Cornwall . . . I can't hear the word Cornwall without suffering what is probably post-traumatic stress.'

'I don't think Cornwall was ever as bad as Nantucket.'

'So stop romanticizing.'

'That's a bit rich coming from a man who dedicates his heart every six months to a different woman.'

'What's that supposed to mean?'

'Only,' she said, choosing her words carefully, 'that it's the romantics who hate the idea of committed love. It's easier – isn't it? – to fantasize about what might be, rather than make the most of what you've got.'

'Maybe I don't want a long relationship. Maybe I find more joy in . . . I don't know, looking at the beauty of apple blossom,' he grinned.

'Apple blossom only lasts a week. Is that what you like? You'd rather that exquisite yearning and melancholy that comes from something that doesn't last?'

He did not answer and they sat in silence. Then Robert went to the fridge and opened a can of beer. 'Nothing lasts,' he said, taking a swig. 'Anyway, what's brought this on?'

'Oh, I don't know.'

But Laura did know. The conscientiousness and sense of duty that had enabled her to look after her children so well for the last seven years were proving harder to find. She had persuaded herself that loving her daughters and losing herself in work for the church, the charities to which she gave up so much of her life, were enough. But they weren't. Not any more. So it was good that she had taken on this work at Hartley High. Very good, she urged herself, checking on the potatoes. She had so much. And she should not forget it. Even at St Catherine's, her daughters' privileged school, there were families whose beautiful homes were desolated by the sickness of a mother for whom there was no remedy. She knew one couple forced to watch their daughter starving herself to death, another in the despair of seeing a child plunge into problems beyond all reach of a parent's love.

She forced herself into a state of cheerfulness. 'So,' she said, draining the potatoes, 'you're off to Paris tomorrow with what's-her-name? Abigail?'

'We're not going till after New Year. Abigail's got to go to India.'

'Got to?'

Robert nodded. 'She wrote an article knocking some clothing company for paying appalling wages to children who spent all day and night sewing sequins on cardigans or whatever. And now these cardigan-makers have gone out of business, so these children are now even poorer and their parents are selling them into prostitution.'

The contradictions of life swirled around Laura.

'So what's she going to do?' she asked.

'She's no idea. So, be careful at Hartley High,' continued her brother, 'fools rush in and all that . . .'

Laura sat down. She wished she might go home and just lie in bed reading Jane Austen.

Instead, she said, 'That's an excuse for doing nothing.'

'It might have been better if Abigail had done nothing –' began Robert, when they were interrupted by their father's big voice booming behind them.

'There you are!'

Laura turned her attention to her father. He had been so engrossed in his work, she had not seen him for a couple of months. She was used to this. As a child she had learned to be thrilled if he left his studio and simply turned up in the house.

'Dad!' she said, hugging him.

'You look great.' He always said this to his children. But she looked far from great. 'And so do the girls. And you, Robert.' He gave Robert a slap on the back. 'Work all right?'

Robert just shrugged.

'Good,' smiled his father. 'Good.'

When they were at school, Laura and her brothers had been the envy of their friends because not only was their father famous and met famous people, he either approved of everything they did, or simply ignored it. When they had bad grades he just assumed they would do better next time. If they had spells of what Patrick called 'not going to school' – playing truant, in other words, and something both Mark and Robert indulged in – he turned a blind eye. When summoned to meet their head teacher, although he didn't demean himself by using the phrase 'university of life', Patrick made it quite clear that he thought that you frequently learned more outside the structured school environment. Patrick himself had left school at fifteen and trumpeted it frequently.

Once, in a magazine interview, when pressed about his family, he had said his acceptance of his children was absolute. Though Robert said he would not call it acceptance but arrogance – they were the children of Patrick Cusack, how could they be anything but perfect? – and Mark said acceptance could also be another name for downright laziness.

But whatever you called it, Laura thought that this approach had somehow worked. Certainly, both her brothers appeared contented with what life had given them and, to Laura, this seemed a wonderful gift. And as she looked at some of the children in her daughters' class, who even at seven were being urged to jump the next hurdle in their little lives, something in her wanted to cry, 'Let them be!'

'Now, where's your mother gone?' asked their father. 'She hasn't told you, has she?'

'What?' cried Robert, and Laura caught a lost look on his face which she had not seen since he was ten years old. 'Mum's all right, isn't she?'

'She's fine. You know your mother . . . Darling!'

'Mum,' began Robert, as Venetia came into the room and Patrick put his arm around her, 'is there something you're not telling us?'

'Darling, don't look so worried. It's wonderful news. Show them,' she said to Patrick, pulling herself upright and smiling. And Patrick took a letter from his shirt pocket saying that he was being awarded a knighthood in the New Year's honours list.

Robert muttered, 'Well done, Dad,' and left the room.

But Laura hurled herself into congratulations, something she was very good and much practised at when it came to her father's life. Then Mark and Jane arrived with their own news, which rather put Patrick's in the shade.

They were not just having the one boy, but a girl as well. Everyone was duly delighted, and among the loud excitement was much discussion about the unreliability of scans and the surprises of nature.

'Fortunately,' Jane explained, 'both the night nurse and maternity one can stay an extra six weeks. You see, I don't want to be too tired to enjoy them. And everyone tells me how quickly the time goes.'

'Yes, it does,' replied Laura, aware she was lying.

Then Jane had to take a call from her office and Laura went to check on her own children, who were sitting quietly, heads bowed, colouring together.

'They can draw,' said her father, who had followed her out of the kitchen.

Laura suspected he felt the glory of his knighthood had been somewhat undermined by the announcement of this extra unborn child.

'Yes,' said Laura absently, relieved her daughters had been so quiet all morning and had absolved her of the need to appease and amuse. Her throat was scratchy and her limbs ached as if she had a cold coming on.

'Laura,' her father was saying, looking over the girls' shoulders at what they were drawing, 'this is very good. Seriously, look at the faces. They notice things. See how they've both got the mouths.'

At once both girls sprawled forward, covering their pictures.

'Grandpa, go away.'

'Leave us.'

'We've not finished.'

'They'll show you when they're done,' smiled Laura.

'But they're good,' said her father. 'You should be proud of them. And the way they concentrate. That's quite something at just nine.'

'Seven,' murmured Laura. 'They'll be eight next month.'

She rested a hand on each of their bent heads.

'Mummy . . . Go!'

'Please.'

'They need to think,' grinned her father, taking a rare delight in his granddaughters.

Perhaps, thought Laura, now they were getting older, her father might take an interest in them.

'What's the art teacher at their school like?'

'Talented – very much so,' she said, thinking of the incredible sets at the school concert the other night. 'Oh Dad,' went on Laura, reminded of something she had to ask him. 'One of the mothers at school has begged me to show you her daughter's paintings. She wants an opinion, thinks her daughter's a genius and, if she is, that you might let her watch you work or something . . . I know, I know. I said you always worked alone. But have a quick look, will you? Please. Let me know what you think. Or the mother will be hounding me.'

'Tell you honestly what I think?'

Laura smiled. 'Yes, but I'll temper it, if I need to.'

She fetched the folder of Rose B's work from the car along with one of her own paintings of apple blossom against a stormy sky. Robert was going to try and sell it to one of his clients.

'They're not bad,' said her father, looking at Rose B's drawings. 'Really. In fact, they're quite well done. What do you think?'

'She's been well taught.'

'She has, but I wouldn't get too excited about them. How old is she?'

'Fifteen.'

'You were better than her at that age.'

She said nothing.

'And that's yours, isn't it?'

'Robert's going to try and get someone to buy it.'

Patrick picked it up and studied it closely. For a while he said nothing. Then, at last, he murmured, 'Nice, my dear, very nice . . . but –'

Laura could not stop herself. 'But what?'

'But . . .' he trailed off. 'When did you do this?'

'Earlier this year.'

'Hmmm,' he muttered. 'Your flowers always were good. Very good, in fact. But your work was always so . . . well . . . so focused. But you've let things slip.'

Laura held herself perfectly still.

'I mean,' he continued, 'you'd paint a simple flower and, somehow, its . . . I don't know . . . its life, I suppose, came across. You could capture spontaneity in a way that I . . . well . . . anyway, you've got the details, you were always very good at that, but you're not touching me like you used to, it's too fractured in some way.'

A tremor crossed Laura's face.

'But my time's so fractured,' she found herself stammering. 'With twins there's just so much to do and . . .'

And, she wanted to say, you may love the way your grandchildren sit so quietly and patiently, but they have learned to do that because

I have sat with them, so quietly and patiently. They notice the shapes in a face – at the age of just seven – because I have noticed the shapes in a face with them. And that has taken time – my time – time when I could have been doing my own painting.

'Of course, my dear,' he was saying, 'don't take it amiss. Of course, you give them masses of time and it's bound to show.'

There was nothing Laura could say to this, and a silence fell between them until her mother called to say lunch was almost ready, and would Laura help serve?

# 16

'Is there any more business?' asked Phillip Snowe, sitting at the head of the table in Hartley High's airless staffroom. It was five to eight on Monday night and he was drawing the governors' meeting to a close with his habitual efficiency. He noticed Laura glance at her watch and her look of relief that they were ending on time. But Phillip's meetings always finished punctually. He could advance ideas with the expertise of a champion sheepdog rounding up a flock – collecting the ditherers, persuading the dissenters, encouraging the idlers – making everyone proceed in the direction he chose.

One governor who had been silent all evening started shuffling her papers, preparing to say something. Phillip cut her short. 'Right,' he said, standing up sharply. 'Thank you all so much. Meeting closed.'

Phillip had other issues on his mind. Late last night, Julia had rung from Boston – just after he had fallen asleep – and they had chatted briefly, only mentioning Rose to agree not to talk about boarding schools while Julia was away. But, it occurred to Phillip, Julia was always away. She might be lying next to him in bed but she could just as well still be in the States. And he was not quite sure how this distance had grown. Or when.

After nearly twenty years of marriage it was inevitable that however much you loved someone you did start taking them for granted, just as you might a lamp on a bedside table. And that, thought Phillip, was not all bad. Far from it. True love you could take for granted. You could reach for it in the middle of your darkest night and know it would always be there for you. Wasn't that the miracle of marriage? One minute the person you loved was as familiar and ordinary as a piece of furniture, but the next they could transform into this soulmate who overcame you with the most elemental passion. But right now that miracle was as distant as a summer's day.

'Phillip.' The head caught his eye for a private word and Phillip, as if he had tossed a coin, switched his mind to the head's question on truancy.

Then he turned to find Laura, standing in a corner blowing her nose. She had spent most of the evening dealing with a streaming cold and had said very little. But, when asked, she had agreed to deliver leaflets about the school's International Food Fair to the three tower blocks where many of the pupils came from. It was a slog of a job, lugging a ton of papers up and down on a cold winter's day. He had asked for volunteers and, not surprisingly, no one had come forward. So, with gentle ruthlessness, he had asked Laura directly. And she had agreed.

'Thank you again for doing this,' said Phillip. 'I really appreciate it.'

'That's okay.' Her voice was heavy with cold and, in her dull, crumpled skirt and sweater, she looked utterly fed up. It occurred to him he had landed too much on her. Bringing up twins on her own, even with her parents' money, was not a piece of cake. And, judging by her old coat, there was probably not a lot of spare cash either.

'Let's go to the art room and I'll carry those leaflets to your car,' he said with a friendly grin. A couple of times over the last few days it had occurred to him how much he had enjoyed chatting with her in the car, waiting for her windscreen to be repaired. 'You can tell me what you made of the meeting,' he said, wanting to discuss it with her. When he ran his own business, he had a raft of colleagues to run things by. But not any more, and he missed it.

'So was that what you expected, or worse?' he asked, opening the door for her and switching on his phone. 'Oh, sorry.' He had two messages. 'I'd better get these.'

Both were from Julia. The first was to say that her lunch with the publisher had gone so well she was being commissioned to write a book on corporate responsibility in the Internet age. She was thrilled. He could hear it in her voice. But Phillip was livid. A book would absorb every moment that wasn't monopolized by her regular work. Julia would write in her study at home, and do so at every opportunity because she would – he was certain – have agreed to too tight a deadline. And she had not even thought to ask his views or consider how writing some legal book – as if her love affair with the law was not all-consuming enough – would impact on the rest of the family. He took a deep breath.

The second message was that she would have to stay yet another extra night. Once he would not have thought twice about her change of plans. It was the nature of her work. And once it had been the nature of his. Yet now he wanted Julia's help with Rose. And he wanted . . .

Phillip's thoughts ranged back to Sunday morning when that damned David had rung, interrupting their weekend yet again. And at night these days, when Julia was actually in the same bed, she would be sitting up, beautifully straight, in a fine linen shirt, besieged by a deep sea of legal papers, so to reach her –

'Phillip?' He was brought back to the overheated staffroom. 'I've a babysitter waiting,' Laura was saying, 'so if you just tell me where those leaflets are, I'll go and get them myself.'

'No, no. I'm sorry. We'll go now.'

He made himself put aside thoughts of Julia as Laura suppressed a yawn that he hoped was tiredness, not boredom.

'So how did you find it tonight?'

'Interesting,' she said, as they walked off to the art block.

He suspected this was a lie.

'The deputy made her *EastEnders* departure.'

'Yes,' she replied guardedly, remembering how easily he could draw you into a sense of warm alliance. But his powers of observation and his sharp eye had made her wary of what he might say when he turned them on her.

'We are grateful for you getting involved,' he ploughed on.

Laura met this with silence, and Phillip wondered if she had even been listening.

'Tonight was pretty typical,' he continued doggedly, but his thoughts were returning to Julia. What he really wanted was to pick up the phone and rage at her not to do this damned book, although he and Julia never lost control and raged about anything. Yet right now he would like to yell his socks off. He forced his attention back to the school.

'The art block's over here,' he said, pushing open the door to the playground. 'Good God, it's cold. Come on.'

And with their heads down against the wind they hurried across the tarmac.

'You wait here, I'll go and hunt out the leaflets,' he said, oddly irritated with Laura as well as his wife now. He needed an ally on that deadly board but she was being so unforthcoming. Phillip regarded himself as very skilled at bringing out the best in people. But those skills were not working on Laura tonight. She seemed wary of him, a little distrustful. What was the matter with her? And he felt all the physical signs of unexpressed anger as he strode off, his jaw clenched, his breathing shallow, his temples throbbing.

When Phillip returned with two weighty boxes of leaflets, Laura was on her hands and knees, searching through a pile of paintings dumped on the floor in the corner.

'What are you doing down there?' he called out.

'Oh Phillip,' she said, looking up at him and giving him the sort of smile he had been hoping to charm out of her earlier. 'Turn all the lights on, can you?' Her eyes were suddenly free of her weariness, all the lethargy and listlessness with which she had sat through the meeting quite gone. 'Please!'

'What is it?' he asked, arrested by the change in her.

'That picture. There,' she said, getting up and, to his surprise, taking his arm and standing him in front of a picture tacked up on the wall.

'What about it?'

'It's wonderful!' she said. 'Really. Dear God, this is so exciting.'

Phillip cast his eyes over the painting of five teenagers lolling up against a wall behind a wire fence.

'Yes,' he hesitated. She was staring hard at him. He was not sure what she expected of him. 'What of it?' he asked.

'It's brilliant!'

He looked again. But to Phillip the picture simply represented rather predictable adolescent angst. It was just very dark, he thought, too dark.

'This painting,' Laura was saying. 'It's seriously good. And this girl can only be fifteen, sixteen. Truly, Phillip, this is special. Is there anything else by her?'

He glanced at the name: Isabel West.

'I doubt it.'

'But why? There must be –'

'We had to exclude her last month.'

'What?'

'Exclude – expel her.'

'Oh Phillip, no! You can't do that.'

'Actually, I can. And, well, I had to.'

'No, no, you can't. Look at the picture she's done, Phillip. Properly. It's extraordinary.'

He made himself concentrate on the gang of five teenagers. He thought it was the sort of scene you saw the moment you walked out of Hartley High school gates. He looked harder. The boys' faces, he supposed, were interesting, ranging from the utterly apathetic to the downright aggressive.

He turned back to her. 'I think art was always her best subject.'

'Of course it was.' Laura got to her feet, with that smile still on her face. Phillip returned it. She had come alive now with the sort of energy he needed on the school board.

'Can't you see,' she pressed, 'how exceptional this is?'

'Not really, I'm afraid I don't,' he said, just as interested in the change in Laura. 'Help me.'

'What's so exciting,' she spelled it out, 'is that this girl hasn't just painted some stroppy teenagers caged behind this fence. And even if she had, quite frankly, it would still be brilliant for her to get all that emotion in those faces. But what she's done is control all that anger about what has been done to these boys so that there's a beauty there.'

'I don't see much beauty.' He would not have run his business so successfully if he had mildly accepted the views of others, and he was fully versed in creative work. 'To me,' he pronounced, 'it's just a typical teenager's picture.'

'No, Phillip, this is very special. Just technically it's incredible for someone her age. Didn't one of her art teachers see what she could do? All her potential?'

'The art teachers were forever changing.'

'So she taught herself? Or someone at home did?'

'Maybe. I suppose so.'

'Then that's all the more reason for you not to dismiss it. The girl didn't have a chance. This picture damns you, me, all of us.'

'And her – Isabel West.' Phillip had sat in on countless meetings discussing how best to deal with this troubled girl.

'That's why it's called "self-portrait". The anger's not just with us.'

'Well, she was given a lot of chances.'

'Give her another chance, then.'

'She was too disruptive . . . So no. I can't.'

'Let her come to school and just do art all day.'

'I can't do that.'

'But what's the point of her sitting in on media studies and God knows what if she's just wasting her time? And everyone else's when she could be doing paintings like this.'

'It doesn't work like that,' he explained, aware he was reverting to full chair-of-the-governors mode. 'We can't be seen to have someone doing just what they want. There'd be chaos.'

'So what's this girl doing now?' asked Laura. 'Playing truant from some other dud school and getting in trouble with the police, if she's not already?'

'It's not that simple. Just one student can make it impossible for the rest in the class to learn a single thing. And Isabel West was a nightmare . . . violent, aggressive.'

'Who wouldn't be? With a talent like this, and no one's got the slightest understanding of what you can really do.'

'But you can't turn a blind eye to the curriculum, give different rules to one student. It's not fair on the others.'

'As if fairness was ever possible,' said Laura. 'To be given this sort of ability isn't fair. But not to be able to realize it is tragic. And if this girl doesn't, you'll be partly to blame. It's not as if talent was like . . .' she cast around, 'like litter in the park. Everywhere you look.' Then she turned away to try and find more of Isabel's work.

## 17

Phillip was not used to people turning their backs on him when he talked.

'I can't put this girl outside the system,' he insisted. ' He was irritated. Laura was proving unexpectedly naive. 'What about the ones with no special talent? It's my job –'

'What's the situation with this girl's family?' she interrupted.

'It's my job,' he repeated, ignoring her question and also not used to being unable to finish his sentences, 'to protect the ordinary child too.'

But he remembered the family well, what there was of it. Isabel lived on the Hartley Estate, where Julia had grown up. The father was long gone and the mother was confined to a wheelchair with some dreadful disabling disease – just as Julia's mother had been, he had found himself thinking when he had met this woman in her flat. The lift in the tower block was broken and Isabel's mother was unable to get out so he had visited her at home to formalize her daughter's exclusion.

'But you must know people,' Laura persisted, 'who've had awful childhoods but someone – a good teacher, a good school – has given them a chance.'

Phillip stopped himself wondering how even Julia, for all her brilliance, would have fared at Hartley High, instead of the academic hothouse she had been both clever and lucky enough to escape to.

'Look,' tried Laura, taking another approach. 'You were in advertising, weren't you? You must have pushed things to the edge. Twisted things to your advantage with a bit of imagination and courage? Taken a chance?'

To Laura, this was a fair question. But Phillip read into it all the self-doubt that had led him to giving up his business. He had made a lot of money doing something which did not always stand up to close scrutiny and now he was trying to make amends by do-gooding, and he felt she was mocking him for it.

'For God's sake,' he muttered, answering not what she had said, but what his questioning conscience asked. 'There's no comparison between this and advertising, and it's not helpful to try to make one.'

'But you were saying the other day that you wanted to make a difference. And if you do this one thing, and help this girl, that will be more than many of us ever do. I sat in that meeting wondering if I was wasting my time. And now I see this and realize I wasn't.'

*Wasting my time?* echoed Phillip. So that's what she was thinking – the same question that needled away at him.

'Look, let me show this to my father,' said Laura, resorting to a tactic she despised. 'If he rates it, perhaps you'll believe me. You've got to do something.'

'But I can't!' Suddenly he was furious. Not, he assured himself, because she doubted his abilities and imagination, but because she was being ridiculously obtuse. 'How many times do I have to explain it? I've a thousand of these kids to worry about, not just the odd genius who catches your eye.' His habitual restraint deserted him. 'I'm responsible for the whole school. You've no bloody idea! Half the time it's a miracle if these kids leave being able to read and write.'

It was so long since Phillip had raised his voice, let alone lost his temper, that he had forgotten what it was like. Julia and he never argued like this. At work, too, it had always been his style to remain calm and controlled. But it occurred to him that he was gunning for a fight. He had been for ages, just to relieve some of the strain of self-doubt that was wearing him down. But there was no one to have it out with. Until now.

For a brief moment he felt ashamed, he should not have raised his voice. But Laura did not seem the slightest bit bothered. Instead, she was looking at him as if he was a sudden firework display and wondering if he had finished. He had not.

'I accept it's a good likeness,' he roared on, 'but I don't see any imagination in this, the great creativity you do. Nothing that tests your boundaries or takes you out of yourself.'

Laura had grown up with a father who was forever bawling his head off with the abandon of a toddler and self-indulgence of a teenager. No one else was allowed the privilege but she frequently wished she too might scream the house down. Now, looking at Phillip, she was torn between wanting to laugh at his red and angry face with, she noticed, a smudge of blue ink on his nose, or simply joining in the battle.

She opted for the latter and went full tilt for it. 'Takes you out of yourself?' she mimicked. 'I've never heard such condescending, pseudo-art speak. Just because it doesn't make you buy things you don't want.'

'What do you mean by that?'

'You know exactly what I mean. You made a mint from advertising, for God's sake,' she said, moving towards him and staring right up at him.

Laura could just as well have punched him. Then, once he was down, she hit him again, right on target, also giving up on any attempt to temper her feelings.

'For once, just take a chance,' she said, her face close to his. 'Because what's the point of all your great plans and bowing and scraping to Ofsted if someone comes your way whose life could actually be transformed and you won't bend the rule book? No wonder your precious attendance figures are looking so much better if you just kick out the problems and dump them on a scrap heap.'

'What the hell do you know?' he flung back. 'You've not the slightest idea of what I'm up against.'

In her family, Laura would have ducked the argument, but she had not wanted this governor's job. It had been foisted upon her, and if she was going to do it she was going to speak her mind.

'So you deal with these problems, do you,' she asked, staring up at him, mocking and scornful, as if deliberately goading him on, 'by smoothing them over? You made a lot of money by being so brilliant at presentation, making things appear to work. And here you're clearly doing exactly the same.' And with that she edged past him and marched off down the corridor.

'You sound like every other damned do-gooder I've had the bad luck to sit next to at every damned dinner party,' he heard himself shout after her.

But even as he tried to write her off as another ignorant idealist, he did not want her to go. He ran after her, as best he could, carrying the boxes of leaflets, because he wanted the fight. How the hell *do* you make a difference? This was the debate that kept him awake at night, but there was no one to have it with. But she was up for it. It occurred to him that she was the sort of woman with whom you could say what you wanted. He ran faster and caught her up.

'Aren't you on a prison board too?' she was saying, holding the door open so he could carry the boxes out to the car park.

He nodded.

'It's a good job, because you can keep an eye on her in prison next. Help her according to your rule book.'

She stood there defiantly as he stepped into the doorway.

'Listen,' he said, now trying to keep his voice reasonable, 'helping people . . . it's not simple. Because people need so much. And so many need more than we have to give. If I give to Isabel, then someone else will go without. And if all I seem to be doing is weighing things up – if I give here, then do I make a compromise there? – then I do it in the belief that at least some are better off. That's the best I can do. Sometimes you have to accept the limitations of the system.'

'But by accepting – resigning yourself, more like it – you fail the Isabel Wests of this world,' said Laura. 'It makes a mockery of all you are claiming to do.'

'And,' persisted Phillip, 'you have to accept . . . resign yourself, as you would say, to your own limitations too.'

He paused, expecting her to argue back. But, to his disappointment, she did not respond. Instead, he watched her face revert to the worn-out expression she normally displayed.

'Maybe you've never had to do that – put up with your own fail-ings,' he went on.

Laura did not reply. Her head dropped. What had he said? Her energy had disappeared as quickly as if he had clicked his fingers.

'Laura?'

Laura felt she spent her life putting up with her own failings, never reaching her own standards. But she was silenced by contra-dictory desires: to tell him or to say nothing; to be open or to be circumspect; to keep her distance or to foster a little friendship. He had been trusting with her and part of her would like to be the same with him. For a moment she was torn. But he was the sort who was clearly very practised at persuading you to open up, tell all. No, he did not need to know about her. It was time to clam up.

'Look, I'm sorry,' she said. 'I'm being glib. Sorry. It's just that I didn't want to be a governor, so if I'm going to do it, I might as well do it properly – or at least properly as I see it. Otherwise, what's the point?'

To his surprise he found himself laughing. 'What's the point?' he echoed. 'You're sounding like me.'

And he smiled at her kindly. All that passion was a godsend. She was a woman he did not have to tiptoe around on eggshells.

'I must hurry,' she was saying, taking the leaflets from him. 'I've got a babysitter waiting.'

He opened her car door. She walked round to him and was about to climb in when he suddenly found himself saying, 'Laura.'

For a moment they faced each other and he thought, she has the looks that transform according to the landscape behind the face. He tried to think of something else to say, to keep her.

'Yes?' she said, getting into the car.

He hesitated as Laura pushed her hair away from her face – light brown curls, he noticed for the first time. So many of the women he knew were deliberate creations of grooming and styling. But there was a naturalness about her, and it was oddly beguiling. Laura's scruffiness suited her. Her sweater, her skirt, he realized, were not so characterless as they had first appeared but showed off a softness, a give and take in her unfashionably well-covered, shapely body. She slung her coat on to the back seat and her sweater rode up her back and he caught a glimpse of creamy-white flesh – receptive flesh, he found himself thinking, that would spring back in your arms when you held it close.

'Yes?' she said again.

Unusually for Phillip, he was at a loss for words.

'Oh,' he said uncertainly, as if he was missing something. 'Nothing . . . . It's nothing.'

## 18

Isabel West, the subject of Laura and Phillip's argument, was finishing off a bag of broken biscuits from the Under a Pound stall at the market, cramming stale bourbons and custard creams into her mouth. The sickly, floury taste caught at the back of her throat. She knew she might be sick. Certainly she was going the right way about it. But at least she wasn't drunk. Though that's what she wanted, to be completely out of it. But then she wouldn't be able to look after her mother, and if she couldn't do that . . .

Her stomach convulsed. She would be put into care. There was no family to take her in, no father, no friends. But she would kill herself before that happened. She had the means. She'd made sure of that. Though what worried her – on top of everything else – was that her mother would want the pills for herself, that first she would have to help her, fetch a beaker of water, lift it to her lips.

Isabel curled up on the bathroom floor. She wouldn't think about that. But the point was, she was still under sixteen, not yet able to look after herself. According to the law. Though that was a laugh. Ironic, the English teacher at Hartley High would have said, on the day he was explaining irony to anyone who would listen – no one – and Isabel had thrown a copy of *Twelfth Night* at him, giving him the biggest black eye her class said they had ever seen.

But for three years now she had done more looking after than anyone else she knew because she cared for her mother, stuck in the flat, stuck in a wheelchair, stuck in her bed. Unless she moved her. She alone. Because there was no one else to do it. Sometimes the social workers did make it to the no-go estate and walk up the eight flights of stairs, as the lift was broken. But they didn't get their hands dirty doing what Isabel described as the dirty work. They liked to talk, have a cup of tea, empathize, build up a relationship.

Though it would be more use if they got out the bleach. Or cooked a meal. That would be helpful. Instead of going on, asking her how she was – wasn't it obvious?

Though it was not obvious, and that was down to Isabel. When anyone came to the flat she made sure the place was clean, that her mother was properly dressed, wearing lipstick, perfume, that she and her mother were just fine, fine, fine. Though you would have to have a pretty odd definition of fine. But, thought Isabel, show people what they want to see – no violence, no abuse – and they turn a blind eye to the rest.

Isabel had been twelve when her mother became ill. At first her eyesight began to go and it didn't seem that big a deal. She just thought she needed glasses. But within a year almost every muscle in her body failed. It was a rare neurological problem – very rare, in fact – one in a million. As if exclusivity made hell any better. Now her mother could not take any weight on her legs and that meant Isabel had to . . .

Isabel retched. All the shit she had to deal with. Sometimes she was afraid she would hit her mother the way she had hit Miss Black, her PSHE teacher. That was why they'd kicked her out. Hitting that cow across her sallow, thin face was the final straw for Hartley High. So Isabel was excluded. But she never hit her mother. Never. And she never would. Because she had worked out a system to cope. She would imagine herself in this brilliant light, enveloped in golden sunshine, and although she knew exactly how pathetic and pitiful that sounded, how else could she escape as she heaved her mother up and down, as she helped her dress, as she wiped . . .?

She threw up, retching into the toilet. All those biscuits.

She lay her hot cheek on the cool lino. That was better. And no one need know. She could feel her ribs heaving in her skinny chest. There was barely anything of her, so her mother said. And now she felt so light she might disappear into the thin air and be taken away from it all. But damn it. The noise had woken her mother, and she barely slept now. She was in too much pain or her legs would twitch and jerk and she could not control them.

'Izzy.'

She heard her mother's voice, like an old woman's. She was only thirty-two, though she looked nearer eighty-two.

'Coming,' she called.

'Are you all right?' her mother asked, trying to raise her worn face.

She wasn't too bad today. You never knew how she'd be. Unpredictability is all you can predict about this illness, the website had said when Isabel looked it up on the school computer when no one was looking. And today was a good day, better than yesterday when her tongue and lips seized up and she could barely speak.

'Fine, Mum.'

'You should be at school.'

'I told you, it's the holidays,' she lied.

She gave her daughter a long look. Grief and anger and love resided in that stare. 'Isabel . . .'

She was supposed to have changed schools, to be going to some new place, a dump so bad it made Hartley High look good. She had given it one day and it was a total waste of time with supply teachers going on about whatever and knowing no one was listening to a word and living only for the pay cheque at the end of the month.

'Isabel,' her mother began again, then gave up.

'You need anything?' Isabel asked, hoping the answer was no.

She was in luck. Her mother just wanted a drink and Isabel gave her the child's plastic beaker she used. She could manage that herself today. Isabel watched her mother take two sips, and then drop the beaker, exhausted.

'You're a good girl,' said her mother, as she had a million times before.

Isabel handed her back the beaker, wishing she might chuck it flying out of the window because she hated these plastic beakers in their gross, lurid colours. They were for children, not adults.

But she just said, 'Try and have a bit more, Mum.'

To begin with, her mother had tried to hide her illness, to play it down. But one afternoon Isabel came home from school and found her collapsed on the floor, unable to get up, her face ravaged with tears.

Isabel had just turned thirteen and the child in her cried like it had never cried before. 'What will happen to me if you die?' But the adult in her knew. She would be put in care and she had heard . . . the stories she had heard . . . and she felt her mother's fear for her little girl, so slight and so fragile, with her plain, mousy hair and love of drawing.

Her mother had fought with every ounce of her waning strength. But no strength on earth could fight the illness taking over her body. And now she was defeated. She did not cry or berate her daughter. Though Isabel would have preferred it if she had. Then she might be spared some of the unhappiness in her mother's smile, or the ugliness that crossed her face as if she loathed herself because she could not be a mother to her darling daughter.

When Isabel had been excluded, the head teacher and some do-gooder – the chair of the governors, Mr Snowe – had come to the flat and tried to play upon her guilt. Think about the worry you are causing your mother by your behaviour at school, the distress, the disappointment.

She had switched off after two minutes, otherwise she would have laughed in their faces. Because what did they know about guilt? Nothing. Not a clue. Real guilt – the sort that gets under your skin so deeply it changes your whole vision of the world – is walking down the street knowing the one person you love is imprisoned in a living grave. Real guilt is drawing a picture – art was the one thing the teachers said she was good at – and being incapable of forgetting that your mother can't even hold a pencil to write her name and needs you to forge her signature. Real guilt is being unable to enjoy the sun on your face because your mother is incarcerated for now and always. Real guilt means you lose the right to your own life.

'You know,' said her mother, rousing herself. 'If I went into a home it might not be too bad.'

'No, Mum,' she interrupted as an all too familiar panic rose in her. For the last few weeks they had been having this conversation.

'Mum, no. Please.'

'It won't be for long. A nice family.'

'Mum, no.'

'You could live, well, a more normal life for a girl your age, not have to do all the things . . .'

At school, Isabel would have screamed and yelled, lashing out in her anger and frustration. But at home she had iron control. She could make herself sit and listen. Besides, her mother could not talk for long and when she had finished, Isabel did what she always did. She put her arms around her and said, 'Let's give it another month or so. Mum, please. We'll talk about it then.'

And this way, thought Isabel, things will stay . . . stay what? Of course they wouldn't stay the same. Her mother would get sicker and weaker and then she would die. And then what would happen? How would she live without her mother? The flat was ugly and small. She never invited anyone back. But with her mother, and her mother's love, it was bearable. But without her?

Isabel had always been a loner. Her contemporaries at school bored her. All they wanted to do was get legless and get laid, and then talk and text and tweet about it for hours on end. It was the last thing Isabel wanted. Even if she could. But the problem was these girls also frightened her, and she could not be indifferent to them. So she had found her place by being rude and disruptive, and by treating the teachers not as human beings but as targets she could unleash her aggression on. And until the exclusion it had been a successful strategy. Safer to be a bully than the one who got bullied. But now what?

She had always liked art. For the last few years it had been something into which she could pour all her misery and fear. Now even that seemed pointless.

She waited for her mother to doze off and wandered into the kitchen. There was the foul smell of drains and she went to the window. The broken latch always stuck. But Isabel could push and pull and manoeuvre it open to let in the damp December air.

She looked out at the seagulls scrabbling and fighting for rubbish to eat. They were a nuisance, and everyone in the flats had had a note from the Council threatening fines for feeding them. Though who would enforce that round here?

She shivered. Being too thin she always felt the cold. She went to find another bag of broken biscuits and threw half a digestive out of the window, then closed it again. A group of squawking, hungry birds dived down. But one was fastest, catching the biscuit with perfect precision, then rising with the grace of an angel, flying away over the rooftops as Isabel watched it through the grimy glass.

## 19

Anna Snowe was drinking iced lemon tea spiced with vodka on the cerise sofa in her friend Phoebe's bedroom.

'Go on, Anna, try it,' yelled Phoebe from her bathroom where she was applying a new gold-glitter rinse to her hair. 'There's plenty here. And it washes out if you don't like it.'

Anna did not move. Phoebe was always harping on about her hair and what she should do to improve it. And if it wasn't her hair, it was her shoes, her nails, her glasses, her eyebrows. Having a mother edit a fashion magazine meant Phoebe felt entitled to dictate on everyone's looks. And for the past six weeks, since they had been working together on the magazine, she had been relentless, seizing on Anna as if she was her project, a guinea pig whom she could practise upon.

'Highlights would suit you,' persisted Phoebe.

'She's right,' piped up Lottie, who was sitting on the floor painting Stella's toenails midnight blue.

Lottie and Stella, who were taking gap years, had also been in Anna's class at St Catherine's and they were all getting ready for Phoebe's boyfriend's best mate's birthday party. Not that Anna had any intention of going. Or letting Phoebe make her over. A bit nearer the time she would fake a headache.

'At least let me blow-dry your hair for you, and get the frizz out,' said Lottie.

'No, thanks,' said Anna.

'You should,' called out Phoebe.

'Oh, leave her alone,' said Stella. 'Now, are you sure I can have these?' she asked, waving a pair of false eyelashes Anna had been given as a freebie at the magazine.

'Sure,' nodded Anna, as Stella adorned her pale blue eyes with great long fringes.

Since they were twelve, Phoebe, Stella and Lottie had been participating in these rites of decoration, and, Anna guessed, they would still be as girly at sixty. The conversations might vary – boys/men, lack of boys/men, engagements, marriages, children, divorce – but that intimate, confiding atmosphere over the lipsticks would not. She supposed it was how women bonded. Though she had never really managed it.

She was only here now, invited into this exclusive little set, because they had all done maths A level. Anna had been useful because she would painstakingly explain the finer points of differential equations. And now she was a convenient foil to their confident loveliness, and made their lives easier because their parents approved of her. That's why Phoebe's mother had offered her the job on the magazine – not Stella or Lottie. Clever, reliable Anna was regarded as a good influence on Phoebe. Though that just showed, thought Anna, exerting herself to join in, how utterly deceptive appearances could be.

'The eyelashes look great,' she said. 'Really great.'

Better than on me, she added to herself, ashamed of her pathetic self-pity. What was it with her that she wanted to be like Stella? Or Phoebe? Or Lottie? But she did. Right now she would love to be Phoebe with her good-looking boyfriend who was modelling his way through university with money to spare. Though he did write awful poetry, invariably about the Apocalypse. Not that it mattered to Phoebe, who found it wonderful. But I could pretend to like it, thought Anna.

Or perhaps, if she was like self-regarding Stella, she would be happy. Stella, with her blue eyes and translucent blonde curls, was so pretty, a chocolate box of a girl. Anna watched her purse her rosy lips in front of the mirror. But even she is not nearly as lovely as my sister Rose.

No one was as lovely as Rose. The point about Anna's sister was that she was pure beauty. Girls as well as boys had crushes on Rose, all longing to be close to every inch of her. But it was not as simple as just being beautiful – though, dear God, it helped – because Lottie really had to struggle to keep up the good looks and had already had plastic surgery, on her nose, for her eighteenth birthday. And everyone loved being around her because she was so brilliant at making the boys laugh. Whereas she, Anna, who was supposed to be the brilliant one, could never think of anything to say. Let alone anything remotely clever until it was at least half an hour too late.

'Lottie, please, do me a favour,' said Phoebe, appearing out of the bathroom. 'Put this on for me, will you?' she asked, handing Lottie – who was renowned for her steady hand – a jar of gold eye-liner, another acquisition from the magazine.

'Oh, and me,' said Stella. 'Can I try it?'

'Sure,' said Phoebe, teetering around in high mules on her long, thin legs.

Anna watched them all from under half-closed eyes. They had bodies as vulnerable as Bambi, yet eyes as knowing as Cleopatra. But what exactly do they know? More to the point, how had they acquired this knowledge? It wasn't just sex. It was more than that. It was knowing how to get what you wanted and right now that meant knowing how to work a party, how to get into the right restaurants and nightclubs, how to behave and what to say when you got there.

From an early age, Anna had always learned with a speed and agility that had marked her out. At two she was apparently so worried about dying she had been taken to a child psychiatrist who – to her parents' relief and delight – informed them that the concept of death in one so young was, in fact, a sign of quite exceptional intelligence.

By the time Anna was ten she was proficient in Mandarin and at thirteen she had completed an Open University course in physics and was being encouraged to try one in chemistry. (Though she overheard her mother saying that this told her more about the Open University than about Anna.)

But although she could grasp mathematical concepts like a shot, she was acquiring social ease with such excruciating slowness she suspected it was beyond her – like playing tennis, which she detested, or ballet, which she had refused to do after the age of five. And later, when she was thirteen, jazz. Or indeed any form of sport or dancing, because it was all torture.

'I love this,' said Stella, putting on some music and moving with a lithe grace to a song which Anna secretly thought moronic.

'You like this, don't you, Anna?' asked Stella.

'Sure,' murmured Anna, as Phoebe joined in, singing along, word-perfect.

Having to go to parties and talk and dance was one of the many reasons she hated Christmas, along with all the preparation required for an evening when she was only ever noticed by the other misfits and geeks. Because what she really wanted was a man who was normal, not one who only chatted to her because he needed help with his maths A-level, or some boy like her – awkward and spotty with a brain that made him an outcast too. It was not that she did not try to fit in. She hesitated. Well, she tried a bit. She was here, wasn't she? In Phoebe's bordello-like bedroom, supposedly getting ready for a party. Socializing with her peers.

Part of her wanted to be like them, to throw off her image as the girl who kept her face plain and her clothes shapeless. And yet, if pushed, would she really change places with Phoebe? Of course she would adore a boyfriend who looked like Phoebe's, but to live in Phoebe's brain would bore her rigid. And Stella's egotism, for all her prettiness, would get its come-uppance soon enough. And if she was Lottie she would have to feel the insecurities that made you risk plastic surgery at just eighteen.

But the truth was, she had never really bothered to make the effort to fit in because in the end she had not seen the point.

Though her parents had.

They had never said as much to Anna, but she knew they had done their homework – read the books on gifted children, taken her to special events for equally bright children, solving maths problems or writing plays in teams or playing chess. And she had quite enjoyed all the attention – not least because the chess tournaments meant she had been able to stop the charade of letting her father appear to beat her. Her parents had tried hard. They had arranged parties and invited the whole class, bought her the sort of clothes her contemporaries wore, taken her to the places the other girls talked about.

But they had not really solved the problem. And this was where her mother was downright stupid, thought Anna. Her mother thought cleverness was a gift – cleverness combined with hard work. But it was not. However much Anna tried, she would always be different. A line separated her from the other girls at school and she knew it and, thought Anna to herself as there was a knock on the door, the other girls knew it too.

'Hurry up!' Phoebe's father called out from behind the closed door. 'If you want a lift to this party you'll have to be ready by eight-thirty.'

'But, Dad, that's way too early,' screeched Phoebe.

'Well, make your own way, then.' And Anna heard his footsteps stomping back down the hall.

'But I never go out before ten,' yelled Phoebe. 'You know that. For God's sake, I'm not a child.'

Lottie and Stella glanced at each other. Phoebe's father was a legend at St Catherine's. When he and Phoebe's mother attended events at the school they appeared to perfection, she in the sort of chic clothes that Anna knew her own mother could not help coveting, and he in his fine tweed jacket, holding her arm, being courteous, attentive. In the best possible taste they displayed the sort of intimacy that, according to Lottie, was intended to make the blood of his other lovers boil. For Pheobe's father was not, as Stella said frequently, 'merely unfaithful to his wife – he's health-hazard unfaithful'.

This story had been fuelled by a variety of accounts from older sisters, mothers' friends, friends of friends, aunts and divorced cousins – he was utterly catholic in his tastes, so the reports went. And dangerously successful. Even though, as the St Catherine's sixth form pointed out when trying to fathom why he was such a draw for women, he was short and growing fatter by the month.

Phoebe's father was a maths professor who moonlighted

lucratively in the City, drawing up models of chaos theory for hedge fund managers. Stella's best friend's cousin had been one of his students and had allegedly spent an unforgettable afternoon with him. This same woman also knew someone who had been considerably cheered up by him after her third baby. And, according to Lottie, her mother's aunt's god-daughter who worked at the bank he advised had a weekend away with him after her husband left her for his secretary.

Anna had dismissed the talk as hyperbole but now she was not so sure because, to her dismay, despite his girth and stature, she could see his attraction.

A couple of months ago he had invited her to attend his lectures on turbulence at the university. She had been in two minds, but one bleak October afternoon, when she was supposed to be preparing for her Cambridge interview, bored and feeling she had nothing better to do, she had turned up. And been spellbound.

His best work was done, so everyone said, but his gift for explaining complex and, to Anna, utterly fascinating ideas and then communicating his enthusiasm was richer than ever. He was electrifying. Anna could not remember when she had been so excited. She had not missed a lecture since.

Yet, even if the stories about him had any truth, it was quite clear to Anna that his interest in her was, she grimly realized, purely mathematical. After that first lecture he had sought her out in the throng of students and asked if she had found the subject interesting. To which she had replied yes. And he had said that she was very welcome to attend as many lectures as she wished.

And that was that. At subsequent lectures he had always acknowledged her, given her a nod or a smile or briefly said it was good to see her. After one lecture, he mentioned he had heard she had an interview at Cambridge and would she like to have a coffee with him to talk about it? They had sat together in a busy, steamy café with people pushing past and knocking into her. After twenty minutes he had said he doubted she would have any problem getting in – and he was right. But after that he had to go, as he had a seminar. So they had got up, made their way through the crowded tables. At the door, he held it wide open and for one all too brief moment Anna was aware of his hand on her arm, guiding her through. Then he was gone, rushing off to his students and leaving Anna confirmed in her bleak view of herself. Even a man who was notorious for his interest in every variety of woman was immune to her.

Yet she was far from immune. To have a man who knew his way around women, who understood what she was thinking, who loved numbers as things in themselves and wouldn't want her to help with his homework before going off to snog one of her friends . . .

'Damn him,' said Phoebe. 'We'll have to go in a taxi.'

It was unbearably humiliating to find yourself having an infantile, unrequited crush on your friend's father, particularly one whom everyone else gossiped about and who was short and fat into the bargain.

'It won't be too awful,' said Lottie, 'if we split the fare four ways.'

Anna stirred herself. If she wasn't going to this party she needed to exert herself now and fake this headache. She often did get headaches, so pretending she had one was a piece of cake.

'I think,' she began, rubbing her temples, 'I might have to go home . . .'

No one heard her as Stella was trying unsuccessfully to squeeze herself into a leather dress and needed help.

'Perhaps if you cover your body in talcum powder,' Lottie was suggesting to Stella. 'Then it might go on more smoothly.'

'My head . . .' began Anna once more.

Dear God, thought Anna, as Stella began hurling about clouds of talcum powder, it was hard telling lies like this. Though she should find dishonesty easy enough now. She had been a million times more dishonest this past month than in her whole life to date, and in both her parents' lives as well. A figure of how much money she had made – though 'made', she knew, was the wrong word – welled up before her and she was hit by a wave of nausea. It was a colossal amount. First it was in the hundreds, but now it amounted to thousands – tens of thousands.

She quashed the panic erupting inside her. She would be all right. Of course she would. She had covered almost all eventualities.

But the truth was that Anna, quite simply, was stealing.

At the magazine where she was working, clothes, bags, jewellery and so on were sent in for fashion shoots. Just one individual item could be worth thousands. To safeguard all these valuables, a designer would send out an inventory of everything that had been lent. Then, when the magazine had finished taking the pictures, the goods would be returned to the designer, where they would be checked off on the original inventory. It was regarded as a very efficient system against theft, designed to be foolproof.

On her second day at the magazine Anna had had to take back six ludicrously expensive handbags to the designer's showroom. Watching the young assistant register their return on the computer she had noticed his password. Late that night she had been unable to sleep and had wondered idly if she could hack into his computer. And she found, without too much difficulty, that she could.

To test herself she then attempted to get into the records of another designer, but without the password. This was harder – much harder – and she had had to work into the early hours. And that night she had failed, and the next. And the one after. But on the fourth night, just as she was wondering whether to give up, she had cracked it.

She was thrilled with herself, pitting her wits against this impersonal machine and getting the better of it. Beating the system at least gave her a sense of power, and power was something she had never really tasted. So she had taken hacking into the computer one step further.

She had started with a plain blue cashmere cardigan, deliberately choosing something innocuous and easily overlooked. One night at home, she altered the designer's original inventory, deleting the blue cardigan. Officially it had never existed. Anna had taken the cardigan home and sold it on the Internet – quickly and far too cheaply, but she did not want it being traced.

After one success, she wanted another. And another. She was

careful not to take anything actually used in a fashion shoot, and she made sure she took the more modest pieces that would not be noticed until it was too late, if ever. Then she got rid of the stuff within twenty-four hours.

The only flaw in the scheme was keeping the clothes at home overnight. Just the other day her father had come into her room and spotted a pink leather coat which she had carelessly not hidden away. But she would not make that mistake again.

Now, in a very short space of time, she had made all this money. Her three years at university were paid for if she wanted. Or she could spend the money on a nose job like Lottie, or have her thighs slimmed like another girl from St Catherine's, or have something done to her ears like one of the girls who had been in her class. Though Anna could never quite see what the problem was with the girl's ears. They weren't that big, certainly not as big as the girl thought they were. But, thought Anna, if I reconfigure my face . . .

Tears pricked Anna's eyes. She did not want to have plastic surgery. To court that pain, to take that risk, and for what? It was madness. Frustration flared within her. How could she be so stupid as to think that changing her face would change her? She forced herself up off the chaise longue. She had been awake until four last night attempting to get into the system of a popular shoe designer who she knew was making a delivery to the magazine tomorrow, and it was proving exceptionally difficult. She would go home, she told herself, and have another try. Then at least she would escape this party and dent the boredom.

'I feel sick,' she announced bluntly, as Stella began pirouetting around in the dress she had finally pulled on, as unstoppable now as an arrow released from its bow. 'I've got to go.'

'Oh no,' said Lottie. 'Are you sure you're all right?'

'Yes, I just want to go home.'

'Do you feel very sick?' asked Stella, who was going to read medicine, edging away with evident distaste.

'You do look a bit grey,' said Phoebe, running her hands through her glittering hair. 'Let me call you a cab.'

'No, no, really. The bus is fine. Have fun.'

And with that she left them, flying down the three flights of stairs from Phoebe's bedroom to the front door where Phoebe's mother was just arriving, and her father was on his way out.

'Anna,' called Phoebe's mother, 'are you all right?'

'Oh yes, well, no. I've got a headache.' She caught Phoebe's father giving her an appraising look, as if to say he didn't believe her. She put her hands to her eyes as if in pain. 'I don't feel great.'

He had seen through her, that was obvious.

'Let me give you a lift home,' he said, looking for his car keys.

'No, honestly.'

'Don't argue,' he said. 'If you're not well I'm not having you get the bus. Now, come on. Or I'll be late myself.'

With a peck on the cheek for his wife, he held the door open for Anna and with great solicitude, as if she was genuinely ill, he helped her out to his car.

With his arm holding her he was so physically close, her legs turned hollow and she walked as gingerly as if she was crossing thin ice to the car.

'Hold on,' he said, lifting a plastic Sainsbury's bag full of papers off the passenger seat. 'There you go.' He hurled them into the back.

'Thank you,' she said and sat down, aware her hands were shaking.

'Are you cold?' he asked as he got in the other side, nodding at her fingers clenched together in her lap.

'No.'

'Just say.'

'Sure . . . thanks.'

'It's Ash Hill Square you want, isn't it?'

'Please.'

And with that he drove in silence and she stared ahead. She wondered where he was going afterwards. To meet someone more interesting than her, that was for sure. For the entire ten-minute journey she tried to think of something to say and failed. And then they were outside her home. And it was all over.

'Here you are,' he said, still keeping the engine running.

'Thank you.'

He gave her a half-smile. 'Not at all.'

She reached for the door handle, then he stretched over and put his hand on hers, and for one delighted moment she thought he was going to kiss her.

But instead he said, 'You know, Anna, I don't really like parties either. But it's a mistake to write them off totally. You might go to one and find someone there who feels just the same about things as you do. And it would be a shame to miss that person.'

The weight of her disappointment was frightening. Here she was, alone with him, but what could she do? She bent her head.

'Wouldn't it?' he said.

Dear God, she thought, let him kiss me.

'Anna?'

She just shrugged.

'I mean it,' he went on. 'I know you feel the odd one out. But you never know, there might be another odd one out too. Not just you. If I was only . . .'

Only what? She made herself look at him directly. In this half-light his eyes seemed made only for seduction, and nothing in the world would have made her say no.

But then he said, 'You'd better go.'

So she got out of the car, saying politely, 'Thanks for the lift.'

## 20

In the back of the Mercedes picking her up from Heathrow Julia was straight on the phone to Kate, her assistant.

'They're wonderful,' she said, looking through photographs of a villa in Corfu Kate had emailed her. 'Exactly what I wanted.'

While she was in Boston, Julia had asked Kate to arrange a week's holiday for her and Phillip next June.

'They had one with a larger private beach,' Kate said, 'but this villa, I thought, was gorgeous.'

Truly gorgeous, thought Julia, enchanted with the absurdly beautiful primrose-coloured house overrun with bougainvillaea, the mountains behind it every shade of blue and violet, and the cool sea in the bay below. Julia closed her eyes a moment imagining herself and Phillip there, together in that glorious Mediterranean light.

She glanced again at the price of the holiday. It was the sort of money that her mother would have had to eke out for a year. But Julia had it to spend on treating herself and her husband to seven days in perfect beauty, without even worrying about the cost. And she had made this money herself. No one else.

She eased out her long legs, picturing Phillip's pleasure. She could make everything all right, she knew. Because everything was not quite all right. On Sunday, Phillip had been reluctant to see her go. He wanted to talk more about Rose, to have more time with her, alone.

And she would like more of her husband too. It could be blissful with Phillip, even now. Almost twenty years on, she could find herself in thrall to his hands, the sweetness of his flesh.

But she had been terribly preoccupied for a while. She had no choice, what with the Clifford James case taking up so much of her attention. But she would sort it. And this holiday would make things right again with Phillip.

Julia flushed with excitement. Seven whole days in June! It was a pity she could not book anything earlier but she would not take on any work in June. She would make Phillip that promise.

She checked her iPad, responded to five urgent emails and then contemplated once more the villa's garden full of irises and poppies, with forget-me-nots spilling down the old stone steps to a terrace overshadowed with wisteria where there stood very comfortable cushioned chairs. Or at least, she thought, looking more closely, I will try not to do any work. But those soft, easy chairs were made for reading and, by June, she hoped to have the bulk of her book written, and that perfumed terrace would be perfect to sit quietly and edit her manuscript. That wasn't exactly work and, anyway, he would read himself, those Scandinavian detective novels he loved when he wanted to unwind, though lately he had taken up again with his Tolstoy –

'The road's blocked up there,' said the driver, interrupting her thoughts. 'A burst water main. So we'll have to go through . . .'

'Don't worry,' she murmured, as he rattled off names of streets she did not know. 'It doesn't matter.'

It would sound too gauche and naive to admit how much she enjoyed travelling. But Julia loved the luxury of flying first class, the thrill of being on the move and part of a continuous flow of life from the ease of a leather-cushioned limousine. They crossed a bridge and she glimpsed the canal below and a houseboat lit up with red and green Christmas lights. To Julia, they were exhilarating, these short December days, with all this activity going on under cover of darkness. I must take the girls out one night, she thought, perhaps to one of those swish restaurants Rose was dying to go to. It would be fun for them all to be part of this glamour, dressing up, enjoying the pre-Christmas excitement together. A vast building site came into view with half-finished towers of gleaming glass and cranes reaching skywards. A Father Christmas dangled from the arm of one, and another glittered with flashing stars, lighting up the outlines of the spire of a Georgian church in the distance. That was the beauty of London, there was so much happening, nothing in her could grow slack and stagnate.

But now the car was crawling along busy, narrower streets, passing row upon row of small houses, not the pretty bay-windowed sort that come at great price with stripped floors and restored fireplaces, but dreary and dark, semi-detached and double-glazed to keep out the noise and hold in the heat, with gardens cemented over for parking, weeds growing through the cracks. The line of traffic slowed yet again and came to a standstill. Julia reached for her phone. These airport journeys were an opportunity to make non-urgent calls and Angela had left a message for her – nothing important, she said. Julia called back but the line was engaged.

The car edged forward.

They were moving so slowly she was able to glimpse inside the cramped front rooms of the houses, at a mother trying to calm a screaming baby, another unloading shopping into kitchen cupboards. In the street a woman, considerably younger than Julia, her exhausted, pretty face set in rigid lines, was pushing a wheelchair holding, Julia guessed, her father, while at the same time trying to control a little boy grabbing at the last of the leaves swirling around the pavement.

Women's lives could be too bitter and too hard. All that caring to do – of the young, the sick, the old – while engaging in a never-ending battle to keep everyone clean and fed. Thank God, thought Julia, grateful to something she did not believe in, and responding to more emails, that she had managed to carve out a different destiny for herself.

The car began to pick up speed, and Julia called out, 'It's better if you go left here. Then straight through the lights, and sharp right.' Her phone rang. 'And keep in the right-hand lane,' she instructed, answering the call. It was her sister again.

'I'm sorry I've not rung for a while,' began Angela, in her soft, patient voice.

'Don't worry, I've been so caught up.' They were both always sorry for not being in touch sooner – although they lived just five miles apart, they rarely saw one another. 'It's been the same here.'

They were each used to the other being 'so caught up'. Normally this was due to work, but life had dramatically changed for Angela since adopting Mirela and she had taken most of the past six months off to look after this orphaned child she had brought back from Romania.

'So how's she doing?' asked Julia, while at the same time flicking through some boarding school prospectuses for Rose that Kate had emailed over.

'She's getting there,' said Angela, non-committally.

'What about you? Is she sleeping any more?'

'Well, yes . . . if I let her sleep with me.'

That was typical of Angela, thought Julia, to get into the dangerously unbreakable habit of letting your child share your bed.

'Well, whatever works.'

'You see,' said Angela, 'she was used to sharing a cot in a great big dormitory, so she was terrified being all alone in a bed in an empty room and so I have . . . look, I know you don't approve,' laughed Angela.

'Don't say that,' said Julia, suddenly chastened, and looking up from the prospectuses to give Angela her full attention. 'You know how I admire what you've done.' And she did. It had taken her sister years of battling bureaucracy and trips abroad and using her medical contacts in order to adopt a child. 'Is she talking any more?'

'She's really coming on. I mean,' Angela backtracked, 'not like other four-year-olds, obviously.'

Mirela was barely speaking Romanian six months ago. On the two occasions Julia had met her, the criminally thin little girl had sat without moving, fearful and silent. To teach her English and help her acquire the bravado to manage in school would require the sort of dedication only someone like her sister could manage. And even Angela might find the task beyond her, Julia suspected.

'But she's incredible, the way she's picked up the language. The other day,' went on Angela, 'she actually said to me, "I love you."'

'Oh Angela!' cried Julia. She could hear all the joy in her sister's voice. 'That's wonderful. It really is. Mirela's lucky to have you.'

'And I her,' responded Angela immediately. Angela never accepted a compliment without qualification. 'Really. Just pushing her on the swings, or sitting with her in my lap in front of the telly, or just, I don't know, going for a walk and watching her take it all in.'

Julia listened closely. Angela invariably sounded happy in a calm and peaceful way. But this was strangely different. Angela was exhilarated – which was lovely – but she was also what Rose would call 'wired', and this was so unlike her elder sister that Julia felt uneasy. She wanted to warn Angela to take care. But she wasn't sure what she needed to warn her of and dismissed the thought as swiftly as it came.

Instead, with her usual practicality, she asked, 'And what about school? Have you managed to get all the extra support?'

'Yes,' said Angela.

Of course she has, thought Julia. If anyone could make things happen, it was her elder sister.

'It was a battle, but it's all sorted now so she'll begin next term.'

'So does that mean you're going back to work full-time?'

'No, just two and a half days. Less, if possible.'

'Less?' But that's almost nothing, thought Julia. 'Can you afford not to work?' she asked, a domestic problem she was genuinely interested in.

Although Angela earned a very respectable salary, she always gave a good percentage of it away, and was a trustee of one of the leading charities for the elderly.

'Yes, I can, as long as I move, which is one of the things I wanted to tell you.'

'Move?'

'That's right.'

'Not out of London?'

'Well, I'll have to – to make the money.'

'But that'll be a new job, a new life,' cried Julia, surprising herself with her concern that her elder sister would no longer be close by. 'Where might you go? Don't say "the country", please. All that mud and scenery.'

Angela just laughed. 'Someone I used to work with has moved to Bristol and he's always urging me to go and join his team there – and he's happy with me being part-time. But Julia, it wasn't just about this that I wanted to speak to you.' She paused and lowered her voice.

Suddenly Julia was alarmed.

'You see, I have to make a new will,' said Angela. 'And I need to make sure that Mirela is looked after. There's money for her because I've taken out massive life insurance, so that's not an issue. But I need to appoint someone as Mirela's guardian, someone who'll look after her, love her. And I know it wouldn't be easy, obviously, a trau-matized child. And Mirela already has so many other issues.'

There was a silence. Julia felt her mouth contract.

'Julia, please, will you be her guardian?'

It was for no more than a second – if that – but to her shame Julia hesitated. The lawyer in Julia came to the fore. Her practical mind saw all the immense difficulties of taking on such a responsibility – a whole new life. But then, overcompensating, she gushed, 'Of course, of course. I assumed I would be,' she lied. 'But Angela, promise me. You're sure you're all right? There's nothing wrong?'

'Yes, I'm fine. Really.'

'You're not hiding anything from me?'

'No, of course not,' said Angela. 'But you just never know.'

Too right, thought Julia. Of course you never know. You have to work so hard to keep the unknowable at bay, to protect those you love as best you can. It was all right for Angela. Her unwavering faith in God kept her steady, regardless. She always found the good in the bad. Whereas Julia knew better. There were not always silver linings. And she endured a rush of irritation towards her sister who dealt with life with the assurance of Mr Micawber, blithely assum-ing everything would be all right. Because how would she be all right if she suddenly found herself looking after Mirela? Of course she could employ help, masses of help. As, indeed, she had with Anna and Rose. But it was not as simple as that.

She pictured the sharp reality of Mirela living with her, sharing her home, her life. She did not want to have to worry about children sleeping or not sleeping. She was past all that. But she could imagine Mirela screaming in the middle of the night. Or even more disturbing, never crying, never talking, but shrinking and silent.

She had had such bright, robust little girls. But Mirela was no such child. And more to the point, thought Julia, I am not like my sister. The presence of this tragic creature would cost her so much – and she did not mean money. It was the continual necessity of care, the relentless responsibility, and with Mirela there would be more than the usual share of worry. But she owed her sister. Julia knew that. Angela had been positively saintly the way she had taken on the care of their mother.

She steadied herself. 'Of course I will be her guardian,' she repeated. 'Thank you for asking me. Though I'll have to speak to Phillip of course.'

'Actually, I did speak to Phillip. You see, I rang you at home and he answered so we chatted about Mirela and I said why I wanted to speak to you and I told him.'

'That you wanted me to be her guardian?'

'Yes, because obviously it would be difficult for you if he was against the idea.'

Julia was in no doubt that Phillip would have agreed. Being the guardian of such a disadvantaged soul was the sort of challenge he could not resist right now.

'He's a kind man.'

Julia did not respond. As they turned into the quiet square where she lived, with the first of the magnificent Christmas trees lighting up a huge bay window, sign of a goodwill she was now far from feeling, she just said, 'Well, that's settled, then.'

## 21

Julia sat at the large kitchen table with her legs crossed and twirling a high-heeled shoe on her toe.

'All I meant,' she said to Phillip, with half an eye on some documents Kate had had delivered to her home, 'was that you might have consulted me first, rather than simply agreeing to me being Mirela's guardian.'

'It didn't occur to me that you would even give it a second thought,' he said, giving some coriander seeds a great whack. He was following a recipe for curry he had read in the Sunday papers, making an effort, because he wanted them all to sit down and have a family dinner on Julia's return from Boston. But her first evening home was not going as either of them had envisaged.

'It's not that, it's just that we should have discussed the reality of what having Mirela would actually mean.'

'So your own sister asks for your help and you have to think about it.'

'Not exactly,' she said looking at him, bewildered. She had the awful impression that he was picking a fight with her. 'I just have to –'

'Have to what?' he asked, as coriander seeds shot across the kitchen floor.

'I just think,' she said, 'we should have talked about it together. That's all.'

How they had got on to this argument only minutes after walking through the door she had no idea. She watched him tip the coriander into the frying pan and great clouds of black smoke billow up. He's got the oil's too hot, Julia thought irritably. But she contained herself as he went on, 'I don't get this, I really don't. I thought you were the sort of person who could handle this.'

'I am. But you don't just agree to turn our lives upside down without asking what I think about it.'

'But what is there to think about? Honestly, Julia, how could you say anything other than yes?'

'I did say yes.'

'So what's the problem?'

'There's no problem. It's just . . .' Julia hesitated. She did not want to be having this argument. She had agreed to be Mirela's guardian. So why was he harping on at her? What were they really rowing about?

'Just what?'

Just, thought Julia, that this is not purely an emotional decision, which is how you seem to view the world these days. There are practicalities too. Phillip's philanthropic turn to his life had changed him. They had always worked so well together, but now she was not sure where he was heading.

She said, 'Just that this is not some token gesture like being a godparent, sending the odd cheque with no thought and zero commitment. This is life-transforming. What if something really does happen to Angela? Seriously, what if she dies? We'll have a four-year-old living with us. Can you remember what that was like? And this is one with problems we can't even begin to imagine.'

'Oh, come on. We'll cross that bridge when we come to it.'

'Cross that bridge?' echoed Julia. He sounded as if he was talking from some trite self-help manual.

'Of course we will,' he said.

But some bridges are too difficult, she thought. I spend my life imagining bridges my clients might need to cross, preparing for all eventualities. But I've seen too many people fall to be under any illusions that there is always a way to the other side.

'For God's sake, Julia, you are one of the most capable women on the planet.'

She supposed he meant that as a compliment.

'Just think what you've achieved.'

But the fear never goes, she wanted to say. And if you had lived as I have you would understand.

'And this is your sister.'

'I know it's my sister. I mean, how could I ever forget . . .'

My perfect, holier-than-thou sister, she thought, her anger spilling out towards Angela. Then she was ashamed of herself. Angela was about as good as it was possible for someone to be, and Julia recognized that and was grateful. But her feeling of moral inferiority to her sister could be such a reminder of her angry, frustrated childhood.

Once before – only the once – Angela had asked for Julia's help when their mother was sick. And Julia, just down from Cambridge, had said she was too busy, overloaded with work in a new job, fighting for her corner among other extremely talented trainee lawyers. After that she had never really found the time, except for breezing in and out occasionally with a colossal bunch of overpriced flowers that would barely last the day in the overheated flat. And there had been plenty of opportunities to help – four years of opportunities, in fact – as her mother had struggled on for ages, lying under some monstrous quilt Julia could not stand the sight of.

Now Angela was asking for her help again. And it terrified her. It was all right for Phillip. He had absolutely no idea what a great incubus family need could be. His parents never seemed to want anything and his sturdy, buxom mother, who always looked as if she would relish yet another ten-mile ramble, liked to boast she had not known a day's sickness in her whole life. 'I'm like you, dear,' she would say to Julia in a conspiratorial way, 'far too busy to get ill.' As if, railed Julia to herself, it was that simple.

But right now, all she wanted was to ease this tension with Phillip.

'I'm sorry, sweetheart, I don't know what I'm saying, I'm probably just tired.' The words stuck in her throat but she did not want to argue. 'I'm fine about Mirela,' she lied, 'really, I am.'

She got up and walked over to him, her shoes crunching on the coriander seeds Phillip had spilt all over the place, and leaned her body into his.

Phillip held Julia close. He could feel her long dark lashes brush his cheek. Her hair smelled of the vanilla shampoo she ordered from Rome. But as he kissed her, he realized he did not have a clue what his wife was actually thinking.

While Julia was away it had startled Phillip how much he missed her. He had found himself staring at a photo he had taken when they were in Regent's Park rose garden at the end of one summer. Her head was bent to look at the soft, fading flowers and her expression was uncharacteristically nervous. This apprehension touched him deeply, but she disliked the photo and much preferred the one taken for a law magazine, which sat on his desk. With her strong, direct gaze it was the perfect affirmation of a highly intelligent, beautiful woman who could give every bit as good as she got.

The first time Phillip set eyes on Julia she stood so tall and aloof, her shining black hair coiled up above her lovely face, giving no sign of what she was feeling or concealing. He watched her standing on her own by a window, a glass of wine untouched in her hand. Suddenly he wanted access to that glossy hair, to that pale body, to that aloneness. And to his relief and joy Julia granted it with great experience and generosity.

Yet on the first morning he woke next to her she was already sitting up in bed reading a legal textbook, wearing one of his sweaters and nothing else. Engrossed in some aspect of contract law she was quite indifferent to him lying beside her after a night that, for him, had been anything but indifferent. When he reached for her she gave him a pleasant glance, smiled, but then gently pushed his hand from her thigh, saying, 'Let me finish this chapter.'

*Let me finish?* Phillip had never been turned down before, let alone for a finer point of law. He was devastated. He wanted her, there and then. But watching her with his head on the pillow it was clear that the book commanded her full concentration, that he should keep quiet, let her finish, but he could not help himself. He was as desperate as a man in the desert taunted with a clear glass of water placed just out of reach.

'But Julia . . .'

She ignored him.

'Julia, for God's sake.'

She glanced up over her book. 'What?'

Phillip had never pleaded in his life. Good-looking, bright and with a cheerful disposition, he found that women were just there in the path of his life and he had taken up with them – or rather, they had taken up with him.

Some of his encounters had dragged on for what seemed like for ever. He was a lucky man who pretty much had only had kindness shown to him, and so much kindness had coloured him. He never wanted to be the one to end it. But what he was feeling for this woman lying in bed beside him, who was more interested in preparing for an essay than in him, was unlike anything he had ever known. He watched her reach for a pen and make notes in her bold, rapid script, as if he was not there. This, he realized, was how crimes were committed.

'Wasn't,' he tried again, 'wasn't last night . . .? Wasn't it . . .?'

She frowned, still reading. 'Wasn't it what?'

'Well . . .' This was one of the most humiliating moments of his life, but to hell with it. 'Well, wasn't it . . .?'

Then she turned to him, and a smile appeared on her face that was actually more of a grin. 'Yes it *was*,' she said with a look that, to Phillip, was closer to triumph than anything warmer. 'I wouldn't still be here otherwise.'

That was not, for Phillip, a particularly satisfactory answer but he suspected it was the best she would give. But then she slowly marked her place in the book and put it precisely on the bedside table.

'Listen,' she went on. 'I thought, or at least I certainly hoped, that I would spend quite a lot of time here. And if I do, I'm still going to have to work and you've got to understand that and . . .' Julia hesitated. That she found his sweetness utterly compelling and that his gentleness made her heart lurch in a most unfamiliar way, he did not need to know. Nor did he need to know that, of course, she would rather be between the sheets with him than getting to grips with contract law. She had to guard her thoughts like a pot of gold, as not a soul needed to know her fears or where she had come from. All that mattered was who she now was and where she was going. She had better things to do than let her feelings run wild, and she could not let herself forget it.

When Julia arrived at Cambridge she had absolutely no intention of falling in love. All around her she watched couples in such states of passionate ardour or hopeless deprivation, they lost their appetites or ate too much, could not sleep or work, their emotions written all over them in what looked to Julia like large childish letters. She would never expose herself in such a way. She did not have the time. She had work to do and a first to earn.

But she stroked the hair out of Phillip's eyes. There were golden freckles, she noticed, on his cheekbones. Then he took her hand and began, very gently, to kiss the knuckles, one by one. She would, she realized, have to keep a tight rein on herself. But she was well practised at that.

'The thing is,' she went on, retrieving her hand, 'I can't mess this up. I'm not going to get a second chance.'

'We get millions of chances,' he said, putting his arms behind his head, and propping himself up on the pillows, 'we just have –'

'No, we don't,' she interrupted sharply. 'At least I don't. And I'll certainly never get this one again, and I'm not throwing it away. For . . . anyone. So I have to do this . . . the work. And if you want to see me again, that comes first. My work. That's the deal. And if you think that's pompous and priggish, tell me and I'll go and you need never see me again.'

But Phillip had no intention of letting her go, because what he heard that morning was her raging, naked need. From that day his hidden lover was that lonely young woman desperate to control the world with her unyielding intelligence. He saw all her beauty and fierceness and vulnerability and never had he wanted anything more ardently in his life. But he, too, knew better than to let on.

She had returned to her book and he could not see her expression. So he touched her chin lightly, turning her face towards him.

'Look me in the eye,' he said, 'and tell me you don't want to stay.'

She did not let herself look him in the eye. Instead, she looked at the clock. She had time. She slipped off his sweater, put her cool white arms around him and her lips against his.

Twenty-five years on, standing in their large, expensively lit, expensively furnished kitchen with all the accessories of shared family life, Phillip wondered what Julia was hungry for now, whether that eager questing girl was still yearning. She seemed happy in her work, her home, her family. And she seemed happy in him. Indeed, she always had done. Yet for Julia, the ups and down of marriage were things you take in your stride by not giving them too much thought. Or if she did, her own view of love and its complexities was so internal, she would not speak of it. With Julia, he knew he had to ask her what she was thinking, that although in most respects Julia was the epitome of the modern woman, she was not in this. She kept her feelings so hidden he might ask and still she might not say. That was the way she was, and he had always accepted it.

But now her work . . . no, he reminded himself, desperate to be fair, his work as well as hers had cramped them in many ways, made them both hard to reach. They might make one another a cup of coffee, ask how their day had gone, exchange a bit of news, fall asleep in one another's arms, but their minds were elsewhere. And he had never noticed how repressive this was. Until now. Now, he realized, he was tired of her distance. And that unnerved him. Now he wanted her close, even if it was to have a flaming row.

'Let's go away,' he said on impulse. 'Just you and me. As soon as we get back from my parents'. Over New Year. Five days or so.'

She looked at him aghast. 'What?'

'Go to Venice.' Suddenly he was full of possibilities. 'Lisbon – we've never been there.'

'Lisbon?' she repeated, as if he had suggested the moon.

'Yes, why not?'

'Because for starters there's the Clifford James case.'

'Well, some nice hotel nearby. Dorset. Drive down there. It'd only take a couple of hours.'

'It would take more than that. Much more,' she said adamantly. 'And we've got to go to your parents'. I've barely got time for that.'

'Yes but that's . . . that's family. I'm talking just us.'

'But I can't,' she said, pulling away from him. 'You know I can't.'

'Call in sick.'

'Phillip! I've never done that.'

'That's why you can do it this once.'

'I can't just shoot off on a whim because the mood takes me. I don't do that. And nor do you. You've never done that,' she said, turning the tables on him. 'Have you?'

He shook his head. 'No, but –'

'So why are you asking me?'

'Because . . .'

Because, he thought. Because . . . he did not want to acknowledge it. He loved Julia's sense of responsibility and the way she stuck by her high standards. She embodied so many qualities that he valued. She never passed the buck, never flattered or fawned, never compromised or said second best would do. And yet.

He did not want to question the worth of all he had. Here he was with his wonderful wife, in his fabulous home, about to eat a fine meal. Millions would look upon him as having a gilded existence. And they would be right. Yet it occurred to him that he had spent nearly all of his working life telling people how to buy happiness but he, himself, was not happy. And that was a dreadful thought.

'Please, Phillip,' she said, 'you must understand.'

Of course he understood. In Julia he could not have chosen a better companion for life. They agreed on what was right and wrong, believed in the values of hard work and honesty, had almost identical views on how to bring up their children. But now he felt like an outsider in the world he had made. And that, he could not understand.

'Look.' Julia was showing him her iPad. 'I was going to save it for

Christmas. As a present. For you. For us. I've booked us a holiday. Because I know we need it,' she said, full of the excitement of giving someone a gift you think they will love and of having solved a problem. 'Look . . . Corfu.'

'Lovely,' he said, trying to inject some enthusiasm into his voice. 'But when have you actually booked it for?' he asked, realizing he already knew the answer.

'Well, June,' she said. 'Not till then, I'm sorry. But I won't take any work . . . well, not to speak of. I knew you'd love it. You do, don't you?'

'How could I not,' he said, keeping his eyes focused on the pictures of the Greek sunshine. He was unaccountably angry. His wife had just bought them a week in a gorgeous villa in Corfu. How could you be angry with someone for that? 'Lovely,' he repeated, because it was churlish and childish, thought Phillip, condemning himself as harshly as he could, to be angry with someone because after twenty-five years you have come to the conclusion you want them to give more of themselves. But he found himself saying, 'Why can't we do both? Go away now as well?'

'Darling, you know I can't.'

Then Julia had to answer her ringing phone, and he hurled some cumin seeds into the pan, stirring them up with the blackened coriander.

## 22

On the other side of town, Angela was sitting in her office on the geriatric ward of the vast London teaching hospital replaying the conversation she had just had with her sister about being Mirela's guardian.

That morning one of Angela's patients had called her 'a saint'. She had laughed it off. But 'a saint' was how she was generally regarded. Though right now a devil was nagging at her. Was she asking too much of Julia?

But who else, besides Julia, could be Mirela's guardian? No one. She knew Julia would look after Mirela to the best of her ability. But Julia was so . . .

Angela did not want to think badly of her younger sister. Or indeed anyone. Do not judge what people do, only what they suffer. That was her principle. That was why she had taken on the burden of their mother's illness – not Julia, who had run and run and never looked back. Julia's spirit would have broken and Angela had accepted her absence. She doubted she could do her job so well if she had not sat those long hours beside that shell of a woman. But right now she had to do all she possibly could to protect Mirela if the worst should happen. Because the thought of her darling child enduring yet more distress was terrifying.

Fear was virgin territory for Angela. Fear was lack of trust in God. Fear was powerless before faith. And Angela's faith had never been in question. Until Mirela.

'Are you sure about this?' a friend had asked when she adopted the child.

And Angela, holding the trembling girl close for the first time, her fragile ribs heaving, replied, 'Yes,' with such certainty, she realized that she had never before been truly sure of anything.

For Angela's entire existence, God had been the object of her love – her north, her south. And the sick, the poor, anyone in need had been the children upon whom she lavished herself, body and soul. Even among the ugliness and grim monotony of her ward, Angela had believed in the nearness of God. But Mirela, with a blink of her troubled eyes, sent the compass of Angela's life spinning. Because God could not compete with the joy of hearing this child laugh, or seeing the trust in her smile.

'Don't die, Mummy,' Mirela had begged her last night, 'don't die, please don't. You won't . . . will you?'

And how do you answer that? thought Angela, sitting at her desk. Except with a lie. Because no amount of prayer could prevent Mirela's worst fears being realized. Some day. Sooner or later. And it would not matter one jot if Angela entered the golden gates bathed in God's love, because there was no place in heaven where she could escape Mirela's need for her.

For the twenty-eighth time that day there was a knock on her door and she wrenched herself back to the problems of the moment.

'Come in, James,' she said, getting up from behind her desk to greet the tall man blustering into her dingy, overcrowded office.

'Thank you,' he said, taking her hands in both of his.

He was about Angela's age, in his late forties, and his well-cut pin-stripe suit suggested a man for whom the lights in life had always turned green. But now he was up against old age and the slow dwindling of reason in someone he loved. His mother's condition was deteriorating and Angela knew she had to spell this out.

'You'd think,' he said, 'that it would get easier coming into a hospital. I mean, I've always hated hospitals. Even when my children were born I couldn't get out quickly enough. But I've been here so much now. You'd think it wouldn't be so bad. But it is.'

'But you still come,' she said, telling him what he needed to hear. 'It's been a great comfort to your mother.'

He smiled at her gratefully. And this gave her the cue. 'James, I'm afraid we need to make some decisions about the best way to manage . . .'

She watched him gulp. She was used to being the bearer of bad tidings, had been well trained in meeting disaster in others but, she thought, talking him through the painful facts, I am incapable of facing it in myself. Or not so much myself. How would she feel if someone was telling her Mirela was in pain? Or dying? She shivered, suddenly bereft of faith, a seizure of the spirit beyond her control. But God's love was one of hope, she tried to remind herself while explaining the scant options available for the mother of this man sitting beside her. God was the all-protective Father. She had to trust Him.

Instinctively she reached for the tiny seed-pearl cross around her neck because, if that trust was scattering to the four winds, she had to pray for it, pray for the habit of prayer which she was losing daily – and worse, much, much worse, was not even particularly bothered about.

'That's what I advise,' she said, trying to concentrate on the man whose eyes were drifting up to the grimy office window as she spoke. She touched him lightly on the arm. 'James, do you have any questions?'

'Not really.'

'You might later,' she said. 'You probably will. Please call me if you need to.'

'Thanks, yes, I will. Thanks.'

He got to his feet and shook her hand. Then he hesitated, and stepped over to the window. To the left rose the great concrete slabs of the new psychiatric unit – a sight to send anyone over the edge, according to the local paper. Directly opposite lay the Victorian workhouse which had been the original foundation of the hospital and still housed the A&E department within blackened brick walls.

'How you can tell me you take heart from that view, God only knows,' he said.

She looked at him in surprise. Had she said that? Then it came back to her. In one of their first meetings, more than a year ago – before she had Mirela – she had told him how she would look out of this window and not see ugliness but hope. She would think that if it wasn't for that aesthetically monstrous psychiatric unit, the prisons and gutters would be even more overflowing; that however hideous the building, much of the work in there had averted even greater torment of spirit. She would remind herself, too, of the many families defeated by the relentless duty of care, whose burdens had been eased by the help they had found in that hospital.

'Well,' she said, joining him by the window, 'I suppose I try and see all the good that is done here. Otherwise . . .'

I have to think, she reminded herself, that in the A&E department, lives which only a short while back would have been lost are saved and handed back intact. Children, who might have grown up without a mother or father, now know the love that once would have been taken from them.

Angela truly had taken comfort in the phenomenal achievements of the place. And if the achievement was not enough – and it could never be enough – she had not let that undermine her spirit and energy for the work she could do. The problems were obvious, but if she was to do her job, her defence was either to remedy what she could, or accept what was beyond her power. And for almost twenty years, since she had qualified as a doctor, that is what she had done.

But then Mirela came into her life and that wonderful universal love she felt for her fellow men was crushed by her love for this one, damaged little girl. All she could see now was God's power to hurt, not to heal, and some days she could barely bring herself to look at her patients because she would see Mirela lying there instead, sick and helpless. Or she saw herself, while Mirela screamed, unheard and ignored.

'You'd have thought . . .'

She was aware James was speaking to her.

'. . . at least they might have put in some sort of garden, just so patients could get a taste of fresh air, see a bit of greenery.'

She turned her attention to the tarmac courtyard where a woman was pushing a wailing child round and round the one lifeless, leafless tree. Angela watched the weary figure. How could anyone speak of the joys of motherhood when those joys were transfigured by fear? Love, which had always been the guiding light of her life now gave her no peace, no answers, no safety.

In her first week as a newly qualified doctor Angela had dealt with the suicide of a young mother who had thrown herself and her child in front of a train. At the time, Angela felt nothing but pity for that unhappy, terrified woman. But now she felt recognition. You can be so frightened for the one you love you only find safety by ending their life. Of course that was extreme, she reminded herself. That poor woman was desperately sick. And every day she saw mothers who looked far from afraid, striding along with babies in buggies, dropping bonny little children off at school, laughing with leggy teenagers. Indeed, her own sister marched through life, head up.

But, she wanted to know, did those women stumble as she did, only stifling insurmountable fears with hundreds of thousands of other hurried little worries? Is there milk in the fridge? What's for dinner? Where's the homework?

'I mean,' James was saying, 'if you didn't see the good, you couldn't do your work.'

She nodded politely.

'And I'd better let you get on and do it.'

As soon as he left, she went to check on a man who had had a third stroke that afternoon and now could not speak or move.

'Good evening,' she smiled.

The panic in his eyes subsided a moment as they rested on Angela.

'How frightening this is for you,' she said, taking his paralysed hands in her own. 'Can you squeeze my hand?' she asked mechanically. He could not, but she said, 'Very good,' trying not to edge away.

But the touch of his lifeless hands was suddenly repellent. She gulped and clutched at the cross around her neck. Such oversensitivity was dreadful. This dribbling husk of a man, she impressed upon herself, was happily married for thirty years, was a respected history teacher, played cricket for Middlesex. No doubt he had once been a beautiful young man with lips that kissed, hands that caressed.

Dear God, she prayed, but not in the manner she was used to. Why does illness take even love by the throat and throttle it? Why does it all end with this appalling corruption of youth and health and beauty? The danger was as present as the sky overhead. It was the careless driver, the strange lump, the pain that would not go away. It would come to them all. It would come to her, at any time, to hurt the child she loved.

She leaped up too quickly and saw the desperation in his eyes.

'You're thirsty, aren't you?' the caring professional in her said.

There was a glimmer of acknowledgement on his face.

'I will ask the nurse to bring you something, to make you more comfortable. And I will see you tomorrow morning.'

And with that lie she left him, because she doubted he would survive the night. '"For the poor always ye have with you",' she thought. John, chapter twelve, verse eight. And the sick too. And the dying.

But she had not always had Mirela. If she left now she would be home in time to read her a bedtime story.

## 23

Laura was on her knees at the back of the Roman Catholic Church of St Joseph doing the cleaning as elderly, female voices rose ever more stridently from around the altar.

'If we leave the tree by the heater it won't last till Christmas Eve,' snapped the retired head of a leading girls' school.

'But no one will see it behind the pillar,' cut in a retired professor of archaeology.

Laura kept her head down. For most of her life she had known this collection of brilliant women, all friends of her mother. But since having children she had tried to keep out of their shadow. Nothing had ever been said, but she felt diminished in the presence of these single women who had embraced all the opportunities of feminism, become leaders of their professions, whereas she . . . What had she done? 'Stupidly got yourself pregnant with twins,' is the response she imagined these women would give. And they'd be right. Which is why she preferred to be here, away from them at the back with the dustpan and brush.

'What about the lilies?' a former diplomat was demanding.

Laura glanced up. She had to hand it to these women. The decorations were stupendous. Whatever they did, even if it was just organizing tinsel and baubles, the result was awe-inspiring. They filled their retirement years constructively – running charities, fundraising for medical research, acting as JPs, petitioning for maintaining libraries and other good causes. And yet, thought Laura. And yet.

'But if we put the lilies . . . Oh, what do you think, Father?'

The priest, Father Eoghan, a tall man in his early fifties, with all the grace of a fine sportsman – as he still was – was walking from the vestry.

'Good morning, one and all,' he called in his rich Irish voice.

At once the women gathered about him.

'How wonderful to see you, ladies.'

Heavily lined, determined faces dissolved into soft smiles and Laura paused to watch this man of God wield his power over these women who had spent their lives putting the fear of God – though not necessarily in a biblical sense – into employees, public officials, difficult students.

'Anything I can do to help?'

'This tree's bigger than ever,' declared the professor of archaeology, 'so how we are going to get the star to the top –'

'Lie it flat again, and attach it on the ground?'

'What we need,' said the professor, with the air of a woman who thinks she is going to say something funny, 'is a nice young man.'

And, indeed, everyone did laugh and Father Eoghan said, 'Well, that counts me out.'

They are flirting with him, thought Laura, and a lesser man might feel quite daunted. Every one of these women had the physique and build of terrifically strong swimmers and, indeed, a number of them swam all year round, ice permitting, in the ponds on Hampstead Heath. But these indefatigable Amazons capitulated to the allure of Father Eoghan. They are like the elite girls in a sixth form, thought Laura. As, no doubt, they once had been – the whole world before them, with their brains and education.

Some of them, Laura knew, had made the choice to be alone, not wanting the constrictions and drudgery of marriage and maternity. These women had faced life's crises with energy and courage. They had not faltered. But had life actually delivered on its promises? In the end, had these once gifted young women who won their much-vaunted places at Girton and Somerville been short-changed? When the diplomat was awarded her OBE, she had asked Venetia, as her closest friend, to accompany her. No loving man, no children.

But they had their worthy work, Laura reminded herself, picking up some squashed fruit pastilles. Which is more than I have. But then she overheard the professor talking about being kept awake by the storm last night.

'I was awake too,' said the doctor of philosophy. 'But I wake so early anyway.'

'I'm normally awake from four,' said the ex-head teacher.

'Four?' repeated the JP. 'That's hard.'

The ex-head teacher nodded and, for a moment, her imperious features looked tired. 'The days can seem so long when you wake that early.'

'Well, I listen to the World Service,' the JP was saying. 'I tend to leave it on all night.'

'Oh, thank God for the World Service,' murmured the doctor of philosophy. 'A genuine prayer, Father,' she laughed with a sad smile.

And suddenly Laura was ashamed.

It had always amused her that such domineering women who had conquered so much were, despite all their achievements, so competitive and desirous of the attention of a man whose job it was to give everyone exactly the same attention. Yet today, preparing for Christmas, they appeared pitiful in their loneliness. She glanced at the altar. Oh, please God, don't let me end up like this.

But it was not that simple. If only, she thought, resuming her sweeping with a vengeance. She knew of more than enough marriages where the loneliness was devastating, where little seeds of resentment grew into great imprisoning forests. Without a doubt, in this very church, too many men and women had walked down the aisle with unreal dreams that left them more isolated than ever. Too many marriages only survived if you hid behind a mask, concealing your weaknesses in fear of showing your own true face.

And yet, thought Laura, bashing away with her broom to dislodge some raisins stuck to the floor, we cannot escape it, this longing for something to love. Thank God – another genuine prayer – she had her daughters. Her wonderful, beautiful daughters. Because if not, who would she love?

There was always God, of course. Always, always, she thought, trying to address herself to a God she had not given proper attention to for twenty years, despite regularly going to church. That was the thing about Catholicism. Once it was in your blood – or rather, your conscience – it rarely left you. Still, she went through the motions. But that was not enough. And that thought depressed her until she came across an empty juice container stuffed under a beautifully embroidered kneeler, and depression gave way to fury against the carelessness of modern children and their parents. When Laura was a child she and her brothers had to sit perfectly still in church and listen, or at least learn to give the appearance of listening, not scoff little picnics. Though Laura had been a religious child and, for her, the attention had been genuine. At least for a while.

She had loved the drama of the music and the glorious building and the cadences of a language she could not understand. But her fervour had not survived adolescence and being confirmed, mumbling vows with the certainty of concrete – she had wondered if she would be struck dumb for lying.

On Sunday mornings when she stood mouthing the Creed, she would look around and see highly intelligent people like these women here speaking out clearly and she would wonder, do you really believe in that one God, the Father, the Almighty, Maker of Heaven and Earth? And if so, how? But the moment soon passed and that was as much trouble as her lack of faith gave her. She had not bothered to question or grapple with it, but simply let doubt sidle in and take up more and more space. Yet going to church was a habit she did not want to break. Not least because for the hour the girls were in Sunday School, she could switch off her phone, nothing would be demanded of her and she could have her thoughts to herself. The peace of God came in many guises.

'Careful!'

A shrill cry came from the ladies at the front of the church and Laura looked up to see a young man standing precariously at the top of a very tall ladder. So, thought Laura, they have found themselves a nice young man, the problem of attaching the star to the top of the tree solved by asking for help from a labourer on a nearby building site.

'Concentrate!' roared the ex-head teacher, when the ladder

wobbled and the young man's laugh rang out merrily through the church. A lovely, fearless laugh.

Laura did not move. She watched him, entranced, his arm outstretched, reaching to the top of the tree. So much power and grace rested in that young male body and to Laura flashed the thought, he's beautiful. And suddenly she desired the impossible, that she too was twenty-one and gorgeous, that his hands were held out to her, his smiling eyes looking into her own, and that she could take him up in her arms and lose herself in all the fierce, self-absorbed joy of young love.

'There!' he called out triumphantly, putting the star in place.

A round of applause broke out and he raced down the ladder, bowed with great bravado, then ran out of the church, not even noticing Laura.

She watched his retreating back, covered by nothing more than a torn shirt – in this cold weather he should wear a jacket, her maternal mind clucked away. But a brief pain pierced her with the thought of what she had never had. She flushed. Oh, the wild prayers for love, she thought angrily. No one was spared them, and they wore you down and made you useless for getting through the demands of the day.

She barely ever gave the father of her daughters a thought now. She had forgotten him long ago. She had been naive, she had been careless, she had been an idiot. There was no point in going over it. It was not him she craved, far from it. Besides, she had her wonderful daughters. But she resented the way motherhood somehow left her lonelier than ever and although on some days she could barely tear herself away from her girls, on others she would find herself longing for them not to need her so intensely.

Before she had children, Laura had had a few good girlfriends – a couple from work, a few she kept in touch with from art college. But then motherhood hit her with the full force of extreme weather. She was every bit as powerless and overwhelmed as if in the path of a tornado. In the face of the twins' incessant demands, her girlfriends had – quite understandably, thought Laura, when she was able to keep her eyes open long enough to think of anything – all drifted away and now she saw them about once a year, if that.

But no one had ever taken the place of these friends, and her children could not be companions in any real, adult sense. Instead, they increased her sense of isolation. The continual need to disguise her dark thoughts, to put up a front of happiness and serenity so that her young daughters might see only joy and calm, was, thought Laura, enough to drive the sanest person mad.

Though maybe, she sighed, it would become easier as they got older. When her children were grown up, she might not have to edit herself in the same way.

She saw Venetia entering the church carrying a large box to help with the decorations. And the idea of actually having an open and truthful conversation with her own mother seemed so ludicrous she almost laughed. Not once had she ever confided in her. So, true to form, as if without a care in the world, Laura greeted her mother with a smile upon her face. Except the smile vanished immediately.

'Mother, are you all right?' she asked, hurrying over and taking the box from her.

'Yes, of course I am.'

'But you look . . . you've lost weight.'

Normally, her mother held her own among the hefty party at the altar, but today she looked utterly diminished.

'It's this diet.'

'What the devil are you on a diet for? There's nothing left of you.'

'It's so much healthier to be thin when you're my age. Really, Laura, don't look like that. No extra weight to wear out the hips, knee joints . . .'

Laura ignored her. 'What,' she demanded, 'does Dad say about you being so thin, or hasn't he even noticed?'

'Don't be so mean about your father. Sarcasm never suits you. And I'm fine. Now please, open that box.'

Laura contained herself and did as she was asked. Inside the box was a hand-carved nativity scene, a wistful Mary, a Joseph tense with longing.

'What do you think?' asked her mother.

'Lovely,' said Laura truthfully, examining them carefully.

'Aren't they? The children will adore them.'

Laura said nothing.

'Won't they?'

Laura hesitated, then replied with what was required of her. 'Oh yes.'

'Don't say it like that,' her mother snapped back. 'What is it?

'Well . . . they're beautiful, really. It's just that it's the adults who'll love these wooden ones. Children will probably prefer what we've got at the moment,' said Laura, nodding towards the altar, 'where the kings are all wearing colourful clothes and there's a soft, fluffy donkey with a sweet little nose. But I love these, really.'

'See? If you don't expose your children to good taste, they'll never learn it,' said her mother, sounding, to Laura's relief, more like her old self.

'The Joseph is perfect,' she said. Laura had always thought Joseph got a raw deal, made to saw and hammer away in his carpentry shed, firmly on the outside of the charmed circle he had to support.

'He looks exhausted,' said her mother, 'and sad.'

'Well, all he does is work, yet he is still left out.'

'Good grief, Laura. What a depressing way to look at it. You know,' continued Venetia, easing herself down on to the pew. But then she winced sharply.

'Mum,' cried Laura, 'are you all right?'

'Oh, stop fussing. I'm fine. But you . . . hold on,' she said, reaching for her beeping phone. 'Oh, it's Phillip Snowe,' she said, reading the text.

'What's he want?'

'Just to thank me. Some legal thing I clarified. He's such a nice man. Really,' she smiled to herself, 'they are very lucky to have him at that school.'

'Yes, if you want education to be controlled by someone who knows how to tick all the right boxes,' Laura muttered.

'That's not true at all. What are you talking about?'

'Oh, nothing.' But her mind had returned too often to the argument she'd had with him about Isabel West. And the more she thought about the bloody chair of the governors, the more she disliked his easy smile, his gracious manner. People like him were dangerous. He had set himself up in a position to help, yet his inability to use common sense in the face of bureaucratic nonsense meant he had done harm to that poor girl, not good. Yet the worse she found him, the more her mind turned to him.

'He's doing real good,' said Venetia.

Laura shrugged. She was not up for an argument with her mother. 'He just seems to me,' she said, 'one of those people whose do-gooding is about them, rather than those they are trying to help.'

Venetia gave her daughter a long look. 'The two don't have to be mutually exclusive.' Then she said in an uncharacteristically uncertain voice, 'Laura, you know, I think you need to meet more people. Have a social life.'

What? Laura was completely taken aback. Her mother never spoke to her like this. They never discussed anything more personal than what they were having for dinner. Besides, she did not want a social life. What she wanted was . . . She hesitated. What she wanted was one other – one man – with whom she could be absolutely naked, and she did not mean just in the obvious sense. But to be with someone whom she could trust to accept her with all her unreconciled thoughts and cluttered life. Oh, for that she would need a saint.

'Mum, I'm all right, really,' she said. 'It's you I'm worried –'

'Stop it, I'm fine. Now listen,' her mother went on in a hurry, 'the girls' birthday.'

The twins were born on New Year's Day and were about to turn eight.

'I know what it's like having a birthday so near Christmas, you always feel short-changed, and this year I want to give the girls something really special.'

'Mum, you've already bought them bikes. That's more than enough.'

'But they're Christmas presents. I want them to have birthday presents too, and I've got the most brilliant idea.'

'Mum, no! You can't. They've got masses.'

'Honestly, Laura, where did you get this puritanical streak? Not from me. That's for sure.'

Laura hesitated. There were some battles worth fighting, but she doubted this was one. She compromised. 'Take them to a show or something. They'd love that. But no more toys.'

'I looked into a show but there's nothing worth seeing till the end of February if you want decent seats.'

'February's perfect. A real treat at a really bleak time.'

'No, I don't want to wait till then. And so I've already booked . . . now, don't look like that, Laura. I've got three nights at Disneyland – the Paris one.'

Laura's heart sank, not just because the idea of three nights at Disneyland filled her with horror, but because her daughters were unusual. And if her mother had ever bothered to spend time with them, thought Laura irritably, she would know that although Laura had sat them down in front of *Cinderella, Snow White, Beauty and the Beast*, you name it, in the hope of having some time to herself, her girls had never been that bothered by princesses.

'They grow up so fast,' continued her mother, 'so I want to go now, while it will still be magical for them. And I couldn't believe how quickly time passed with you three.'

That was because you were never there, thought Laura, leaving the thought unvoiced.

'And I'm sure they'd love to see Sleeping Beauty and go to a magic palace and so on.'

Laura looked at her mother as if she had gone quite mad. What had come over her? If she'd been all high and mighty and said it was time her granddaughters saw Paris and the *Mona Lisa*, it would have been in character. But Mickey Mouse?

'Apparently, you can have a princesses' lunch in an enchanted castle,' her mother was saying, 'or something like that. And Josie said she would come and help.'

'Josie?' Josie was her parents' housekeeper, efficient, capable, mother of three grown-up children. 'Who'd look after Dad?'

'He'll be away painting that . . . oh, that awful woman. What's her name? With the football team. And she's flying him down to her hotel in Madeira. And he fancied getting out of England, so we'd go then. And if Josie came, you could have a break.'

What? Laura could not quite believe what she was hearing. 'You mean,' she asked, scared that she had not quite understood. 'You mean I needn't go?'

'Not if you don't want to.'

Had her mother taken complete leave of her senses? She hated looking after children.

'And Josie really wants to come. You see, I've been thinking about you, Laura. I mean it. You need to get out more.'

But Laura was not thinking of going out. No. Her spirits soared to a guilty high. She could not help herself. She stopped questioning this sudden change in her mother. Three days! She had not had this long to herself since the girls were born. Three whole days when she would not have to think of anyone else but herself, she could eat any old rubbish and she could just paint and paint and paint.

'Oh, Mum,' she said. Tears pricked her eyes. 'Thank you.'

## 24

I shouldn't have come, thought Phillip, sitting with Isabel West and her mother in their cramped flat. Ever since his row with Laura after the governors' meeting, her accusations that he had failed this girl had tormented him. But the more he relived the arguments, the more he floundered in his attempts to dismiss Laura as a misguided do-gooder. So, that morning, when a meeting was suddenly cancelled, he decided he would visit Isabel and her mother and see what he could do.

'Piss off,' Isabel snarled, when he turned up at the door. 'You've no right to be here.'

Of course he hadn't. But Mrs West called out to let him in. Stuck in a high-rise block of flats with the lift still not working, she was clearly desperate for something different in her day. So Isabel, conceding with a grace she never displayed at school, did not slam the door in his face.

Now he was here, drinking instant coffee from a mug tasting of washing-up liquid, he wasn't sure what on earth he thought he might achieve. His feet alone seemed to be taking up all the available floor space and Isabel was looking at him with unconcealed hatred.

Phillip, who had always prided himself on his ease with people, was struggling. Sitting there with his health, his worldly success, his well-intentioned concern, he had nothing to give. And this young girl knew it. And, soon enough, her sick mother would know it too.

When Phillip's father, the Reverend James Snowe, was asked why God allowed so much suffering, he would respond, 'Don't ask what God does. Ask what are *you* doing to relieve such suffering?' And although by the time he was twelve Phillip had dropped the idea of God, he had imbibed the idea that it is up to human effort to redeem cruelty and injustice.

Yet what could he actually do in this dark, stifling room? He sat sipping his coffee and loathed himself for his arrogance and naivety in thinking he could help. Before him were the brutal facts of life: a woman trapped in a comfortless, sunless flat too incurably ill to be a mother to her daughter; a girl full of a talent that he feared would never be realized, let down by social workers and teachers. And now by him for conniving with a system which, from where he sat right now, seemed to be more about protecting the jobs of those running it than helping those who needed it.

But if he was despairing, how on earth did Isabel and her mother feel? On the wall were half a dozen charcoal drawings in cheap frames. At some point, one of them had determined to rise above this defeat and bring beauty into this ugly room. He needed to do the same.

He hauled himself out of the uncomfortable chair to look properly at the pictures.

'I did those,' Mrs West said, watching him. The sketches were of rivers and seas with great, wide horizons. To capture such beautiful, expansive landscapes, once her mind and body must have ranged free. 'Years ago,' she murmured.

So that's where Isabel's talent came from. 'How wonderful,' he said, 'for your daughter to have you to inspire her.'

'Yeah, right.'

Phillip winced. There was no mistaking the disappointment in the sick woman's voice.

But then she softened and went on, 'I liked art at school, but since then . . . I mean, the teacher said I was good, but . . . well. It was a hobby for a bit.' She picked at a loose thread on her cardigan.

I thought we were supposed, Phillip found himself thinking, to find and help people like Isabel's mother. She was clearly clever, had had promise. Yet we have failed her, he thought, and now we are failing her daughter.

'And anyway,' she went on, 'I wasn't a patch on Izzy. She's the one with something special. That's what I always tell her.'

He turned to Isabel, 'Do you do art at your new school?'

To his ears the question sounded priggish and forced. If Isabel was as brilliant as Laura thought, there was no way such a school would foster her abilities. They struggled to get a teacher to stay more than a term, let alone a year.

Isabel shook her head.

'But I thought –' began her mother.

'I learn more from you, Mum,' Isabel said hurriedly.

'But I can't . . . .'

'Mum, please. Leave it.'

Silence fell between them.

Phillip pressed on. 'That's a shame you're not doing art. You're quite exceptional, I'm told.'

To his amazement, Isabel turned and gave him the only smile he had ever seen on her pasty, pinched face. 'I do citizenship classes instead now – not art.'

'Citizenship?' muttered her mother, exerting herself. 'What on earth –?'

'Mum, it's fine,' interrupted Isabel hurriedly. 'Really,' she said, addressing Phillip directly, 'it's a lot more use.'

Phillip felt at even more of a loss. He wasn't sure if Isabel was being ironic. But she was sitting there so innocently, childlike, holding her mother's hand. Except, of course, she wasn't a child. She was fifteen, yet she was so tiny and thin, she could have passed for twelve. She was the same age as his own daughter, Rose, though she looked far from it, wearing none of the make-up or provocative clothes that Rose and her friends flaunted. Their maturity was alarming. And yet, he found himself asking and feeling discomforted by the all too obvious answer, how would they cope in this girl's cheap, ill-fitting shoes? How many of them could care for a parent? Or run a home with all the ghastly restrictions of poverty?

Phillip recalled reports from social workers saying how well Isabel looked after her mother. Their love was evident. But Phillip had the quite clear impression that Isabel was outmanoeuvring them all.

'Don't you miss art?' he pressed on.

Isabel just shrugged, as if there was nothing else to say.

And Phillip was forced to acknowledge, there wasn't. He fidgeted with the buttons on his jacket. His good intentions ran round his brain, mocking him. Then, as if confirming his defeat, it was Isabel who took control.

'My mum's tired,' she said. 'Aren't you, Mum? So unless there's anything else?'

He reached for his coat. For once, his physical ease and size made him feel awkward as he stood holding the old but fine navy cashmere in his arms. He could not bring himself to say, 'If there's anything I can do,' or equally meaningless offers of help. Happy Christmas seemed even more ludicrous.

Isabel was holding the door open. They wanted him gone.

'Thank you,' he murmured, 'for the coffee.'

Isabel slammed the door behind him and he walked slowly down the dirty staircase. At least he would ring the Council to see if he could harangue them into fixing the lift. But, as he walked out of the building into the drizzle, even that seemed pointless. Who would want to go out into these filthy streets? And, as if in answer to his question, he trod on a large piece of chewing gum.

Uncharacteristically he swore. A young woman in pink with a pushchair grinned at him, as though his words were funny. Her blonde little girl, also in pink, smiled too, kicking her legs in sparkly tights and looking up at him.

Then the child repeated what he had said. 'Fucking hell.'

To hear his foul words being copied by a child was suddenly intolerable. 'Oh, sorry,' he cried, as hundreds of Isabel Wests appeared before him, let down by the inadequacies of an adult world in which he fancied he played an important part. 'Sorry,' he said, as the mother laughed at her daughter and the child gave him a sweet smile.

But what use was an apology? Apologies were just sops to make the perpetrator feel better.

I'm useless, he thought. Laura had been right. He lacked imagination and courage. All he did, she had taunted, was make things look good and dump the problems on the scrap heap. But damn Laura. He had tried to help.

As if to hammer home his impotence, every time he took a step his shoe stuck to the pavement, but the wretched stuff was impossible. He would not be able to clean it off until he got home.

Except he did not want to go home. But he did not know what else to do with himself. He speeded up to escape the feeling that he had nowhere to turn, that in the midst of his perfect life with his gorgeous, successful wife, his brilliant elder daughter and his beautiful younger daughter, he was, in fact, lonely and futile. He could feel Isabel's tired, knowing eyes boring into him. What had all that perfection actually masked? Now, what was he really achieving? Sadness enclosed him, because he did not know how to make things better. For Isabel. For anyone. He loved his wife but right now she felt as close to him as a crater on the moon. And what worried him was that it had always been like that. Had he just been too busy to notice?

His thoughts were broken by a piercing scream. He turned and saw the young woman with the pushchair yelling at a man charging right towards him, holding the woman's pink bag.

It would have been wiser to let the mugger simply run away. But, for one of the few times in his life, Phillip did not think. He swung his arm at the man's face. Phillip, who had never before hit a soul, was surprised at the softness of the flesh, the ease with which it crumpled. But the punch seemed to have as much impact as a fly, because next thing Phillip was aware of the closeness of the man's breath as he was grabbed by the shoulders, then shoved forward. His legs buckled as he was kicked in the knees and he went crashing down on to the road, face-first, his head bouncing off the kerb, his skin grazing the tarmac.

He lay in the road, his senses reeling. He was aware of blood streaming from somewhere, a car screeching to a standstill, just inches away. Then he heard voices around him. 'Oh God. Are you all right? Jesus . . . are you okay?'

He rolled himself over. He couldn't be that hurt. He could move, but there was so much blood. He stared up into the sea of faces and tried to lever himself up on to his elbow.

Then a voice which, to his surprise, he knew but could not place said, 'You're all right. Now stay still.' And a woman was taking off her coat and kneeling down beside him. 'Put your head on this.'

He did as he was told, lying back on the old sheepskin coat she had folded up for him. As she smoothed his hair off his forehead, he closed his eyes.

The voice he vaguely recognized suddenly spoke sharply, 'Open your eyes. Now!'

'Oh God,' he murmured. In the confusion of shock and pain, he had not realized that it was Laura. But he could not mistake that voice now.

Laura was in the area delivering the wretched school leaflets and had almost finished when she saw a crowd forming around a body lying in the road. Her first instinct was to hurry on. Someone else was dealing with the problem – and besides, she wanted to get home as the washing machine had broken again and an engineer was coming to fix it. But she could not turn away. She saw the blood and instinctively rolled up her coat to place it under the man's head. And then she realized who it was.

'Phillip! It's Laura . . . Laura Cusack. You've got to keep awake. You can't fall asleep, however much you want to. Do you understand me?'

'I'm all right,' he grimaced, trying to get up. 'Really.'

'Just wait,' she said, putting her hands on his shoulders to stop him moving. 'You've been hurt. The ambulance is coming.'

'But I don't need an ambulance.'

'Phillip, just stay still. You need to be checked out. Is there anyone you want me to call? Your wife?'

'For pity's sake it's just a nosebleed. But, oh God,' he groaned as the ambulance pulled up.

Phillip had barely known a day's illness in his life. And when he had, he had never been allowed to make a fuss. As a child his mother refused to countenance what she dismissed as 'pampering and molly-coddling'. And in his marriage, if he was ever sick, Julia would tell him to rest and drink lots of fluids, then take herself off to the spare room so she would not catch whatever he had because, she always said, 'There's no point us both getting ill.'

'I'm so sorry,' he protested, as a paramedic jumped out of the ambulance. 'Honestly, there's nothing wrong. It looks worse than it is . . .'

The paramedic smiled at him with a practised calm. 'Why don't you just tell me what happened?' she said, sitting down on the kerb beside him.

So Phillip explained, with the help of the young mother whose bag he had failed to rescue but who kept thanking and thanking him.

'Let's get you to A&E,' said the ambulance woman.

'No, please! I don't want to spend hours sitting around in A&E.'

'At least get in the van and we'll make sure you're okay.'

'But I don't think I need . . .' he muttered as she and her colleague helped him into the ambulance. 'I'm so sorry to waste your time –'

'This is the end of my shift,' she interrupted, 'and this is the first call all day when I've not wasted my time and just been a glorified taxi service. So don't apologize.'

'But it's just a nosebleed.'

'You've had a bang on the head, so we need to be sure you're not left alone. Is there anyone at home?'

Phillip hesitated. Their housekeeper was off sick today. And every six minutes of Julia's day was accounted for – meetings, phone calls, coffees, drinks. He did not want to disturb her.

'You seem okay,' the ambulance woman said slowly, 'but just in case you suddenly feel sleepy, or nauseous . . .'

'I know,' murmured Phillip. When Anna was younger she was forever falling and banging her head. He knew all about concussion.

'How did you get here?' went on the woman.

'Car.'

'It's not a good idea for you to drive for a while.'

'I'll get a cab home,' he said, climbing out of the ambulance. 'Really, I can probably pick one up at the lights.'

But Laura, who was waiting outside, overheard him. 'Phillip, you can't get a cab,' she said, 'not after what you've been through. I'll take you.'

'Great,' said the paramedic, latching on to Laura, and addressing her now, rather than Phillip. 'I presume you know each other, right?'

Laura nodded.

'So can you stay with him, or make sure someone does?'

Dear God, thought Phillip, listening to himself being discussed in the third person as if he was a problem to be solved.

'I'm fine,' he said, taking charge. 'Really, don't make a fuss, please.'

'Phillip, sorry,' said Laura, turning to him. 'I'm not making a fuss. I just think you should come back to my place for a while and I'll give you some tea or whatever. Then I'll run you home.'

'No, I don't want to be any trouble,' he said. Yet the idea of being made a cup of tea was suddenly very appealing and he could not understand why on earth he was not just saying thank you. It was so easy. But something was stopping him. 'I know you're busy and have got the twins to collect from school.'

'It's no trouble. Besides, my brother's taking them swimming and he's bringing them home.'

The last thing Laura wanted to do now was play the Good Samaritan. She had set aside today to do tedious chores – firstly the church, then deliver the damned leaflets and later this afternoon, while waiting for the washing machine repairer to arrive, do her brother's accounts. She had a grudge against Phillip for landing the leaflet job on her. Also, she resented the amount of time she had given that argument with him about Isabel West. Not that it was his fault her mind dwelled on him. It was hers. But today his face was grey with shock, and the idea came to her that if she let him find his own way home and he was suddenly taken ill, it would be on her conscience.

'Well,' he began. 'Well . . .' It was just a cup of tea. 'Thank you, that would be lovely.'

## 25

'Are you sure you're okay?' asked Laura, as Phillip climbed into her car.

'Yes, yes,' he said, trying not to snap. Laura's kindness and patience embarrassed him. He had wasted her time, the ambulance workers' time, police time. Two officers had arrived and he had given an utterly useless statement – he couldn't even describe what the mugger looked like.

'Be careful, sir,' the young policeman had said, 'taking on people like that. You could have got hurt – seriously hurt.'

Phillip closed his eyes. 'Don't fall asleep,' said Laura.

'No, no. Don't worry,' he said, exerting himself to chat. 'I'm glad you happened to be around. But why? I mean, what were you doing there?'

'Delivering those leaflets you asked me to.'

'Oh God. Sorry!'

'No problem,' she said. 'But what about you?' she asked, thinking it was hardly his usual stamping ground. He was dressed for strolling around Hampstead. But be kind, she told herself. Ease up. Half an hour ago he could have been killed.

Phillip steeled himself. 'I went to see Isabel West. You know, the girl whose paintings you liked so much. And I thought about what you said and . . .' He trailed off.

So he listened to me, she thought, heeded my advice.

'And . . .?' she pressed.

'She as good as slammed the door in my face.'

'Surely you didn't just turn up out of the blue, did you?'

He braced himself for Laura's derision. But however he had played it with Isabel, he was in no doubt Laura would find fault with it. 'Yes . . . yes, I did. But if I'd phoned before,' he continued, justifying himself before she could launch in, 'I wouldn't have even got through the door. So I had to risk calling on the off chance. Don't you see?'

Laura hesitated. He had tried, she reminded herself, and this was not the time for an argument. 'I suppose,' she conceded. 'Maybe.' And with that they lapsed into an uneasy silence.

He turned away and opened the window, then closed it again as exhaust fumes from the lorry ahead blasted in.

'Do you need more air?' she asked.

'No, I'm fine, just tired.'

Then with Laura knowing she had to keep him awake, they moved on to a desultory conversation about the weather.

From the corner of his eye, as they talked about whether it would get even colder, or warm up, or rain, or be a white Christmas, Phillip watched her. The hem was coming down on her short skirt that was riding up over thick tights which had a ladder above the knee that grew every time she put her foot upon the clutch.

On Julia, clothes sat with calculation and precision. Laura, by contrast, was a study in dishevelment. Around her neck was a string of beads which, he guessed, her daughters had painted, and her curly hair was held back not very efficiently by a slide that was slowly slipping out. When they turned into Laura's street of tall red-brick houses and could at last stop discussing the weather, he realized he had been watching the slide, transfixed, wondering whether it would stay in place.

As he got out of the car, the cold hit him like a slap in the face.

'Your coat!' he cried. 'We left it back there. And I ruined it, didn't I? It was covered in blood.'

'It doesn't matter, I always hated it,' she said, letting them into the warm flat and clambering over scooters, balls, wellington boots and picking up the card from the washing machine repairer to say he had been but no one was in.

'I can't let you lose your coat because of me.'

He wanted to reimburse her, but was worried she would take offence.

'You've just been thrown in front of a car. You could have lost your life. I can lose my coat. And I've been looking for an excuse to get rid of it – the girls hated it. Now take a seat,' she said, leading him into the small sitting room.

Phillip sank into the sofa. In the warmth and comfort of soft cushions he was aware that it was not only his head that hurt, but every bruised and battered part of him. His hands stung from where he had grazed them trying to break his fall; the skin on his left cheek was raw; and he suspected that by the end of the day he would have a pretty dramatic black eye.

'I'll make some tea,' she said.

'Thank you.' He smiled at her but Laura just stood there, assessing him gravely. Some childish part of him wanted to see if he could make her face light up. He tried again. 'This . . . this is a really beautiful room.' But still she seemed to be eyeing him with suspicion.

What he did not realize was that Laura was telling herself that Phillip's smile was just an accident of bone structure, an arrangement of muscle, a movement of lips. An odd millimetre's difference here or there, the artist in her was hammering home, and that smile would have none of its potency.

She had to turn away. 'Thanks,' she said and retreated to the kitchen.

Her sweater, he noticed, was coming apart at the shoulder. What was the story here? He thought of her genius of a father, the philanthropist lawyer of a mother, those exuberant, demanding twins. Who was their father? Not in the picture, he knew that much. And twins on your own would explain why she always looked so worn down. And yet she had energy and fire when she needed it. He recalled, with an odd pleasure, how much he'd enjoyed arguing with her the other evening. But when he was lying hurt in the road she had been so unassuming in the way she insisted he came home with her. He looked about the room he had just described as beautiful, though in truth he was not sure what to make of it. The detail was overwhelming: flowery wallpaper; paintings hanging at crooked angles; crammed shelves. On one window sill alone stood part of an old wasps' nest, a miniature double-decker bus, a vase of wilting anemones and what looked like a Dresden shepherdess.

In his home, surfaces were clear, kitchen shelves neatly arranged with glass jars for six varieties of tea, three of sugar, four of rice and so on. Sheets, towels, china were white; pictures were perfectly straight; even the bed was made in such a way that you could balance a glass of wine upon it – not that he ever had. Indeed, most of their friends' homes were the same, and so flooded with light Phillip felt he had a permanent squint.

He swatted an embroidered cushion into shape and put it at the back of his head, when Laura appeared with a large tray on which she had arranged a teapot, a jug of milk, tea strainer, cups and saucers, a bowl of sugar and a plate of hot buttered toast.

'Oh my,' he said, sitting up. 'That looks wonderful.' And it truly did. None of the china matched, except that it was all covered with flowers. 'It's like a still life,' he went on, wondering whether she went around collecting all this incredible china. He didn't know anyone who collected things these days. Most people he knew were endlessly decluttering and taking their dustbin bags full of unwanted possessions to charity shops which, in his bleaker moments, he saw as an indictment of a world that overworks and underpays ninetenths of the population and leaves the rest so bloated they clog it up with rubbish. He rubbed his head. Except it wasn't that simple. People needed jobs; the hospice he worked for made a lot of money from their second-hand shops, enough to –

'Here you are,' said Laura, interrupting his thoughts and giving him some tea. It was strong and rich and scalding hot.

'It's delicious. Thank you,' he said, feeling the warmth run through him. 'I was cold.'

'Shock, probably – it's not actually that cold in here,' she said, going to the radiator and turning it up.

Her face was flushed, he noticed, and she had taken off her red jumper and was now in a sleeveless T-shirt revealing peachy shoulders. The unsettling thought occurred to him that Laura was one of those women for whom clothes do nothing and that he would like to put his cold hands under that frayed T-shirt. He brought his mind back to interior decor.

'This is a lovely room,' he said again. At first he had thought it ludicrously over the top, but it was growing on him as if he was looking at a wood carving. Slowly, more and more emerged. The room lives, he thought, truly lives. From all this untidiness and mess she had created a world of vitality and colour and shape.

'My God, I've only just noticed the wallpaper,' he said, realizing it was hand-painted with extra flowers and butterflies and birds. 'All that detail, like Elizabethan miniatures. Did you do them?'

She nodded.

'They're fantastic.'

'Thanks,' she shrugged.

'No, don't look like that. They are,' he said, getting off the sofa to look at them properly. 'The precision is extraordinary.' And so at odds, he thought, with her chaotic appearance.

'Thanks,' she said again, thinking this was when people usually started asking about her famous father. They moved on from her painting to his, as if from minor to major, asking about his latest work on some face of the moment, whether he really was as 'frank' towards his sitters as the papers reported. 'Rude' would be more accurate. Laura suspected her father spent a lot of time composing his malicious, racy remarks to boost his reputation as an eccentric genius who existed outside normal conventions.

Just that morning her mother had complained about a diary story in which her father had described on Twitter some luscious Oscar-winning actress he had painted as no more sexually charged than his gas bill. 'Absolute nonsense,' her mother had said.

And it probably is, thought Laura. These days most of his adlibs were invented for him. But Laura guessed he was delighted, as he never bothered to contradict them and, instead, tried to live up to them.

But, to her surprise, Phillip was not interested in her father.

'You should be painting all the time. Really, these are . . . Oh sorry, are you meant to be working now? Please,' he said, 'don't let me stop you. I don't want to waste any more of your time. Just because I've been bloody stupid.'

'Bloody stupid?'

'Well, yes,' he said, sitting down again, 'I can't think of better words for it. I know that's what my wife will call it. And she'd be right.'

'Don't you do "bloody stupid", then?' asked Laura, looking at him closely over her teacup.

'Well, you know . . .'

Laura leaned back in an armchair. 'And there was me thinking you were a man of the world.'

'Well, of course I've been stupid, I mean . . .'

Phillip hesitated. He had made some wrong calls in his business, he supposed. But nothing that could be described as stupid. He cast back. Before he met Julia he had once found himself waking up next to a woman he did not recognize. It turned out she lived two hundred miles away in Leeds. And that encounter was bloody stupid because afterwards he had taken the train up to see her every other weekend, hoping she would soon tire of him, but that took six interminable months.

'Well, I . . .' The truth is, he thought, I don't do 'bloody stupid'. And he did not understand why he should see it as a failing.

While running his business, Phillip had not been used to brooding or reflecting. He was a man of action. Wasn't he? The sort who got things done. But during this last year he had changed.

He rested his aching head on his hand, and Laura was taken aback by how sad he suddenly looked. He's beating himself up, she realized, and he's not used to it. And her better nature came to the fore.

'Sometimes,' she said carefully, 'not often, if I can help it, I look back on things I've done and it's like walking on broken glass. There are so many stupid, idiotic . . .' She trailed off.

For the last seven years and for a good while longer her entire life would pivot on one careless mistake, one unplanned encounter. Though no one plans on winning the lottery, she thought, fingering the beads the twins had painted, and her gorgeous girls were just like winning the lottery.

'Anyway,' she said, 'chasing that mugger wasn't stupid.'

'It was,' he countered. 'I've got responsibilities, children who –'

'Don't go on about how you could have got hurt. I know all that. But that girl whose bag it was. You didn't see it because you were in the ambulance, but she was so moved by what you did. Seriously. I don't think she could believe you would risk yourself for her – a complete stranger. That connection with another human being, just wanting to look after them regardless of your own safety . . . it's heroic. It's bloody stupid as well, yes. But you gave that woman something to make her feel good about.'

'My God!' said Phillip. Normally, Phillip saw it as his job to restore people's confidence. He had never seen himself needing such af-firmation. 'I don't know anyone else who'll see things quite so dramatically or, indeed, so generously, but thank you. My head doesn't hurt so much now either. Amazing!'

And at that Laura laughed.

Phillip had never heard Laura laugh before. Her face was nearly always stiffened by . . . by what? Loneliness? Sadness? But with a laugh like that, he thought, she should be causing quite a stir. And he wanted to hear more. 'You know,' he said, 'I think your pictures are truly incredible.'

'Not as good as Isabel West's.'

'Laura, take a compliment, please. Just for now.'

But Laura was not used to praise. Her face closed down.

'Seriously,' he said, getting to his feet, and studying a single white rose. 'This reminds me of the Redouté rose prints my parents have in their bedroom.'

'Don't be daft.'

'No, I mean it.' I've misjudged her, he thought. And because she had been so good to him, because she had made the effort to under-stand him, he wanted to do the same for her. 'Something so ephemeral and lovely,' he went on, 'you feel you could smell its per-fume. I don't suppose . . .' He picked up a watercolour of mauve lilac on a midnight-blue background. 'I love this. Is it for sale? I would love one. To buy one,' he stressed.

'Because I've given you a lift home?' asked Laura.

'No! Because they're beautiful.'

'I suppose . . . yes. But not the lilac. That never worked. Not really. I mean, what sort of thing? Do you like flowers?'

'How can you not like flowers?'

'As paintings, I mean.'

'Yes.'

'Are you sure?'

'Laura! These are brilliant, truly.'

'Well, I've got about a dozen or so here. I can get them.' She tried to hide the eagerness in her voice but she could not stop herself. 'Lately I've been doing watercolours and they're, well . . .' A look of worry returned to her face.

'Don't tell me they're no good. Let me be the judge of that. I'm the one who'll be living with it.'

'Okay, I'll –'

But what she would do had to wait as the doorbell rang and five seconds later the room was full of her daughters, flushed and excited.

'Someone was sick,' yelled Alice. 'So the pool was closed and we weren't allowed in.'

'Really sick,' cried Eliza, pretending to retch all over the place.

'That's enough! You two, stop it. That's horrible,' said Laura, introducing Phillip to her brother.

'It's good to meet you,' said Robert, making room for himself on an armchair stacked up with ironing.

'Mum, please, can we have something to eat?'

'Just a minute.'

'So you took over from our mother at Hartley High?' said Robert conversationally to Phillip.

'We're starving, please, please,' pestered the girls.

'Okay, okay,' said Laura, leaving Robert with Phillip and disappearing into the kitchen with the girls.

★

Phillip, it occurred to Laura as she began more making toast and tea, was the first man who had sat in her sitting room who was not a member of her family or married to one of her friends or from the gas board or come to repair something.

'Mum.' Eliza was pulling at her skirt.

'Yes . . . yes . . .' she muttered, thinking Father Eoghan called round too, of course. But that was it. And it was wrong. She should not be living in quarantine like this. Not that Phillip really counted because he was so obviously married. But she had realized, chatting to him, that she had almost forgotten what it was like to talk to a man, to feel that male physical presence. And most of the time it was manageable. She had got used to loneliness. But occasionally it reared its hungry head and could rip her to shreds.

'Thank you, Mummy, thank you!' cried Eliza.

'What?'

'You just said "yes",' crowed Alice, 'that we could watch television all night.'

'No, I didn't,' said Laura, putting raisins into a bright blue bowl and red grapes into an emerald one.

'You did, you did,' insisted Alice.

Laura looked into her daughters' clear, fresh faces. What did she want for them, more than anything else in the world? Interesting work, of course, work that they were good at and enjoyed. That was a true blessing, a great gift in life. And good health, obviously. But most of all, she thought with a pang, don't let them be lonely. Dear Lord, please, spare them that. Let me be lonely in their place, but not them, so eager and trusting and –

'You're *not* listening,' cried Eliza. 'You can't be, because –'

'Come on in and eat this,' said Laura, kicking open the door with her foot and returning to the sitting room with a large, crowded tray in her hands. 'Help yourselves,' she said, as the girls pounced on the toast. 'Phillip, would you like anything?' she asked, not catching his eye. He looked so at home, as if he would quite happily settle in that spot, stay on that sofa, chatting away, with her . . . Oh stop, she told herself angrily. Stop!

'No, no thanks,' said Phillip, conscious that he was oddly put out by this great spread suddenly placed before him. He had been touched earlier when Laura had presented him with such a beautiful tea. He thought the effort was for him alone. Now he realized she did it for everyone.

'Robert promised,' Eliza was saying with her mouth full, 'that he would watch *South Pacific* with us while you do his work for him.'

'Because we can't go swimming because someone was –'

'Enough!' warned Laura as Eliza put her fingers in her mouth.

Alice began singing 'Some Enchanted Evening'.

'*South Pacific?*' asked Phillip.

Laura was aware of the blood rushing to her face. 'They love musicals,' she said.

'And so do you,' said Alice. 'You know all the words.'

'*South Pacific* is her fourth favourite,' explained Eliza. 'First is *Carousel* – which is mine too.'

'But I like *The King and I* –' said Alice.

'You can watch it, of course you can,' interrupted Laura.

'Now?'

'Soon.'

'While you do Robert's work?'

'I'm so sorry, Laura, I hadn't realized you have work to do. I'd better go,' said Phillip, getting out his phone to ring for a cab.

'It's all right,' she said. 'But are you okay now? Stay a bit longer if you need to.'

He certainly wanted to. Right then, all he asked from life was to sit talking in this warm, crowded room. He looked across at Laura and he was aware he was contemplating her with pleasure, her cheeks burning with wind-lashed colour, her soft curls, her bare arms encircling her daughters.

'No, no,' he made himself say, 'I must be off.' And soon he was forcing himself to his feet as a cab was waiting outside.

Phillip followed Laura out into the hall.

'I really would like,' he said, when they were on their own, 'to come back and buy a painting.'

'Of course,' she smiled. She was not happy, she told herself, because he would call again, but because he wanted a picture. 'I'll dig out some more, so you've got more choice.'

'Great, thanks. And thanks again for taking me home. I feel so much better.' He was, he realized, reluctant to leave. 'You know, I've never seen *South Pacific*.' He and Julia went to the opera, and as a child his parents had taken him to choral evenings. 'Nor your favourite. *Carousel*.'

Laura said nothing.

'Anyway, shall I call you, then?' he asked, putting his coat on slowly.

'Call me?'

'About choosing a picture?'

'Sure,' she said, not looking at him but picking up gloves and scarves that had fallen on the floor. Then she asked, 'Phillip, you know, Isabel West, what are you going to do about her?'

'How do you mean?'

'What are you going to do next? For her?'

'There's nothing I can do.'

'But you can't just give up.'

'But she didn't want me there.'

'Of course she didn't – to begin with. You can't think you'd win her trust in just one meeting. But that doesn't mean you can't go again.'

'No, I'm not going to intrude like that.'

'But you must.' Her heart was beating fast – too fast. She had this desire to fight him. But was this the time? Of course it wasn't. The poor man had just had a serious knock on the head. But he said he was all right. He had been up for a big row the other night. And a row was a desire she could give in to. 'Otherwise,' she asked, her voice rising, 'what was the point of going in the first place? Unless it was to make you feel better, rather than her?'

'That's not fair,' he said, taken aback. There was a look in her eyes of what? Scorn? Dislike? What exactly? They had been getting on so well. And his self-recrimination was bad enough without her ladling it on. 'I went there with the best intentions –'

'That's the most pathetic argument of all,' she interrupted, a rush of anger invigorating her. 'Best intentions are useless if they achieve nothing. They're purely about the person feeling them, not about the person needing help. Of course Isabel was a nightmare at school. She has to be a saint at home when most girls her age are being absolutely vile to their mothers. She had to find an outlet somewhere.'

'Laura, I'm beaten by this. Knowing what battles are worth fighting.'

'And you call stepping down off your middle-class pedestal for half a morning a "battle"?'

'I can't argue with you on this. I've fought all I can for one day.' And he opened the front door and walked out into the rain.

'Good God, give the man a break,' said her brother, appearing in the hall behind her. 'He's almost been killed.'

'What were you doing listening?' she said, turning on him.

'I couldn't help it, the way you were screeching your head off.'

'I was not . . . I . . .'

'Honestly, Laura, that was so unnecessary.'

Of course it was. She knew that. What was she thinking? Yelling and having a go at him. 'I just can't stand . . .' she trailed off.

'What?'

'Just . . . oh, nothing. I don't want to talk about it.'

'Laura, stop,' he said, following her into the kitchen. 'Ease up.'

'What?'

'You like him, don't you?'

'Don't be absurd.'

'Just a bit?'

'No! How can you possibly . . .? He's so full of himself and arrogant and . . .'

'He clearly didn't want to leave,' said Robert seriously. 'Just be careful, Laura. He's married and –'

'Jesus,' she muttered. 'That's ripe coming from you. When was the last time you went out with someone who *wasn't* married?'

Robert ignored this. 'But you'll get hurt,' he said.

'And you don't? Or, more to the point, you don't cause hurt?'

'I only mean,' he said in his calm voice, 'that you will hurt more, because you will love more.'

'I don't know what you're talking about. Anyway, I've got work to do. And turn that telly down, will you?' she said as the girls began calling for Robert and singing 'I'm Gonna Wash That Man Right Outta My Hair'.

## 26

It was almost ten and Julia had only just come in from work, with a bag full of papers that had to be read by morning. Her head was pounding, but with Phillip standing before her bruised and battered, she tried to push the pain crashing across her forehead to one side.

'You could have been killed,' she said, taking off her narrow shoes. 'Honestly, what were you thinking of? I can't believe . . . Anyway, are you all right now?' she asked, not wanting to argue and going to the kitchen cupboard. 'Have you eaten?'

'No,' he said, realizing he was suddenly hungry and had had nothing since toast at Laura's.

But if he hoped his wife was about to make supper, he was disappointed.

Julia reached for a couple of painkillers and then collapsed on the kitchen sofa. It had been one hell of a day. She had been briefed on a complicated new case, another one was about to come to trial with a client who kept changing his mind. She had also spoken on the phone for the first time to the new boss at Clifford James. Julia had been dealing for years with the previous CEO, an American, and they had liked one another in as much as she ever liked her clients or they liked her, knowing how much she was costing them. But he had retired and now she had his replacement, British and a woman, to contend with.

'Well, do you want anything to eat?' Phillip asked, muffling the resentment that he was the one cooking when that morning he had been punched, pushed and thrown in front of a car.

'Oh, please, darling. I'm ravenous. I think that's why I've got a headache,' she said, as he began taking bacon, eggs, mushrooms and tomatoes from the fridge. 'But what I don't understand is why you were there, right in the middle of the Hartley Estate.' She tried to contain the sharpness in her voice because why did he have to get involved in the place she had used every cell in her body to escape and forget? 'I mean, what makes you think you can help this girl, anyway? For goodness' sake, Phillip, you made a decision about her, stick to it.'

'But the more I think about it, the more I know I made a mistake. Of course, she was a nightmare at school – I should have realized. Who wouldn't be, given what a saint she had to be at home?' he said, aware he was echoing Laura's words. 'And for a talent like hers to go to waste.'

'Who says she's so talented?'

'One of the governors,' he said, splashing water everywhere as he washed the mushrooms, reluctant, for some reason, to mention Laura's name.

'If this girl's so exceptional,' said Julia, 'then she's also failed herself. It's not just about talent – you know that. It's about hard slog and self-discipline. So stop giving her false hope.'

'But how can she possibly work or put in the "hard slog", as you call it? The mother's sick, really sick. You know, these days you'd have had to go to a school like Hartley High.'

Julia heard the note of accusation in his voice and sat up as if suddenly hit from behind. 'What,' she asked very quietly, 'do you mean by that?'

He turned up the heat under the frying pan, throwing in the mushrooms, and said, 'Just that if you were in this girl's shoes could you, even with all your brilliance, have escaped? I know I couldn't.'

'What I could do is irrelevant.'

'No, it's not. Think about it.'

'Why? The point is, I did escape. And that's all I need to know. And so did Angela. And she looked after a sick mother. If this girl is as extraordinary as you say she is, she'll overcome all that.'

'But you were given the chance,' said Phillip, 'and this girl wasn't. Times are different. It was easier for you, back then. And for Angela. You both had opportunities – all the scholarships, better schools – to pull yourselves up. But these days, even the clever ones are stuck.'

Julia hesitated. 'Okay,' she acknowledged, 'you're right. It was easier then. For me. And Angela. We've made things harder for people like . . .' She couldn't bring herself to say 'people like me'. She loathed anything that hinted at self-pity about her childhood and hated categorizing herself in such a way. 'And, it's true, if Angela and I hadn't had such a good school, then maybe . . .' But we worked, she thought. You've no idea how we forced ourselves on. 'Look, this isn't about me,' she went on, trying to be conciliatory. 'It's about what's the best use of your time right now. And you would do better concentrating on those you can help. Talking of which, what about Rose? I've been on to some boarding schools.'

'So have I.'

That took Julia aback. She had thought the job of finding a new school would be left to her. 'Thank you,' she said with relief.

'And,' said Phillip hurriedly, 'they don't think boarding school is suitable for her.'

'What?'

'I explained the situation.'

'There's no "situation".'

'When I rang the schools I told them,' said Phillip, turning the bacon, 'that Rose hated the idea and they all said there's no point in sending a child to boarding school if they don't want to go.'

'Of course they're not going to take anyone who smacks of trouble,' she cried, suddenly livid. 'You did that on purpose, didn't you? Well, thank you. Now I'll have to sort it.'

She switched on the extractor fan because Phillip – as usual – had forgotten and the room was filling with the smell of frying, then threw open the window and let in a blast of damp night air. That he had deliberately scuppered Rose's chances of getting into a decent school filled her with rage. But she did not know what to say. She was not used to this sort of confrontation with Phillip. To many people, she knew, rows were an ordinary part of married life and forgotten by the time their heads hit the pillow. But Julia and Phillip did not work things out by fighting. Instead, they reasoned sensibly and talked through their differences.

She began to lay the table in an attempt to restore calm but Rose came racing down the stairs and hurled herself into the kitchen.

'Well, thank you,' she stormed. 'For ruining my life.'

'What on earth,' demanded Julia, 'is the matter now?'

'How could you?' Rose yelled, her face red, tears pouring down her cheeks. 'Sophia's just texted. And she's found out that her mother asked you if I could do some modelling and you said no. How could you? First you say I can't go on television and now this. How could you be so mean? How could –?'

'Sit down,' said Julia, 'and we'll talk about this quietly.'

'How can I talk about this quietly?'

'Because this ridiculous hysteria will get you nowhere.'

'But I'm not like you, who does everything so bloody quietly.'

'Rose, stop it,' said Phillip. 'Don't speak to your mother like that. You must understand. You're too young to do any modelling.'

'For God's sake, Dad, what do you know?'

'I did work in advertising.'

'But do you have any idea how young models start? If I leave it much longer, I'll be past it.'

'Don't be absurd,' said Julia. 'You've plenty of time, if that's what you want to do with your life.'

'Actually, Mum, like it or not, I do want to do that. And what's wrong with it?'

'Nothing's wrong,' said Phillip. 'It's just –'

'I want to make my own money,' cried Rose.

'That's very laudable,' said Julia.

'Very laudable,' mimicked Rose. 'Don't patronize me. You should be glad I want to be independent.'

'I am, we are,' said Julia. 'Truly Rose, really.'

'So why don't you let me? I mean, what if anything happened to you, to your jobs?'

Julia and Phillip exchanged glances.

'Darling, I gave up my job deliberately,' said Phillip. 'And we've . . . we do have plenty of money.'

'And nothing is going to happen to my job,' said Julia. 'Sweetheart, really.'

'You don't know that. Matilda's mum was fired only last week and her dad's been out of work for ages. Loads of people lose jobs. Don't you realize?'

'I do realize, thank you.'

'And Jane's mum's lost hers,' persisted Rose. 'And Lily's mum doesn't stop moaning that she's earning half of what she used to but is working twice as hard. Honestly, Mum. You're not as safe as you think you are. No one's safe. Even if they are clever and work like a dog, like you do, Mum. And you know what? I reckon – and my friends agree – you wouldn't work so hard if you didn't feel worried that you might lose yours.'

'Maybe,' said Julia, bridling at being gossiped about by teenagers, 'I work hard because I enjoy it.'

'Yeah, right. Hand on heart, do you really want to read all that rubbish in your bag tonight because some person with too much money wants a bit more?'

'Don't be so simplistic.'

'See, you don't. I rest my case,' she said, as Anna walked in and then turned on her heels as if to make a quick exit.

'Don't go, darling,' said Phillip.

'But what's the drama?'

'Your sister is indulging in histrionics,' said Julia.

'There's been a misunderstanding,' said Phillip.

'The only misunderstanding,' said Julia, 'is that Rose thinks your father and I are trying to ruin her life whereas what we are actually doing is trying to stop *her* ruining it.'

'But you never let me do what I want,' cried Rose. 'Brilliant opportunities come my way. Things half my friends would kill for. And don't turn your nose up, Anna.'

Anna glanced at the burnt mushrooms and joined her mother at the open window. 'Oh, let her do the modelling,' she said, 'for all our sakes. Or she'll be a complete pain.'

'No,' said Phillip. 'Certainly not at just fifteen.'

'Just because you're pretty,' said Julia, deliberately diminishing her younger daughter, 'it doesn't mean your father and I want you modelling when you should be concentrating on other things. You know what your last report said about how little work you're doing. Your face is a gift, but use it for something worthwhile.'

Julia tried to hide her exasperation. Here was Rose, yet again, looking for some easy option through life.

'You know,' she said, trying to reason with Rose who had flung herself on the sofa, 'most people when employing someone and with two equal candidates to choose between go for the better-looking. And I know,' Julia added, more for Anna's benefit, 'that doesn't seem right, but making the best of yourself does show self-respect, a more rounded personality. But Rose, sweetheart, with your looks and your brains – if you chose to use them – you could go so far . . . I mean, look at those women standing to be MP the other day. Rightly or wrongly, the prettiest one won.'

Anna kept her face straight. Her mother, at times, could sound like an undergraduate making a case at an interview. And the idea of Rose as an MP was laughable.

'Oh, Mum, just let her,' said Anna. 'Can't you see? Look at her.'

Rose had her eyes closed, her golden hair spilling all around her, as lovely as a disappointed Madonna.

'It doesn't matter what grades she gets, how she does at school. She'll be fine.'

'Of course it matters. These are difficult times. Rose . . . Rose!'

Rose opened her eyes and looked at her mother with defiant indifference.

'Think of all the people you've just listed who've lost jobs – the competition is so great. If you used all your gifts . . .'

It occurred to Julia that she could talk to Rose all night long, use every sensible, intelligent argument in existence, but to her daughter they were nothing but chaff on the wind.

She heard Anna say, 'Mum, listen to me. I said, "Look at her." Don't you see? She'll get married.'

'Yes, she may. And I hope you both find people you love and who love you,' answered Julia, neither looking nor listening but turning off the bright overhead light that was making her eyes smart and her head throb all the more. But it was her heart that was aching.

How could my beautiful, privileged Rose have grown up so facile? How could I have let this happen?

Julia glanced at Anna, dressed in her uniform of shapeless black, and with a pang she wondered what secrets Anna was harbouring in her exceptionally well-tuned brain, what walls she had built up between them. Am I blind here too? wondered Julia. Are both my children strangers to me, cynical and negative?

'Mum,' Anna was saying, 'Rose will get married, full stop. That's it. Marriage will take care of her.'

'But Anna,' said Julia, not without a trace of bitterness, 'this is the twenty-first century.'

'What else do you think she'll do? Become a lawyer? Doctor? Run some business? Get real, Mum.'

'You can do both,' said Julia, habit and instinct proving stronger than her self-doubt, and not letting her give up on an argument.

'She doesn't want to. She just wants to be beautiful and adored.'

'But you can't just want to get married.'

'Why not?'

'Well, do you?' asked Julia, thinking, please tell me my brilliant elder daughter has more sense.

What do I want? thought Anna to herself. If you had any idea what I truly want . . . I want to want to go to parties like other people, I want to have a brain that knows the right thing to say and not one that grasps quantum physics but is incapable of holding a man's attention for more than twenty seconds. And I want . . . I want Phoebe's father to grip me close in his arms, clasp my face in his hands, open his lips and press his dangerous tongue against mine.

To her mother she simply said, 'This is Rose we're talking about. And maybe getting married will suit her just fine.'

'But you're not, thank God, in some Jane Austen novel where the only option is marriage.'

'These days loads of girls just want to get married,' said Anna.

'Not ones with all your advantages, all your education, all your opportunities.'

'Actually, Mum, they do.'

'I don't believe you.'

'You know, my darling,' said Phillip, joining the conversation – not before time, in Julia's opinion – but in the sort of voice that made it clear he was about to put her down, 'you're being a bit disingenuous here. You may not approve of it any more than I do, but you know full well how lots of girls just want to be celebrities and marry footballers.'

'Of course I know,' said Julia, trying not to display her irritation with him, 'but not . . .'

Not *my* daughters, Julia wanted to say. Of course she knew that for many young women marrying a rich man could still, even now, be the best escape from the dull job, the lethargy of housework, the exhaustion of child-rearing.

'My sister the WAG,' smiled Anna. 'Think, Dad, of all the football matches you'd go to.'

He laughed, and Julia had what she told herself was a ludicrous sensation that the three of them were ganging up against her. But however ludicrous, however sensational, it hurt. And she was not sure where to turn.

'You hate football.'

'But if Rose could get me good seats, I might learn to like it,' he said with a smile.

But Julia noticed his normally light eyes had gone dark, as if there was an incoming storm.

'Anyway, the point is,' he continued, 'there are countless ways of finding happiness and fulfilment. And marriage is one of them – and possibly the most important. To have love –'

'Yes, of course,' snapped Julia, unable to stop herself, 'but we are talking clever, highly educated women, who have the opportunity to go to great universities, to have fascinating jobs.'

'Oh God, Mum,' sneered Rose, 'half the time now, university's a complete waste of money.'

'Not the good ones. Ask your sister.'

'Yeah, right,' laughed Rose, as Anna hurriedly left the room. 'You know what degree Sophia's brother got from a good university?

Cambridge – just like clever you and clever Dad and clever Anna. Double first in philosophy, and now he's chief elf at the Christmas Grotto in Center Parcs. At least he gets to be chief, says Sophia.'

Julia ignored this. 'Look, what I'm saying is that marriage alone, however wonderful,' she added with a perfunctory glance at Phillip as he served up their late-night breakfasts, 'won't satisfy you. And if you think that it will, you're making yourself so vulnerable. You need something of your own. For the money you can make – but not just the money. For the emotional independence, for the sense of self-worth, for –' She stopped in mid-sentence. 'I cannot believe I'm having to spell this out to you. Life can be so difficult and women have had to fight so hard.'

And what, my darling wife, thought Phillip, methodically working his way through eggs and bacon, are you still fighting for? As she lectured on, marriage – marriage to him, for God's sake – seemed so low on the list of her priorities that as he sat there, he felt his chest tightening, his head hurting.

'Do you want some tea?' she asked, dunking a tea bag in a mug.

'Please.'

'Here you are. And Rose, will you clear up, please? I must go and work. Thank you for dinner, darling,' she added as she picked up her briefcase.

Phillip watched her back as she walked down the hall. They had rowed as they had never rowed before. Surely, he thought, she can see that. But she is retreating, as usual, into her work. How dare she? he thought angrily. Who the hell does she think she is?

'Dad,' Rose was saying carefully. 'The modelling . . .'

'No,' he said. 'Categorically no, and I never want to hear it mentioned again.' And he stormed out of the room and collapsed in front of *Newsnight*.

## 27

Julia sat down in the chair specially designed for her back. When things troubled you, you went to your desk. That was her golden rule. Though it was not so much that she lost herself in work, it was more that she found herself. But tonight work had lost its magic. Not even her innate resilience could help. Because why had her husband spoken to her so dismissively? He wanted – just as much as she did – for his daughters to achieve their potential. He, too, hated cynicism and indifference. Why else was he suddenly trying to save the world? Surely he was disappointed in Rose? He knew what gifts she had, that with a bit of application she might achieve so much. And why was he making such a fuss about that girl Isabel and then being so hard on her – his wife, who knew more than he ever would what it was like to grow up somewhere like the Hartley Estate – because she would not go along with his sanctimonious sentimentality? If he knew what she knew.

Recollections pierced her. She and Angela fighting for space at the kitchen table to write essays that had to be marked 'A' – anything less was not good enough. Trying to work through the racket from the neighbours and when it grew too violent taking themselves off to the library. But then she heard Phillip saying in a priggish voice, 'But Isabel can't do that, there are no libraries now . . . *It was easier for you.*' A blow, as much physical as emotional, struck her. What was wrong? Why was he finding excuses to put her down? Why was he not supporting her over Rose?

She bowed her head but in so doing she caught sight of the time. Gone eleven. She had to work. She arranged her papers in orderly piles in an attempt to focus on the immediate job. But she was too confused and anxious. Concentration eluded her. There was a problem with Phillip. But she did not know what it was. And if she could not identify the problem then she could not solve it.

She forced herself back to her legal conundrums. A weak will achieved nothing. But a job well done could be a cure. Doggedly, she began slogging her way through the papers. Tomorrow, although it was Saturday, she was seeing a client who had booked the entire floor of a London hotel so that his meeting with a lawyer would go unnoticed. She read on.

It was almost two before she finished and even then, she knew, she had not mastered the arguments. But she was exhausted. She went up to the bedroom where Phillip was fast asleep.

Breathing deeply, his eyes closed, he looked so young, like a bruised child. And, she thought, with horrible clarity, so very far away. A presentiment of loss clouded her face. When they were first married and living in a tiny flat, each with their new demanding jobs, they would sometimes take their work to bed together. Propped up on the pillows, assessing difficult cases but with her husband at hand's reach filled Julia with the sort of joy she thought she would never know. To have such access to that wonderful, agile mind and strong, tender body made marriage seem the greatest gift on earth. Now, of course, they each had their own study.

She got carefully into bed, nervous of waking him. She did not want to have to speak to him. Her feelings for Phillip were the most profound she had ever known and now she was angry with him, her sense of betrayal almost took her breath away.

But he opened his eyes and gave her an inscrutable look.

'Sorry,' she said with formal politeness, 'sorry. I didn't mean to wake you.'

'Be quiet,' he said, 'Julia, please. Just be quiet, and come here.'

He held out his arms and instinct made her respond to a gesture she knew so well. She moved towards him. And, for that moment at least, there was no distance between them.

But just a few hours later – Julia's alarm went at six – while she was getting dressed, Phillip said, 'Look, darling, I've been thinking.'

She sat next to him on the bed, drawing on fine stockings. 'Yes?' she smiled.

'Great legs,' he said, tracing his finger around her ankle. 'I've missed them – you.'

She laughed.

It's all right, she told herself, stretching out her hand and stroking the faint freckles on his bruised cheek. Last night's row was an aberration. Overworked and overtired, they had been like two children squabbling over a toy, and the disagreement had been as meaningless, cured by a good night's sleep, or not so much sleep . . . She kissed him gently.

'Don't go,' he said. 'Might we just once have a Saturday morning?'

'I must, you know I must. I'll be back by twelve,' she said. But everything was fine. The relief she felt was so intense it almost hurt. And once things were more sorted with the Clifford James case, she would make time – for him, for the two of them. She had got things out of proportion last night. That was all. It was her headache – which was fine now. Everything was fine.

'No but seriously,' he said, 'I've been thinking. About Rose.'

'Oh yes?' Her smile broadened. He has seen sense, she thought. Boarding school is the best option.

'This modelling lark. Perhaps Anna is right. Perhaps we should let her get it out of her system.'

'But I thought . . . I mean, we agreed. You were so against it.'

'Yes, I was. But maybe Anna has a point. What else is Rose going to do?' he asked, as she moved out of his reach. 'Let's face it, she's not as clever as Anna.'

'None of us is as clever as Anna, but that doesn't mean Rose's only option is to be a model.'

'But sometimes you have to give people a free rein and let them run with it.'

'No, you don't. Particularly a fifteen-year-old incapable of holding a sensible thought in her head.'

'Don't exaggerate.'

'But why do you keep changing your mind?'

Suddenly the atmosphere chilled, as if the room was bating its breath.

'Julia,' he said in an unnervingly quiet tone, 'that's not fair.'

'But you were adamant about Rose and the modelling – just last night. And you got yourself beaten up because you changed your mind about that girl Isabel and went to see her.'

Phillip said nothing. He got up and pulled back the shutters to look out on the dark streets. Then he replied in the same cool manner, 'Changing your mind is not some capital weakness. I wish one day you'd see that. It can be flexibility, an acknowledgement that you're wrong.'

Julia turned her attention to her pearl earrings. But her hand was trembling. In just five minutes she found herself pitched once more from calm waters into this unpredictable sea where her husband was a stranger. He never criticized her in this cold manner. A few hours ago, as he took her in his arms, all their arguments had melted away. It had seemed so simple. She had woken early, and found herself yearning for her husband and he was there beside her and so loving she thought their differences were as meaningless as a bad dream. But they were not.

## 28

Oddly, for just this minute, Venetia was in no pain. As her taxi went hurtling down Harley Street, she felt strangely light and young, and for one witless moment she thought, it's all a mistake. Doctors get things wrong. I'm fine. I will live.

The taxi swung round a corner and her beautiful bag slid towards her. The bag was an obscenely expensive present from her husband, chosen by his PA on his behalf, because you, extraordinary genius Patrick Cusack, thought Venetia with the anger that had become as much a part of her as the dreadful pain, would never give up your invaluable time to go shopping. She watched the bag tumble on to the floor as the taxi negotiated another bus, the finely wrought clasp straining shut, the butter-soft leather bulging at the seams, crammed full of the heavy load of drugs she was bringing home.

There was no denying it. Six weeks the doctor said. Six weeks. Last spring – on April 14th to be exact, as there are some dates, Venetia knew, you can never forget – the doctor had given her a year, but now she would be lucky to make it to February. Normally, she hated February – such a mean little month, she always said – and she used to beg Patrick to go away somewhere warm with her. But he had always been too absorbed with his portraits, and she had given up asking him.

Now she longed to see another February. Because how could she have been so careless? How could she not have appreciated the grey, short days? Cold, drizzle, dullness were all transformed into a wonderful affirmation of existence as her life began closing in on her. Dear God, why did I not realize the blessings of what I had?

She felt the pain rising up again and for a moment she thought she might be sick. She tried to open the taxi window, but it was locked.

'Please,' she said to the driver through clenched teeth, 'can I just let in some air? I need . . .'

The window wound down without the man saying a word.

Venetia looked at the back of his head.

I'm dying, she was tempted to screech at him. Dying! And one day you will too, and all those you love. And you will know what I know and it is terrible.

When she was pregnant, an experience she found uniformly ghastly, she had looked at people on the streets, thinking each one of you had to be born. We all arrived in this dreadful, painful way. But now as she gulped in the damp, cold air from the open window she wanted to remind the passers-by, shoving and hurrying to do their Christmas shopping on this busy Saturday morning, every single one of you will die. For some of you, your death will be at the right time, with dignity, knowing your life has been well lived – what her own mother in Dublin used to call a 'good death'. But the odds on it were slim. For many it would be terrifying, agonizing, lonely.

She did not want to think about it. But she had to.

'I really wish you would tell your family,' her pretty, sympathetic doctor had said earlier. 'There are decisions you need to consider. Where you want to be, at home, or go to the hospice.'

Where I want to be bumped off is what you are actually asking me, thought Venetia. Because that is what happens, for all the moral debate and hand-wringing argument in public. Though that was not necessarily a bad thing. When she was alone in the middle of the night waiting for the painkillers to kick in, she was often tempted just to take the lot and be done with it. But that was Catholicism for you, when it lay as deep-rooted as in her. You had to battle on, never letting the sin of despair cloud your actions.

'To keep it from your family for so long,' the doctor had said, 'I think you've been terribly brave.'

And Venetia had smiled, as if accepting a compliment.

But it was not bravery, Venetia knew. It was an act of revenge. Her husband, the great artist who could depict a face and bring out both the weakness and the magnificence of human existence, whose profundity lay in his sensitive rendering of our vulnerability. Huh! The rubbish she had read about him in newspaper profiles, the clap-trap she had listened to as critics discussed his work in interminable documentaries. It was all a farce. The genius whose portraits were said to be so full of love they seemed to be guarding his sitters from death, could not see what was right under his nose: his own wife was dying.

She would show them. As if being an artist meant you had any greater sense of the human condition, thought Venetia, doubling over as a spasm of pain took hold. Life was fragile, happiness ephemeral, and you did not need to be a genius to spot that. Any fool stuck sitting in a hospital waiting room would have every bit as much understanding. Because if you, Patrick Cusack, knew what I now know, you might have thought more of me, have noticed me.

Venetia closed her eyes, begging the pain to ease, and indulged in a fantasy she had entertained with more and more relish these last months. She would imagine herself taking a red felt-tip pen and scrawling across one of his works, adding a moustache or bushy eyebrows. What an uproar would ensue. What sacrilege she would be committing! What destruction of beauty! And yet, there was no uproar when he hurt her, a living, human being. Day in, day out of their married life together he hurt her. When she was younger she would weep with sorrow but now she was beside herself with fury. Because how could a lifeless picture, dead to the touch, be more precious than another loving soul? *Her* loving soul?

Not that he ever laid a finger on her – that was all too true. But he barely spoke to her, except in an absent-minded, avuncular manner to exchange domestic information. After almost forty years of marriage she doubted whether he had any proper grasp of how she filled her day, all her work as a barrister specializing in protection of vulnerable children. When their own family was small and at home, he had no idea how she struggled to appear cheerful and disguise her feelings whereas he could rant and rage or disappear to his studio in a sulk because he was an artist. Thank God he was an exceptionally prosperous one too. So she could afford help around the house – because he certainly didn't lift a finger to do anything he didn't want. Thank God a million times over she had never had to worry about money, and she did not need to be told what a privilege that was.

But it was not as simple as money. Her husband had never loved her the way she had loved him, and the pain of that was irremediable. They had had a terrible marriage. Perhaps not by some standards – they had children, they were still together, he was never physically violent. But he had never loved her. Never. Not in the way she had been brought up to love.

She was still not sure why he had chosen her. It couldn't have been because he wanted to paint her. When they met in seventies Dublin, hordes of young women were queuing up to take their clothes off for him. Venetia was pretty enough, but nothing out of the ordinary, just another nice, clever girl studying law at Trinity College in thrall to the gorgeous golden painter, the lone wolf, the motherless, fatherless boy raised in an orphanage.

Why me? she would rail to herself as the reality of her marriage swiftly dawned on her. I was no different from any of the other eager, willing convent girls, whose highly educated minds could not stop them falling for the brilliant artist from the wrong side of the tracks. The only answer she could come up with was that she was chosen because she was so ordinary. Raw and discreet, she was ideal, the box he could tick in the experiences of life, then return to his portraits. He did not want one of the gorgeous girls with green eyes who would have gone to bed with him at the drop of a hat. Such gregarious, popular women would have found him out, known right away what it took her a while to realize – that their inept fumbling was the first time for him and not just her.

But however naive, their pathetic union one summer night on the cold sands of Dublin Bay resulted in their son, Mark, nine months later. And in the moral climate of seventies Ireland there was little option but to marry.

He could have turned his back on her and the child but later she thought that with her conventional loving background and her abilities, he'd decided she would provide him with the stability to do the only thing that mattered to him – paint. And she fulfilled her side of the bargain in that she gave him a family life he could dip into if the mood took him, as well as a beautifully run home where he was shielded from the drudgery of daily life so he could quarantine himself in his studio with his art.

But what a marriage.

On their first night together as husband and wife she and Patrick arrived at the hotel and he went down to the bar while she stayed in the room. At the foot of the bed was a table with a vase of pale pink roses and she placed the flowers in her then long, dark, wavy hair. Next, she removed all her clothes and she lay on the bed and waited.

In the back of the cab, Venetia winced.

'Oh God,' she murmured, closing her eyes in anguish at the memory she could not obliterate. What a sorry sight she must have made.

When her new husband at last came back he just stood staring at her bare, blushing body. So she came towards him, shy and audacious. She put her arms around his neck. But he removed her hands and put them by her side. And it was there they had to stay.

He was not interested. He was never interested.

But what about my loss? she thought, stifling the rage that felt like bombs exploding within her. She learned to manage it of course. Even on their honeymoon, as the man she had committed herself to was exposed with glaring, unflinching clarity, she realized she would only survive by finding a way to escape inside her marriage.

In the hotel lounge she came across a copy of *Middlemarch* and retreated into another world. And that was the beginning of their married life. Her new husband painted her, over and over, as she lay on the bed reading as if her life depended on it.

Just one year later, this series of paintings – simply called 'Venetia Reading' – was deemed his breakthrough into greatness. In these pictures of his new wife Patrick Cusack, the genius, emerged. They were wonderful for the tremulous tenderness, the loving detail with which he captured her every strand of hair, every nuance of her youthful, creamy skin. But he felt no love for her. Ever.

Thank God she fell pregnant so easily or she might never have had Laura and Robert. Even though she had a husband who hardly ever came to her bed, theirs was cited as a perfect marriage. In all the profiles of him she was described as his mainstay, the bedrock on which his genius could flourish, the sort of phrases used in obituaries, she thought grimly, turning her wedding ring around on her bony finger. But in this world of full disclosure she kept the reality of her marriage a secret.

There was no one she wanted to tell.

Except for the priest. Confession – that was a good thing about Catholicism. Her faith meant she could not bring herself to construct some dubious arguments for divorce but at least she could spill out her heart to Father Eoghan. But her pride would not let her confide in anyone else.

Though she suspected her parents discerned the truth. Their life together had been what Venetia in her naivety – and what she now called her stupidity – assumed marriage was. Even when her father was dying, her parents shared the small bed in the small room whereas Venetia had never got used to the way she and Patrick slept in huge empty beds in separate rooms at opposite ends of the house, each with its own en-suite bathroom. When her father left for work in the mornings he always kissed her mother goodbye – not just a quick peck on the cheek but a great smack on the lips. And before he returned home at night her mother would, without fail, go up to her dressing table, brush her hair, apply her lipstick, spray on the Worth perfume. Then, when her father came through the door, the first thing he would do was seek out his wife, put his hand on her waist, and she would circle her arms around his neck and they would kiss again. And to Venetia, lonely in her large bed and luxurious room, this kiss seemed priceless and all the fabulous show of her life, utterly worthless.

Sometimes she thought if Patrick had had affairs, it could have been better. Or if he had been gay. At least there might have been some passion left over for her. When she lay naked and he painted her, what to her was a moment of the richest erotic potential was to him just his damned art. Those first drawings of her were now worth a fortune. The love, the sensitivity, wrote the critics, his ability to capture the fleetingness of beauty. Well, it was fleeting, that was for sure. Her body now was abraded to the bone. Not that he had noticed. And would soon be ashes. In no time she would be nothing.

But how had it all come to this? How had she lived more than six decades never knowing a man's love?

For years she had overcome the disappointment of her marriage with work. She could comfort herself with the knowledge that, thanks to Patrick's material success, she could specialize in one of the least lucrative areas of the law, child protection, and that she had done good things. At night she could rest her tired head knowing her efforts and expertise had spared some children the hell that Patrick had endured. Not that he ever talked about it. His childhood was beyond reach. 'You knew who to avoid,' was the most he ever said to her of the priests who ran the orphanage he had been placed in at birth.

But Venetia could draw her own conclusions. When bitterness threatened to engulf her she would tell herself that Patrick had not just married her because she made an excellent project manager for his life. He also wanted to be a father to his own son because he knew too well what placing a defenceless little boy into the hands of other men could mean behind closed doors.

And that was a dreadful truth.

Venetia had tracked down a boy who had been in the same home as Patrick and she put together an all too likely and horrifying scenario. So she made it her life's work to spare more children what had happened to Patrick. And this mission had consoled her and given her the grace to make excuses for her husband, over and over. She could love him as you might a lame, wild creature. Until now.

On April 14th, the day she was told how finite her own life was, sympathy for her husband died. On that day she realized that the evil of his upbringing did not stop with Patrick.

I have been crippled too, she thought. She had sacrificed her life, this beautiful ephemeral thing that her husband was said to portray so perfectly on canvas, and she wanted it back. But it was fading away with a terrifying speed.

The Catholic funeral is not an end but a beginning. She had heard that so many times. But whatever may or may not lie ahead, she cried, I want *this* life. I want . . . she wanted what it was too late for her ever to have.

But she would have her revenge on her husband. Just you wait, she thought. I'll expose you as the fraud you are.

When she was first diagnosed, she had tried to tell him, to explain that she was having tests, but he was terribly dismissive and said she was probably imagining things. Later, on April 14th, when she received her prognosis, she had gone home in terror and sought him out. But he was in his studio with some Cabinet minister and, of course, that was far more important. When the Cabinet minister had left she tried again, but it was clear from the glare he gave her that she could not possibly interrupt his creative flow.

So at first she thought, I've enough to deal with without his rage or distress. I'll wait for a better time. But there was never a better time and, over the weeks, as the pain grew, her secret knowledge had festered into this colossal revenge, which she nursed like a miser his gold.

Thanks to her, all those people who queued up to be painted by him would learn the truth about the brilliant artist they so revered: he was as blind as a bat. He could not see that his own wife was dying before his very eyes.

She shivered. She was suddenly cold and she put up the cab window and wrapped her thin arms about her frail body.

But I have had the love of my three children, she thought. And that was wonderful. Although the truth was – another truth only the imminence of death enabled her to admit – her own children did not stir her heart in the way the neglected, the abandoned and the orphaned did.

Of course she had made sure they were well fed, well educated, well clothed, well housed. But she had never given them the family life she had adored as a child. To do that, she could not have worked as she had. And that would have meant burying her best soul deep underground and then she would have been nothing but some diminished, nervy little thing buffeted about by petty worries in an impossible task.

Besides, my children are fine, Venetia told herself, pulling herself upright as the pain died down slightly. Right now Mark was making yet more of a fortune in the City and he had his wife whom he loved, twins imminent. Robert was presumably decorating – somewhere near here, she guessed, as they drove past colossal Primrose Hill mansions. He was talented and personable enough to be doing so much more, but he was still young. His breezy love of life was worth millions. And Laura . . .

What no one ever tells you, she thought, is how to relate to your own child when you have nothing in common. With her sons she had accepted it, but she had imagined a daughter might be a friend. Laura was so much like her father – forever drawing as a child and following him around, desperate for him to take notice of her pictures.

I never have any idea, thought Venetia, what my own daughter is thinking. Have I failed her in some way? At least Laura had the sense not to trap herself in a loveless marriage. And Laura always seemed to be coping perfectly well. 'She's an incredible help to me,' Father Eoghan was forever telling her. And only yesterday he said Laura had saved the parish a fortune by sorting out some accounting error.

Laura may not have pursued a career but she has made, thought Venetia with satisfaction, a life of caring for others beyond herself and her children. She was always helping those less fortunate than herself. Like me. Just like me. And yet . . . and yet I am so unhappy.

'Which one?' yelled the driver as they turned into her street.

'On the bend, please,' replied Venetia. 'With the black door.'

And they pulled up outside her large, empty home.

## 29

Laura sat on her daughters' bed, flicking through their book with pictures of a boat tossed by the billow on a lonely coast, an eagle catching the sunlight on the arch of its wing, sun glancing through bars of cloud above a dark forest. Then she caught sight of the overflowing laundry basket and slammed the book shut with a bang, making Eliza stir.

'Don't wake,' begged Laura, glancing at the clock – nearly ten.

It was Saturday night. The girls had come home full of excitement after a party and, as usual, it had taken ages for them to calm down until she intoxicated them with this romantic vision of the world. She looked at the book dubiously. Of course you had to foster children's imagination and all that. But she wondered, not for the first time, whether she was doing as much harm as good. She read and read as a child. And then as a teenager. When she first met the girls' father, her irreverent mind saw a rather too well-fed Heathcliff. Read too much Brontë and du Maurier at an impressionable age, she thought, you learn too late that one woman's Heathcliff can be another's woolly jumper. She returned the book to the shelf which, she noticed, she ought to dust, and edged to the door so as not to wake the girls.

'Sweetheart, please,' murmured Laura, as Eliza began throwing her arms around.

But then Eliza began chuckling in her sleep and Laura was transfixed. All night she had wanted nothing more than for her daughters to go to bed, but that private laughter was so touching Laura stood still, her heart dangerously expanding and contracting because one moment she was desperate for some distance from her daughters while the next she could not drag herself away from staring at their soft, untouched faces.

Slowly, Eliza's laughter subsided and she put her arms around her sister and they lay together as if mounting guard beside one another, in readiness for another day.

Soon, thought Laura, all too soon, they will be jumping and shouting and dancing and fighting and singing. Life – everyday, mundane, ordinary life – was a great adventure to them and for a moment Laura felt terrified that she would slowly but surely snuff out all that spirit. Once, I was just as full of excitement, she thought, taking herself downstairs. Incredible loves and selfless heroics had not seemed beyond her. But now . . .

She began unloading the tumble dryer, thinking, you start out believing life is wonderful, but end up folding vests.

But perhaps that was the point of laundry and all the mundane tasks – to take your mind off impossible dreams. Washing, cleaning, doing accounts . . . Phillip. A tremor of guilt and annoyance went through her. She was sick of thinking about Phillip. It felt wrong to give a couple of brief encounters so much attention. But at odd times now she kept going over her damning words to Phillip. Why couldn't she speak to him without criticizing and condemning? Some pathetic inferiority complex that made her need to cut him down to size? Even after he had been mugged, she had had to have a go at him.

She slammed the dryer door shut and shoved Phillip to the back of her mind. Her brother was coming round to collect his accounts on his way to a party. And she did not want him ringing the bell and waking the girls. So she went to the front door to look out for him.

The wind was raw and the sky black, the sort of night that offers you nothing. Yet she did not want to be inside either. She looked up and down the road at the cars driving too fast, then closed her eyes a moment, huddling into her jumper.

When she was younger and was unhappy, Laura would take herself off to a land of her own making. She could wander through snowdrops flowering under arms of great beech trees, see daffodils blowing on a windswept plain, almost taste the bluebells spreading down to rivers running brown with peat.

Laura had long dismissed these fantasies as the stuff of yearning adolescents, but as she stood waiting in the shadows it occurred to her that her painting was in the same league as these clichés. Her efforts to portray a flower, to capture some immaculate conception of life, were just as childish, the same immature hunger for a perfection that could never be found, exposing her to vanity and humiliation. Face the facts, she told herself, seeing a mangy fox run by with a half-eaten burger in its jaws. Believe the evidence before you. Your painting is ordinary. Nothing more.

But I have an incredible love, she reminded herself. I have my beautiful children. But the reality of that love was their relentless demands upon her. And selfless heroics were her duties to the old and the sick she met through the church. Just that morning Father Eoghan had rung asking if she would take two old ladies shopping and, disguising all her bad grace, she had been unable to refuse him. But, she thought, appalled by her selfishness, am I always going to have to think about other people? She turned to go back into the house to throw herself into clearing up the kitchen when her brother came hurtling along the pavement.

'Laura! What are you doing standing out here? Are you all right?'

'Sure, sure, come on in,' she said with false brightness, as he began thanking her profusely for sorting out his accounts and shoving ten fifty-pound notes into her hands.

'This is way too much,' she insisted. 'I can't take all this.'

'Rubbish – you know how I hate doing this stuff. So I want to pay you properly. Spend it on yourself. Go out for an evening. I know babysitters cost the earth.'

'Yes, but . . .'

Laura baulked at the cost of babysitters, yet at the same time she thought they were obscenely cheap because she was entrusting what she loved most in the world to someone who was paid less than a plumber to fix a leaking tap.

'Laura, take it. Have a night out.'

'You sound like Mum. She was on at me the other day about going out. I wondered if she was all right.'

'Seriously?' he hesitated. 'I mean, do you think she's all right?'

'Of course she is,' said Laura. 'She's just spent her life telling people what to do, she can't stop herself.'

'Don't let her get to you,' he said, putting the money on the kitchen table. 'Get a baby-sitter so you can paint. Your kids are perfect, anyway. And we were all right as well.'

'Were we? I do wonder if any of us . . . I don't know . . .'

'What?'

What Laura wanted to say was, have any of us achieved our potential, done what we should with our lives? But it sounded so melodramatic, she confined herself to, 'I was thinking about Mark. He was always brilliant at art. Of the three of us, he could have been so good. Like Dad.'

'That's enough to put anyone off.'

'He could have been great. But he just wasn't interested.'

'Do you blame him? Who'd want the self-centredness of Dad's life?'

'I'm serious.'

'So am I. I'm sure that's why Mum was always out attending to other people's suffering. Sitting on committees and writing memos to escape Dad.'

'Don't say that. Anyway, Dad was never there.'

'He was – or rather, the weight of his bloody genius was there. And you're as talented as Mark. More so, in fact. You just don't give it the time. You know, Laura, you don't have to keep doing good turns for people just because Mum did.'

'I don't do good turns.'

'Come off it. What's Father Eoghan roped you into this week?'

'Yes, but . . . I can hardly call that a good turn. I hate it.' That's the truth of it, she thought. Any kind act of mine is soured by resentment at the time it takes.

'So? You virtually beat up that Phillip the other day for feeling good about doing his good works. You can't have it both ways.'

Why did she have to be so hard on Phillip? She had been putting together a picture of the man with every scrap of information she had and he was universally liked, respected, rich, and generous with his time and money. There were the daughters, one brilliant, the other a beauty, and of course there was the wife – beautiful and, no doubt, brilliant too.

'He just got to me,' she said to her brother, 'and what if he does more harm than good?'

'That's different. But let him feel good about what he does.'

'But there's something so ... well, smug and ... oh, I don't know.'

What did his motivation really matter, as long as he achieved something? And how was he feeling now? Was he still in pain? Or was he out at some dinner party? The theatre? Sitting happily watching telly with the family?

'Perhaps,' suggested Robert, 'he's like Mum and is unhappy at home so he needs to go and save the world, or at least one person in it.'

Laura shrugged.

'Or maybe,' he went on, 'he's just good?'

She laughed.

'It's possible.'

'It is,' she conceded. 'Anyway,' she said, trying not to dwell on Phillip's life, 'you go to this party. Or whatever it is you're off to. I mean, what sort of people have parties at this time of night?'

'People without children.'

She smiled.

'Are you going on your own?' she asked, not expecting to be answered. She was not exactly close to Robert, and she certainly was not to Mark. Their relationship was simply a result of having known each other for so long. But she was curious. Robert – and Mark too – had the air of men who had cracked the art of leading happy lives.

'Nope.'

'Who with?'

'You don't know her.'

'Married?' she asked, knowing she would be snubbed.

'None of your business.'

'But don't you ever want something more?'

'What? To be married like Mark and Jane?' He put a fatherly arm around her shoulders. 'The thing is, if you get married, what do you long for? What do you brood over in the dark hours of the night? Double-glazing? Which worktops you want for the new kitchen? No thanks.'

'It's not that simple.'

'Of course it's not, but I've got to go.'

And with that he was gone, and Laura went inside and upstairs to kiss her sleeping daughters.

## 30

'Come on, Rose, get a move on,' said Phillip, parking the car near his daughter's school on Monday morning.

'You know, Dad,' said Rose, climbing out of the car with practised slowness, 'sometimes I think school is just respite care for parents who need a break from their kids.'

'Expensive respite care for privileged kids like you.'

'The cost is to assuage the parents' guilt.'

Phillip contained himself. 'Just hurry up.'

'It's such a waste of my time at the end of term. The teachers are just clearing up and . . .'

Phillip put his head in his hands.

'Oh Dad! Are you all right?'

'Yes, of course.'

'But you've still got a horrible bruise.' For one rare moment Rose actually looked her young age. Her enormous eyes were wide and anxious.

'It's nothing,' he said, though his head did hurt. He rubbed his temples.

'Are you sure you're okay? I mean, if anything happened to you –'

'Sweetheart, I'm fine.'

'It's just . . . I'm sorry . . . I . . . sometimes,' she said in a small voice, 'I just get so cross with you, with Mum, and I . . .'

But then one of her friends called out, 'Rose!' And with that she ran off.

For a moment he watched her, laughing and chatting, back in her own world, and he felt a presentiment of fear. Where would life take his dangerously beautiful little girl? Who would she turn to for love as she grew apart from him? And what could possibly be solved by his wife's simple solution of sending her to boarding school?

It was three days since he and Julia had argued. Over the weekend, neither had said much, and at night, they might lie side by side, but when they spoke it was only with self-conscious politeness. Then at six this morning, when Julia's car arrived and he heard the door close behind her, Phillip realized that not since he was a child and packed off to boarding school, had he felt so lonely.

There was a knock on his car window. It was Laura, and to his surprise he was relieved to see her.

'Phillip! Can I have a quick word? Please?'

'Of course,' he said – anything to be diverted from his own thoughts.

'I want to apologize for the way I spoke to you the other day. I'm so sorry. Are you okay? Your head?'

'I'm fine. Really. But you?' he asked, struck by how tired she seemed. 'Your car? Is it all right?'

She looked at him blankly.

'You walked,' he said in explanation, 'in this awful weather.'

'I always do.'

'That's a hell of a long way. I know it's hard to park round here but I normally find somewhere.'

'It's not that. It's . . .'

'What?'

'Most of the parents here are forever on their high horse about saving energy, but none of them walk.'

A smile, like a fish darting through water, flickered across his face. 'Well,' he said, 'it's very noble of you, walking to save the planet.'

And at this, Laura laughed. 'The real reason is that the girls sleep so little I need to tire them out.'

Phillip thought the girls always looked as if they were just getting warmed up and Laura was the one who was tired out.

But she was saying, 'I was out of line with what I said. Especially after all you'd been through. I'm sorry. And please, this is for you.' She handed him a small package.

'What is it? Oh my!' he cried, unwrapping one of her paintings.

'You shouldn't. I mean, I'm the one who should be giving you something for all you did looking after me. Look, get in the car, please,' he went on as the drizzle suddenly turned into full-scale rain. 'I'd hate to get this wet. It's . . . it's perfect. My God! It's beautiful.'

'You said you'd like a painting,' she said, once in the car.

'I said I'd *buy* one,' corrected Phillip. 'And I really meant it. I'd love to. You shouldn't be giving me this. It's . . . it's truly lovely. Please, let me pay you.'

'No, no. It's nothing.'

He looked closely at the tiny, postcard-size picture. 'Don't say that.' White hawthorn, glowing with light, grew along the side of a stream glinting in spring sunshine, the clear running water and the lovely, soft blossom spilling over the frame of the canvas. 'It's so incredibly peaceful. What a gift to be able to capture that.'

'It's only an imaginary peace.'

'What on earth do you mean?'

'Just that you don't get peace like that in real life. Everything perfect.'

'So? I feel peace looking at this, and that's not imaginary. It's a wonderful thing to give someone. Don't knock it. You know,' he went on, 'you're always putting yourself down. Do you realize you do?'

Laura looked away. Don't be kind to me, she thought. Argument and discord were manageable, but goodness disarmed her. She was always telling her daughters that in an ideal world tears are only ever caused by kindness.

'You shouldn't underestimate yourself,' Phillip was saying. 'To me, this is really, really special.'

Laura gripped her hands in her lap. No one spoke of her painting like this. Don't stop, she wanted to plead. He did not.

'I've never once created anything as beautiful as this. Or so truthful. Or that brings such pleasure.'

And impulsively, he took her cold hand and the heat from his grasp sent a shiver of fear through her because she could not delude herself any more.

Sitting in his car as the rain lashed down, Laura surveyed Phillip silently as the realization sank in. You don't think about someone almost constantly, be it unconsciously or not, without reason. Her brother was right, she did like Phillip. There was, she was forced to acknowledge, such a warmth about him. Kindness came to him naturally and he was extravagant with that kindness.

But she wanted that warmth directed at her specifically, not just as part of some general love of humanity. And that knowledge made her utterly miserable. The knife that turned in her would not even touch him. She had come to a decision in the early hours of last night to apologize to Phillip, and in the merciless judgements of three in the morning she had seen herself through his eyes, homely with tired brown eyes, plump body, her plainness growing and growing, as exaggerated as the shadows cast by the street light breaking through the edges of the curtains.

She wanted, she saw all too well, something she could never have, and she was in no doubt what torment that would bring.

'Please,' he said, her hand still in his, 'let's go and have a cup of coffee – if you've time. I don't want to keep you away from your painting. But we keep getting off to wrong starts and I'm not explaining myself well. And if we are going to work together at Hartley High . . .'

Self-preservation made her extract her hand and force out the words, 'I'm sorry but I really ought to get home. I must . . . Thank you, though.'

'Oh,' said Phillip. 'But let me drive you home, please. If you walk in this rain, you'll be drenched.'

She had little choice. It was pelting down now. She would look stupid if she insisted on walking. 'Well, thanks,' she said, sitting primly upright.

They pulled away slowly.

'Dreadful, this rain,' said Phillip. 'Like driving into a wall. And apparently it's going to get worse.

'Oh,' said Laura, thinking perhaps we will make yet another

journey confining ourselves to conversation about the weather and I can be as composed as a breeze block.

'More rain, that's what it said on the news,' continued Phillip, going on to tell her the likelihood of snow over the next few days, until they came to a stop in a line of traffic and fell into silence. More minutes passed by with nothing but the sound of the hammering rain and hooting motorists.

'So,' attempted Phillip, 'are you doing anything for Christmas?'

'Going to my parents'.'

'That's nice. Or is it?'

'It's fine. What about you?' Laura asked politely. 'Are you here for Christmas?' Probably not, she thought. He'll be off somewhere exotic.

'Same as you, actually – to my parents', in Yorkshire, to a freezing house my wife and daughters can't stand. And a small chicken as my parents make a point of not subscribing to what they go on about as the destruction of the true Christmas message. So they won't spend the money on a turkey. And even the small chicken will be burnt. Plus my father's a vicar,' he added, 'so he'll be working as well. Though he's *always* working.'

And before she could stop herself she was saying, 'Like mine. Not just Christmas and Easter, but weekends, evenings, holidays.'

With that Phillip gave her his frank, open smile, and before she knew it she was smiling back.

## 31

I should have gone for coffee with him after all, thought Laura. There would have been a table between us and other people around. I wouldn't be sitting beside him, alone, as if in the confessional and in danger of saying too much.

'But does your father actually enjoy his work?' Phillip was asking.

She was surprised at the question. 'Of course he does.'

'I only ask,' Phillip said, 'because sometimes you get into habits of working and providing and you don't know how to break them.'

Laura thought her father's only habit was his own artistic fulfilment. 'I'm not sure he'd want to break them.'

'What I mean is that such single-mindedness takes its toll.'

'On those around him, certainly.' Laura stopped herself. She never spoke disloyally of her father. Indeed, she never spoke of him at all if she could help it.

'Maybe he's making compromises you don't know about,' he said. 'You'd paint more without the children, wouldn't you?'

'Of course.'

'I only meant that you've chosen to compromise on your painting and he's chosen to compromise on family. Maybe he's aware he's not been around – for his children, his grandchildren – but he doesn't know what to do about it, and maybe he regrets it.'

The thought unsettled her. It had never occurred to her that her father had done anything in his adult life but please himself.

'I mean my daughters,' Phillip was saying, 'I'd like to see more of them. But it's just so hard to change those family patterns. I worked long hours. I still do, I suppose, though nothing like I used to. But your children fix you in a certain role and it's difficult to break out of it and that makes me sad. Anyway,' he said, changing the subject and turning off the engine, 'it looks as if we'll be stuck here a while. Let me see what's going on.'

He stepped out of the car, then threw himself back inside, the rain blasting in with him and the wind slamming the door shut.

'Dear God, it's apocalyptic out there. I don't think,' he said, looking at the traffic now all backed up behind as well as in front, 'that there's much we can do. It's a burst water main by the look of things. Do you have to be home for anything important?'

'Only –' she began. This was the morning she had promised Father Eoghan to take out two housebound old ladies to buy Christmas presents. 'Oh, nothing. It doesn't matter.'

'What?'

'I just said I'd take a couple of people shopping. But not till eleven.'

'That's kind of you.'

'Not if you do it with my bad grace.'

'Then why do it?'

'Because . . . oh, I don't know . . .' she trailed off.

'Because what?'

'Because I have so much, I feel I have to give something back.'

'Yet you hate it.'

'Yes. I hate caring for people. No, I don't mean that. Of course I don't.' What was she saying? 'I adore caring for my children. But . . .'

'But sometimes they're hard work?'

'Not the way some people have hard work,' she retorted. 'But because I'm healthy, have a car, and can do things like take lonely old ladies shopping, I feel I should. When you've had an easy ride like me you have to do something to stop –'

She held her breath. He was the sort of man, she thought, who was probably used to lonely women having crushes on him and baring their hearts because he gave them two minutes of his attention.

'To stop what?'

'Guilt,' she muttered. 'Oh, I don't know if it's that. Not feeling you deserve it.'

She turned away to the steamed-up window, rubbing at the condensation. She had had enough of this self-disclosure.

'Lots of people manage just fine,' he was saying, 'and are simply pleased with what they have.'

'I don't give a damn about lots of people. They don't have to live with being me. It's the way I see it. So I give up the time I'd rather spend painting. And it's probably no bad thing. Because the world hardly needs another second-rate picture.'

'Not second-rate,' he protested. 'Certainly not to me. And besides, none of us really deserve what we have. It's all gift. I know you have to work hard, use your intelligence, and so on, but so much of it is just that – gift. So, Laura, don't feel guilty,' he said, giving her hand another squeeze. She almost choked. 'My father always says that guilt is lack of faith in God.'

'Lack of faith?' She contorted her face into a light smile. 'That's me.'

'But you do all that stuff for the church. Go to services and all that.'

'I like the poetry,' she shrugged. 'The music, the art, the opiates – for want of a better word. But everything else – God and all that implies – only leads to more questions I can't answer. Anyway,' she would not be drawn any more, 'I think I'll walk.'

'But . . .' he said, as she opened the door and the rain lashed her like a whip in the face.

'I don't mind the rain, honestly, and I'm dressed for it.'

'Give it five more minutes,' he said. '*Please.*'

Sitting here talking in a way he had not talked to anyone for too long, he felt like a parched man given a long, cool glass of water. He wanted to know more about her, and with that he gave her something of himself she could not run away from.

'Just because you've got food and shelter,' he said, 'even the very best food and shelter, you still have to work hard at doing the right thing, and if you get it wrong you've got all the more reason to be even harder on yourself. I mean, I suppose I started on all this – Hartley High, the charities and so on – for the same reasons as you. Wanting to give something back. To make me feel better. All that. But also. The opposite too. Maybe faith in God . . .'

Phillip hesitated. He had not even told Julia this. His uncertainties seemed too fragile to expose to her logical scrutiny. But Laura was looking at him, as if she might know what he meant.

'With my father and my mother – so devout, so undoubting, as far as I could tell – I turned my back on it all. I thought, how dare they be so sure? But with selling my business, getting out of that mad life, I've had more time. And sometimes I walk into churches, go to the odd service, go through the motions. But nothing happens. No revelations. Nothing. It's not made a blind bit of difference, sitting in church. But that's what I remember my father saying, just say the prayers, don't expect anything back. Just do it. So I did. I do.

'In the end, I think you just make a choice. You ask yourself if you're going to believe or not. And I suppose I've chosen to believe again, though I can't give you any rational reason for doing so. And sometimes I wonder if it's all a figment of my imagination just to make me feel better. And in my bleaker moments it is. But I carry on acting . . . acting as if I do believe. Hoping it might be true. But I keep it to myself because the Anglicanism I was brought up with has gone almost underground, it's so unfashionable.' Then he laughed deliberately. Suddenly he felt he had said too much and wanted to change the subject. 'Unless, of course, you use your faith to get your child into a good school.'

But Laura's face remained grave and serious. She was taken aback by this unexpected vulnerability and it only made her want him more. Don't let this moment end, she begged, but the moment the idea of loss entered her head the car behind them began hooting. And the one behind that.

'We're on the move,' said Phillip, and they wiped the condensation off the windscreen and set off again into the rain in silence.

Laura was staring firmly ahead but he wanted to catch her eye. There was a contradiction about her he could not understand. Now her tired face, her shabby clothes, suggested a woman who was forcefully alive, not the down-at-heel soul she gave the first impression of being. Far from it. Even her stricken conscience and her self-doubt gave him a sense of some hidden fortitude. It must be hard, he thought, noticing the paint ingrained on her fingers, having the sort of talent that rarely brings much reward.

'Please,' he said, as they arrived outside her home, 'I know you're busy now and I've got a meeting but I meant it when I said I'd like to buy one of your paintings. I really would. So may I call you to find when would suit you, so I can choose one? Or what about tomorrow even?' She nodded. 'Fine.' His face was close to hers, as if he might kiss her goodbye. She wondered how he might go about it. He moved nearer and placed a light kiss on the side of her cheek. She kept her face like stone, though she wanted to put her fingers to the skin his lips had touched.

'I'll see you tomorrow, then,' he was saying. 'Take care of yourself, Laura. Now hurry on in. Or you'll get wet through.'

And he drove off with a wave through the driving rain.

Laura watched the bright lights of his car disappear into the dark December morning, a sickening sense of disappointment chilling her – once Phillip had chosen his picture, he would have no reason to visit her again. But she wanted his conversation, his confidences, his closeness, his . . .

She had to stop right there. She wanted much more than that. But that was madness. How had she let this happen, allowed such a man to win so strong a hold over her? And in such a short time? She did not need the pain and humiliation of struggling through a mire of useless feelings for a married man. But, whether she liked it or not, she had.

Laura was fully aware of what she was exposing herself to. For months on end she could derive warmth from the one squeeze of his hand. She could spin out his odd kind word to find comfort in his goodness on interminable empty nights. She could relive the peck on the cheek, the touch of his skin, the comforting smell of him . . . oh, she did not want to remind herself. But she knew too well the nonsense she was capable of, a secret passion kindling in her for years, choking all possibility of genuine happiness.

She had to act to extinguish this feeling. And she had to act fast.

Standing in the wet street, it occurred to her how to begin. Good student of English literature, she recalled Jane Eyre who painted a picture of herself alongside Blanche Ingram, the beautiful, accomplished woman Jane believed Mr Rochester loved. Whenever Jane longed for Rochester she could compare the two pictures and remind herself of the impossibility of him ever wanting her.

Laura would do the same. She would do one of Phillip's wife and another of herself. And the two portraits would remind her to exercise her common sense. True, she had only seen Julia a couple of times. But she had a good memory for faces and she had not forgotten Julia's. She hurried indoors. If she concentrated she could sketch herself in the time before she took the two old ladies shopping.

## 32

A couple of days later, Venetia stood on Laura's doorstep staring at her daughter's flushed face. She had never seen her look like this before. Laura's plumpness usually made her seem homely but today suggested a buxom goddess.

What's going on? Venetia wanted to ask, as into her mind flashed a vision of Venus surrounded by cheeky cherubs with Zeus hovering over disguised as a swan.

'Good grief, Mum! What are you doing here?' asked Laura. Her mother never turned up out of the blue. 'Is everything all right?'

Venetia was suddenly at a loss. She was a brave woman but her bravery did not run to saying, the truth is that last night I lay awake hating my husband and thinking what a stranger my own daughter is to me and soon it will be too late. And looking at you now, I realize more than ever how little I know you.

What had happened to her daughter? Was it a man? She could not get the image of that great swan out of her head. Though perhaps that was the painkilling drugs shooting through her veins. But no. Laura's eyes were truly bright and intense. Whatever the cause, there was no mistaking her daughter's happiness.

'Look, come on in,' Laura was saying. 'But are you okay?'

'Yes, fine,' she said quickly, negotiating a number of Laura's pictures stacked along the hall. Perhaps she's been painting, thought Venetia, and that is what has made her so alive. Her father's daughter. She repressed a sudden chill of jealousy. 'I was supposed to be having lunch and then it was cancelled so I wondered whether you'd like to join me.'

Laura looked at her mother in equal surprise. They never had lunch. Venetia always said it messed up your whole day. Besides, Laura had no idea what they would talk about alone for an entire meal. They only had long conversations when her mother wanted her to do something.

'That would be lovely,' said Laura, also lying. 'But I've got the girls home. There's some bug going round the school and both of them are off sick,' she said in explanation. 'You could have something to eat here,' she added, hoping her mother would say no.

'Well, yes, thank you,' said Venetia. 'I'd like that. But what's wrong with the girls?'

'Just a slight temperature,' said Laura. But she, too, was feeling fevered, though that was from sorting out her pictures because Phillip was coming to choose one at half past twelve. Arranging this had necessitated a number of phone calls. He had come round yesterday morning and ended up staying for lunch but in all that time he had been unable to make his mind up. He had rung last night to discuss seeing the paintings again today. Then Laura, who never forgot minor details, had to ring him back to check whether he had said twelve or one. Then he had rung again.

Laura knew, of course, what had hit her. And she knew it would only lead to suffering – hers. Yet, try as she might, she could not ignore the stirrings of life in her once more, the sense of movement after a long period of paralysis.

'Your pictures,' Venetia was saying. 'Why are they all out?'

With her back to her mother, Laura just said, 'Someone wants to buy one.'

'Oh yes?'

'Yes,' murmured Laura. Venetia was the last person she would tell about Phillip.

'Who?'

'Oh that chap, you know, the governor at Hartley High.'

'Phillip?'

'Yes.'

'Phillip Snowe?' said Venetia, oddly put out.

She looked upon Phillip as her find. That he wanted to buy one of Laura's pictures established a bond between him and her daughter. Despite herself, she resented this intimacy.

With an effort, she said, 'That's nice of him.' She noticed Laura's shoulders tensing. 'I don't mean "nice" in that he's doing you a favour. Not at all. Of course not. Just I'm pleased for you. They're lovely. And you've . . . well, good God . . . you've certainly given him plenty to choose from.' Now I'm sounding patronizing, she thought.

'I said I'd dig out some more for him to look at,' said Laura, 'because yesterday he couldn't decide which he liked best.'

He was here yesterday? And today he needs to look at watercolours and choose pictures *again*? Could something be going on between them? wondered Venetia. Surely not. Phillip is so obviously happily married. He is also, Venetia could not help but think, the sort of man I could have . . . oh, how I would have loved . . . She stopped herself. But with a curiosity she would despise in others, she could not let the subject go.

'So . . . um . . . which pictures did he like?'

Laura coloured. 'He liked lots. He just wasn't sure which he liked the most. That's all.'

That's all, Laura repeated to herself. It really was all. For him. Phillip was a married man and she could not forget it. Every night she concentrated on her portrait of Julia, recreating those lovely features to remind herself of her place in Phillip's world. Someone he clearly liked talking to. But nothing more.

Yesterday they had just talked about painting – or rather, *her* painting. He had come round in the morning and somehow that had spilled over into the afternoon. But now she had her mother here and she wondered whether to call Phillip and ask him to come another time. But to postpone his visit because she had her mother and children at home seemed to suggest she thought there was some other agenda. And that was not so. Certainly on his part. But on hers?

Laura's life was very busy, but there was little in it of her, and yesterday had been blissful, like being lost and at last finding yourself after years of telling yourself it doesn't matter, really, I'm fine, I'm not lonely, not at all – well, not much – lots of people go without . . . without so very much. But now she longed for Phillip's attention.

Yet here was her mother, settling herself down on the sofa, saying, 'I always liked your miniatures.'

'Thanks.'

'Does Phillip?'

'What?'

'Like your miniatures?' replied Venetia, trying not to show her impatience.

'Quite,' said Laura.

'The flower ones?'

Laura pursed her lips. 'They're all flowers.'

'Of course. But Phillip might have liked one of the others,' said Venetia, refusing to be snubbed and unable to curb her interest.

Oh, what was the matter with her that she wanted to know if anything was going on between Laura and Phillip? And the odds of that were so remote. She hoped her daughter was not going to make a fool of herself and let her imagination run riot over a man like Phillip Snowe.

'Have you met his wife?' asked Venetia, pointedly.

'Not really, just said hello once at a St Catherine's thing,' shrugged Laura, her face inscrutable and making Venetia think, not for the first time, that in another life Laura could have done well in MI5.

But, persisted Venetia, Phillip had been here yesterday. He and Laura had talked about art – or, more to the point, Phillip had clearly talked about how much he liked Laura's art. Perhaps, surmised Venetia, they really were just choosing pictures. Or at least deluding themselves that was just what they were doing.

But clever though Phillip was, there was surely no way he would realize that a love of her pictures was the way to win Laura round. Laura was normally so cagey about her painting. Or did he know more about her daughter than she did? Tears smarted her eyes. Oh, what secrets and lies were they all carrying? Phillip's marriage looked so perfect. But I am the last person to be fooled by appearances, thought Venetia. I know what goes on.

Julia, on the few occasions Venetia had met her, was always so clearly fulfilled, so adored, so assured. The opposite, thought

Venetia, from my daughter. But perhaps that was the attraction – the very difference. She stared at her daughter's soft, serious face and then, to her horror, the most appalling envy invaded her heart. She longed for a man like Phillip to want her, to choose her, to exercise his charms on her. Oh stop, she begged herself. To be jealous of your own daughter was too degrading, utterly wrong. She was better than this. But she wanted her life to hold possibilities, opportunities for romance, for love, for fulfilment. But it was all over. There was no hope. No hope! It was too late for hope.

'Oh, please may I have a coffee?' Venetia cried in a rush to change the thoughts in her head. It was this monstrous illness, she tried to tell herself, warping her judgement.

'Of course.'

'Thank you,' murmured Venetia. Dear Lord, have pity on me. But as she followed Laura into the kitchen Venetia caught sight of herself in the mirror, gaunt and pale with – uncharacteristically – a touch too much make-up to disguise that paleness. How can I feel as if I am just twenty? Why am I beset with all the desires of some lovely young thing, yet cursed with the body of an old dying woman?

It was not fair. I should have had affairs. But I observed the sacrament of marriage because I believed I should. It was so bred into me. You have no idea, Laura, she was tempted to say, what I put up with from your father. The emptiness I have endured. I kept us together as a family. Because I believed it was right. Although the hatred I feel for your father is like a depth charge within me.

She removed one of Laura's paintings propped up on the kitchen chair. It was of a glass vase of white lilac on a black background.

'This is good,' she said, 'truly lovely.'

Phillip Snowe just wanted a picture, she reasoned, and she was reading too much into it. More importantly, it was none of her business. Who was she to judge? She shouldn't begrudge her only daughter some happiness. Because her daughter was lonely. That was clear. They didn't need to have some heart-to-heart lunch for

Venetia to work that out. Oh, Phillip, don't make her unhappy, she thought. Please.

But however much you hope for your children's happiness, she knew, it is not really in your power. When they are little you give them love and security – life and circumstances permitting – but in no time their happiness is as beyond your control as the weather. You can guide them, help them with their demons – perhaps – but they have to find their own way to happiness. And some may never find it. But there is nothing you can do. Oh take care, my darling, she thought. Take care.

'Laura . . . dear . . .'

'Yes?' said Laura, a little too sharply.

But she wants me to go, thought Venetia. Of course. I should have realized. Venetia suppressed the rising hurt and, instead of the gentle words she wanted to give her daughter, she reverted to type and said briskly, 'I don't think that I will stay for lunch, after all. With the children ill, with Phillip coming.'

'Oh,' said Laura, trying to disguise her relief. 'Are you sure?' she asked, suddenly guilty. She knows I want to be rid of her, thought Laura. 'It's no trouble,' she said, overcompensating. 'Really, do stay, I've got a chicken. I'll make sandwiches.' She had bought food specially, thinking – or rather, hoping – Phillip might stay for lunch again. 'Stay, Mum, please.' It will serve me right, she thought, for these stupid feelings.

She took her mother's thin, mottled hand, trying to make amends. Her mother suddenly seemed very old, too gaunt and weary. 'The girls can't wait for Disneyland,' lied Laura, trying to be kind.

'Lovely,' replied Venetia. Though if she was feeling this ill, it would be a nightmare. She had not realized she would deteriorate so suddenly, and she wished now she had just decided to take the girls to the ballet. But she said, 'I'm looking forward to it too.'

'Good,' said Laura, as there was a great yell from upstairs.

'Mummy! I need you! Mummy!'

'Damn,' said Laura, as there was the noise of a herd thumping down the stairs. 'They've woken up.'

'Grandma!' shouted the girls, giving her a quick kiss, but then throwing themselves into their mother's lap.

'Hey, stop!' said Laura, as they began fighting for prime place. 'Stop! Calm now. You're still very hot,' she said, stroking their foreheads. 'You must go back to bed in a minute. Just sit still.'

'Are you looking forward to going to Disneyland?' asked Venetia, in the gushing way she spoke to children other than her own, and which always grated on Laura.

'Yes, thank you,' replied Eliza, to Laura's relief.

'Good,' said Venetia, thinking, I cannot disappoint them. But anything may happen in the next two weeks. Soon she would tell Patrick the truth. And the thought of his response when she announced she was dying and he had not noticed gave her a satisfaction she thought she would never know again. So what if it's a malicious pleasure? she thought, as the girls began fighting again in their mother's lap.

'Stop it,' yelled Eliza.

'You started it,' screeched Alice.

'Now be quiet,' said Laura.

'But she keeps pushing me,' cried Alice. 'She doesn't let me alone. What's wrong with her?'

'She's not feeling well,' explained Laura. 'And when you're not feeling well, everything seems wrong. Doesn't it, Mum?' And Laura smiled at her mother for confirmation.

Yes, it does, thought Venetia. Everything is wrong because terror and pain destroy you – as they are destroying me.

But she just said, 'Your mother's right.' Then she put her hand to her stomach, a gesture that was all too instinctive to her now. And she added quietly, 'You have to be quite an incredible person not to let feeling rotten change you, make you cross and bad-tempered. So if someone who's ill behaves badly, tell yourself it's not them, it's their nasty illness.'

Laura looked at her mother in surprise.

'Mum? What are you saying?'

'That you're right, that's all. Don't look so worried. Everything's fine. Now you two girls,' she said, rising briskly and going through the motions of departure, 'do as your mother says. And Laura . . .' There was so much Venetia wanted to say to Laura, but she had no idea of the right words today. And she feared she never would find them now. So all she could do was depart from her daughter with just a quick peck on the cheek.

Laura watched her mother walk out to her car.

'Close the door! You'll let the cold in,' her mother called back.

Laura did as she was asked but she had the sensation that she was shutting out more than the cold wintry day. But she had no idea what.

She hurried her daughters back up to bed, guilty that she was so desperate to have both her mother and her children out of the way, and Phillip to herself. But she would not let herself grow any fonder of him. She would not.

## 33

Julia did not really have time for this breakfast meeting but her client, Jonathan Branson, had said in the seductive voice that made him one of America's highest-paid film stars, 'Come on, Julia, I'll take you to the Wolseley.' Usually, her parent company in New York oversaw all his legal problems, but she had taken on this case against a British film company that owed him royalties. She should, she knew, have delegated it to one of her juniors but so much of her work was done behind the scenes – the only glamour in the number of noughts involved – that Julia, even though she was conscious she was being foolishly star-struck, wanted to meet the man herself. She justified her behaviour on the grounds that the case would be high profile, and success with him might encourage other 'wronged' celebrities to beat a path to her door.

'Is this the correct table?' she asked the waiter. It was set for three.

'Yes, madam,' he said, checking for her, 'three is correct. Now may I get you something while you wait?'

She ordered tea, looking around at the well-preserved women picking at scrambled eggs. For Rose's benefit, she made a mental note of a television presenter's tweed suit in a highly fashionable but, to Julia, hideous amber and also a newsreader walking in swinging a much-coveted handbag. But she was concerned because Jonathan had not mentioned bringing a third party. So was there a problem? The production company now recognized they were in the wrong and wanted to settle, but Julia was advising against it. She could command considerable damages if they went to court, and she would enjoy the exposure. She could see herself standing on the steps of the High Court in the Strand with the television cameras, the photographers' lights flashing as she announced, 'On behalf of my client . . .' And this was not like Rose's hunger for celebrity, she assured herself, because she had earned this.

She noticed heads turning as Jonathan entered, a pretty young woman on his arm. Julia who, of course, had done her research, recognized Indigo, his new wife, the daughter of an old rock star who in his younger days belted out anti-capitalist rants and now lived in the States as a tax exile. Indigo spent her time managing a charity aimed at reducing conspicuous consumption in the West – though not her own, surmised Julia, noticing Indigo's diamond bracelet. Also, clearly inheriting her father's business sense, Indigo had set up and now ran an extremely lucrative 'ecologically aware' fashion company – whatever that meant.

She soon found out. Throughout breakfast Julia listened assiduously to Indigo's interminable principles, but with her eye on the clock since she had non-stop phone calls booked from ten o'clock and a meeting with her associates at one. Julia barely got a word in, apart from admiring and approving all Indigo had to say. Come quarter to nine, however, after hearing about some new eco-hotel in Anguilla where Indigo had decided to photograph her next autumn-winter catalogue, Julia knew she had to raise the subject of the law suit.

'Jonathan,' she asked, 'I know you are both very busy so what is it you wanted to talk to me about? Is something worrying you about the case?'

'Well, no . . . it's not, actually,' replied Jonathan, 'not at all, in fact. I'm really not worried. Because the thing is, I've decided to settle, though I know you think we can get more.'

'I'm certain I can get you more – a lot more.'

'How can we ever really be certain about such things?' asked Indigo in such a sweet voice Julia had to rein in a desire to kick her.

'I know, Indigo, you're right, absolutely right. Of course we can't be certain,' she said serenely. 'But I'm certain that the amount they're offering is derisory compared with what Jonathan deserves. Think about it, please,' she continued, playing on his initial fury.

'They tried to pull a fast one – compromised your artistic integrity, I believe you said. And if you look at similar cases – ones I've won – I could get you at least twice –'

'But it's not just about the money,' said Jonathan.

'And, anyway, the money was all going to charity,' piped up Indigo.

'All the more reason for settling for as much as we can,' smiled Julia.

'No, the point is,' said Jonathan, 'I want to spend more time doing . . . well, being with Indigo. And life's too short to sit around in court.'

'I'd be the one doing that,' said Julia confidently. 'You don't have to be in court, or even in London, just decide which charity you'd like to donate the cheque to.'

She saw Indigo take Jonathan's hand and shake her head. It was all too clear. Indigo, the pretty new wife, was calling the shots now. Julia had lost long before this meeting started, and for a moment she felt a bitter, childish grief – the wonderful party where she was going to shine had been called off.

'I'm sorry, Julia,' said Jonathan. 'I'd have loved to see you in court. It was a performance I'd have enjoyed. I'm sorry for both our sakes. But there are things that are more important.'

'Isn't this important? The principle, at least?' asked Julia, making one last effort. 'Truth, treating people with respect, valuing hard work. I remember you were quite clear about that earlier on. You wanted to be decisive, outspoken, tough –'

'And you,' interrupted Indigo, 'Julia, you are – you really are – all that. But the thing is . . .'

Julia looked at her as if a monkey had spoken, and braced herself for whatever nonsense she was going to have to listen to next.

'. . . the thing is, decisive can be dictatorial, outspoken can be, well, rude. And tough,' Indigo pursed her pretty lips, 'well, tough can be intransigent.'

Julia wondered whether Indigo had been rehearsing this put-down. It sounded like it.

But one thing was clear to Julia: she was not going to waste her time any longer. She had learned detachment in a hard school. When you lose, you put it behind you as fast as you can so as not to expend energy needed for the next battle.

With a warm smile on her well-trained face, she said, 'Don't worry, I'll wrap things up very quickly for you.' And, getting up to leave, she said what a pleasure it had been to meet Indigo, that she would speak to the lawyers at the film company right away. Then, on impulse, she turned to Indigo and said she would look out for her new fashion catalogue.

'It sounds gorgeous,' she gushed. 'But when you do the shoot, will you fly there – to Anguilla – with all the models, and make-up people and whatever else you need?'

Indigo looked at her blankly. 'Of course.'

'Of course,' echoed Julia.

'Whenever Indigo flies,' Jonathan explained, watching Julia guardedly, 'she always does the carbon off-setting thing, don't you, darling?'

'Oh, of course,' said Indigo. 'Of course.'

'Of course,' smiled Julia. And with that she hurried out on to the grey, December street and stood shivering in the damp air, looking for her driver.

She was hurt, and even more annoyed with herself for being so. She knew the score. Business was business. She need not have taken that cheap shot at Indigo. It was beneath her dignity to let that smug little hypocrite get to her. But what had Indigo said? That her decisiveness could be dictatorial? That her toughness . . . oh, what did it matter what the silly cow had said? She should not take these things personally. And yet.

To sit and listen to all her strengths being turned into weaknesses and not have the opportunity to answer back was unfair. If I had turned on you, thought Julia. Oh, to hell with Indigo. The point was, she would have won the case and it would have been fun. Fun, she thought, with a vague yearning. Fun.

Now she had to decide how to play this back with her colleagues.

Because this was undoubtedly a professional setback. She climbed into the car and asked her driver not to take her to the office, but back home. She would collect her thoughts in the peace and quiet, perhaps have a quick word with Phillip while making her calls, then head to work for her meeting at one.

Julia was fully aware that she and Phillip had barely spoken in days, and an anxiety that for weeks now had lain like a sleeping dog began to rouse itself and start worrying away at her once more. No, not now, she thought, pushing it back down. But she would definitely speak to Phillip – this very morning – and she began framing the conversation she would have with him. She would make him laugh. He would enjoy the nonsense of Indigo. And Jonathan. Her natural robustness began reasserting itself. So what that she had to settle, rather than enjoy a great victory? She would see the funny side and turn human absurdity to her advantage.

But when she got home Lillius, her housekeeper, said that Phillip had gone out. She did not know where. Julia tried his phone again but it was off. Where was he? However, Lillius told her, Anna was at home.

'Why isn't she at the magazine?' asked Julia, hurrying upstairs, wondering whether Anna was unwell. The door to Anna's room was shut – as usual.

'Anna,' called Julia, knocking gently. There was no response. 'Anna,' she said, more loudly. Still nothing. Julia was worried. It was so unlike her diligent daughter to take time off to sleep in the day. She opened the door carefully, so as not to wake her.

Then, from behind her, she heard Anna yell, 'Mum! What the hell are you doing?'

## 34

'What is it?' cried Julia, shocked at Anna's tone as she rushed out of the bathroom. Her daughter never spoke to her, or indeed to anyone, like this. 'Darling, are you all right?'

'I'm fine . . .'

But it was clear to Julia that her daughter was horrified to see her.

'. . . just fine,' Anna repeated, hurrying to close her bedroom door.

But from the threshold Julia glanced in. Lying on Anna's bed was a stunning emerald dress. 'That's gorgeous!' smiled Julia, stepping into the room to look at the dress properly. At last, she thought, Anna is starting to make the most of herself. She is learning something on that magazine, acquiring some style. 'You'll look lovely in that.' The deceptively simple cut and expensive colour would suit Anna's pale complexion. 'Really lovely and –'

Julia stopped short. Hanging from the picture rail were more brand-new clothes – at a glance, three coats, all beautiful and costly – and on the chair was a collection of silk and cashmere. All over the floor were flat-pack boxes and bubble wrap.

'All these clothes,' continued Julia. 'They're . . .' Wonderful, she thought. But suddenly Julia was uneasy. She had always assumed that Anna spent hours in her room reading, or something equally admirable. But Anna could not possibly afford such gorgeous garments. And even if she could, when would she wear them? 'What are you doing? I mean, whose are they?'

Dreadful suspicions began crowding in on her. Anna was always quiet and reserved but it occurred to her that she had been even more secretive of late. Julia told herself that was normal and desirable. An eighteen-year-old should have things she did not want to tell her mother. Julia never told her own mother anything from the age of about twelve.

Please tell me, thought Julia, these clothes are in aid of some man Anna's met. Despite her lecture to Rose the other night about not setting her sights on marriage, not looking to a man for answers, Anna was different. She could do with being taken out of herself, having her confidence lifted.

But instinct told Julia this wasn't about a man. It looked as if Anna was in the throes of packaging the clothes to put in the post.

'Darling,' she said, feeling the cold in the warm room and pulling her coat about her, 'what are you up to?'

Anna stalled. 'It's not like you to be home, Mum.'

'I'd a problem at work. But don't change the subject, just tell me what you're doing.'

Anna had prepared a story if she was found out. She would say she had been on a fashion shoot nearby and had been dropped off at home with the clothes as it was easier to cab them back to the designers from her place than lug them all into the office. It wasn't that plausible a story. But it was plausible enough. But now that Anna actually had to tell the lie, face to face, she could not. She was used to doing no wrong in her mother's eyes. Her diligence, her brilliance – these were qualities Julia revered and loved. But now her mother was standing there with worry and incomprehension on her face. Hacking into a computer was a piece of cake. But to look at her mother, so rigidly honest and upright, and not tell the truth was beyond her.

'Anna?' repeated Julia. Her daughter's expression now left Julia in no doubt that whatever Anna was up to, it was wrong. 'These clothes – they're not yours, are they?'

'Of course not. I'm not the beautiful daughter, remember,' said Anna, a sharp edge in her voice. Guilt and shame brought you down. But anger could be energizing. And Anna was angry – angry with herself because she had told herself that she would stop, that every computer she hacked was the last. It really was. She was going to post this final batch this morning. And then she was going to stop.

'You've not got some scam going on, have you?'

Slowly Anna clapped her hands. 'Well done, Mum! Very clever. You've worked it out!'

'Sweetheart, please! What exactly are you up to?'

With forced casualness, Anna shrugged. 'I hack into the designers' computers. I alter the inventory forms designers send out with the clothes so no one knows they've been lent to the magazine. And then I sell the clothes online. Simple as that.'

'Simple as that?' echoed Julia.

'Pretty much. The hacking takes a bit of effort, though I've got better at it.'

The strength seemed to leave Julia's legs. She sank down on the bed. 'But I don't understand.'

'I change the forms the designers send the magazine listing what they've given us. So if I want an emerald dress like that one, I delete it from their inventory and then –'

'No, not that. But why?' Julia put her face in her hands. 'You could go to prison for this,' she said, almost inaudibly.

For one awful moment Anna thought her mother might burst into tears, and she had never seen her mother cry. Her mother was supposed to be impregnable but she seemed to have aged ten years. Dear God, she begged. Don't let her cry. Make her strong like she always is. Not this dreadful diminishing, her voice fading away.

'My darling, why?' pleaded Julia.

'Because . . .' began Anna, horrified at her mother's tone. Never had she seen her so small and hurt, and this was like kicking a dog when it was down. If only her mother would get angry. Anger she could rise to.

'Because . . .'

Because it was a challenge at first, she wanted to cry, something to relieve the boredom. Because I want to be like everyone else and hang out with friends I like, rather than just pretend to like. Because I long for a man. Because I want some weirdo like Phoebe's father who barely even looks at me. Because I want to be pretty. Because.

'I did it because I could,' she said. 'And if people are stupid enough to leave their computers so accessible, what do they expect? Anyway, I get a buzz from it. The way you get a buzz from beating up someone in court. I mean, you're always going on about getting a thrill from being clever. Well, it's escaped me – till now. It's just a pain. And I don't drink, I don't do drugs the way half my so-called friends do, I don't . . . I don't do anything. Some people hack into government departments and broadcast secrets around the world. All I've done is get into a few clothes designers' systems. It's not that big a deal.'

Julia was at a loss. Her daughter had turned into a stranger who, with undeniable criminal intent, had deliberately set out to defraud and steal. Even her voice had changed – become coarse and lazy – and her face, lips upturned with a couldn't-care-less contempt.

'But you're so clever,' said Julia in desperation.

'So?'

'Your abilities, they're such a gift. You could have so much.'

Anna gave a grim laugh. 'The trouble with you, Mum, is you think that being clever makes you happy, that life is like arithmetic, some simple equation. Put a certain amount into it and then you get a certain amount out. But guess what? A shock as it may be, you're wrong. Believe it or not, I'm unhappy.'

Julia knew Anna was not happy but had put that down to her age and her brilliance. She had assumed all that would change once Anna went to Cambridge and mixed with like-minded souls. She had not realized her daughter's misery ran so deep. And I should have realized, she thought. But that was still no excuse.

'What makes you think that being unhappy gives you special rights? Lots of people are unhappy, feel lonely, that no one likes them. But they don't steal. How much money have you made? Stolen, rather?'

'Not sure exactly.'

'Don't lie to me. Is that why you did it – for the money? You could make lots of money honestly and relatively easily. You must know that. With your brains you could make loads.'

'The thing is,' Anna said savagely, thinking this, at last, would rouse her mother into her usual self, 'I'm not like you. I don't want loads of money.'

Anna was right. The blood began mounting under Julia's white face.

'Do you have any idea,' said Julia, 'how hard some women work just to earn the money you and your privileged little friends squander on . . . I don't know . . . a couple of cappuccinos? The reality of their lives? They work all day – and not at the stimulating stuff you are lucky enough to do. They sit on tills in supermarkets, they stare at computers in stuffy offices. They get down on their knees cleaning other people's houses, and then clean their own homes in the sort of places you have never had to set foot in because I have made money – and made it honestly – because that's what I wanted to save you from. Because it's awful. And I know –'

'Here we go,' taunted Anna, having got the reaction she wanted, 'your dreadful childhood.'

'That's unfair, and you know it.'

Anna did know it. She was being cruel and monstrous. Her mother never went into much detail about her childhood, though Anna wished she would. But at least this was the mother she knew, fighting back.

'And Mum, you're always going on that these job placements my friends and I do for no money are an exploitation of a whole generation, just slave labour of young people. So I'm turning the tables and exploiting them instead.'

'Don't flatter yourself. What you're doing is straightforward theft.'

Anna gulped, then she took a line she knew would enrage her mother yet more. 'Do you have any idea what happens to the people who make these clothes? The factories children work in? The dyes and all that toxic stuff thrown into rivers?'

'Don't you dare,' interrupted Julia, so furious it was all she could do not to slap her daughter's face. 'Don't you dare justify what you have done on those grounds, that because they do wrong you can too. And how can you be so . . . so naive? Do you think if those children were not making those clothes and being paid a pittance they would be at school, learning to read and write? They'd be starving. If they hadn't been sold off into prostitution. For God's sake, Anna, I thought you were more intelligent. If you really care, go and earn some money and build a school, go and . . . I don't know . . . go and help your father with all his charity stuff. Oh God, your father . . . this is going to break his heart.'

And with the thought of her father's distress Anna's hostile, unrepentant pose broke down. 'No, Mum, no. Please, don't tell him. Mum, please, anything. I'll give the money back. I haven't spent it. I promise. But not Dad. I beg of you. Oh Mum.'

'But I have to tell him,' said Julia. I need to, she thought. I need him. I need to talk about this.

'But Mum, you're right. It'll break his heart, please.'

'Then why didn't you think of that before?'

'I don't know. I was stupid.'

'But you're not. That's the point. You're so clever. Much cleverer than me. Even down to hacking into a computer. I wouldn't know where to start.'

'I could teach you.'

'No! For God's sake, have you learned nothing?'

'That was a joke, Mum!' And with that Anna was the one who burst into tears.

Julia watched Anna's thin shoulders heaving. Instinctively, Julia lifted her arms to hold her, but then stood still, as if embracing a ghost.

'I can't forgive you for this,' she said, letting her arms fall to her side. Her love was too laced with rage and disappointment for her to move. 'I can't. The dishonesty, the deceit, the arrogance, what this will do to your father.'

'Mum, please, I know. I'm sorry. Really. I'll pay it all back. I promise. I will. I can. It won't be difficult. I spread it all around, so it can't be traced. And it's all there. I've not spent a penny.'

'How much are we talking about here? And don't you dare lie to me this time. How much?'

'My university fees are paid for.'

'All three years?'

Anna nodded. 'And I could afford a PhD if I wanted.'

Julia was appalled. 'That much? How long have you been doing this?'

'About six weeks.'

'And you made all that in just six weeks?'

'Yes. But Dad, that's the one thing, I beg you. Please, don't tell him. That I could not bear. Mum, please!'

Julia hated the idea of having secrets from Phillip. They had their differences but she thought of themselves as so open and honest.

'Mum, I beg you. I know I've done wrong. But not Dad – think how it will hurt him.'

'Of course it will. To learn that his precious daughter is some high-class shoplifter.'

*Some high-class shoplifter.* Occasionally, Julia wondered how she would have raised the money if she had had to pay for herself to go to university. Or rather, she had a pretty good idea what she would have resorted to, and it was not a happy thought. But she had spared her daughter all those worries, those experiences, those memories that would dog you later in life.

'Mum, I do know what you've done for me,' cried Anna. 'I do. How hard things would be, if you weren't so generous. But please, Mum. Not Dad.'

Julia desperately wanted to tell him, to talk it through. But Anna was right. He would be devastated. 'All right, I won't tell him,' she said fiercely. 'But it's for his sake – not yours. Do you understand that?'

'Mum, thank you,' Anna was sobbing. 'Thank you.'

Julia had nothing to say. She felt voiceless and helpless. She could never have expected this in a thousand years. Was Anna really so unhappy? When she was young she had always been awkward with children her own age, preferring the company of adults. But now that Anna was older, Julia thought life was getting easier for her.

Oh God, cried Julia inwardly, how wrong have I been?

## 35

It was eleven in the morning and still Venetia had not got up. But she had a vital job to do. Now. And she could not afford to delay much longer. All night her conversation with Laura and the twins had played in her head. Couched in childish language, advice she had meant for her seven-year-old grandchildren had brought home the nature of her loathing for her husband. 'You have to be quite an incredible person,' she had said, 'not to let feeling rotten change you, make you cross and bad-tempered. So if someone who's ill behaves badly, tell yourself it's not them, it's their nasty illness.'

Lying in bed, unable to escape her own words, her lulled and drugged reason had begun to reassert itself. She had been obsessed with showing her husband up as a fraud. But during the long night, when she was able to think of something other than her own pain, she had demanded of herself, who am I to judge and punish him? What sort of monster have I allowed myself to become?

Body and spirit, Father Eoghan had reminded her the other day, are so profoundly connected they cannot work alone. Maybe a saint can love in dreadful pain and frustration, in the freezing cold on an empty stomach. But most of us can't. And trying to find a comfortable position in which to lie during the interminable dark December nights, the simple, awful fact was clear – malignancy had crept into her mind and warped all her goodness. Illness had so diminished her she was nothing but rage and revenge. If she did not want to die this vindictive woman, she had to act. And soon. To free herself of this hatred, she had to lie to her husband. Again. She had to tell Patrick that she had only just learned she was dying.

And he will believe me, she thought, as slowly, trying not to retch, she heaved herself up off the bed. They all will – the children too.

For years I have lived the lie of a loving wife and none of them have ever doubted me. There is no reason why they should start now. And she forced herself downstairs, out across the drear, lifeless garden to her husband's vast, brilliantly lit studio.

Patrick was engrossed in a portrait of some actress Venetia vaguely recognized. He doesn't even know I'm here, she began railing with familiar bitterness, then stopped herself. She was here to make peace.

'Patrick,' she began.

'Oh, hello,' he said, in surprise. 'Everything all right?' he asked, returning to the painting.

Venetia looked at his back. He's getting a stoop, she thought. He, too, is mortal. Then she forced herself to speak loudly. But her voice just came out in a hoarse whisper. 'No, it's not all right.'

'Oh darling,' he said, concentrating on the actress's nose – plastic-surgeon job, thought Venetia. 'Just a minute. I'm right in the middle . . . can't it wait?'

'No. This is important. It won't take long,' she said, failing to remove the sarcasm in her voice.

'But I'm almost finished, and if I leave it now . . . I really am busy.'

This, thought Venetia, is the story of my married life. In one sentence. You are always too busy. But she had got this far. She would get his attention.

She took a deep breath and then she shrieked, 'For God's sake, Patrick, listen to me!'

Venetia never shouted. In fact, she still prided herself on never having raised her voice to her children. It was always Patrick who bawled his head off. Not her. But, she thought, there is a lot to be said for it.

'Listen! For once in your self-important, self-obsessed fucking life, listen! I'm ill. I'm very ill. In fact, I'm dying.'

The effect on Patrick was devastating. He began shuddering uncontrollably, dropping his brush on the floor. 'Sorry,' he said in a terrified voice, a little boy again, back in the orphanage with a black-cassocked Brother yelling at him. He stood hesitating, looking at her as if he needed her to tell him what to do, whether he should pick up the brush.

Venetia was horrified. She had never known she had such power. 'Patrick, please. It's all right. Leave the brush. Here,' she said, picking it up for him and putting it on the easel. 'It's fine. Please. Come and sit down.'

With a meekness she had never even suspected he possessed, he followed her and he sat down on one end of the sofa and she on the other.

'Sorry, sorry . . .'

'Patrick, stop, you don't have to say sorry. Patrick, please. Just listen.' She tried to take his hands but he had clamped them together.

Thank God she had not exacted revenge on this lamentable creature, shaking before her. Thank God, she thought, with a gratitude she had not known in a long time.

'I . . . Patrick, darling, I'm very ill,' she tried again. 'It's cancer and it's spread. Everywhere. I'd no idea. No one did. But I'm . . . I've only just found out – just yesterday. Just yesterday,' she repeated, emphasizing the lie, 'yesterday afternoon, that I'm dying.'

'No! Oh my dearest, dearest.' He never called her his dearest. He fumbled for her hand. Nor did he hold her. 'You can't . . . no.' Tears were falling down his cheeks. And she had never seen him cry. Never. 'Oh God! Tell me it's not true. Tell me.'

'It's true.'

'But . . .' He choked in trying to speak. 'Are you sure? What about other doctors? What about –?'

'No,' she interrupted him.

'But there are second opinions. They get it wrong.'

'Patrick.' She forced herself on. 'Listen to me. They say nothing can be done. They say six weeks.'

'No! No!' he cried, his great man's body racked with sobs like a despairing child.

Venetia knew Patrick would be distressed. She did not underplay her importance to him that much. And death – when you learned it was going to knock at your own door, and soon – was always shocking and cruel. But she had not expected him to act so out of character.

'You mustn't . . . you mustn't take it so hard. Patrick, please. I've had a wonderful life. I've had . . .' Her litany of complaints and sorrows all disappeared in the face of this man looking at her so desperately.

'Why didn't you tell me before?'

She could no more have reminded him that she had tried, but he was too busy, than have kicked a child. 'There was nothing to tell. I didn't think it was anything,' she insisted, with a calm she was not feeling. 'Just a bit of pain, you know, I ignored it.'

'Pain? Is it bad? I mean, the pain? Now?'

'No, no, not so bad. And it passes. I've been lucky.'

'Can they give you anything?'

'Of course. And really, it doesn't hurt too much at all,' she lied. 'It's so advanced now, the way they manage pain, truly . . .' she trailed off.

'But why?' he pressed on. 'Why didn't you tell me?'

'I only found out yesterday,' she repeated, as if it was a mantra.

'But I could have gone with you – to the doctor's, you must have had tests. I could have been there for you,' he insisted. 'You'd have been there for me, if I'd been ill. You always are. Always. For everything. I can't do anything without you. I mean . . . none of this . . . my work. I couldn't do it without you.'

'Of course you could,' she smiled, not believing him for one second but treating him like the damaged, frightened children she was so good with through her work. 'You were painting long before me. And you'll carry on doing so. You don't need me for that.' She could not say that he barely noticed she was there most of the time. But instead, clutching at the practical and prosaic, she explained, 'As little as possible will change. Josie will stay on and run everything. Your home. Your daily routine. I'll make sure of that. And you'll be all right. You must paint and carry on painting, and that will give you comfort.'

He looked at her blankly. 'What on earth do you mean?'

'Just,' she explained once more, 'that nothing will have changed in that you can still do your work.'

'Nothing will have changed?' he repeated. Then, with a sadness she had never heard from him before, he said, 'Everything's changed.' And he went to his desk, picked up a great pair of scissors and, with one sudden movement, slashed through the portrait he had been working on.

'Patrick!' But no sound came out. Suddenly she was frightened. He had a dreadful temper. But he was never violent – not physically. At least she had never seen him so. But now . . . this was madness. He held the scissors aloft once more and cut through the painting again.

'Stop!' she cried. But he wouldn't listen. She made herself approach him. What did it really matter if he turned the scissors on her? But as she placed her hand on his arm, he dropped them.

'There's no point now. In this . . . all this,' he said, gesturing around at his work.

'Of course there is. More than ever.'

'All that matters is you.'

'But you can still paint. You must. I mean, that's what you do.'

He shook his head. 'Not without you. You made it great.'

She was not sure what he meant, but she said, 'That's not so.'

He was not listening. 'You never needed me,' he went on. 'Never. Not even when you've had the worst news you can have. It's always been one-way. Even when you're dying.'

'But I have needed you.'

'Then why didn't you say?' he cried plaintively.

'Because . . . but I do need you.'

'You don't get it? Do you?' And he clutched at his head, wrenching his hair. 'I can't paint without you. Don't you see? It's you I paint.' He pointed at the painting he had ripped in half. 'That's you.'

Don't be absurd, she was thinking. That luscious, vain woman isn't me. I'm wrinkled and withered and haggard. And I am dying.

Then he said, so gently she could barely hear, 'The best bit is you. It's always you. Look,' he said, taking her by the shoulders and standing her in front of the torn picture. 'Look!'

'Patrick, please, you're hurting me.' His fingers were digging into her shoulders and her skin now was so sensitive the slightest pressure was painful.

'Sorry, sorry. But look.'

She stared at what was left of the portrait. It meant nothing to her.

'Who is she?'

'What's it matter who she is?' he cried in desperation. 'Don't you remember?' he began, trying to compose himself but only gripping her tighter. 'That first night in the hotel – you and me. There were those roses in your hair – pink ones.'

How could she forget one of the most pitiful images of her life?

'I remember. But please, let me go.'

'You were so perfect. And I'd seen that perfection violated.'

For a moment she thought he was going to sob again. But instead, he turned cold.

'I saw,' he said, letting go of her now, 'too much. But you, you were untouchable. I could not touch you. Don't you understand? Your beauty –'

'I was never beautiful. Not like so many of those girls.'

He ignored her. 'To me you were so open and innocent and the picture of love. And I could not. I couldn't . . . I'm sorry, Venetia.' He sank down on the sofa and closed his eyes. 'I'm so sorry, but don't you see? You are what I paint. Because I'd never seen anything so lovely and so vulnerable and so . . . so . . . innocent. Or when I had seen it before . . .' He got up and walked away to the window and stood with his back to her. 'I saw it destroyed. But that night with you . . . it's always with me. And that's what I paint, over and over. Your fragility, your – I don't know – your beauty, your innocence. Not all those exasperating celebrities. No, that's not fair, some are all right but . . . Don't you get it? What people like about my paintings is the way I paint you in all of them.'

She was completely lost now. 'I don't understand.'

'It's not the wrinkles, or the texture of the skin or their maddening personalities that I paint. Any decent technician can do that. It's what I saw in you that day. The beauty of all that love. I mean, don't you understand why people like my work? Why I'm . . . why I'm great, Venetia? Why I'm bloody great? It's because I can paint that love – that love you had for me. I remember you lying there, so intensely alive. And my whole life I have wanted to capture that life and love and . . . and I do. Don't you see?'

'But,' she blurted out, 'how was I to know?'

'How could you not know?'

'Because you never said!'

'Then what do you think all this is about?' he cried, picking up a paintbrush and hurling it across the floor. 'I don't see you getting . . . well, getting . . .'

'Old? Ugly and horrible?'

'No, no! When I look at you –'

'But you never look at me!'

'Of course I do. For God's sake! And I see your . . . I don't know . . . your spirit,' he said, latching on to the word. 'The beauty of your spirit, and that's what I always see – that wonderful loving girl – whatever age does to you. Those first pictures, "Venetia Reading", they were better than anything I'd ever done before. That was what made everything take off.'

'Yes, but . . .' They are only pictures, she wanted to say. 'But I didn't know. How could I? Why did you never tell me?'

'I do. All the time. In the pictures. I don't do words, I can't. You know that.'

Venetia said nothing, but if ever unseen hands were looking after her, they were that morning. She forgot the waste and the loss and the unnecessary unhappiness that all stemmed from the misunderstanding of her husband and her marriage. Instead, she simply thought, he loves me, he loves me.

And with that overwhelming glimpse of human happiness she dropped her face into her hands and cried.

## 36

Phillip walked back to his car, parked outside Isabel West's block of flats. A sense of failure assailed him. He had brought pens, pencils, paper and paints for Isabel, doing everything properly, asking permission from Isabel's mother beforehand. But still it had gone wrong. Isabel, no doubt obeying orders, had been outwardly polite and thanked him as she sat opening up bag after bag of expensive brushes and beautiful oils. But he also heard her mutter, 'There's too much.'

And as he sat in their overcrowded room, Phillip realized she was right. There was not even space to store the stuff, let alone use it.

But what was he supposed to do? You hear a cry for help. Then what? He could pay for Isabel to have art lessons, pay for some care for the mother. But that seemed too intrusive, an even clumsier attempt to salve his own conscience.

He drove off into the evening rush hour. He would like to stop a moment, and talk to Laura. He buried that thought immediately. He would call Julia. But she had made her views quite clear on how much help he could be to Isabel. She would only say that she had been proved right about his middle-class philanthropy. Anyway, he had phone calls and emails to deal with. But his thoughts returned to Laura.

Phillip had never really had women friends. He had never wanted them because most of his adult life he had had Julia. But Julia was so busy and Laura was easy to talk to. Yet with that temper of hers, she was also the sort of woman a man could let himself go with.

His phone rang. He did not answer it but listened to the message, a follow-up from his meeting with the prison board. That morning they had made a decision to install new showers for inmates but now the prison officers were up in arms because nothing was being done about their showers, so he would have to go back and appease their demands all over again.

His head was hurting. He opened the car window and the breeze eased the dull ache. I'm just tired, he thought. Not long ago, he had loved his new work and it had energized him. But what good was he doing now? Spending half a day talking about showers? Perhaps he should have kept his advertising business, just made the money and paid for the damned shower block himself. That might have been more use, and he could have spared himself all that endless negotiation.

As he let himself into the house he realized that Julia, unusually, was home and he could hear raised voices from the kitchen, his wife and daughters, all yelling at one another. For a fleeting moment all he wanted to do was turn and run. That he should feel that way about the people he loved most in the world, almost a stranger in his own home, frightened him. And that fear propelled him into the kitchen full of smiles.

'Darlings!'

'Oh, hello,' said Julia, barely glancing at him.

'Dad,' said Anna, not looking up from the *Guardian* crossword.

At least Rose came up to him and slipped her arm through his.

'Don't think you can get round your father,' said Julia to Rose. 'I've said no.'

'What's the problem?' he asked, kissing Rose on the top of her golden head.

'A pair of shoes,' explained Julia, 'that I'm not buying for Rose.'

'I don't want you to buy them. I want you to let me earn my own money,' protested Rose.

'Listen to your mother,' said Phillip, as Rose extricated her arm. 'But . . .'

'Where've you been?' asked Julia, ignoring Rose.

Phillip hesitated. He did not want to tell Julia that he had been on the Hartley Estate to see Isabel. He knew what sort of response that would elicit.

But Julia's question was purely rhetorical. 'I must hurry,' she was saying. 'Lillius has left some stew or other in the fridge for you to heat up.'

Phillip felt a flash of anger. I am not, he thought, some family pet who just needs to be fed to be kept happy. But Julia looked so grim and exhausted, he contained his irritation and made himself walk over and kiss her cheek. 'I didn't think you'd be home so early,' he said, squeezing her hand.

'I'm not here for long,' she said. 'I've got to rush.'

He held her hand more tightly and noticed she was wearing the plain white-gold bracelet he had given her when Anna was born. That seemed a century ago. Then, if either of them had been troubled, they could help one another. But now? If she was feeling as low as he was, their duty, surely, was to comfort each other. And that duty could be a joy. But these days he was at a loss to know how to reach her. She looked so unhappy, he wondered what resentments and reproaches she held against him. Perhaps it was a good job they saw so little of each other. Perhaps their busy, separate lives had covered up essential differences that they were too preoccupied to notice. If she gave him more time, might that even make things worse?

But he could not countenance that thought. 'Do you have to go?'

'Of course I do.' She looked at him uncomprehendingly and retrieved her hand. 'I told you this morning. Remember? I've got to meet the new CEO at Clifford James.'

'Oh God, yes, sorry, I forgot. Well, have a good time.' She rolled her eyes and he corrected himself. 'Well, as good as possible.' He made one final effort. 'I remember giving you that,' he said, fingering the bracelet on Julia's wrist. He noticed Anna glance up and catch her mother's eye. Anna seemed as unhappy and shattered as her mother. What was wrong with them all?

'That was a long time ago,' said Julia. Then, to Phillip's surprise, Julia turned on Anna, who now had her head down again in what he could only describe as some complicated sort of Sudoku thing. 'For God's sake, Anna, can't you do something more constructive than those stupid puzzles?'

Julia never spoke to Anna like this. But – equally surprising – Anna did not retaliate. She just put down her paper and went to the fridge and asked, 'Do you want me to put your dinner on, Dad?'

'No!' What was this insistence on feeding him? 'I mean, no thank you, darling. Good God, what's the matter with you all tonight?'

'Mum's in a bad mood,' snarled Rose, 'because that case of hers with Jonathan Branson has fallen through and she thought she was going to be on the *Ten O'Clock News* and be all starry and generally show off and now she can't. So now she knows how I feel about not being allowed to go on that show, and it serves her right. She gets all holier-than-thou about me wanting to go on telly but it's all right for her –'

'For God's sake, Rose,' interrupted Anna before Julia herself could put her down, 'it's not all about you.'

'Oh darling,' said Phillip, 'I'm sorry. What happened? I know you were enjoying the case.'

'It's nothing,' lied Julia. 'Really, he was a pain to deal with. And the new wife's even worse. And there was no money to speak of.'

'Is it the wife's fault you've been ousted?' asked Rose with a hint of malice.

'I've not been ousted.'

Rose gave a hollow laugh. 'So much for the sisterhood.'

'Don't be ridiculous, Rose. And talking of money, it's not simply the cost of those stupid shoes I object to.'

'But I want to earn the money myself.'

'Not by modelling. And what I don't understand is why you want shoes everybody else has. It's naff to be really fashionable, to follow it slavishly like some idiot. Any fool can go to a shop and write a cheque for what they've been told to buy. But someone as clever and pretty as you should be making their own style, if that's all you care about, which it seems to me you do.'

Rose glared hard, to stop herself bursting into tears. This is what was so annoying about her mother. Sometimes she could be right. It was naff to want these shoes. Oh, to hell with her.

'Ease up,' murmured Phillip in Julia's ear.

'Okay, okay. But I'd better go. And I've got to work when I get back. Did you have a good day?'

'Fine.'

'Where've you been?' she said, glancing at her watch.

He mentioned the meeting at the prison.

'Prison?' muttered Julia with a pointed look at Anna.

'Mum!' cried Anna. 'You'll be late, you must go.' Julia stared hard at Anna but said nothing. She went out to her waiting cab.

'I'd better go too,' said Anna.

'Where are you off to?' asked Phillip.

'Phoebe's.'

'I didn't think you really liked Phoebe.'

'I don't.'

'Then why?'

Anna shrugged. 'It's something to do.'

'She's not going to see Phoebe,' said Rose. 'She's going to see Phoebe's dad.'

'Why?' asked Phillip, suddenly alarmed. 'What on earth for? I mean, make sure he behaves himself.'

'Don't be gross,' cried Rose.

'For God's sake, Dad,' said Anna, who also looked as if she, too, might be on the verge of tears.

'All right, all right,' said Phillip. 'But what are you seeing him for?'

'Because he's explaining something to me. And I'm not seeing him – well, him specifically. Phoebe invited me for dinner and her dad's going to be there. It is his house.'

'But what do you need explaining? Especially by him.'

'Something about turbulence, of course. What do you think? That's his speciality. You know that.'

'Yes, of course, but . . .' He felt completely out of touch with his family. Had it always been like this? Or had he changed? Had they? 'Does your mother know about this?'

'Of course. And she's delighted I'm doing what she calls "proper work". Oh, for God's sake, Dad, what are you in a state about?'

'It's just . . .' A new thought crossed his mind. 'You're not worried about Cambridge, are you? Keeping up? Because you mustn't be. You don't need to start doing lots of maths work. Really, you're more than capable. This is a time for you to be . . .' Having fun with people your own age, is what he wanted to say. But to say that to Anna was like asking a fish to fly. 'Oh darling, I just mean . . . oh, never mind. I don't know what I'm saying. I've got a bit of a headache.'

'From that fall?' asked Anna, suddenly anxious.

'No, no. Maybe just a bit of bruising, that's all. But turbulence,' he ventured, 'it always sounds so interesting. Is it?'

Anna nodded.

'I mean, I've never understood quite how you study it. I mean, what the concepts are. Where you begin, even.'

'Oh please, Dad, you wouldn't understand, it's terribly complex. Really.'

'All right, I just wondered.'

'Sorry, Dad, sorry. It would take ages to explain. But if you really want,' she said, 'maybe over Christmas I'll sit down with you and talk you through it.'

'That would be lovely, thank you.'

And with that she pecked him on the cheek and she, too, was gone.

'Well, it looks as if it's just you and me tonight,' he said to Rose. 'Shall I heat up that stew Lillius left us?'

'I'm going to Sophia's.'

'You, too, are leaving me?' It was pathetic, but he didn't want to be left alone.

'Sorry, Dad.'

'You know if Sophia's mother asks you about modelling what the answer is. You can't.'

'Don't, Dad . . . don't start on that any more.'

'All right.'

'But Dad.'

'What?'

'I do worry about money.'

'Darling, that's my job and your mother's.'

'Don't patronize me. I'm serious.'

'I know. But Rose, I made . . . I made a great deal of money. Truly, you don't have to worry.'

'But I want to earn my own. And don't say I don't need to. Because things change – you just don't know what's going to happen. You might need my money, and when I say that to Mum she won't listen as she just thinks she's invincible and will always earn a packet.'

'I don't think that's quite true.'

'It is. She thinks that all she has to do in life is work and everything will be just fine. But Dad, bad things happen. And I can help.'

'When we need your help, I'll ask for it, I promise. Now,' he said, to change the subject, 'how are you getting to Sophia's?'

'Well . . . I could get the bus,' she said with a questioning lilt.

Phillip recognized the cue. 'Do you want a lift?'

'Oh Dad, thank you.'

'Now come on, hurry up,' he said, relieved he had an excuse not to sit in the house on his own. Sophia's home, he recalled, was near Laura's. Perhaps he could drop in on Laura afterwards. The idea of sitting chatting with her again was suddenly very appealing. He had ended up having lunch at her home twice last week as he tried to choose a painting.

His spirits lifted but then Rose said, 'You don't mind being on your own tonight, do you, Dad?'

Phillip simply had to say that he would not be alone as he was going to see Laura to choose a picture. It was perfectly innocent. But, looking into his daughter's lovely, open face, he at last acknowledged that there was nothing innocent in his desire for Laura's pictures. There might once have been. But not any more. The pictures were a pretext. I want, he understood with undeniable clarity, the pleasure of Laura's company, I want the pleasure of her . . .

What did he want? An affair?

Phillip's entire life, bright and beautiful women had stood in his path, available and willing. But he loved his wife, in his eyes more bright and beautiful than them all. He had not wanted the lovely, talented women with a canny eye on him – or what he could do for their brilliant careers – or rather, working late in the office, alone with some leggy young woman discussing the artwork, he decided he wanted the damage and destruction of an affair even less.

Phillip had friends and colleagues for whom the only question in an affair was, can I get away with it? They told themselves their wives never found out, or that they accepted the affairs and no real harm was done. But in an affair, Phillip believed, someone was always being deluded and that meant someone was always being hurt. And the hurt was not worth it. What he had with Julia and his daughters was too precious to jeopardize. So he resisted suggestions of after-work drinks *à deux*. Love and trust steadily built up over years and years, he told himself, were too dear to put in such danger.

But he saw himself sitting in Laura's kitchen. Laura who was so slow to smile, so at sea, so thwarted in her work, so appallingly dressed, so tough on him, so hot-tempered. Laura, who was also so very soft and tender, had taken him by surprise. With Laura he felt alive. With Laura he could be himself. With Laura . . . He hesitated. Questions began clawing at him because, with Laura, what was he thinking? What had actually happened? What were their arguments, their chats, their discussions on painting really all about? What were they, in fact, negotiating? Had he, without knowing or courting it, fallen for her?

All the signs were there. Right now he wanted nothing more than to pitch himself into her arms and into her life, but that desire only made him profoundly sad. Because what did that reveal about the life he now had and had worked so hard to create?

No, realized Phillip, he did not want an affair. If only. What he wanted was a different life. When he thought of Laura he wanted to be with her, in her home, her bed. He wanted to discover everything about her. He wanted that intimacy, and that knowledge was so subversive, so dangerous to the family he loved, he almost doubled over with the pain.

'Dad?'

Phillip could not lie to his beautiful daughter and say that he intended seeing Laura in order to choose one of her pictures. Nor could he lie to himself. Instead, he said, 'Sweetheart, of course I'll be fine on my own. I've got loads of work to get through.'

So Phillip took Rose to her friend's house and then he returned directly home and sat at his desk until ten o'clock. Then he attempted to eat the hard, dried-out stew that he had left heating up too long. He poured himself a beer, wishing he liked football and might escape in front of the television watching sport. But instead, he stared at the whorls in the wooden kitchen table that he and Julia had bought shortly after Rose was born. At the time he had loved the idea that the table would become part of their family history – birthday parties, Christmases, celebrations and tragedies would all be played out sitting around that table. They had found it in an antiques shop outside Cambridge and Phillip had also wanted to buy what he thought was a beautiful green jug, but Julia had dissuaded him as she said they already had more than enough clutter.

The jug, like so much of the stuff in the shop, was from a house clearance and it had distressed him to think of this lovely object just being discarded. It occurred to him now that it was the sort of thing that would appeal to Laura. He rested his head down. You are born, he thought, you go to school, get married, make a home and fill it with things and, before you know it, you die and all those things you have worked so hard for and have cherished are just chucked away.

He got up and put his plate in the dishwasher, his head aching, and he hoped he might be sickening for something as that might explain why his marriage looked so bleak. Illness always brought you down. Perhaps it was as simple as that, and for a moment he clutched at that thought.

Phillip had always liked being married and, more importantly, he believed in marriage. At his wedding, the vicar had likened marriage to the great copper beech tree that stood in the far corner of the churchyard. The tree had been struck by lightning; gales had wrenched away great overhanging branches; nails had been hammered deep into its trunk to prop up fences; fungi, beetles, woodlice, owls, ants had all used the tree for their own purposes. But instead of being brought down by these assaults, the tree had enriched itself through all the scars of its history and was beautiful. Marriage could be the same. Absorb the hard times – which no marriage escapes – and with maturity and wisdom you could create something enduring and glorious.

The vicar was right, of course, but sitting in his empty kitchen the plain fact was that Phillip felt redundant – to his wife, to his daughters – and it was bitterly hard to feel this way. Yet he was expected to endure it.

Other people – hundreds, thousands, millions – had, of course, despaired of their marriages. A man like his father would pray for guidance and strength. But that was not an option for Phillip. His faith was such a half-hearted, broken little thing, he was ashamed of it. He could not turn to it now. But he could turn to his desk.

As we grow older, he thought grimly, making his way back to his study, we acquire techniques to help us through the bleak days. And he had his work, the way others might have golf or gardens. Or, of course, he could turn to Laura. But, thank God, she had never shown any sign of interest in him. Thank God, he thought, though fully aware of his weakness – the choice was being denied him, so he could take no credit for not taking it further.

What he would do, he decided, was go round to her house tomorrow and buy both pictures so he could not be accused of letting her down. And that could be done in five minutes and he could just give them away, not keep them at home. Thereafter, he would not have cups of coffee with her, talk meaningfully about hopes and ambitions and all that nonsense. He would just chat politely at the school gates and the odd governors' meeting. And that would be the end of it.

## 37

Early the following morning Anna was the first in the office. She was sorting shoes. The work suited her oversensitized mind because from the hour her mother had discovered that she was stealing from the magazine, Anna had been afraid – and if she kept focused on the mundane and monotonous, she could keep the fear at bay.

No matter that the worst was over. Her mother had found out, but no one else. Though that was not the point. The point was, if she could exercise her brain – and she had not even exercised it that hard – to do what could land her in gaol, as her mother had hammered home, what else might she be capable of? What if she really tried? And that was terrifying.

But I have Cambridge, she reminded herself yet again, boxing up the last of the shoes and starting on the swimwear. More maths would keep her occupied on nice straight lines. But she was growing weary of maths. She did not want to spend three years exploring abstract patterns in an academic sect only to . . . to do what? Teach? Research? But what else was she fitted for? she thought, trying to find the other half to a gold-mesh bikini top. Going out into the big world and . . . she had no idea. Because she would look about her at the way others led their lives and wonder, who would she like to be?

The phone rang. Anna was required in the editor's office – this very minute. She froze. She had been discovered. She knew it. The police would be there. She would be arrested, put in handcuffs, her cleverness irrelevant, her life over. 'Mum!' she whispered, her heels clacking as she walked down the corridor, suddenly desperate for her mother.

But instead of accusing her of theft, the editor simply told her to hurry up and find something decent to wear from the fashion cupboard as she was honouring Anna with an invitation to breakfast in the boardroom and Anna needed to be there in five minutes.

'Oh, thank you, thank you,' Anna found herself babbling.

She could have wept with relief. She would never do wrong again. She would find a good way to live. She would! She would not let her mother down again. Or herself. And this was the most propitious opportunity.

The editor's monthly breakfasts were legendary, invitations reserved for idols and icons, one of whom, a best-selling novelist, had cancelled at the last minute, fog-bound in Rome, and Anna was to fill the empty chair. No matter that the editor's secretary made it clear Anna had only been asked because no one else was in the office as early as a quarter to eight. Anna didn't care. What she needed in her life right now was inspiration and direction. And that was the purpose of these breakfasts. The contemporary elite were brought together to bounce ideas, to discuss and debate.

I will learn from them, Anna insisted to herself, see how they have used their gifts to do good. Unlike me, she thought, riffling through the fashion cupboard for the perfect outfit. But I will listen, drink in all their wisdom and experience, she gushed for the first time in her life, unpacking a pair of high heels she had just boxed up. I will no longer indulge in this self-pitying teenage angst and despair. I will find a way of weaving together a fulfilling life, she urged herself, tottering upstairs into the boardroom.

She hovered at the door. Actually seeing these movers and shakers in their flesh and blood made her hesitate.

Such hair! Such teeth! Such heavenly dresses – plain but clinging, exercises in mathematical precision, engineered to display honed bodies and honeyed skin. Such an incredible sense of well-being in the long elegant room with views of the London skyline, exotic parrot tulips spilling from Clarice Cliff bowls, antique porcelain platters of ethically farmed mango, papaya, goji berries.

Expectation was in the air. Who will I meet? Who will I sit next to at this long table, so polished you could almost see everyone's reflection, all gleaming and dazzling with the silver and glass?

There was a flurry of kissing, delighted greetings.

'How lovely to meet you . . .' New contacts, old friends. 'You do look gorgeous . . . I loved the book . . . the speech . . . the shoes . . . the film.'

Waiters circled the room, dispensing tea, coffee, decaffeinated, herbal, lapsang, champagne . . . Anna smoothed down her borrowed white dress and hurriedly took her place. Anonymous hands proffered her a plate of sushi. The man beside her, with a prosperous air of Harris tweed and expensive aftershave, boomed, 'Now who are you?' and introduced himself as the editor of an arts magazine.

Anna explained herself as the intern, the humblest of the humble.

'Well, if you ever want work experience with me – unpaid, I'm afraid – but that's the way things are,' he sighed. 'Send your CV to my secretary – I'll see what I can do.'

'Thank you, I wondered –' she began, about to ask him about an artist featured in his magazine but, with the slightest turn of his back, he was already giving his full attention to the grand BBC reporter opposite.

Anna turned to her other side, to a famously left-wing actor. But he was deep in conversation with an old Etonian friend of Prince William's about an orphanage in Africa. She caught the eye of the award-winning film director opposite and smiled at the woman who, stretching out her toned arm, said, 'Would you pass me the water, please?'

'Of course,' murmured Anna. 'I so enjoyed –' she ventured.

But Anna was beaten to it by a fashion designer saying how very important she found the director's latest movie, set in the slums of Calcutta, and the two were up and away discussing extremes of wealth and poverty in India.

Anna looked about her, turning left and right, right and left, searching for someone to speak to. A waiter asked if she would like poached eggs, scrambled, egg whites only.

'No, I'm fine, thank you,' she said, glancing down the table.

Croissants were being picked at, yogurts toyed with, teas sipped.

Anna concentrated on putting wild raspberry jam on her toast as, back and forth from the kitchen, waiters ferried salmon from the Outer Hebrides, Prince Charles's organic eggs, Suffolk apple juice.

'At the hospice . . . if we can only raise enough money . . . opening a new wing . . . granting opportunities . . .'

On and on they went, vigorous with their sympathy, awash with understanding. Then, from the highly photogenic human rights lawyer came a shift in conversation.

'Of course, I hate the idea of private school but you have to put your children first.'

'I know, I know. And with a job like mine – the hours I do.'

'So, though I'd have loved to send them to the local comprehensive, I simply couldn't.'

Heads nodded sadly, knowingly.

'Of course, of course.'

Then, from education it was a short jump to the cost of school fees and money and how to make it and how to keep it.

'I've got a wonderful guy in Zurich. He's saved me . . . well, I'm embarrassed to say . . . but it's a fortune.'

'I use a chap in London, as I never fly – if I can help it, that is. I got him from a mate of Tony Blair and he's brilliant.'

'But you give so much to charity.'

'As do you.'

'Thank you.' Self-congratulatory smiles. 'But there should be more financial help for creatives like us.'

'Good God, yes.'

'But what is the government going to do?'

And with that everyone turned to an MP, a 'face of the future' in politics.

'Jane, come on, tell us. You're in the know.'

The MP's lovely face – before becoming an MP she had been a children's television presenter – fell grave.

'In these hard times,' she began, trotting out the same pious line Anna had heard her give on *Question Time*, 'we all have to do our bit, shoulder the burden. It's the duty of you wealth-creators –'

Snorts of derision erupted.

'For God's sake. I've worked so hard for my money.'

'What about your promises on offshore investments?'

'Sometimes the reality of a situation –' persisted the MP.

'If you had any idea of where I grew up, what I suffered,' began a former rock star. 'How my poor parents . . .'

The editor put her hand on his, caressing and gentle, then murmured something for his ears alone, and at once he burst out laughing, altering the mood at the table.

'One of the reasons I wanted to see you all,' the editor continued, taking her guests off the chase of the floundering MP, 'is the magazine's tenth-birthday celebration.'

And with that politics and the poor were pushed to one side and they were up and away, discussing details of a party, conversations splitting again, the editor engineering the social process, smiling, listening, curving her neck in a magnificent gold choker, checking her illustrious guests were happy.

The actor on Anna's right got on to a particular hobby horse of his – press invasion of privacy.

'The way these newspapers just make up stories, distort the truth and get away with it. It's got to stop. Though I have to say, I did love that interview with me your editor ran last month,' he said, looking for the first time at Anna with his pale, insipid eyes. In the magazine his eyes had been airbrushed to an electrifying blue and there had been no mention of an unfortunate incident with a couple he met in Cambodia.

'I'm so glad you liked it,' said Anna, when there was a sudden screech of pain from the rock star as a waitress, having to stretch across his knees – he always sat in the lotus position to preserve his back – spilled coffee into his lap.

For a moment there was a vacuum of silence. Then it was filled by the rock star's voice. 'For Christ's sake, you stupid –!'

'Oh God!' said the editor, losing her poise for a moment.

'I'm so sorry,' spluttered the waitress.

'That bloody hurt! Jesus!'

A man dressed in a butler's uniform pushed forward, barging the woman aside. 'Sir, I'm sorry, sir, please,' he said, fluttering linen napkins about and hissing at the waitress, 'Get out!'

'Are you all right?' pressed the editor. 'I'm so sorry. We will, of course, pay for this to be dry-cleaned. Or reimburse you for a new suit.'

Then she leaned towards him with a soft thrust of her strong shoulders, whispered in his ear, and he bellowed a hearty laugh and they were smiling together once more. Everything was all right. Normal conversation resumed.

Anna sipped at her tea. She had one of her headaches starting. She could feel the throbbing beginning insidiously in her temples and wanted to take some painkillers before it got too intense. So, very quietly, she rose to her feet. Unnoticed, she left the room.

The waitress who had spilled the coffee was also in the Ladies.

'Are you okay?' asked Anna.

The woman did not speak, but Anna was sure she had been crying.

Anna rested her hot cheek on the cool mirror before taking her pills, then she forced herself to return to the boardroom. But in the corridor she saw the waitress being given an envelope and pushed towards the exit by a man who was clearly the boss.

Anna watched the money change hands and the woman head for the lifts.

Anna hurried towards the man. 'You're not firing her, are you? It was an accident.'

'Maybe, but we'll lose the contract if she does it again,' he said, turning his back and returning to the kitchen.

'But . . . but . . .'

But what? Anna was at a loss. Who was this woman? Anna just had a vague impression of a tired face, reddened hands, like millions of women. Not especially intelligent, always working for others, never knowing success.

What do I do? thought Anna. Protest on the woman's behalf? Run after her? But the woman had already gone.

So Anna went back to her seat at the table where a novelist was holding forth on how he loved Hampstead, the area where he lived, because of its social diversity until the editor began engaging everyone's attention with, 'This is Anna, everybody, one of our most talented interns. I'm told on good authority – my husband's . . .'

This prompted a friendly laugh.

'. . . Anna is a mathematical genius. We may have the next Turing in our midst. Or even Vorderman!'

More laughter.

'But seriously . . .'

The laughter died, faces were rearranged.

'. . . I'm fascinated by your views, Anna, how young people see the world.'

All eyes were upon Anna. She had never had an audience like this before, and they were smiling, welcoming. But they were also, she realized, looking to her for approval, for yet more congratulation and admiration for what they had done. How greedy were these people? They had everything, but they still needed to be told how great and good and wonderful they were. How, she wanted to demand, can you manage to be on such excellent terms with the ways of the world, extract so many of its delicious offerings, yet remain so blind to the contradictions of your own way of living?

For rather too long Anna said nothing, though she knew she should be singing for her place at this table, showing off her creativity, her originality.

'Come on, Anna.' The editor was insistent now. 'Don't hold back. Put us in our place, tell us where we've gone wrong and how your generation will put your talents to better use.'

Still Anna hesitated, acutely aware of the criminal use she had already made of her talents. But suddenly that seemed insignificant among all the hypocrisy and lies she'd heard that morning. These people took and took and yet they had no shame.

Very calmly, she stood up. And then, her headache easing, Anna gave voice to her own thoughts.

## 38

Laura sat in her kitchen looking at her finished portrait of Phillip's wife. She had taken a perverse pleasure in painting Julia Snowe. She had drawn her own picture in less than an hour but she had gone to real trouble over Julia.

The portrait was not great. She certainly was not her father's daughter in this respect. But she had, at least, captured the intelligence in Julia's light grey eyes, the erotic sway of her long black hair, the challenge in her smile. The evidence was before her: Julia was lovely, and she was not. Phillip was the sort of man who wanted a woman who had made her own way in the world with her wits and intelligence, who had carved out a great role for herself – like Julia, of course, Laura went on, thinking she might curb her infatuation for him with this sort of reasoning.

But her thoughts were pierced by the doorbell ringing and she went to the front door, expecting the postman with the girls' Christmas presents she had ordered online.

Instead, it was Phillip who, without even looking at her – and before she could say hello – rushed out, 'I was just passing, and I don't normally turn up at people's houses without warning. But I've decided. I would very much like to buy both of those pictures, please. Both. Please. And I must hurry. I really must.'

So this is it, she thought, taken aback by his abruptness. This is the end of this pathetic charade of mine.

'Fine, I mean, thank you,' she said, forcing a great smile on to her face. 'I'll get them. Come on in and wait there. Just there,' she added, to be sure he stayed in the hallway and did not see the portrait of Julia in the kitchen. 'They're just upstairs. I won't be a minute.'

But then her phone rang and, to give Laura some privacy as she talked, Phillip walked into her kitchen.

'Phillip!' Laura was too late. 'Please don't . . . Oh Mum, I'll ring you back.'

She raced after him, but he was already staring at the portrait of Julia.

'I . . .' she began, then stopped. She could feel her colour rising, her heart thumping oddly.

He turned to her and met her eye.

'But that's Julia,' he said. 'I mean, it's . . . well, you've got her in many ways. But . . . but why? I mean, why have you painted her?'

A number of options flitted through Laura's mind. She could attempt to save her pride by saying she was experimenting with portraits, drawing faces she had only seen a few times. She could spin a number of lines. But what was the point? End it now, she told herself. Let him know how you feel and he will run a mile and be out of your life for ever. The humiliation will pass. Pride recovers and this longing will end.

Crossing her arms, she told him the truth. 'This is to remind me why you go home. To your beautiful wife. So now go, please.'

He did not move.

'Please,' she repeated. 'Phillip, please . . . I told myself I just wanted you to come round to buy a picture. But I was lying. I wanted to see you. I like you. I like . . . I like talking to you.' But this was not really what she liked or how she felt. Be honest, she told herself. Anything is better than this pathetic, painful yearning. 'I like . . . I let . . .' She shrugged with embarrassment and, as though to undermine what she was saying, added 'I've let myself fall for you. And it's stupid. So now you know, and please will you go.'

Phillip's chest tightened. He had spent the night lying next to his wife, sleeping fitfully in her ironed linen shift, and he had thought about Laura. Some people, he knew, committed adultery because they enjoyed the excitement and there was no more to it than that. Others said they could not help themselves, that circumstances and emotions overwhelmed them. But Phillip was not interested in a cheap thrill and he could no more lose control than could Julia. If he stepped towards Laura and took her in his arms, he could not delude himself that he had got carried away, that he did not know what he was doing.

They stood an arm's length apart. One step and they would be together. When you are younger, you can flirt and tease, play to-ing and fro-ing, even if you are earnest about love. But reach a certain age and you know that time is limited, that the good things of life are all too rare and fleeting. For a moment of weakness Phillip wished his hand might be forced – that the phone would ring again, that Laura herself would turn her back – so he would not have to make the decision for himself and accept the responsibility.

But nothing happened.

On Laura's face was an expression that suggested she had just heard terrible news. And even if nothing ever happened, if he did just leave, Phillip knew that in some way a betrayal of his wife had already taken place. Certainly he had to sacrifice that fine image of himself as a man who had never once considered walking away from his family. What he felt now was not like being in the office, watching one of the designers lean over her work, her glossy hair parting, and wondering what it would be like to kiss the back of her neck. This was a moment of joy.

Laura had blown away his despair like a puff of smoke, and he was buoyed up with gratitude. To love someone and then hear you are loved in return changes your landscape utterly. Standing in Laura's kitchen, with the weak, wintry light filtering through the window, life was beautiful. But the beauty, Phillip was all too aware, would also bring its opposite. Being with Laura would mean hurt and heartache, and he would have to accept those consequences.

So he knew exactly what he was doing when he took a step forward, placed his arm around Laura's waist, drew her close, tilted back her head and kissed her in such a way that left her in no doubt that he felt every bit as strongly as she did.

Slowly, Laura put her arms around him too. She was conscious of his height, the warmth of his body, the way he pressed her into him. It's not real, she thought. And she wished she might make herself slender and lithe, like Julia, then he might not let her go. Because

I can't bear this to end, she thought. When it does, I am lost. And she shut her eyes, wanting to imprint every sensation on to her memory, terrified he would stop kissing her. But the closeness of this body she had desired so dearly suddenly was too much, and she opened her eyes. And if she needed any reminder of how grim and painful love with a married man could be, it was the sight of the picture of Julia. She made herself pull away.

'I could go, if you want,' said Phillip.

Laura felt on the brink of tears.

'But I think,' he went on, 'I've fallen in love with you too.'

'Yes,' she said, not sure whether she was overjoyed or devastated. Compromises would have to be endured, decisions made, and they would be all too difficult. 'I didn't want to,' she said, playing for time. 'I don't even know you that well.'

'I don't think there are formulas for these things.'

'No,' she said, looking down at the floor. 'Believe it or not, I don't make a habit of falling for married men.'

Phillip did believe it. The loneliness was written so large on her face he believed it was a long time since she had fallen for anyone.

But they were both such novices. He, too, declared himself. And although it was a cliché, it was the truth when he said, 'I haven't felt like this before.'

She was tempted to say, when you go home you will feel awful and guilty and torn and it will be hell. But, from the seriousness of his face, he seemed to know that.

'I told myself I was just buying a picture,' he said. 'Nothing more. But I kept thinking about you, wanting to tell you things – stuff that had happened, or you might find funny, or ask your opinion. Or I'd see something and think, Laura would like that, Laura would be interested in this. Or I'd wonder what you were doing . . .' He hesitated. 'I didn't realize what I was actually feeling. Why you were always on my mind.'

Then he took her in his arms once more. She smelled of lemons and paint. And he kissed her as if his life depended upon it.

## 39

Laura lay under the heavy duvet and began shivering, not from the cold but adrenaline, terrified that she was going to do something that might grate on Phillip. Now they were in bed, neither knew quite how to behave. So much, thought Laura, for a rapturous union of bodies and souls. I have yearned for this man, dreamed of him. But this was a nightmare, lying inches apart, not moving – or at least, not intentionally – exposed by the grim light of day in what she knew was awful washed-out underwear, even by her standards.

They had stood kissing in her kitchen, then Laura had reached for Phillip's hand and led the way to her bedroom. But after they had edged their way awkwardly through the narrow doorway, they somehow found themselves on opposite sides of the bed, as if they were an old married couple about to go to sleep after a hot drink and the *News*. They each took off some of their clothes. He unbuttoned his shirt, she struggled out of her jeans, their eyes politely on the floor – though Laura did catch sight of Phillip actually folding his trousers and laying them neatly on the chair. Laura retrieved the old T-shirt she normally slept in from under the pillow and slung it out of sight.

With them both staring at the ceiling at quarter to eleven on a grey Tuesday morning, she wasn't sure how the next move would be accomplished. Might he tap her politely on the shoulder? Rugby tackle her round the waist? And for an appalling moment Laura thought she might break into idiotic giggles.

But what if he was about to say he had made a dreadful mistake? Just to catch his eye now seemed too dangerous, because she might see him preparing to get up, say goodbye and walk out, leaving her embarrassed, humiliated, bereft. Then the doorbell rang. And with that, they each turned on to their sides.

Suddenly, their faces were barely apart on the pillow and Laura could feel his breath on her cheek, the heat of his body, all the nearness of him. But, as if she was chatting over the garden fence, she found herself saying, 'That's probably the postman. I expect it's a package.'

'Do you want to get it?' asked Phillip.

'No, no,' she said, as he shifted a fraction and accidentally kicked her in the shin.

'Sorry, sorry.'

'It's all right,' said Laura, moving her leg away, although it most certainly was not. The bell shrieked once again, as if the postman was leaning his shoulder against the door. 'He's going on a bit. I'm so sorry. They're Christmas presents for the girls, I imagine, and he doesn't want to be stuck with them,' she said, forcing the words out in as normal a tone as possible for a woman discussing the postal service while lying next to the half-naked man she desperately wanted. 'If it's the usual postman,' she went on, wishing she could shut up, 'he'll hide them behind the dustbins under the hedge.'

'Unless it's a temp,' Phillip suggested. 'I used to work as a postman at Christmas when I was a student. Did it for three years, in fact.'

And with this, whether it was thanks to nerves or hysteria or some basic instinct coming into play and telling her the surest route to Phillip, she burst out laughing. 'Dear God,' she cried, 'this is romantic.' And her beautiful laugh had the desired effect.

Phillip enfolded her in his arms and, like two souls who have not known love for centuries, they were together.

Later – much later, as it was growing dark – Phillip was standing by Laura's front door, kissing her goodbye.

'This is not just a fling,' he said, 'you understand that, don't you?'

His lips brushed hers. A different sort of kiss, she thought, not so much passionate, but protective this time, thankful.

'Laura?' he said, stroking her hair out of her face and running his fingers through her curls. 'I knew you'd be gorgeous. But . . .' He hesitated.

Laura braced herself. So this, she thought, is when the guilt kicks in and he tells me it was a terrible error of judgement.

But instead, he was saying, 'You do want to see me again? Don't you?'

'Yes.' She tried to sound perfectly calm. Yes! Yes! 'But it's been so quick, so sudden,' she said, attempting to appear as the voice of reason. This is the role she would play, the sensible woman with her feet on the ground who could face reality. She had certainly played it before – and very well. But inside she had lost all her bearings. She wanted to scream, leave Julia! Leave her! Tell me your marriage is over, quite dead. But she simply said, 'You might get home, think this is all wrong –'

'Stop!' he said, kissing the top of her head and pressing her into his chest.

She fitted herself against his warm body. Last time she had been to bed with a man he, too, was married and look what had happened – she had ended up a single mother with twins. But, oh Lord, she thought, how I would love to have Phillip's child. And with that impossible wish, tears pressed at the back of her eyes. To have the opportunity to bring up a family in the conventional way, not to have to do it all alone – but with him. With Phillip. With love.

But all she said was, 'You might be full of regrets. And, if you are, it's okay.' She hid her face in his neck so that he would not see she was lying through her teeth.

'Regrets?' he echoed. 'My lovely, lovely sweetheart. How could I possibly –?'

'But you came here,' she interrupted, determined to face the facts at their worst, 'to buy two paintings so you would not have to see me again.' He had told her that was what he had intended doing once he realized he had fallen in love with her. Fallen in love? He had used those very words. He loves me! He loves me! she wanted to cry. But she simply said, 'You made all those resolutions, but now, in just hours, we're talking about having a weekend alone together.'

After hours in each other's arms, being such organized people, they had sat up in bed with their diaries, deciding when to meet again, the best ways of contacting each other, and that when Venetia took the girls to Disneyland Paris they would go away. It was as if, thought Laura, they had been arranging their lives with one another for years.

'I would understand,' she said, unable to meet his eyes, 'if you got cold feet.'

'Listen,' he said, pulling her away and forcing her to look at him. 'And listen carefully. I do not regret this. I am so happy, you have no idea. I mean it when I say I've never felt like this before. Of course it's horribly complicated.' For a moment he looked devastated.

He's going to say it now, she thought, he's sorry, terribly sorry. She had the measure of the man now. She was in no doubt that such contrary truths could tear him apart.

But he said, 'Of course it's all those awful things. But at the same time you are also the most wonderful thing that has happened to me. So we are going to do what we said –'

'Take stock,' she interrupted. 'Take it very slowly.'

'Yes, we are. Dear God, I'm under no illusions about what this means. But I'm going to call you tonight. And I'm going to come here tomorrow morning, and after Christmas – when your daughters are in France with your mother – I'm going to take you away and it will be just us, you and me, together. So, my darling . . .'

My darling? Laura called the girls her darlings. But to hear 'my darling' whispered in her ear by a loving man.

'My darling.'

Such beautiful, hopeful words.

Dear God, she prayed . . . though what was the use of prayer? But I will go back to the church right this minute, pray as hard as a nun for the rest of my life, if I might only have Phillip by my side and in my bed. Though that is hardly a pact I can suggest to Father Eoghan.

He gathered her into his arms. 'We are going to give ourselves some time, my luscious Laura. Did you know that there is the most gorgeous spring to your lovely, soft body.'

So Julia is too bony and thin. Oh, stop such comparisons, such ugly thoughts.

'My darling,' he was whispering in her ear, serious and concerned now, 'when were you last told how very, very beautiful you are?'

She said nothing. Not for years and years, she thought. I could have found someone, I suppose. Somebody. But I wanted love. Even though it sounded immature, neurotic, that was the truth. I was waiting for love, and that might have meant for the rest of my life I would have to live this lonely, virginal existence. Oh, don't make me go back to that! Just keep holding me, she thought, as he began kissing her again, expertly, voluptuously.

So many types of kisses. She had forgotten. Or rather, trained herself to forget.

Some repressed identity was asserting itself. She could feel it within her. This was the life after death, the long-promised miracle. And she wanted to live again more than she had ever wanted anything. She had been dead for so long now, telling herself that she could do without. And of course she could. But if she had to kill this life off yet again, shove it back down in some place where it died, ignored and unloved . . . She dropped her head.

'Laura,' he said, lifting her face and tracing her lips with his fingertips. 'You know, I'd see you at the school looking down like this and I'd wonder what you were thinking, and a couple of times I tried to seek you out but you always seemed to avoid me.'

She smiled.

'So, you were avoiding me,' he said. 'That smile of yours. You know, your whole face transforms, lights up. But don't avoid me now . . .' he went on, in a beginning sort of voice.

Nudging his shoulder with her forehead, she said, 'Not now. You'd better go. I've got to get the girls.'

He put his arm around her. 'I know. We'll speak later. I promise.'

And with that promise he left.

Instead of rushing out to the school, Laura sat down in her dimly lit kitchen. Around her was the familiarity of paintings by the girls, the girls' chairs, the girls' laundry, remnants of the girls' breakfasts. Yet her home looked strange to her. It had become the stuff of another life, of another woman. And she shut her eyes to it all, and the claims it made on her time, her energy, her love. She would be late for the girls. She who was always there for her daughters. But today they could wait. For this miraculous moment she would not be defined by her past, or by what was to come.

I love him, she thought. He loves me. And right now she would treasure this gift. They had been so open with their feelings, they were like two teenage innocents. But, of course, they were not teenagers. There were years and years of life between them – marriage and children and Julia.

Julia.

To her surprise, Laura suddenly felt a wave of pity for Julia. Laura knew just how she would feel if she watched Phillip leaving her home, never to return. And yet she was prepared to inflict that pain on Julia.

While working on the portrait, Laura's thoughts had revolved around Julia with the unflinching precision of a dentist's drill. The Julia whom she had painted was so successful, so beautiful, so accomplished. Julia who had managed to arrange her life so she enjoyed the great career and the perfect family, all the good of feminism, while I, Laura had berated herself, ended up with the other side of the coin, a one-night stand and single motherhood.

Laura opened her eyes and saw the portrait afresh. Now she saw it as a simplistic caricature. No one could be read that easily. Love, whatever its consequences, can give you a better understanding, even of the person you are wronging. Far more must have been going on in that marriage, she realized, than she could ever have imagined.

If not me, would he have fallen for someone else? Laura wondered. Quite possibly. But, just then, it didn't matter. What, oddly, did matter to her was Julia's portrait. The purpose for which she had begun the picture was irrelevant now. There was a vulnerability about Julia and she had missed it and she wanted to get it right.

Yet she had to fetch the girls.

She flew out of the house, ran to the school, heard her daughters' account of their day as if she was on planet Mars, plonked burnt fish fingers in front of them, ignored the message from her mother asking her to ring back, and got the girls to sleep by nine.

Normally at this hour she was exhausted, but right now she did not feel she would need sleep for weeks. She knew what she had to do. She returned to her portrait. The smile was wrong – too confident, too certain. That smile needed a hint of wistful strain.

Laura got out her paints. But it was difficult work. She ploughed away, losing track of time, until one of her daughters called for her.

Only then did she look at the clock. It was nearly midnight and Phillip had not called.

## 40

Phillip drove home from Laura's, his mind swirling in confusion. Already difficult decisions loomed. If Julia asked him what he had been doing during the day, would he lie? Or, at least, lie by omission?

It was a point of honour to Phillip always to tell the truth, not exactly easy for someone with a career in advertising. His entire life he had tried to live by an exemplary standard of conduct. And, not quite unconsciously, he had judged those who did not. But now he, too, had fallen and the longings of his soul felt as dangerous and divided as the Middle East.

Laura had a heart to break. He had never doubted that. But now, having lain in her bed, with her in his arms, he realized exactly what damage he could do. He had stumbled across Laura in her warm, crowded, crazily decorated home like a cottage in the woods in a fairy tale. If he disappeared out of her life she would continue living just as she had always done, loving her daughters in her loving home, except he would be responsible for wrenching away yet more of what little faith she had in herself. And that knowledge, that she felt so strongly about him, filled him both with terror and with joy.

At some point, he would have to choose between Laura and Julia. There was no escape from that, and all the shoddiness of love outside marriage stared him right in the eye. But to live without Laura meant he could see nothing ahead but a deadening flatness.

He was so unhappy with Julia. The dreadful truth of this took his breath away. He had not been able to admit it before. Or even truly see it. He loved Julia. They had, in many ways, grown up together. They had created a family, a home. But that morning, he had been reminded of what it meant to be happy, and that had put the reality of his life into stark relief. It seemed to him that so much of his time was spent repressing disappointment and frustration, trying to compensate for the emptiness. He was weary of skirting around her, trying not to have an argument. He was partly to blame, of course. He had connived with Julia in the life they had created. And now he was pulled apart, because alongside the ugliness of an affair was the fearful beauty of loving and being loved in return. His feelings might be pure and right – how could love not be? – yet they could have no moral standing, no public context. But in that contradiction, in that undoubted wrong, he was also embracing what felt like a gift from God.

He pulled up outside his home and looked out at the light rain. Was it wrong to be so happy? But how could it be a mistake to be shown again how wonderful life is? And he saw himself standing at the window of Laura's small bedroom. She had her arms around him, her head resting on his chest, and he was watching the clouds over the rooftops. They stood perfectly still, looking out at the overcast sky, and to Phillip the ordinariness, the greyness, possessed all the colour and beauty of life.

Already, he wanted to speak to Laura again, to hear her voice and reassure her. And himself. Because was she all right? He wanted to know how she was feeling, what she was thinking, he wanted to know about her past, her painting, her future. He wanted to know all there was. But he would ring later tonight, as he had promised, when her children were in bed. She had not wanted Eliza and Alice to have any hint of what was happening.

He winced, brought back to practicalities, and made himself get out of the car. At least the house would be empty, and this evening he would simply avoid Julia.

But Julia was home, her coat slung carelessly on the hall chair, though normally she always hung it up in the cupboard. He was puzzled. He looked in the kitchen but she was not there. So he headed for the obvious place – her study. That, too, was empty but the desk lamp was on as if she was around.

As always, the room was immaculate. Pens were upright in a pot, stationery stored in labelled boxes, even the newly opened post was neatly aligned. Yet the place was not a showcase for work but a veritable factory of industry.

To Phillip's surprise, the sight of his wife's study filled him with pity. One minute he had been all too aware of Julia's failings, but now her desire for control, even down to her spotless desktop, seemed oddly pathetic. He knew what lay behind that precision and order – the desperate childhood, the hunger to succeed, the struggle for a different life and the fear that it could be taken away. Somewhere within that carapace of perfection Julia, too, had a heart to break.

Glancing at her tidy desk, wondering what particular legal quagmire was engaging her now, he noticed an invoice for next term's fees at a girls' boarding school – one he knew that Julia thought suitable for Rose.

At once pity turned to fury. What the hell was she playing at? Sorting out Rose's education without his agreement? Then, for the second time that day, he did something he had never done before. He looked at his wife's chequebook. On the stub, in her clear, precise hand, she had written the name of the school and an amount of more than £10,000 – a whole term's fees.

How dare she! Julia had gone behind his back and arranged for Rose to go to this boarding school in Wiltshire. He had never really known what the phrase 'incandescent with rage' meant until now. He wanted to slam doors, tear papers, kick walls.

'Oh darling,' said a voice behind him. 'I'm so pleased you're back. I really wanted . . .'

He started and turned. Julia had not spoken to him so lovingly in ages. She was wrapped up in a towel after taking a shower. Quite what she was doing home in the middle of the day like this he had no idea, but if she thought she could win him round with a few sweet words, she had never been more wrong.

'What's this?' he demanded, as she came towards him, about to put her naked arms around him. 'This cheque?'

'It's for someone at work,' she explained. 'Robert Weston – you've met him. One of the clerks – very tall, with glasses – you know, a nice man.'

'But what for?'

'Because he's got . . . Oh, another time, I'm so glad to see you. I need to tell you something.'

'No, Julia! What the hell is this?'

She looked at him in shock. 'Robert's mother has Alzheimer's,' she said quietly, 'and he and his wife have looked after her for ages, but they can't take any more. They've got two other children – young ones, on top of the girl they've got at boarding school – so they're having to put the mother in a home and that takes every last penny. Look, I know it seems odd but his wife works as a receptionist so you can imagine how much that brings in and they're struggling to keep their eldest at this school. She got some music scholarship but that's only tokenism, you know what it's like, and they're really struggling to find the money. So I just thought . . . you know, sometimes people come your way and I just thought I can help and so I said I'd pay the fees . . .' She paused. 'Did you think this . . .?' She gave him an aggrieved look. 'Oh Phillip, surely you didn't think this was for Rose, did you?'

'These days I don't know what to think.'

'But I would never . . . Oh Phillip, darling, how could you doubt me like that?'

'You're so damned busy, I barely know what you're up to, let alone what's actually going on in your head. You certainly can never be bothered to find time for anyone but yourself.'

Suddenly Julia looked nervous. She moved towards him in alarm.

But he exploded with, 'And I don't understand why you're the one having to pay for this man's child to go to an expensive school like this.'

Julia had no idea what to say, how to talk to him. She was used to reading between the lines, and the meaning here was as clear as day. Her husband's words may have been brief, but they harboured long, long resentments against her, grievances that she had known nothing of – or rather, had kept ignoring. He was accusing her of gross selfishness, that she did not give him enough time. This was utterly unreasonable, but she was at a loss to know how to make things better. Then the lawyer in her told her to answer his second complaint first – she was on firm territory there.

'I'm paying the fees because the Westons are the sort of people who have spent their life working, not taking a penny from anyone. The daughter's bright, and if she didn't go to this school she would be at one where they speak twenty-six different languages – and I don't mean posh languages like the "Euro-Richoes" who go to St Catherine's with our precious princesses . . .'

She hesitated as he grimaced at this description of his daughters, but to protect herself from an onslaught from Phillip, she persisted with her own attack. 'And they're not closet racists like the well-heeled hypocrites round here who express such pretty opinions on the benefits of diversity but for some reason their little darlings can only be educated with others exactly like themselves.'

Julia paused for breath. But now they had started, the floodgates had opened, and she was scared to stop as she was in no doubt he would want his own back. So she ploughed on.

'Didn't you say to me the other day about that girl you've taken on – the Hartley Estate girl, Isabel, or whatever her name is – that she could have been me? Well, this Weston girl could have been me too. I'm sorry, Phillip, but it's not, as you seem to think, just the really poor who need help. You only go for the big story – the violent, brilliant girl with the dying mother in a sink estate – and, by the way, I know more about that than you will ever, ever know, so don't you dare lecture me. But believe it or not, there are also millions of ordinary people who slog their guts out, never taking from anyone. But they, too, need help sometimes. Though you'd probably dismiss them as middle class – far too unfashionable for you to care about. Or, quite frankly, almost anyone. They are just there to be taxed to death and expected to behave and not complain that their schools are packed and that hospital waiting lists are endless while their savings hit rock bottom. So that's why I'm helping the Westons, and don't you dare knock it. Don't you bloody dare.'

She could go on and on. She was right. And Phillip would know it. But so what? What was this argument really about?

She felt slightly unhinged. How do you claw your way back together after words like this? When younger, if she and Phillip had a disagreement, after resolving the issue – without such piercing personal attacks – they would spend the afternoon in bed. And suddenly that presented itself as a solution. They had not gone to bed together in the middle of the day for so long, it did not bear thinking about.

'Oh Phillip, please, I can't bear talking like this. I'm sorry. Really. Don't look at me like that.'

He just shrugged and said, 'A lot of what you say is true.'

He looked at her eyes blazing, as articulate as ever, as if she was in court. Of course he knew she was right. And that she had just written a cheque to help this man without telling a soul was the sort of charitable deed that could get you through the eye of the needle. How could he fault a woman so quietly generous?

'Look,' she was saying, 'I didn't mean all that. I'm sure you're doing a lot of good, I really am –'

'Don't patronize me.'

'I'm not,' she said, flinching at his tone. But once more she tried to get near him, taking a step closer, but he only stepped quite deliberately back.

'Phillip, please,' she cried. He was repelling her. There was no doubt about it, and she wanted to cover her face with her hands and sob. But she would never do that to gain his attention. 'I'm sorry. But I've had a dreadful morning. A dreadful week,' she added, thinking of Anna. 'Please, sweetheart, don't look at me like that. But this morning . . . the reason I'm home . . . you know the Clifford James case –'

'How could I not?'

Julia forced herself to ignore the sarcasm. 'I met the new CEO last night, remember? At dinner?' she reminded him. 'And she was a complete nightmare.' She shuddered, partly for effect but also because the woman had been really hard work, matching Julia in energy, drive, intellect and confidence.

'Well, this morning I got a call that she's decided she wants a change in lead counsel – to get shot of me, in other words. The case has been going on too long, she says, and she thinks it's my fault. Though she's wrong on that. Utterly. And she'll find out soon enough. But that's not the point. She's dropping me and bringing in some friend of hers. This man she's used to dealing with. So, there you go. All that work, thrown over. And what with the Jonathan Branson case going pear-shaped as well . . . So I came home. I'll work from here while I decide how to play it. But it's a disaster, whichever way I look at it.'

Phillip knew full well how much the Clifford James case meant to Julia in terms of money and prestige. And if he hadn't, it was now written on her face. This was a dreadful blow for her. Suddenly, his indomitable wife looked unusually vulnerable and scared – as young as twelve years old, yet also as if she had aged a couple of decades. She had never been taken off a case before, and to be removed from one that was so public – at least, in the legal world – and profitable was downright damaging.

But it was also a dreadful blow for Phillip. The Julia who was successful, controlling, in command was the sort of woman he could walk away from. But this woman before him now was weakened in some fundamental way, as if what made her uniquely Julia had taken a fatal battering. For all her strength and intelligence, Julia was as fragile as the next person. He turned to the window, to hide his distress. How could he inflict pain on Julia? How could he possibly leave her?

'Phillip, please!'

He looked back at her and she threw her arms around him with all her strength, embracing him as tightly as possible, and pressed her face into his chest, just as Laura had done.

She breathed deeply in an attempt to calm herself. She breathed once more. And she breathed in a lemony scent she did not recognize.

Another woman.

## 41

Julia's arms fell to her sides. She thought she might be sick. Another woman. Of course! How could she have been so blind? It had never occurred to her before. But now it all fell into place – Phillip's distance, his argumentativeness. Of course she knew women found him attractive, and she was in no doubt that he had had plenty of opportunities. But, she thought, he always turned them down. Not because he had not been tempted. But the point about Phillip, in Julia's eyes, was that he was naturally good – not a saint, but about as decent a human being as it is possible to be.

Julia believed that she, on the other hand, was not a good woman. She had to work at goodness, really hard at times. There were areas in her life – admittedly a long, long time ago, to do with her mother – that she was desperately ashamed of. Terrible memories, like shards of glass, lay embedded in her brain so deeply she knew she would have to live with them for ever. She could make endless excuses for herself – she was young, she knew no better – but the truth was there were times in her life when she had not behaved well. She had turned a blind eye to her mother's suffering and in so doing she had shut the other eye to Angela.

But she could not think about that now, except that she had always believed Phillip was the sort of person who would have acted better. Phillip was a genuinely good man. He didn't have to struggle to do the right thing, the way she did. Goodness came naturally to him. And with his moral vision of the world, she had thought, came absolute probity. But she was wrong. Oh dear God, she wanted to cry out loud. She was wrong, wrong, wrong! She had been wrong about so much.

'You're seeing someone, aren't you?' Her voice was unrecognizable to her, unusually light and high, like a child's when scared of the dark.

Phillip froze. This was not supposed to happen. He was not going to have this conversation today. Nor tomorrow. Not for weeks . . . maybe never. But it was as if Julia had pushed a large rock from the top of a mountain and, whether he liked it or not, the rock was rolling and might destroy all in its wake.

'Who?' whispered Julia. 'Who is she? Don't lie to me.'

Looking at his wife's distraught face, it occurred to him that this was actually the beginning of his adult life. His strong convictions, his high-minded ideals were easy when you lived in the tents of prosperity. But now, for the first time, he was the one scrabbling for a way through paradoxes and pain. He braced himself. He did not lie. 'It's Laura,' he said.

'Laura?' Julia didn't know any Lauras. 'Who?'

'Laura Cusack,' he said. 'You met her at the school the other week.'

'Not that painter's daughter?'

'Yes.'

'But . . . her? You've slept with *her*?'

'Yes.'

She looked at him incredulously. 'But . . . for how long, you two?'

'Not long.'

'What's that mean?'

'Since this morning.'

'This morning? Don't treat me like an idiot.'

'I'm not. I would never –'

'This morning ? You mean, it began just now? Today?'

'Yes.'

'But why? I mean . . . for God's sake, Phillip. What have you done?' she cried, but the guilt on his face made it obvious.

Julia had had far too early an education in meeting unhappiness and disappointment. But that her beloved husband should be the one to inflict such a blow was appalling. In the shock of that terrible moment, all Julia's natural diplomacy, her innate intelligence and common sense failed her. Because if she had wanted to contribute yet more to the collapse of her marriage and make Phillip hate her, she could not have chosen words more effectively.

'She's the woman with the twins who lives off her parents, isn't she? The wannabe painter, trying to be like her dad?' she sneered. 'I've got it right, haven't I?'

Phillip said nothing. One step at a time, that is what he and Laura had decided, to cherish what happened between them, but to make no grand assumptions or sudden moves. He knew what a massive choice he had to make. But certainly not now. That would be madness. He and Laura both had the sense to know that they needed time, to consider what they had done, to reflect on what they might do. But here was Julia, needing – as always – to take control, to force things along according to her timetable.

'I remember her,' Julia was saying. 'Everyone made a fuss because she'd made a chocolate cake? Jesus Christ! All this time . . . did you want me making cakes? Have you hated me? All my . . .? All I've done?'

'How could you possibly think that?' he murmured.

'Quite easily, since you're having an affair with a woman whose greatest achievement seems to be her ability to bake great cakes.'

He shook his head. 'I've been so proud of you.'

'And yet you fall for Little Miss Cupcake.'

His voice rose. 'That's the trouble with you. You just latch on to one thing – glibly dismissing someone – completely incapable of seeing the whole picture.'

'The picture's quite clear,' she cried. 'When it comes down to it, you're pathetic. You think you want a strong woman but, actually, what you want is someone to stand in for your mother, listen to your whinges and your moans and comfort you so you feel better about yourself.'

'Don't be absurd. You know my mother. Jesus! When did she ever think of comforting me? Even you were a better mother.'

'What the –?' He might just as well have struck her. 'What the hell do you mean by that?'

'Just that if you wanted comforting the last person you would turn to is my mother. She was too busy looking after others.'

'But me? What are you saying, that I was a rubbish mother?'

'No, of course not.'

'Then what?'

'Just that you had other things in your life as well.'

'Of course I did. I had to. Because it's all right for privileged Miss Cusack Cupcake, dabbling away at her painting, sponging off Mummy and Daddy with not the faintest idea of what hardship is. God, how I hate those upper-class dilettantes, never really working at anything. But all I've done – my whole life – is work.'

'Because you love it! And don't you dare pretend otherwise. Laura gives her energy and her creativity and her . . . passion to her children. You gave it to the law.'

'And you blame me for that because I wasn't at home cooking comfort food?'

'Do you have to be so damned simplistic? I'm just saying Laura did things differently.'

Julia's phone began ringing.

'And because it's not your way doesn't mean it's wrong. Typical!' he cried as, instinctively, Julia reached for the phone. 'Here's our marriage at stake and your work takes precedence.'

'I'm not going to answer it,' she said, 'even though I have probably had the worst day of my entire career. But I'll have to deal with that later, because you come back and tell me you've been sleeping with a school-run mum. Dear God, Phillip! How many others have there been?'

Phillip shook his head. 'None.'

'Oh, come off it! What about all those gorgeous girls who used to work for you?'

'Really, I promise you.'

'I don't believe you.'

'Julia, please, don't destroy everything we've ever had.'

'But why should I believe you? I mean, how can I? How can I believe anything any more if you've . . . How can I?' Julia looked him in the eye. 'Do you love her?'

Phillip had thought he had not made up his mind, that he had not known what to do. But, almost without realizing, he was running to a decision at breakneck speed and there was no way to stop or turn back.

'Yes, Julia, I do.'

Now the words were out there.

'But why?' she cried. 'Oh God! Her? I mean, why *her*? For God's sake, Phillip. You owe me this. Why?'

'I don't know exactly. It sort of . . . crept up on me.'

'So I've been dumped for an "I don't know" that "crept up" on you? You risk all this – your family, your daughters. Did you even bother to think about them? Or were you just too busy thinking of yourself?'

Phillip took a step towards her and for one second Julia thought he was going to throw his arms around her and say it was all a terrible mistake, that he was sorry, he did not know what had come over him, that he was desperately, desperately sorry, that he loved her, and would she forgive him? He could not have chosen a woman more unlike her, and the insult to all she believed in and held dear could not be more clear. But she would forgive him. She would. This world she had created, and so painstakingly constructed, would not be destroyed. Dear God, please! Let him come to my arms.

'I'm sorry, Julia, I am.'

So he was going to apologize.

'I'm sorry,' he repeated.

It was going to be all right. She would make it all right, somehow. This was a glitch – a terrible glitch, admittedly – but people overcame these problems, and she would.

But he avoided even her eyes. He just sat down at her desk and rested his head on his hand.

'The truth is, Julia, I can't stand this life we lead any more. The way your work . . . There's more to our life than your work, you know. But it's everywhere, all around us, in your moods, even in our bed. I just can't bear the way it takes over everything.'

She could have hit him. So he was not sorry in the slightest. 'So it's my fault?' she yelled, fear making her lose control. 'Of course, I might have guessed you'd put it on me.'

'No, not just you, of course not. But we never make time –'

'You found time for this Laura. God, it's all right for her. She doesn't need to work.'

'Oh, don't start on that again.'

'And she's such a flake she just gets herself pregnant and gets other people to look after her. I'd never let that happen to me.'

'Don't be absurd – that could happen to anyone.'

'No!' She was in tears now. 'I had to be careful. All my damned life I've had to be careful . . . careful about everything.'

'You know, maybe that's the difference – she bends with what's thrown at her, but you're so damned controlling.'

'Now who's being simplistic?' She stopped as she heard the front door open.

It was one of the girls.

'What about *them*?' she hissed. 'Shall I tell them what their father's been up to? How he's been fucking –'

'No, please,' he interrupted. 'Please!'

'Ashamed now, are you?' she muttered, not caring what she was saying. 'Ashamed of what you've done?' All she wanted to do was hurt him back for hurting her. But then, where would this end? Did he want to divorce her? Of course she wouldn't tell the children. She almost doubled up in pain. Her children. *Their* children. She could not bear, ever, to tell them. He could not leave her. Oh dear God, don't let him leave me! Please!

Phillip shook his head. No, he thought, I am not ashamed of this love. Every fibre in his being insisted that to deny such love would have been to turn his back on life itself, and a familiar image of his childhood flashed across his mind of Christ nailed on the cross. I might, he thought, be torn apart but I have to thank Laura for the survival of my soul. Then the grandeur of his sentiments brought a smile to his face.

He was just an ordinary man – like millions – muddling through life, this incredible, miraculous, phenomenal journey, stretching for years and years, and over in the speed of light. But he had left Laura's transfigured. In the betrayal of loving Laura he had found a saving grace.

Just now, the success of his work no longer mattered. Just now, he could see his beloved daughters growing up – becoming the old women he would never know – and, for once, he told himself he would find a way to accept what was thrown at them. Just now, he could regard his parents' dictatorial do-gooding with generosity. And Julia, his beautiful, brilliant wife . . . There was so much they should have done – together – and he wanted to tell her that all the work she believed in would, ultimately, fail her. And he was overcome with compassion and he went to take her in his arms, but suddenly his head hurt. He felt dizzy.

'Actually,' he murmured, 'I don't feel too good.'

There were beads of sweat on his forehead.

Let him suffer, thought Julia. Serve him right. 'It's guilt,' she sneered. She turned her back on him, muttering, 'Now I'm going to see to our children and keep from them the fact that their father fancies a mum he's picked up at the school gates.'

She choked, then hurried out of the room. She was shaking. She did not know where to put herself. She was crying, her body wrenching with sobs, and she locked herself in the bathroom, turning on the taps to drown out the noise.

She lay down on the cool floor, as she used to do as a child when the world was too hard. Then she would lie on scuffed lino. Now she rested her head on creamy marble, but the view was no different. All she could see was failure everywhere – her daughters, her work and, now, her marriage.

And it was her marriage that she mourned the most. Phillip, I love you, she wanted to cry. I really love you. How could you?

But Julia had been trained to see both sides of an argument. She might want to crucify him mercilessly, to scream and shout at him for betraying his family, to tear his hair out for falling for this woman. But she was at fault too – for being self-absorbed, work-obsessed, not bothering to make time for him, for them, making him feel redundant. No wonder he was unhappy. And it was her fault. If she lost him . . . Dear God, she needed him. To live without him . . .

Tears streamed down her face. How could she have let this

happen? How could she have been so thoughtless, so blind, so downright stupid? Why didn't I see? she sobbed. And I'm sorry. I'm so sorry. Phillip, I need you. Come back, she implored. Come back.

She would go to him, promise to change, beg him, she who had never begged in her life. Because the idea of life without him was unbearable. She could make her marriage work. Couldn't she? He and this Laura . . . it was just the once, or so he'd said. Marriages survive much worse. Though if he really loved Laura . . . She would have to win him back. And she could, if she put her mind to it. She could bend too. She could.

She dried her eyes, brushed her hair in a feeble attempt to compose herself. For at least an hour she had lain on that bathroom floor, so he too might be calmer and they could talk. Hadn't he said recently that he wanted them to go away together over New Year? Well, she would go wherever he wanted – Lisbon, she recalled – she would make time. And now she had time, with these two cases collapsing. They would have to work at it. But she could work.

I can mend this, she told herself, going downstairs. I can.

She quietly opened the door of his office. But he wasn't there. She looked in the sitting room. He wasn't there either. Nor was he in the kitchen. The house suddenly felt deathly quiet.

'Phillip!' she called out in a hoarse voice. 'Phillip!'

There was no response.

Where was he? Had he already left her? Gone to Laura's? Perhaps she was too late. Please, no!

Then she heard Rose's scream.

'Mum!' her daughter called out. 'Mum! Help me! I'm in your study. It's Dad . . .'

## 42

On the hard wooden floor, Phillip lay unnervingly still, with Rose sobbing by his side. His head was at an odd angle and his eyes were closed. At once, checking her own fears, Julia put her fingers to her husband's neck. She knew what to do. With her usual foresight, she had done a first aid course when the girls were born. He was unconscious, but there was a pulse and he was breathing. She grabbed the phone, dialled 999 and, with her characteristic clarity, explained that her husband had fallen and was unconscious.

'An ambulance will be here soon, it's going to be okay,' she told Rose.

'But Mum, look at him!' cried Rose. 'It won't be okay . . . . I know it won't.'

'Rose, listen to me. I need you to stay calm so you can help Dad. Go and fetch some blankets. And hurry. We must keep him warm.'

Rose tore upstairs. Keep her busy, Julia told herself, using the same tactics with her daughter as she used on herself. Then she will cope.

Julia knelt on the floor chafing Phillip's cooling hands.

'I'm sorry,' she whispered in his ear. 'Dear God, I'm sorry. But it'll be all right. I promise. It'll be all right,' she repeated, kissing his closed eyes. 'I promise.'

But what had happened? His face was terrifying in its stillness. How serious was this? She felt herself about to cry. But that would not help. Was he going to die? But she could not think like that. She would deal with this as she did with every crisis, with calm and control. Then it would be all right. It would.

'Mum!' said Rose, appearing with a duvet.

'Perfect,' said Julia. 'Well done, darling. That's just what he needs. He'll be fine. Absolutely fine,' she insisted, as though her own will possessed the power to make him so. 'Now go and stand out in the road so you can flag down the ambulance when it appears, and keep the front door open so I don't need to leave Dad.'

Rose raced off and Julia was alone with Phillip once more.

She felt his pulse again. Even her unpractised fingers noticed it was far too fast and feeble. Something was very, very wrong. Panic began rocking her. Because he was going to die. And he would die hating her because there would be no opportunity to make things better. The ambulance would not make it in time. There was too much traffic on a wet December evening like this. There were road-works at the end of the street. And everyone knew the ambulance service was overstretched and, as a result, people died.

Even now Phillip's fine face was a ghastly grey, the blood leaching away from the lips she loved to kiss, turning blue before her eyes, and she could stand it no more so she grabbed the phone to ring 999 again to find out exactly where the ambulance was.

'It's only been five minutes since you called,' a woman at the emergency services explained.

Five minutes? Surely not. She had been waiting ages. Hadn't she? She looked at the clock. The woman was right.

'I'm sorry . . . I . . . I . . .'

'Don't worry, love,' said the woman. 'Time can take on a different dimension, when you panic.'

'But I'm not panicking.'

'No, no. Of course not. But actually, you've been very fortunate. The ambulance should be with you any minute. One was close by. Now is there anyone with you who can perhaps stand outside and wave to the ambulance and let them in?'

'My daughter's already outside doing just that.'

'Well done. You've done absolutely the right thing – all you possibly can.'

I'm being patronized, thought Julia, about to bridle, but then she heard Rose racing in. And two weary-eyed men in paramedic green followed her swiftly. One immediately knelt down to Phillip, and the other turned to Julia and introduced himself. His name was John, and his colleague was Elton.

Elton and John? Suddenly Julia's breath came in quick, jerking gasps and she could not contain herself. She was going to giggle like a hysterical schoolgirl and she did not know how she could stop herself.

But Rose was sobbing, 'Oh Mum, he's gone so grey.'

And hearing her daughter's cry, Julia focused her mind as Elton began questioning her with quiet urgency about Phillip's medical history.

'He's always been in perfect health,' she said, steadying her voice to answer his questions with accuracy and concision. 'And looked after himself.'

'Is he on any medication?'

'No.'

'Had he been feeling unwell?'

Julia hesitated. 'Not really. An hour or so ago, he said he wasn't feeling too good, but that was all. He didn't go into any details. It didn't seem . . . well, anything serious.'

'But he had a headache,' cried Rose. 'The other day. He was complaining about it when he took me to school and I was worrying about him and he told me not to worry.'

'What about today?' continued Elton. 'Did he have a headache earlier?'

'Not that he mentioned.'

'A bang on the head?'

'No.'

'But he did!' cried Rose, rubbing tears from her eyes. 'When he was pushed.'

'Oh God, yes,' said Julia. 'I . . .' She had forgotten. How could she? 'He was knocked down by someone.'

'When was this?' asked Elton.

'Thursday – no, Friday before last.'

'In a car?'

'No,' cried Rose. 'He was trying to save this woman who had been mugged and Dad went to the rescue – because he does things like that – and the man knocked him down and he bashed his head. How could you forget, Mum?'

'I . . .' began Julia. 'I . . .'

'People forget things, love,' said Elton to Rose, 'when they're in shock. It's quite normal.'

But I'm not in shock, thought Julia. I'm not.

But Elton was explaining to Rose, 'So what we're going to do is take your dad to the hospital, where they can decide what's the best thing for him and look after him properly.'

'Be careful moving him,' instructed Julia, with the authority she might use to an usher in court. 'Please,' she added, as John looked up at her with a gentle smile.

'Of course we'll be careful. We'll put a head brace on him. But it might be easier for you if you left the room.'

'No, no,' said Julia. She had a sudden hideous recollection of how her mother used to be heaved about, and the thought of Phillip also being treated with the dignity of a lump of old meat was too much. 'Please,' she murmured, 'please just watch his head.'

'Of course. But I presume,' John continued to Julia, 'you'll want to come with us to the hospital.'

'Yes, yes.'

'So why don't you get your coat and so on? So we don't waste time.'

'Can I come?' asked Rose. 'Please, Mum, please.'

'Of course, darling.'

'You too,' said John. 'Get your things together. As fast as you can. That would be a real help.'

Julia realized she was being managed – an unusual experience for her. Nonetheless, she equipped herself for action. She seized her bag, made sure she had her phone, money, a bottle of water – hospitals were always too hot, and she could not think straight if she was dehydrated.

She also grabbed a new notebook. This would not occur to most people – but Julia did not see herself as 'most people'. She remembered from all those years ago, when Angela dealt with emergencies with their mother, that it was crucial to keep track of what was happening in hospitals, to note times, which doctors she spoke to, who made what decisions. And that is what she would do.

Or at least, what she planned to do.

## 43

The journey to the hospital seemed to take hours.

'Go via Merton Street and avoid the High Street,' called Julia from the back, as they hit the early-evening rush hour. 'It'll be quicker.'

'The thing is,' John, who was tending to Phillip, replied, 'Merton Street has so many islands that we can't just plough down the middle of the road like we're doing here.'

'What about going along Ferry Road?' she suggested three minutes later, when they came to another standstill.

'Because with the roundabout at the end you can get stuck for ages. And here, although it's slow, we can keep moving . . . see?' she was told as they set off again. 'The traffic along here can make room for us.'

Then, shortly after, Julia began to say, 'Wouldn't we better off trying the Broadway rather than –?'

'Mum,' whispered Rose.

Julia looked at her husband. Just in this short time, yet more blood seemed to have drained from his skin. She forced herself to say nothing. It will be all right, she told herself, because we'll be at the hospital soon, with experts, equipment. Soon we'll know what the problem is, what to do.

And when they arrived at the hospital she was relieved to hear Elton say under his breath to the nurse on the A&E desk, 'This one's genuine.'

So we will be seen quickly, she thought.

But they were not. For nearly twenty minutes Julia sat by her unconscious husband with Rose crying quietly beside her, waiting for someone to take charge. And when, at last, the curtain was pulled back, there was just a worn-out nurse who could not stifle her yawns of exhaustion as she sat with her clipboard asking exactly the same questions as the paramedics and performing exactly the same procedures.

Julia repeated all she had already said.

'A doctor will be with you as soon as possible,' said the nurse.

'But when?'

'As soon as possible.'

Of course they're going to be here as soon as possible, the lawyer in Julia thought to herself.

'But when exactly is that?'

The nurse gave her a weary smile. 'I'll chase him up for you. And make sure he sees your husband right away.'

Then the nurse shot off.

'That was a complete waste of time,' Julia muttered to Rose, making a note of the time. 6.40 p.m. 'We're no further forward. She could have got all that from the paramedics.'

'Mum, please, don't make a fuss.'

'I'm not making a fuss.'

'Yes, but Mum –'

'Sweetheart, please, can you do something for me?' interrupted Julia. 'We must phone Anna. Let her know what is happening. But don't frighten her.'

'Don't frighten her?' repeated Rose, tears pouring once more down her cheeks. 'How can I not frighten her? Look at him, Mum. Just look at him.'

At that moment, a young woman appeared in a crumpled suit and trainers, with greasy hair and bags under her eyes, and sporting a stethoscope around her neck.

Dear God, thought Julia, is this the doctor? It was. And as Julia began answering the doctor's questions, she tried to calm her anxiety as she explained once more, 'He fell – or rather, was pushed.' You're wasting time, she wanted to scream. For God's sake, do something, don't just go round in circles. But she just said, 'He hit his head – but it was eleven days ago now. And no, he didn't get it checked out, because he didn't think the bang that serious. He certainly didn't complain about it to me.'

But would he have done? she asked herself. He was keeping so much from her, he could have been in agony. Would he have told her? Or would she have even noticed?

'Mrs Snowe?' urged the doctor. 'Does he?'

'What? Sorry,' said Julia. 'What was the question?'

'He has no allergies, is that right?'

'I've already told the ambulance driver, the nurse . . .'

'Mum,' whispered Rose.

For the third bloody time, she thought, he has no allergies, but to the doctor she just said, 'No, no allergies.'

'Okay, thank you. I'm going to put him on a drip and keep him properly hydrated for now and organize an ECG. And I'll check on him shortly.'

'Is that it?' demanded Julia.

'For now.'

'But what's wrong?'

'I don't know, as yet.'

'But when will you know?'

'The registrar will be here shortly and he'll decide the best course of action.'

'But when?' Julia looked at her watch. 'It's been almost an hour since we got here. Two hours since he collapsed. What could be going on? Has he had a stroke? I don't know, a bleed on the brain?' Panic rose in her. Medical terms she had never really known the meaning of crashed through her mind. 'An aneurysm? I don't know –'

'The registrar will be here as soon as possible, I promise you.'

'So he could be ages?' cried Julia.

'No, he'll be here as soon as possible.'

'Of course he's going to be here "as soon as possible".' God help us, she thought, is this a phrase they teach them in medical school? 'But that's meaningless. When is "as soon as possible"? Ten minutes? An hour? Two hours? Please,' she said looking at the girl, for that was what she now was to Julia, who answered with a blank face. 'Please?' repeated Julia. 'This is absurd. We're not getting anywhere. I just keep answering the same questions. And my husband's just lying there.'

'He's stable. His condition is not deteriorating. There are no signs of anything needing urgent attention. His "obs" are what you would expect.'

'How do you know?' demanded Julia, thinking the doctor sounded as if she was reciting from a textbook. 'You've not done a scan, anything. You've just done what everyone else was doing an hour ago.'

'I've followed all the correct procedures.'

'Procedures?' Phillip needed more than procedures. 'Please, I don't want to be rude,' she said, 'but how long have you actually been qualified?'

'Since August, though I don't see that's relevant.'

Julia was aware her hands were shaking. She had to control them. 'August?'

'Yes. But please don't worry. I promise you that as soon as the registrar arrives he will see your husband.'

Don't worry? Who in their right mind would not worry? Her head began to throb and pound as the girl left, saying, 'I'm sorry, I must go.'

Julia, forcing herself to keep her grip, scribbled hard in her notebook, saying to Rose, 'Right, I'm going to get someone who knows what they're doing.'

'Oh Mum,' begged Rose, 'please don't make a fuss.'

'Rose, I'm sorry, but this is your father, and I don't care how much fuss –'

'But that won't help here. It's not like your work. One cross word and they get all self-righteous and say, "I won't be spoken to like that," however much you're in the right, and then Dad will . . . Dad will . . . Oh God! Dad will die!'

Julia put her arms around Rose. 'Listen to me,' she said fiercely. 'Dad will fight with every bit of his strength. He has so much to live for. He loves us so, so much.'

But did he really love them? All her certainties about her

marriage had been ground into the dust a couple of hours ago when he was all set to leave her for another woman. Would he be fighting for that Laura? Not for her? Not for their children? But she could not think about that now. When he came round, she would make it all better, she would. But right now she had to focus. She had to find a doctor who had a clue what they were doing.

'Come on, my darling,' she continued, 'my brave, brave girl. You go and ring Anna, and I'll go to the desk and see what's happening.'

She took a swig of water, forced herself to breathe deeply, inhaling the sour, stale air. She followed Rose out of the cubicle. Now she would find the registrar.

## 44

It had only just gone seven but already the first casualties from office Christmas parties were arriving. Julia intended marching up to the front desk but three young women, all in wheelchairs because they were too drunk to take the weight on their legs, and clutching cardboard bowls Julia thought much too small for the job, had just been disgorged from an ambulance and were taking up all the nurses' attention.

Julia stood back, forcing herself to be patient, counting the minutes pass by, fourteen in all, when one of the girls threw up right in front of her.

Julia leaped back and almost retched herself with a ghastly recollection of Saturday nights on the Hartley Estate, avoiding the piles of regurgitated curry and lager. This was what she had worked so hard to escape from, this confused, out-of-control stream of humanity rushing towards the disaster of A&E where all hopes and dreams could die on a hospital trolley. But now she was stuck here, back in the chaos of life at its worst. She gasped, putting her hand to her mouth, don't let me be sick. Please, don't.

'Yes?' asked a young nurse, not looking up from the computer screen.

Julia explained the situation, relieved she could still speak in the calm, cajoling tone she used at work. But it held no sway here. The nurse said a doctor would be along shortly but they were very, very busy, what with the Christmas parties. And they had people off sick.

I cannot, thought Julia, stand here listening to excuses, and she was about to say so, when a more senior nurse caught Julia's eye.

'What's the problem?' she asked.

Julia went through her husband's history again and made it

known that she was a lawyer. Whatever she said, it did the trick, because the nurse returned with her to see Phillip.

'He's gone even whiter,' cried Julia, the panic that was just skin-deep now rising to the fore once again.

'We've sent for the neuro-team, but I'm sorry the registrar's been delayed,' said the nurse. 'There's someone terribly poorly on his ward. But I'll call him again. If he's not down in half an hour, come back to me. Your husband needs to be seen.'

'Half an hour? That long?'

'I'm afraid so. But why don't you sit down and wait?'

Because to sit down and merely wait, doing nothing, was impossible for Julia, and the look on her face said as much. 'I'll get someone to make you a cup of tea,' suggested the nurse. 'You're probably in shock yourself.'

'I'm not. I'm fine. I'm just worried about the delay in treatment for my husband.'

'Of course. But thirty minutes. All right?'

The nurse was gone.

Julia stood trapped in a harsh, calculating anger. Damn the nurse. And the doctor. This treatment was not good enough. And she raged at everyone who was failing to give her husband the attention she believed he should receive.

But more than anything, her merciless anger was directed at her-self. If she had been more sympathetic when she heard Phillip had banged his head, if she had actually given him her full attention, she might have insisted he went to the doctor and he might not now be lying on this hospital trolley, dead to the world and all around him, and he might not . . .

But she could not let her mind go down those morbid routes, not if she was going to do the right thing now. So she returned to her notes – that took sixty seconds. She went to the Ladies, then came back to the cubicle where Phillip lay.

Fourteen more minutes, she told herself, checking the time and whispering in Phillip's ear. 'Darling, I'm sorry. I'm truly sorry. But it will all be all right. I'll make sure of it. I promise, I'm here now.'

But her platitudes sounded hollow. Aside from the fact that their marriage was most certainly not all right, and clearly had not been for a long while, there was no indication Phillip had heard her – or, indeed, was aware of anything whatsoever. But she had some vague recollection of reading that people can often hear things when they are unconscious. So she tried once more, 'It'll be all right,' she repeated. 'I love you.'

But after ten minutes of this she could sit still no longer, talking to unhearing ears, and she looked out to see if the doctor was coming. There was no doctor, but a number of people were standing around and discussing who should clear up the vomit.

Then Rose, flushed and even more anxious, appeared.

'I can't call Anna,' she cried. 'I'm not allowed to use my phone in here and outside there's no signal and I walked around for ages.'

'Here, take my purse. Use the pay phone,' said Julia, nodding at the one in the corner.

But that phone could take no more money, so Rose went off looking for another. And by now thirty-one minutes had passed. I will wait two more, decided Julia, then go and chase up the doctor.

But just at that moment he arrived. Tall, good-looking, young and full of himself were Julia's first impressions. And all correct, thought Julia after five minutes and doing her best not to dislike him with his officious, seen-it-all, know-it-all manner when he couldn't be much more than thirty – though he did, she acknowledged, seem to be examining Phillip with some authority and experience.

'What I'd like to do,' he finally said, 'is admit him – obviously. Keep him comfortable overnight and then, in the morning, we can start doing some tests to find out what exactly has happened.'

'But what might have happened?'

'There are a number of possibilities, and it would be wrong for me to speculate just now. I'm going to ask the neuro-consultant to see him and I'll brief the intensive care team.'

'Intensive care?' she repeated. She had never had to articulate those words before. 'But . . . but what . . .?' What she wanted to ask was, how serious is this? When will he wake up? Or was she standing by as her husband lay dying? She forced herself to ask, 'Could this . . . I mean, could this – whatever it is – be terminal?'

'Well, everything is terminal in some way,' he replied, as if she had asked the most stupid question he had ever heard.

Julia bit back the retort on her lips and instead she asked, 'But why can't you start the tests now? Tonight?'

'Because his condition is stable and it's not really necessary. And anyway, er . . . I'm afraid the scanner has broken and won't be mended until about mid-morning tomorrow.'

'Broken?' cried Julia. 'But is there only one?'

'Do you have any idea how much these machines cost?'

No, of course I don't, she wanted to screech. Why would I?

She said, 'If yours is broken, I'll take him to another hospital now, where they do have one working.'

'No, that won't do. I'm sorry. But I'll ensure he's among the first in the queue tomorrow.'

'But surely I can take him to a different hospital. Then we can know tonight what's wrong and what can be done.'

'I'm afraid that's not possible. And I wouldn't advise moving someone in your husband's condition.'

'But just to wait around when something might be done . . .'

She looked at the stillness of Phillip's body with a dreadful foreboding. That stillness could be emptiness in no time. And she did not know what to do. Nor did this doctor – except wait for a broken machine to be fixed.

'Just waiting can be hard, I know, I'm sorry,' he said, and then left.

Fury flamed in her. If her husband died because of other people's incompetence she would never forgive them. Nor would she forgive herself. If he died because she shrank from the responsibility of battling to save him; if she meekly accepted the circumstances; if she was too weak to question every decision and fight for him with her quite formidable strength, she would be engulfed in guilt for ever.

But what, in fact, could she do? What, actually, was in her power?

Think, she told herself, think, as she stood trapped in the orange cubicle, hearing the clinking of metal medical instruments and soft murmured voices to her right and drunken angry cries to her left. She was conscious of everything: the smell of sickness under the disinfectant; the glaring brightness of the lights; the impatience and fear riddled through the very heart of the place. But she could not think. She could only stand there, utterly impotent and scared, until the junior doctor put her head round the curtain.

'Hello again,' she said. 'I'm going to put your husband on a drip, keep him hydrated and comfortable, so perhaps you'd better leave. It won't take long.'

'Can't I stay?' asked Julia. 'Please.'

She did not want to leave Phillip. All the millions of times she had rushed from him to get to her desk, because her work had been more important than being with him, rose up and taunted her. How could she have been so careless? How could she have wasted years of his goodness and intelligence and loving body?

'No, no, you can't stay,' said the doctor. 'I won't be long.'

'You're only putting him on a drip. Surely I don't have to leave for that.'

'I'm sorry, but you do. I have to put it into his groin.' It occurred to Julia that this junior doctor wanted her out of the way, as she did not want a witness to her inexperienced butchery. 'I'll be five minutes,' said the doctor, taking Julia by the arm and leading her out into the corridor.

If she hurts him I will shove her down the stairs, listen happily to her screams as she cries for help and step right over her, thought Julia, forcing herself to walk away from Phillip up the corridor, her shoes sticking to the grey lino floor.

Julia looked about. At last someone was clearing up where the girl had been sick, but watching the dirty water scattering across the corridor, Julia felt her nausea rising once more. She could see superbugs, invincible viruses, new drug-resistant infections spreading all over the walls, scattering into the air, on to hands and invading weak, defenceless human bodies. How did anyone get out of here alive? she wondered. All manner of mankind seemed to be surging here in a great, bloody mess of chaos where they ended up in steel beds, soaked in sweat and racked with pain.

At least Phillip was not in pain. Or was he? How could she be sure? What can you actually feel when you're unconscious? she thought, running back to Phillip.

The young doctor had gone. But there was blood on Phillip's gown. She lifted it. There was no drip in place. Instead, his skin was red and raw where the doctor had clearly been jabbing away trying to find a vein.

'Oh my darling,' cried Julia, kissing him and placing his hand on her cheek as if he might caress her once more. 'My darling, what are they doing to you?'

'Mrs Snowe.' She heard the junior doctor's voice behind her. 'Please give us a minute.'

The senior nurse was with her.

You've messed up, haven't you? thought Julia. Something as simple as putting in a cannula.

'What's the problem?' asked Julia.

'There's no problem,' said the nurse. 'Here, I'll sort this.'

They're useless, thought Julia, watching the woman's concentrated face. Phillip was going to die. And these clowns did not have a clue. Bright lights flashed before her eyes. Phillip was going to die and she did not know how to stop it.

'There,' the nurse was saying, 'no problem. All done.'

But Julia had gone.

# 45

Julia's fingers kept slipping as she stood in the busy corridor punching in her sister's number on her mobile phone. Dear God, make her answer, she begged. Please, let her be there.

'Angela!' Julia let out a cry. 'Oh –' She opened her mouth to speak but could only emit a strangulated sob.

'Julia, is that you?' said Angela. 'What is it?'

'It's . . . It's . . .' But when Julia tried to talk she was suffocated by tears.

Angela was saying, 'I'm here. It's okay.'

But it's not okay, Julia screamed inwardly. Her whole body was shaking. Years ago, this would happen to her when she was left alone in the flat and her mother was sick. Then she had learned how to control it. Or rather, she had gone running, in every sense, because pounding as fast as she could on the hard, unyielding pavements brought her calm.

'Julia, where are you?'

'The hospital,' she blurted out. 'Phillip . . .' But whenever she tried to explain, great choking sobs took her over.

'Take your time,' said Angela. 'Or give the phone to a doctor or a nurse and I'll speak to them.'

'But . . .' Looking about there was no one, or at least no one who seemed to Julia to know what they were doing.

'It's Phillip,' persisted Angela, 'is that right?'

'Yes, he's had a . . .' Julia tried to compose herself. 'He collapsed. He had a fall. He got banged on the head. And then he collapsed at home. And I've been here ages, and no one's got a bloody clue. And I need someone to do something. Jesus, Angela, if they –'

'Julia, stop. Slow down. How is he now?'

'I don't know, that's the point. They don't know.'

'But is he conscious?'

'No! No!'

Suddenly a woman in a bright yellow uniform shoved her in the middle of her back.

'Can't you read?' said the woman, pointing at a sign and bringing her face close to Julia's. 'No mobile phones.'

'But I can't get a signal outside,' protested Julia. 'There's no reception there, and I have to speak to my sister.'

'Not in here,' said the woman, waving her finger. 'Use the pay phone.'

'But I haven't got any money – my daughter's got my purse – and I need to speak –'

'Security!' shouted the woman.

'Jesus . . . Angela. It's a madhouse in here. I can't phone –'

'Go to the A&E desk,' said Angela, 'and I'll phone you there. Do you understand?'

'Yes, yes. But will they let you?'

'Of course they will. And I'll also ask to speak to a doctor and find out what is going on. Then I'll come. All right? Are the girls there?'

'Rose is here. And she's trying to get hold of Anna.'

'Good. Let me just sort out someone to take care of Mirela, then I'll be right over.'

Julia hung up. She turned to a security guard heading towards her. 'I'm sorry,' she said, 'about the phone – but I was desperate . . .'

'I know, love,' he said gently. 'It's a nightmare for people.'

'Yes,' she murmured, 'it is.' And she almost broke down and sobbed again, he was being so kind.

'Look, come with me,' he was saying. 'You can use your mobile in my office.'

She had ten new messages, nine from work colleagues – all, she presumed, to do with her being thrown off the Clifford James case. They could wait, but there was one text from Anna. And she was desperate to speak to her daughter.

'Well, thank you,' she said, following him to his office, and she read the message from Anna:

*I've told the truth and been fired from the magazine. You'd be proud of me.*

Julia made a violent effort of will to keep upright. Anna must have confessed to the theft of the clothes. But why? Although Anna had acted dreadfully, she had stopped and she had repaid all the money. Even so, Anna could end up in prison, there was no question . . .

'Would you like a cup of tea?' the security guard was asking.

Julia gazed at him uncomprehendingly, trying to call her daughter. But she could only get through to Anna's voicemail.

'Tea?' repeated the guard, placing a mug in her hands.

'No, no. But thank you,' she murmured. 'I must go.'

'Take your time,' he said. 'You look –' But he didn't finish the sentence, as she hurried back to A&E.

Passing the lifts Julia caught sight of an exhausted middle-aged woman, her shoulders hunched, her brow furrowed, and she felt a moment's pity. Yet even as the thought entered her head she knew it was her own reflection in the shiny silver lift doors. This is what she had become. And in such a short time. In one day.

Her mind charged around at breakneck speed, looking for answers. Tears rolled down her cheeks. She pushed her clenched fists into her eyes to try and stop them, but she was powerless. She was just a perfectly ordinary woman, overcome by her weakness. And she slumped on to the dirty floor.

She had always known that life was an assault course, that unless you were eternally vigilant you went crashing down into the darkest depths beyond the reach of the light. But she had thought she could master it. Indeed, that morning she had woken, as she always did, thinking she had succeeded. Because she had her marriage, her career, her children. They were rocks she had created in the sea of chaos she had escaped from.

But they had crumbled as easily as sandcastles.

## 46

'I'm all right, really,' Julia lied to Rose later that evening as a nurse led the way to the intensive care unit.

'But Mum, you fainted.'

'I was probably dehydrated. I'm fine now,' she murmured, trying to catch what the nurse was saying to Angela as she showed them into a waiting room.

'Here you are,' said the nurse. 'It shouldn't be long now, and you can see your husband shortly. The intensive care team have to . . . well, do their stuff.'

'For God's sake,' Julia whispered to Angela, 'what precisely does "do their stuff" mean?'

'It depends,' said Angela, deliberately vague. 'Attach him to the monitors, give him a catheter . . .'

Julia winced. Just the word 'catheter' brought back ghastly memories of her mother, and now it was being used in connection with her husband. She felt a weight dragging her down in the pit of her stomach and she dug her nails into her hands to stop herself imagining him being invaded with tubes, pulled about by inhuman hands in rubber gloves, enduring all the humiliating cruelties of sickness.

'Sit a moment,' said Angela.

Julia wrenched her mind back to the tiny waiting room, with seats crammed against the wall and a table in the middle that you had to clamber round.

'What a ghastly colour,' said Julia, of the oppressive dark blue walls and ceiling. 'This is a room where people hear some of the worst news of their life. You'd think they'd paint it white, or something innocuous. But this monstrous, monstrous . . . I mean, dark blue? Who would actually choose –?'

She stopped mid-sentence, noticing Angela and Rose exchange glances, and heard the hysteria in her voice.

'Sorry,' she murmured. 'Sorry.'

She made herself sit down and close her eyes. But in the blackness she stared into the dreadful abyss her life would be without Phillip. The loss was too great. She opened her eyes. Yet in the harsh fluorescent light she was still looking into exactly the same abyss. Phillip, please . . . She got to her feet, opened the door and looked out on the corridor, desperate to see something other than the vacuum that would be left by Phillip's death. But there was no escape from the emptiness, and she was sobbing once more, aware of Angela putting her arm about her and leading her to a chair.

Then the door to the waiting room opened and she looked up, hoping to see a doctor, or Anna – someone to give her hope. Instead, a man, about Julia's age, walked in and eyed them blankly, then sat down, bashing his knees against the table, and shut his eyes.

Julia stared at him. He was a man also in hell. *A man of sorrows, and acquainted with grief . . .* The words she had last heard spoken at Easter by Phillip's father flitted across her mind, back and forth, indicting her for all her futile, pathetic ambitions. *He was despised, and we esteemed him not . . .* I despised Phillip's work, thought Julia. I never gave him the credit for all his dreams of creating a better world. I was patronizing, dismissive. And now I despise myself because I should have taken more notice, shown more care, esteemed his love and his time and his body. And I will. Oh God, please bring him back to me. I will esteem him. I will.

And did I fail Anna? But what was I supposed to do? I couldn't police her every second, her every brilliant, stupid thought. Oh, where was Anna, her foolish genius of a daughter?

'You've left messages for Anna?' she said, turning to Rose.

Rose stopped biting her knuckles. 'Yes, Mum. And I've said to come here. I've told you. But you keep asking me.'

'It's not like her. She's usually so –' She was going to say sensible and reliable. But, of course, Anna had proved herself to be neither.

'If she's been fired,' suggested Angela, 'might she be out drinking with her friends?'

Julia wanted to say, Anna doesn't drink that much. And going out with friends was something she had to be virtually forced to do. Or so she thought. But what did she really know about her family?

She supposed she knew Angela, carrying her God within her, used to disease and dying. So did that mean she did not fear death and loss? But she then noticed the anxiety on Angela's face as she glanced at her watch.

'Do you think there's a problem?' she asked. 'Is that why they're taking so long with Phillip?'

'I don't know. Really. They may just be busy. And there's no real urgency.'

'But . . . how can there not be urgency?'

'Because . . . because sometimes there's nothing you can do. You can only wait. And . . .' Angela dried up. And sometimes, thought Angela to herself, all the struggle in the world, all the expertise and medical skill, is not going to make the slightest bit of difference.

She took hold of her sister's trembling hands. Angela was used to such grievous conversations but not with those she loved. It had always been her job to look out for Julia, and she had done so. Not that Julia had needed her help for years. But now she did and, realized Angela, trying not to let her fear show, she had none to offer.

Her little sister was in dreadful pain. And there was nothing she could do to take it away.

Angela had always tried to see beyond the horror of sickness, to rise above the daily tragedies and remind herself of the bigger picture – thanks to hospitals, people were given second chances, offered new lives. Yet that grand vision seemed irrelevant now. She fingered the cross around her neck. Her protestations of sympathy and understanding seemed all too condescendingly Christian. She bent her head. Give him back to her, she prayed. Dear Lord, please . . . but she felt spiritually lifeless. She had neglected God of late. That was Mirela's doing. She had made an idol of her daughter. And now where did that leave her? How could she help her sister? Oh merciful God . . .

She could not find the words and fell back on medical talk.

'Rose, just to warn you both,' she went on, 'because I don't think the nurse mentioned it. It can be a bit of a shock seeing someone in intensive care for the first time. It's such an unnatural sort of place that –'

But she was interrupted by a nurse coming in to say they might see Phillip now.

'I understand his parents are coming?' the nurse said to Julia.

Julia knew the significance of that casual question.

'Yes, I've called them,' she said.

Then she saw her husband, his body covered in a hospital blanket that failed to hide all the tubes and wires connecting him to the bleeping machines by his bed, and a great plastic pipe shoved down his throat. She laid her hand on his clammy forehead. A doctor introduced himself, a model of grave compassion, and Julia forced herself to concentrate, seeking hope in his words.

But there was little. The doctor suspected Phillip had a ruptured blood vessel inside his skull, probably due to his fall the other day.

'But that was eleven days ago,' Julia protested. 'He seemed all right. How could it have taken so long?'

It was unusual, the doctor explained. But not unheard of. Overnight they would give him drugs to help reduce the swelling and then reassess the situation in the morning.

Reassess the situation? What does that mean? That he might be dead by then? She made herself ask with her usual directness, 'How serious is this? I mean, do you think he will die tonight?'

'It's hard to say. I could give you statistics on these sorts of injuries but at this stage everyone is an individual. It depends upon the exact nature of the trauma, which we don't know. Upon your husband's own strengths and weaknesses.'

'He doesn't smoke,' said Rose, desperation written on her face, 'and he's quite fit.'

'All that helps, of course, to put the odds in his favour.'

'What are the odds,' said Julia, barely audible, 'of him surviving this?'

The doctor looked her in the eye. 'About fifty-fifty. Tonight is critical.'

Julia braced herself. 'And,' she forced herself to go on, 'will he be . . .? If he survives . . .? I mean . . .'

But she could not bring herself to say the words and, instead, it was Rose who found the strength to ask, 'Do you think, after this, that he might be brain-damaged in some way?'

'There's a possibility,' said the doctor. 'I'm sorry, but yes, there is.'

Julia's worst nightmare stared her in the face. Brain-damaged? Her husband in a wheelchair, unable to talk, incontinent.

'I can't!' Her voice came out in a wild cry, and she grabbed at her elder sister. 'I can't. You know I can't.'

'Come with me,' said Angela, swiftly leading her out of the ward. 'It's all right.'

'It's not. Because I can't, Angela. I can't look after him like that. Not brain-damaged. Not all . . . not all over again. I couldn't bear it with Mum. You know I couldn't. To have to do it with Phillip.'

'You don't have to,' said Angela, holding her in her arms. 'You don't.'

'But I might. You heard him.'

'Julia, look at me. You don't have to do anything. Not now.'

'But I can't . . . Oh my God, why can't I?'

'Julia, it's all right. Honestly, lots of people respond like this at first.'

'But I'm . . .' Julia put her head in her hands. But I'm not lots of people, she wanted to say. I can cope. Instead, she repeated – over and over – 'I can't. I know it. I can't.'

# 47

Laura lay in her bed, no more able to sleep than fly. Phillip had not called, but no matter, she told herself. What had happened between them had meant something. She was certain. It had been what she always tried to paint, that moment of perfection, however fleeting, and now she knew it for herself. Whatever lies ahead, she insisted, I have had that joy. And it is mine, all mine – and nothing, or no one, can take it from me.

But she wanted Phillip now, living and breathing beside her. He will be with me in the morning, she told herself with a confidence she did not totally trust. He will. Something must have happened that prevented him phoning. He was a man of his word. She was in no doubt.

'Mum!' There was a sudden cry from Eliza. 'Mum!'

Eliza charged into her mother's bed. 'I dreamed I was being chased and there was this monster.'

'There, there,' soothed Laura.

'And he was grabbing me and no one came.'

'Oh darling,' murmured Laura, guilty that all she wanted was for her daughter to go back to sleep so she might be allowed to think. 'You're all right now.'

'But I tried to shout and I couldn't. No sound came!'

'How frightening, sweetheart, but you're safe now.'

Laura enclosed the child in her arms, but her mind was ranging free, picturing herself lying on the sofa with Phillip, putting her head on a pillow and talking with Phillip, going to bed every ordinary night, with Phillip. *With Phillip?* Could it really happen? Not to have to do it all on her own any more? To share her life, adult to adult, man to woman? And to Laura, her senses sharpened to the quick, even the shadows in the dark little room seemed to be affirming yes! Yes!

'Mum? Can I?'

'Can you what?'

'Why don't you listen? Please, can't I stay with you?'

'Sorry, yes, yes. Sleep with me. Quiet now and close your eyes.'

'But what if I wake up and you're not there?'

'I will be here.'

'But what if you're really not there?' gulped Eliza. 'That it's all a dream? All of it? And I've only dreamed you and really I'm being chased by that monster and that's what's real – the monster and not you.'

'Sweetheart, this isn't a dream. I'm not a dream.'

'But how do I know you're not just saying that in my dream?'

'Because . . . because . . . Oh darling, come here.'

And Laura held her daughter tight, stroking her hair and telling her over and over that she was safe until eventually the tension left Eliza's tired little body and she fell asleep.

Laura shifted her daughter from her lap and on to the pillow beside her. But Eliza had wrenched Laura back to consciousness of herself and her situation. Where would her daughters fit in this bright, shiny new world of her own wild dreams? Her imagination could not devise a place where she and Phillip might be together without dreadful complications and compromises. Sharing her life with Phillip meant sharing him with her daughters and his daughters and his wife. *His wife*.

Laura looked once more at her phone. Still no message. But that was not, she told herself yet again, anything to worry about. An image of Julia flashed across her mind. Julia, beautiful and clever, arguing for all the claims of family commitment, would be indomitable, and fear struck Laura like a left hook. How could she compete? But she could not think of Phillip as a competition. That reduced her love for him to some sordid little scrap. But weren't affairs by definition sordid? Didn't dishonesty taint the love from the start?

*

Next morning, she got the girls up, made breakfast, took them to school. She looked for Phillip and Rose at St Catherine's school gates but saw neither. She began the walk home, clutching her phone. They had arranged he would be round at her home about ten o'clock. He would explain then, she told herself, why he had not called.

She hesitated a moment outside an exorbitantly expensive florist's. Last night, when she had imagined this morning, she had told herself she would treat herself, say to hell with the money and fill her room with flowers.

Today the florist was selling soft yellow roses that looked as if they had been picked from a garden rather than a hothouse and costing the sort of money Laura, who was always so frugal, would never normally spend.

She pictured the roses, so sensual but peaceful, in her tiny bedroom. They were perfect in their open beauty. And longing for Phillip hit her like a kick in the stomach and she had to bow down, as if to brace herself from the pain. Because what if he did not come? What if? But she could not admit the possibility that Phillip might break his word and her lovely roses would taunt her foolish dreams.

'The yellow ones, please,' she said, standing tall. She would not let doubts enter her head. She would snatch from life a perfect morning. 'Three bunches.'

And smiling at the florist with a dazzling confidence, Laura parted with her money and filled her arms with golden flowers.

Four hours later, Laura sat in bed trying to draw. But she could barely hold the pencil, her hand was shaking so.

If she concentrated on the roses, she hoped to force herself to forget everything except the flowers before her. But her eyes kept wandering around the room, thinking of what she had hoped the morning would bring and what had actually happened.

She had not heard a word from Phillip. Of course she need not sit passively waiting, she could be the one to call and ask him what was going on. But what would she say? Berate him for breaking his word? Demand apologies? What was the point?

If she had misread him, if what had happened between them was already over . . .

She pressed her face into the pillow. But he had said, she sobbed inwardly, this was not just a fling. He had said. And even though it was now quite clear to her that he was not coming, part of her still believed him. She could see the look in his eyes, hear his invitation, feel his hands holding hers. He was not lying. Deep down she was sure.

Oh please God, she begged, bring him to me.

Because loving him, however briefly, had pulled her back into life, and the thought that it was all over, so swiftly, before it had barely begun, was intolerable.

At the school gates the following morning, she again looked out for Phillip and when he was not there she leaped on the thought that he had been struck down by some dreadful flu and was too sick to call. The newspapers were full of deadly viruses targeting the strong and healthy. But that brief respite passed. He could not, she thought, be too weak to pick up a phone.

He has made his choice, she told herself, as she walked home. I will find a way to live with it. I have no option. And I can manage, I really can, as I have always managed. Then her phone did ring, and she pounced on it as if it was a gift from God.

It was Father Eoghan.

'Laura? I just wondered how you were?' he began.

For a dreadful moment it occurred to her that Father Eoghan knew about Phillip, that some leering, gossiping grapevine, mocking her ache for Phillip's body and his tenderness, had informed the priest that she loved a married man, was contemplating breaking up a union that had been made in the sight of God. So here was Father Eoghan calling to say kindly but firmly that her love was wrong.

'We'd said nine-thirty,' he was saying. 'And I know lots of people are going down with this flu and I just wanted to check you were all right.'

'Oh . . . oh, I'm so sorry,' she said, only now remembering that she was due at the church to help him with the accounts. 'I completely forgot.'

'Don't worry,' he said. 'We can do it at another time. I know how busy you are.'

Busy? She was busy, of course. She could fill every minute of her day with selfless good works. Indeed, her whole life could be crammed full. No matter that it felt mundane and tedious. Her life could be important in its small way. She knew the argument Father Eoghan would use. Be content with your limited abilities, as they are what God has given you. Acceptance of inadequacy is a gift, in the same way as genius like her father's was a gift.

'They can wait till after Christmas,' Father Eoghan was saying.

She suppressed a sigh. 'No, no, it's fine.' She would get the job over with. The mundane and tedious could take your mind off things and the concentration of work was what, she told herself, she needed. 'I'll come now.'

# 48

For four days, Laura heard nothing from Phillip. She looked after the girls, fulfilled her duties with spiritless efficiency. Then, on the Saturday, she and her brothers met at their parents' house to celebrate, so they thought, their mother's birthday. But there was no celebration.

They all gathered together in the kitchen, as usual. Their mother asked them to sit down as if they were children again and were being told to eat their tea, but then, with a strange and uncharacteristic tranquillity, Venetia explained that she had cancer. A very aggressive cancer, she insisted repeatedly, and had only weeks to live.

Later, when Laura looked back on that dreadful day, she realized that she and her brothers had behaved with the predictability of the alphabet. Mark, always domineering and capable, tried to take charge, to believe he could control and beat this awful situation. Robert, so emotional, took his mother in his arms, sobbing. And Laura, sitting in disbelief, hid all her shock and horror.

'But Mum!' cried Robert. 'Why didn't you tell us? I should have seen. I could have sat with you in those monstrous waiting rooms.'

'The doctors have only just told me,' lied Venetia. 'Sometimes, I don't know, maybe that's for the best. Less suffering. I've been so happy in my life, so incredibly blessed and loved, so lucky with your father.' She turned to him and smiled. 'And with you all.'

Laura clutched at her mother's hand. At that moment she would have given every ounce of her future happiness to keep her mother, now so defenceless and exposed, alive. This calm acceptance in the face of death could not, Laura was certain, be genuine. And she felt an almost unbearable pity for her mother trying to persuade her children not to be too sad because she had had a wonderful life.

How, thought Laura, could almost forty years of marriage to a man as self-absorbed as her father have been wonderful and fulfilling? Surely her mother must have longed for a tenderness and intimacy her father was incapable of giving. And as she stared at her mother under the glare of the kitchen lights, almost judgemental in their brightness, she at last saw her with a compassionate clarity.

Why wasn't I kinder? she cried inwardly. Why didn't I understand that her coldness was its opposite? That her overbearing manner was the only way of containing a loneliness and longing that would otherwise overwhelm her?

Now her mother's life was almost at an end – just weeks, she said, and already she was fading fast – and Laura pressed her mother's hand to her lips, as if she might hold on to her, while Mark was insisting, 'Surely there's something that can be done.' He began rattling off names of people he knew, had vaguely heard of, who had discovered miraculous cures. 'There's a friend of Jane's who –'

'Mark, please,' interrupted Venetia, with a hint of her normal vigour, 'don't you think if there was something I'd have found it out? I'm fortunate. I will live to meet my new grandchildren.'

'But –'

'No buts . . . I've had a wonderful life.'

'Don't speak as though you're an old woman,' cried Mark. 'Sixty-one is far too young these days.'

'When someone you love dies, they are always too young,' said Venetia, as if reading from a prepared script. 'I've been lucky. Really. I mean, look at Phillip Snowe. The man who took over from me at Hartley High,' she explained to Mark and Robert. 'Only forty-eight. And with two teenage daughters. That is too young. Whereas I . . .'

Laura stared at her mother, not understanding.

'Mum,' she murmured, her incomprehension enlarging to panic. 'What did you say?'

'Phillip died . . . I thought you'd have heard.'

Laura gripped her chair as if something had collapsed inside her. She had prepared herself for loss, for him going back to Julia, but not this. Not death.

'But I saw him.' He was alive then, so very alive. 'Just days ago.'

'It's a terrible shock,' said Venetia. 'The poor family.'

'He can't,' Laura whispered under her breath. We made love . . .

Brittle winter sunlight flashed off the surgically clean surfaces, a vase of near-black hellebores stood on the window sill, a fly buzzed about manically, crashing into the windows. Laura noticed all these things, the ring twisting loosely on her mother's bony fingers, the new sourness to her mother's breath as Venetia said, 'I'm sorry, Laura, I know you liked him. He'd been knocked down a week or so ago by some mugger. And the bang on the head . . . well, I'm not sure of the medical detail, but he died early Wednesday morning. Apparently, he'd been trying to help some poor girl whose bag had been snatched. He was that sort of man, wasn't he, Laura? So good.'

Laura did not trust herself to speak. She wrapped her arms about her. And this pathetic gesture made her recall what different arms had held her just days ago. But those arms, she was being told, were dead.

'Laura,' Venetia was saying. 'I want to go to the funeral, and I imagine you will too. So perhaps we might go together. They've managed to get it in first thing on Tuesday, so as not to have to wait till after Christmas. As a governor, and as the ex-chair, I think it's our duty.'

'Mum!' cried Robert. 'Your only duty is to yourself.'

'But Robert, I want to go, and I'm sure Laura does too.'

No! No! Laura wanted to cry. There was a mistake. There had to be. Her mother had misunderstood, confused by her own situation.

'Mum, please,' she whispered. 'Are you sure?'

'Yes, dear. The doctor made it quite clear. There's nothing that can be done for me.'

Laura could hardly breathe. All the strength went out of her. Her mother was dying, yet all her thoughts were with her married lover. 'I meant Phillip,' she murmured.

But no one heard, as Mark was saying, 'Mum, won't you at least try and get another opinion? I will arrange it all.'

Laura began to tremble. Phillip! Did you suffer? Were you in pain? She could feel the blow to her own head, the shutting down of her vital organs, and it tore her heart and she could not bear it. She clutched at her shaking hands under the table. No one must see. And now there was so much grief in her, she had no idea what she might do with it. He was gone, for ever and ever. She longed to scream out in anguish, but already a vice of muscles was tightening around her throat.

Then her father grabbed her arm and sobbed, 'What am I going to do without your mother?' And Laura had to stop herself recoiling from him. 'You'll help me, Laura, won't you?'

'Yes,' she said, not thinking.

For so long now she had been a creature of duty, quarantining herself in obligation to her daughters, her parents, to others. But love for Phillip had not been duty. It had been its opposite. In the dishonesty and the betrayal there had been the paradox of an incredible blessing.

'You'll go with your mother to this man's funeral, won't you?' her father went on. 'I'll go too, if it's what she wants. I don't want to miss a moment with her.'

She looked at him with burning eyes. In weeks, she thought, I will have to attend my mother's funeral. She knew her role for that dreadful day when it came – she would be the bereaved daughter. But at Phillip's funeral, who am I? A colleague on a school governing body? A friend? A lover?

*The woman for whom he was about to leave his family?*

But no one knows about me, she thought. Within hours of making love to her he was dead. So no one could possibly know what she felt for him – or he for her. Surely he had not told Julia about her, she thought. Surely he hadn't. Or had he? And it occurred to her that the only other person who might have any idea how she was feeling was the woman who was now his widow.

## 49

In the front pew of the church Julia bit her lip as the organ played 'And all our flesh is as the grass' from the Brahms Requiem Mass. She and Angela had also chosen Brahms for their mother's funeral, though it was played on a CD rather than with a real organ and choir, and the dark, glorious music had sounded thin and tinny in the grim modern church on the Hartley Estate that Julia had been forced to attend as a child. Julia hated that church. The place always felt like a shelter for the down-trodden – not in itself a bad thing, Julia knew, but, to her, the church represented her mother's dumb acceptance of second best, if not defeat.

Yet today, as she sat under the vaulted arches of the Georgian church in fashionable North London, listening to an expensive choir, Julia felt every bit as defeated as she had on the Hartley Estate. Part of the point of funerals, she knew, was to divert yourself with details so you could keep your mind off the dreadful fact that someone you loved was dead. And that had worked for her daughters and Phillip's parents. But not Julia. Her own view – which she just about managed to keep to herself as her daughters and in-laws discussed hymns, flowers, coffins, readings and the rest – was that funerals were about the needs of the living. And Julia's need was to curl up like a dog in a basket, for nothing could disguise the dreadful truth that if you had not met the needs of the dead when they were alive, no amount of Brahms and heavenly voices could help them now. It was too late. She had hurt Phillip, through negligence, through weakness, through her own deliberate fault. He had turned to another woman.

She tugged at her black suede gloves, stifling a sob. Dear God, she prayed to a deity she had no faith in. Let me just get through this, let me get through this day without further distressing my children, and she tried to pull herself together by losing herself in the language of what Phillip's father, who was officiating, was reading.

*Thou turnest man to destruction; and sayest, Return, ye children of men.*
*For a thousand years in thy sight are but as yesterday when it is past, and*
*as a watch in the night.*

It is all over so quickly, he was saying. And everything this church witnesses confirms it, thought Julia, reading a memorial slab to an 'ever loving and devoted wife and mother who departed this life in 1862 aged 57'. Yet, to Julia, it felt that the rest of her life would go on for too many long, long years, living with the knowledge – day in, day out – that it was too late ever to tell her husband how deep her regrets were and how much she loved him. She forgot how Phillip had delighted in her searing intelligence, how he had taken heart from her fighting spirit, how he loved her sense of the ridiculous, how he felt blessed by her beautiful body, because his last words to her were that he loved another woman.

Beset with morbid self-reproach, she saw that as her fault. If I had not failed him, been so self-absorbed, so self-centred. He was not a dishonest man, not a disloyal man. He must have been desperately distressed to have looked elsewhere for a comfort she had been too blind to see he needed.

So he had turned to Laura.

Laura, she thought, succeeded where I failed.

Laura – how she hated the name.

Laura gave him the understanding I did not.

She was desperate to turn round to see if Laura had come to the funeral, not sure she even knew who she was looking for. Who the hell was this woman who apparently could do what she could not? She had a vague recollection of a dishevelled mess in sheepskin at the school concert. She was beside herself, wanting to see what it was her husband preferred to her. She glanced round quickly.

The church was packed, mainly with Phillip's former work colleagues. But a few faces Julia did not recognize. Wearing dowdy unironed black with a grey tinge they were, guessed Julia, contacts from his charity work, and she was scouring these pews for Laura as another phone went off and the embarrassed fumbling reminded her to face forward, not stare around at everyone like a fidgety child.

Of course Laura could not help Phillip either now, she thought. No one could. Julia tried to concentrate on what was directly ahead but the sight of the coffin on a trestle in front of her was also affecting her irrationally. The coffin was made of cardboard. Phillip's parents had suggested this because, with the self-righteousness that always drove Phillip mad, they said cardboard was ecologically sound. Anna and Rose had also latched on to the idea. And although Julia sat in on these discussions wanting to scream, what does it matter what the coffin's made of? she had gone along with cardboard as it was a relief to have one decision actually made to everyone's satisfaction. But now – and it was absurd, she knew – she was worrying whether cardboard was sturdy enough to hold a man of her husband's stature. Phillip was tall and well built, and she had this grotesque vision of the seams giving way and, with a great thud, him falling out. She gasped in appalled horror.

Angela turned to her and Rose clutched her hand. 'Mum?' she whispered. 'What?'

'It's okay,' murmured Julia. 'Really, darling, thank you.' And stroking her daughter's young, white hand she forced her attention back to Phillip's father.

'They are like grass . . .' he intoned. 'In the morning it flourisheth, and groweth up; in the evening it is cut down . . .'

Cut down? Fewer trees are cut down, thought Julia, if the coffin is cardboard, and she supposed Phillip would have approved of that. But suddenly it occurred to her that the long cardboard box looked like a delivery from Amazon – skis, perhaps – and instinct made her turn, as though to tell Phillip, because the idea would have made him laugh.

The congregation began shuffling to their feet as they stood to sing 'Make Me A Channel Of Your Peace', and Julia hoped to catch Anna's attention because this was her choice of hymn. But Anna just kept her eyes fixed on the cold flagstones.

It had been like this since Phillip's death. Whenever Julia tried to talk, Anna would respond in clipped tones that she was as right as could be expected and wanted to be alone. She could not have been more dismissive when asked why she'd been fired from the magazine, except to say it had nothing to do with the theft of the clothes. But then she clammed up – and Julia feared she was lying again.

Bereavement, Julia reminded herself, affects people in any number of ways. Silence and distance were not unusual, particularly in teenagers, even at the best of times. And of course, Anna never spoke much – unlike Rose, with her gangs of friends forever gabbling away in a barrage of chatter. Anna brooded and reflected, as if she was preoccupied in making plans or guarding secrets of which Julia knew nothing.

On a marble bust up to her left was a memorial to another Anna who 'had been taken from this world' aged just twenty-one in 1788. What had gone wrong with that poor Anna who had died too young? What illness or misadventure? And what might befall her own darling daughter, now fiddling with a loose thread on the coat that she insisted on wearing even though it was falling apart and Julia had offered a thousand times to buy her a new one. Where might her beloved Anna end up? What fate awaited her?

Anna had always been so disturbingly well behaved, but now Anna was a thief. She made Julia's own teenage defiance look no more dangerous than a toddler flinging its teddy out of the cot. Anna's first foray into flaunting authority might well have landed her in prison, and that knowledge made Julia icy with fear, destroying all her confidence in the future. She could see perils everywhere for her child because brilliance, Julia now understood, was not always a gift. It could bring destruction in its wake, and bereavement could send someone as finely tuned as Anna completely off the rails. And Julia felt utterly bereft because she had not realized till now how much she depended on Phillip in guarding Anna from whatever demons were pursuing her.

'Darling . . . Anna,' she ventured, desperate to reach out to her daughter as the hymn ended and they all sat down again for the eulogy. 'That was lovely – the perfect choice.' To which Anna responded with a shrug, and Julia's wave of love for her grieving, troubled daughter was thrown back in her face.

But if Anna was untouchable, Rose at least had softened, creeping sobbing into her bed in the early hours of the morning. And Julia found comfort in the comforting of her daughter. She gave her younger child a gentle smile as there was a peal of laughter from the congregation.

An old colleague of Phillip's giving the eulogy had presumably told a joke which Julia had missed. Concentrate, she told herself, as the friend, standing at the front, smiled directly at her.

'With Phillip,' he continued, 'the rhythm of the advertising world was instinctive and those around him counted themselves lucky if they could catch some of his magic and learn from it.'

Julia nodded politely, as he was still holding her eye.

'Because,' he went on, 'no one was better than Phillip at spotting the intellectual flaw in a campaign or the fatal gap in a presentation. The success of his agency sprang from his willpower, hunger for life, inquiring mind, ability to get to the heart of the matter and an intuitive knowledge of what the client really wanted.'

I should have written the eulogy myself, thought Julia. But she had not been able to apply herself. Even now it was hard enough merely to listen because her eyes kept drifting up to a stained-glass window of St Sebastian, whose fair hair reminded her of Phillip's, and she could see Phillip, young and golden, at the party where they first met. He hadn't intended going, she discovered later. He was on his way to the pub and only went because the friend he was with insisted on looking in for half an hour. I might, she thought, shifting on the hard pew, never have met him.

But chance, coincidence, serendipity – call it what she wanted – had brought him to her. And chance had taken him from her. If Phillip had not been on that particular London street, at that particular time ... She almost broke out in the grim laughter of self-mockery because, her whole life, she had thought through every choice and decision with immense confidence and arrogance, dedicating herself to taking control of her life. As if one could control anything.

She gazed up at St Sebastian as if she was also being shot through with arrows. How could she have been so stupid? How could she have permitted herself such a failure of understanding of the most basic facts of life? She had followed her reason, exercised diligence, balanced one alternative against another. But to what end? Her marriage had not been what she thought it was, her career was slipping away like a mudslide, her elder daughter was a crook, and her younger daughter, beautiful and lazy, was interested only in clothes and being adored.

The first notes of 'All People That On Earth Do Dwell', the closing hymn, swept her to her feet.

She had been certain that, with careful planning, she could engineer life to her own will. Now she was certain of nothing. Only that she had a smallness of stature and was a lesser person than she believed herself to be. With the loss of Phillip came the loss of faith in herself, her past and her future. As everyone around her wailed, 'Sing to the Lord with cheerful voice,' she cast about helplessly, with no idea where she might ever find that faith again.

For most of the people here, she thought, this service is closure of their relationship with Phillip. The ritual will help them come to terms with the loss of a friend and colleague. But as soon as this hymn ends, many will race to work or regroup for coffee or head back home.

Time would heal. Time would help close over the loss.

But time, Julia knew, could do nothing for her.

She looked at Phillip's parents singing, 'His mercy is for ever sure,' as if their sanity depended on it. Nor, she felt certain, would time help them. However appalling and deep their grief now, they would feel his loss even more keenly as the years went on, when they missed his phone calls and lively news, when he no longer visited with his warm energy, and when they became frailer, less able and they could not turn to him for his generous, practical love.

And her daughters. The loss of their father, when they still needed so much from him and he still had so much to give as they grew into adulthood, made her want to turn and run. It was such a waste, it would blind and hinder them for years to come. If not for ever. Because, she realized, it is not in this initial dreadful shock of mourning that my children will most miss their father. It is when they have a problem and need to turn to someone who cares for them with that perfect, unconditional, non-judgemental love. It is if and when they marry, have a child and want to share their joy. It is when the world is cruel and they need a place to run and hide. That is when they will truly know what they have been robbed of.

It does not end now, with the funeral service, the cremation, ashes to ashes. It does not end, she thought, as those behind her sang, 'Be praise and glory evermore.'

For me, it never will.

Nor would it end for Laura.

Crushed at the rear of the church, she stood supporting her parents, her mother gripping her arm, her father, sniffing and sneezing, resting his hand on her shoulder.

'Beautiful service,' said Venetia, as the hymn drew to a close.

Mechanically, Laura nodded.

She had listened to the eulogy feeling bewildered, thinking she might have been at the funeral of a stranger. This advertising guru, so brilliant 'at spotting the intellectual flaw in a campaign' and with the 'intuitive knowledge of what the client really wanted' was not the man she loved. The loyal friend of this smart crowd, the husband to Julia whom Laura, seated so far at the back, her view obscured by a pillar, had not even glimpsed, was unknown to her. And she wanted to cry out, *my Phillip* was not so sharp and quick, so assured and successful. Instead he was bruised and bewildered, hungry in spirit. But with an irony so cruel, his desire to do good – to help that woman whose bag was stolen – cost him his life. Now his energy and questing heart were as nothing.

'I do think,' her mother whispered, as the pall-bearers moved slowly towards the altar, 'a cardboard coffin is a good idea. I've heard of them, but never actually seen one before.'

Laura dropped her head, trying to shut her ears. But the truth, however fearsome, was unavoidable. Phillip's body was about to be burned. In that box lay a man who just days ago had lain in her bed, a man who said that he loved her. Phillip, so tender and ardent, who stirred me back to life.

'That's what I want,' Venetia whispered in her ear. 'Cardboard! Tell your brothers, won't you? Your father won't be in a fit state to organize anything. I think he's getting one of his colds. Have you got a spare handkerchief for him?'

Thou shalt have no other gods before me, thought Laura, fumbling in her bag. But it was too late. Phillip, and thoughts of Phillip, consumed her. And she could see no hope because nothing in her experience told her that love came easily. There might never be another chance. Ignore desires long enough and you grow numb, and she saw herself growing more bitter, more repressed, more disappointed. Yet she had a job to do.

She had to promise her children that life could be full of love and adventure. But how could she?

She looked at the altar, the figure of Christ on the cross, with its promise of the resurrection of the dead. But I don't want life after death, she thought. Father Eoghan, of course, would argue that life was here, right now, if she would only open her heart and mind. Like a lover, God quickens and energizes. God's passion and concern for her was every bit as fervent and zealous. God longed to evoke in her all that was good and spirited, summoning her to life and enthusiasm, reminding her of the joy. Just as Phillip did, reflected Laura bitterly. And for some, God did too. Father Eoghan, in his celibate life, was so very caring and compassionate, so very much alive. But me? wondered Laura. Can those unseen hands really touch me? Is the still, calm voice enough? And every fibre in her being seemed to be screaming, no! It's Phillip's hands I want, Phillip's voice. Phillip . . . whose coffin is being lifted, slowly making its dreadful journey back down the aisle for a family-only cremation.

Then for the first time that day Laura caught sight of Julia.

Julia, so wan and lovely, head bowed, as composed as a Japanese still life.

Julia, the principal mourner, following the coffin of her husband.

Julia, the mother of Phillip's children.

Julia, the woman who shared her life with Phillip.

Julia, who had what I can never know.

Tears smarted in Laura's eyes and she fought for self-mastery. I am not the one allowed to cry. But for a moment Laura felt as if she had been cursed like Midas. Her love for Phillip made her incapable of drawing breath. Her heart was thudding too fast, there was a pain in her chest and she gasped. This pretence of detachment was almost too much to bear and she longed to scream out at Julia. Suddenly she wanted Julia to know. She wanted everyone here to realize. He loved me! My warmth, my understanding, my body. He told me he had never felt such ease before. That with me it was so natural, so comfortable. That with me he felt alive!

'Take your mother's arm,' her father began fussing as a portion of her mind goaded her on. Tell them! Scream out your love! You know you want to. All those years of behaving well. The good mother, the good daughter, the good neighbour. What a farce, the voice taunted, as they began shifting along the pew, back down the aisle with the rest of the slow-moving congregation and out of the church into the bitterly cold December day. Go on! Wail and yell, throw yourself on the pyre, knock back the poison.

'Let me find my gloves,' her mother was saying.

As the dead leaves blew around the graves in the freezing wind, Laura could see Julia, supported by friends and family, embraced and comforted. You thoughtless bitch! You failed him! You were never there, you never listened. You had so much, yet for all your cleverness you were too stupid to understand, too blind to see.

Then for a moment she thought she caught Julia looking directly at her, in her eyes a sense of recognition and awful acknowledgement. But the second the thought flashed through her head, Julia had turned away. Julia does not even know I exist, thought Laura, as her mother prodded her arm, asking, 'Did you know Phillip did that campaign for coffee you always found so funny?'

Laura did not. She clutched at the service sheet of a man whom, she thought, I barely knew. Yet I did know him, because I knew his kindness and I knew his love.

But what if she had deluded herself? It was not only the loss. The briefness of their relationship – if she could even call it that – made her question everything. Now, with her mother saying how hard this must be for Phillip's daughters, how those poor girls must be grieving, ugly, crude words rattled round Laura's exhausted mind, demeaning and humiliating. You pathetic, spinsterish old maid, carrying on with a married man. Of course you're in hell. Affairs cause pain. Who are you to think you'd be any different? So what were you to him, anyway? Maybe nothing but an easy opportunity for spicing up a stunted life. A brief sop to loneliness.

Her mother was telling her to go and help her father, as she didn't want him slipping on all the ice. 'It's treacherous out here. Make sure he's careful.'

Laura offered him her arm and Patrick leaned upon her.

'You're a good girl. But no crying, now,' he chivvied. 'So let's be hopeful, for your mother's sake. We've got this new doctor Mark's found to see shortly. He might have – you never know – a miracle.'

But it's Phillip I'm crying for, she almost bawled at him. It's Phillip and the life I dared to dream of sharing with him. Not a life of bringing up children alone, painting the odd picture, doing good works.

'You'll be all right, Laura,' said Patrick. 'You may not realize it now. But your mother and I have been talking about the future, after, you know, your poor mother . . . that we might be able to help one another. You and I.'

Laura heard the appeal in his voice and she almost doubled up in pain. For years, her father had expected Venetia to pander to the every whim of his damned genius. So when she dies, do they expect me, his daughter to dance attendance on him instead? Is this what he and her mother had been concocting?

She looked at his lean face in terror. If he got his way, the future lay before her in an inevitable pattern, because there was no end to looking after people and the relentless necessity of care – of her children, her father, her neighbours, the sick.

'Now we've got half an hour to get to Harley Street,' Venetia was saying. 'Will you go and get a cab, please, Laura.'

There were no happy endings. I have lost him, thought Laura. If I ever really had him. And she wanted to howl in her wretchedness. But instead, she walked dry-eyed through the mourners thronging the churchyard and out on to the road.

Looking for a taxi, Laura's eyes were drawn to a plain-looking girl sitting on the steps of the war memorial nearby. She was in such distress, her shoulders shuddering as she hunched into herself that, for a moment, Laura forgot her own unhappiness. She watched the girl press a mangled ball of tissues close to her tear-streaked face, saw the tension in that thin body, and asked the question she feared people might have asked of her. What is she doing, intruding with her grief, at this funeral?

Or had she even been at the service? wondered Laura, trying to place her as the girl began walking away. She was not one of Phillip's daughters and she had none of the bearing and style of the young women who were clearly his daughters' friends. Was that stifled whimpering, wondered Laura, caused by some dreadful private tragedy? Or was she mourning Phillip and, if so, who was this lost and pitiful creature?

Then it occurred to her. She almost ran to catch her up.

'Excuse me,' began Laura, 'I don't mean to intrude . . . but I think . . . I'm sorry, but I think we both knew Phillip – Mr Snowe.'

The girl flicked away the mousy hair blowing across her face and stared down at her shoes.

'You used to be at Hartley High, didn't you?' went on Laura. 'You see, he was a governor there, and so was I.'

At this the girl looked at Laura with a dull anger.

'It's Isabel, isn't it? Isabel West?'

Laura took her silence as affirmation.

'I thought so. You see, Phillip talked about you, a great deal,' said Laura. 'He and I . . . we . . . He thought you were an incredibly talented artist. When he first saw your work he was so struck by it. As was I. He wanted to help you. But . . . but it's hard to know, sometimes, the best way of helping people. Phillip said that to me once. But I know you were terribly important to him, that he wanted to help you.'

Her words felt clumsy and patronizing. She was not sure what she was trying to say. Simply that she, one mourner speaking to another, was sorry for her loss? But it was more than that. She and Phillip had argued over Isabel, fighting over the right thing to do. If it had not been for Isabel, they might never have truly met.

She looked into the girl's face, a white mask hiding God knows what fathomless feelings. Laura recalled that Isabel's mother was very ill. Was this girl weeping for her mother? Laura wanted to take Isabel in her arms and comfort her, but that was impossible. So she cast about for some words of consolation, but they did not exist.

Then it occurred to Laura, was she saying she wanted to take over from Phillip and help Isabel herself? Hadn't she been the one to insist that he help her? Might that be something she could do for Phillip? For this grieving child?

'Please, please,' she pressed on. 'I know how very important you were to Phillip.' She kept saying the same thing while Isabel appraised her ever more closely. 'He would hate it if you didn't have the chance to carry on with your art. So I could . . . I could help you, if you'd let me. Please.'

'Why?' Isabel spoke at last. 'Why do you want to help me?'

'Because,' said Laura, fighting the tears returning to her eyes, 'you were important to Phillip and that makes you important to me. And because you're talented, and to see that talent wasted . . . that would be wrong. You'll regret it.' The words came out in a sob now. 'And it would help me. It would help me very much to help you.'

## 50

It was seven weeks, two days since Phillip's death – Julia could tell you to the exact hour – and she stood at the door of her drawing room panting. She had only walked up the twelve stairs from the kitchen with coffee and sandwiches for her sister. But now, even a short flight of steps seemed too much of an exertion.

She had never been so unfit. Quite the reverse. But she had completely given up on the gym, swimming, yoga . . . all the activities she used to pack into her schedule. There was no excuse because she had more time on her hands than she had ever known. For the first time in her life, she was not working.

'Chicken sandwich?' said Julia, aware of Angela's professional glance.

'Thanks. But won't you have something to eat as well?'

'I'm fine,' said Julia, putting her hand to her chest. She had indigestion, another first in her life. It was anxiety, she told herself, anxiety for her daughters, anxiety for herself, anxiety feeding on yet more anxiety.

Julia pushed the sandwiches away, concentrating on quashing her rising sickness.

Anxiety also made you nauseous – all the adrenaline racing round the body to fight this invisible foe assaulting her every waking moment.

'Thank you for coming round again,' she went on, truly grateful to see her sister.

'I was nearby anyway – I'm seeing James this afternoon,' said Angela, which is what she invariably said when she called by so that Julia would not think she was checking up on her.

Angela, to Julia's astonishment and joy, was in love with the son of a former patient. How Angela was able to fit James in with all her other loves – Mirela, God, her elderly patients – Julia had no idea. Love, she now knew with all too brutal clarity, requires hard work and generosity with your time.

'Do you see him every day?' Julia asked, aware she clutched at this story of her sister falling in love like a child to a fairy tale. Their lives had swung. Even as teenagers Julia had been the one with the man, the one out on the town leading an outwardly grown-up existence. Angela had stayed home looking after their mother, performing tasks no one at her age should have to do, living a life she was both too young and too old for. Now, however, it was her sister who had all the trappings of the good life.

'Well, not quite every day,' said Angela, 'but we speak a lot.'

That her sister had found a man to love who matched her in ardour and goodness seemed, to Julia, a miracle in a world which had otherwise grown utterly strange and hostile, some justice in a place where anarchy was overwhelming her. 'But you mustn't let coming here take up time you could have with him. Really, he's the priority.'

Angela looked across at Julia wondering how much weight her sister had lost. Where before Julia had had a lovely, lithe grace, in just weeks she had become angular and atrophied. Now she sat on the sofa with her thin arms outstretched to the side, like a broken crucifix, and all Angela's instincts made her want to help.

Julia was suffering dreadfully. That was to be expected, of course. But Angela had thought Julia would respond to the tragedy of Phillip's death by throwing herself into her work, blunting the pain with her powers of organization and control.

Often, she knew, women of Julia's temperament and capabilities allow themselves to be exhilarated by disaster so they can ride roughshod through the initial shock of grief. And that can make the loss more manageable. Whatever works, thought Angela. But whatever Julia was doing was clearly not working. She had not changed her clothes in the last two occasions Angela had visited, and she was not eating. Nor was she at her desk – her usual route to salvation.

It was as if some basic spring in Julia had broken. And it was quite clear to Angela that all too quickly she was spiralling down and down, cutting herself off from life and drowning in what looked like a dangerously morbid depression. Yet Angela had no idea how she might reach her sister in the depths she was so palpably mired in.

She resorted to, 'James and I wondered whether you might come out with us this Sunday? We could go to lunch. Take the girls?'

'I don't know,' murmured Julia in a way that meant no. 'It's very kind of you, but . . .'

'It would be nice to see Anna,' said Angela.

'It would,' murmured Julia.

'Is she still avoiding you?'

Julia nodded, pulling her cardigan around her. 'Even if I did see her, I doubt she'd talk about how she's feeling.'

'Like her mother,' smiled Angela gently. 'You don't tell me how you are.'

With good reason, thought Julia. She did not need her sister to explain to her how dangerous her feelings were. At three in the morning, she lay wide awake with the light on, frightened of the dark because it was then that the dreadful thought would come upon her that she would like to end her life. And that was something she could admit to no one.

She had two children to look after. Admittedly Anna was eighteen, but she needed her every bit as much as Rose. And what if Anna was again up to something criminal?

'You just ask about me and James,' Angela was saying.

'But that's a happy story,' said Julia. 'And . . .'

And it keeps my mind off things. And there were so many things, swooping down on her like carrion crows, pecking at her the moment she was alone, so that she found herself yearning for the emptiness of death. And it would be an emptiness. Unlike Angela, she had no faith that there would be a rending of body and spirit. This was it. She had blown the fleeting gift of life by her carelessness with her most precious blessing – Phillip's love – and she had only herself to blame that he had fallen in love with another woman.

Lying around in inescapable inertia, Julia tried to track the details of his relationship with Laura. The governors' meetings, chats at the school gates, the argument over the girl from the Hartley Estate. Where, when, how had friendship melted into love? She would picture her husband with his arms around this other woman, wanting her hands, her tongue, her conversation, her love . . . And she would have to get herself up off the sofa, or out of bed, and traipse round and round the room to escape the humiliation that was eating her alive.

Once he loved me so very dearly, she cried to herself. He did, he did. It was not all bad. But I lost his love.

If she could just dismiss Laura as a momentary aberration, a thoughtless one-night stand, it would not be so unbearable. But she could not. Nor could she find fault with Laura any more. She had misjudged the woman. She had looked for Laura at the funeral, seeking out the frumpy, failed artist she recalled. But that woman was not there. The Laura she saw in the churchyard was quite different.

Julia, her vision distorted by loss and jealousy and relentless self-blame, could see only the gleaming wildness of Laura's hair, the warm glow of her eyes, her soft curves. Beside Laura's splendid vitality she felt utterly diminished. She was merely neat and conscientious, a very ordinary sort of woman, rather rigid and narrow-minded, lacking the compassion to appreciate that her much-vaunted belief in the power of hard work and intelligence was, in the end, crude and limited. Phillip had wanted her love. He had wanted her gentleness, her kindness, her understanding. But she had been too blind and busy to give it. Even at the end.

Even then, just before his death, she had let him down with her outburst in the hospital that she could not look after him. If she could only tell him how sorry she was, that she would do anything . . .

'For pity's sake, Julia, please.'

She realized Angela had her arms around her and was lifting her head, which had dropped to her knees.

'Oh,' said Julia, 'sorry . . . I . . .' She clutched at the subject of Anna. She could not let Angela know where her mind was taking her. 'I just thank God Anna's got Cambridge. New people will be good for her. A new environment, something to keep that mind of hers occupied.'

'But you,' pressed Angela. 'Never mind Anna just now. Talk to me. For once. I know what you're like. You never talked after Mum died. You just bottled it up then and I never thought –'

'Don't talk about Mum. Please. I couldn't cope with her. You know I couldn't. And then I couldn't cope with the idea of Phillip being ill and sick and brain-damaged and . . . and he knows it. Oh Angela, how can I go on with him knowing?'

'Hold on, what on earth are you talking about?'

'In the end at the hospital, what if he heard?'

'Heard what?'

'That I couldn't look after him – when the doctor said there was a possibility he would be brain-damaged. I said I couldn't . . . because I knew it. If I couldn't with Mum, I couldn't look after him. And I said so, and he would have heard.'

'Stop,' said Angela fiercely, 'this is madness. It's most unlikely he was aware of anything by that point.'

'But he *might* have heard, mightn't he? And that's the point. I'm right, aren't I?' Julia saw the hesitation on Angela's face. 'Don't lie to me. If you lie to me –'

'I'm not lying. And, yes,' conceded Angela, taking Julia's clenched hands, 'he might have heard you. But it's most unlikely.'

'But he could?'

'Yes . . . possibly.'

'So he would have known I failed him. Even then. Again. And now he'll never know how much I loved him and how sorry I am.'

'Julia,' said Angela, 'you were in shock. You didn't know what you were saying.'

Julia pulled her hands away. Then, with dull resignation, she said, 'Maybe I was in shock. I probably was – you're right. But I knew exactly what I was saying. And I meant it. Because this is how I've lived my whole life and now I'm paying the price.'

She looked at the incomprehension in her sister's face.

'You don't see,' she explained, 'because you're happy to take up the cross, to wash other people's feet and all that. But I couldn't do what you do – what you did with Mum. I just couldn't? But I keep hearing Phillip's father with that prayer about how the burden of our sins is intolerable. And I used to think what a load of guilt-inducing claptrap. But he's right. Looking after Phillip – or Mum, even – would be hell. But it would be nothing to how I feel now. That hell would pass. Call it, I don't know, karma, sowing what you reap, but I would be left with the peace of knowing that I had done the right thing. But now I have no peace and I don't know where I will ever find it again. There is no hope for me, Angela. There is no hope.'

'But . . .' began Angela. But she was lost for words. 'That's not true!' she said, almost in tears. 'I promise you.'

But how could she promise her sister any such thing?

What could she possibly say? That we all do our best and all too often our best is not good enough? That most of us can persuade ourselves that we are good because we have not truly been tested? That Julia had been tested and been found wanting but that only meant she had to pick herself up and try again? That there is always hope?

But her words seemed like Sunday School platitudes, a pretty story to protect a child from cruelty and loss.

Angela had based her whole life on the belief that one could suffer on behalf of others. Easter was approaching, when she had to affirm her belief that Christ had suffered for her. Christ had died the most terrible death so that she might be redeemed. This was the Christian mystery, the Christian miracle. But where was the miracle now? Sitting by her suffering sister's side, the brutal truth was she could do nothing to allay Julia's distress but hold her in her arms beside a plate of chicken sandwiches in the hope that at some point she would find the right thing to do or say.

Suddenly Julia pulled herself away.

'I'm going to be sick,' she said, trying to get up, but she swayed and sank back down into the sofa.

'What is it?'

'I'm so scared,' Julia cried. 'One minute I want to die and the next I'm terrified I am dying, that I really am ill. And who'll look after the girls? You will, won't you?'

'Julia, calm down. Of course I will.'

'I can't eat,' said Julia, her tears beginning to fall, 'and if I do, I get these awful pains in my chest and I'm scared, Angela, I'm so scared.'

'Hold on a moment. Just talk me through it. Slowly. What's wrong?'

'Sometimes I can barely breathe, just walking up the stairs, and I feel faint.'

'This sickness,' said Angela, a suspicion dawning on her. 'Do you have it all the time?'

'Almost . . . well, it's not so bad at night. But the girls, if anything happened to me –'

'Wait, wait, one thing at a time. You and Phillip? Is there a possibility? Could you be pregnant?'

'But I'm always so careful,' said Julia appalled, an hour later, after Angela had been to the chemist.

'Nothing's a hundred per cent reliable,' said Angela, 'you know that.'

'But I'm forty-five. I thought it wasn't . . . I mean, I'll be forty-six with a new baby. How could . . .?'

It could only have been that night after the terrible argument about Rose modelling. So this new life, this child who would grow up never knowing its father, had been conceived in bitterness, after a dreadful row. Would that mean an inauspicious beginning – to start your life as an accident, the result of rancour and misunderstanding?

'But I don't want it,' she cried. 'Oh, God help me!'

Anna and Rose had been planned with love and foresight. She had felt joy and achievement, the most glorious sense of enrichment. But this strange being inside her . . .

'I . . . I can't go through it again.'

Julia had been relatively young when she had Anna and Rose, and she had breezed – in as much as anyone could – through the practicalities of pregnancy and childbirth. But she was under no illusions that this would be the same. Her organized mind had come to the fore once more and was already listing the risks. Firstly, her age was against her. The odds of complications rocketed – for herself and for the baby. Nothing was safe, and in all the accidents of birth and death this new life might be another casualty. For one dreadful moment she hoped it would be, that the decision might be taken from her, that this poor creature, the product of an argument Julia had relived over and over in her mind, lacerating herself for her lack of tenderness towards this baby's father, might be too broken and damaged for the world and that she might lose it.

If Phillip had been with her she would have managed. This child, so late in life, could have been a source of wonder, bringing them back together again. She might have learned through birth what she had had to learn through death, that she should have given Phillip the love and understanding he had every right to.

'You do have options,' said Angela, counting the weeks once more.

Options, said Julia to herself. 'Abortion,' she spelled it out loud.

'But obviously, the earlier, the easier,' said Angela in response.

Julia put her head in her hands. What would Phillip say? What would he want? But that was the point. Phillip was not here, to help her, to advise. It was not that she had deferred to Phillip. God forbid! But she had never made the truly important decisions alone. They had taken them together – sharing the triumphs and the mistakes. Only now he was gone did she realize how much she had depended upon that joint responsibility, the stability of his reassuring presence. Once, recalled Julia, I said Laura was such a flake she just got herself pregnant and got other people to look after her and I would never let that happen to me.

She looked up, the lines deepening on her haggard face. 'I can't,' she admitted to her sister, 'do it on my own.'

'But you won't have to,' said Angela. 'I'll be there for you. And the girls.'

Julia could imagine a baby driving Anna yet further from her, resentful and repelled by the idea. And Rose, who always played up to being the baby in the family, could easily turn horribly jealous and difficult at being ousted as the centre of attention.

'Perhaps,' Angela was suggesting, 'the girls can pour all their love into a baby. It might help. Then again . . . Oh, I don't know. But Julia, think, it might be a sort of second chance.'

Julia gave a hollow laugh. 'Once I told Phillip that people like me don't get second chances.'

'Well, maybe – this time – you're wrong.'

## 51

Laura sat in the lounge of the pretty country hotel looking out across the fields at leaping lambs hurling themselves at their plodding, panting mothers. She was waiting for Venetia. That they were here – having a few days away – was, according to Patrick, 'a miracle'. Though it was not. Nor was it a cure. But it was a reprieve. Now the doctors were saying Venetia might have one, two years. Possibly more.

From the moment Laura's elder brother, Mark, learned their mother was dying he had searched for a different medical verdict with all the energy and focus that made him so successful in the City. And he had found one: a different specialist with a different treatment, a different prognosis.

At first, Venetia resisted Mark's interference. She had accepted her fate and wanted to get the end over with, not eke it out, nursed and infantilized, with nothing to do but be ill. She was sick of lying awake in the night, panicking and doubled up in agony.

But Patrick and her children begged her to take one last chance, and she let herself be persuaded. And the new drug regime appeared to be working. She was free from pain, she was free to sleep. She was free to spend time with her daughter.

She had one ambition for this unexpected lease of life. In her work in the family courts, she had directed all her attention to children who had been overlooked, abused, allowed to fall through the safety nets. Her own children, she had told herself, were so privileged they did not need her in the same way. Now, she acknowledged, her own daughter was desperately unhappy, though she had not the slightest idea why. And she longed to know Laura's trust.

So they were having a few days alone together for the first time in their lives. Not that Venetia had admitted as much to Laura. Instead, when suggesting they went away to a nice hotel, just the two of

them, she had joked feebly, 'I could do with a break from your
father – he's being lovely, of course, but there's a limit to how much
tea I can drink. So you'd be doing me a favour if you came,' she had
gone on in a rather contrived manner, unable to say what she really
wanted. 'And I'm so grateful, the way you introduced me to Isabel
and her mother.'

Urgency, need, sickness . . . these were manna from heaven to
Venetia. An unhappy, troubled teenager who wasn't her own. If
anything could make Venetia believe she did not want to die just
yet, it was a problem to solve.

Helping Isabel had been far from easy. The girl was truculent, rude
and suspicious. But Mrs West was desperate for someone to look
after her daughter. So Laura and Venetia together came up with a
bold and generous plan. In five days' time Isabel would come and live
with Venetia and Patrick in Laura's old room, and he and Laura would
teach her art. Isabel's mother would move into a care home nearby,
for which Patrick and Venetia would quietly pay the bulk of the fees.

So much has been achieved over the last few weeks, thought
Venetia, as she moved slowly down the magnificent hotel staircase.
Her own health, a new chance for Isabel . . . yet she was still no
nearer to Laura. It's my fault, she thought, resting a moment against
the banister. I should have made more effort in the past. Precious
days, months and years had simply disappeared. How had she let
the time slip by so carelessly? And tomorrow they were going home.
She tried to speed up but the drugs had stiffened her joints and she
virtually dragged herself into the lounge, where she saw Laura staring out of the window.

I am the one supposed to be at death's door, thought Venetia, yet it
is my daughter who is so colourless. She watched Laura shrug on the
new coat she had bought her recently – as a thank you for coming to
so many doctors' appointments – looking as if she was being bowed
down by a dead weight. There was fatigue in all her movements, in
her every expression, and yet Laura was also tapping her foot, full of
nervous energy. Venetia straightened herself up to head across the
room when Laura began hunting in her bag for her ringing phone.

'The girls,' mouthed Laura, waving at Venetia and going out into the chill March air to take the call from the twins.

She leaned up against the stone lion standing at the hotel entrance and steeled herself for another onslaught of recrimination from her daughters, furious at being left for three nights in the care of Josie, Venetia's housekeeper.

'I miss you,' Alice launched in, as she had every night. 'I really, really miss you.'

'I miss you too.'

'When are you back?'

'Tomorrow. I'll pick you up from school. Like I promised.'

'I wish I could be there with you,' persisted Alice. 'Why did you have to go?'

'I wish you could be here too. You'd like the lambs,' said Laura, placating her daughter. 'But you have to go to school,' she continued, nodding at her mother, who was moving with a fragility that made her seem older than her sixty-one years. She's aged, thought Laura.

But there was no loss of strength as Venetia said loudly, 'Stop worrying, Laura, the girls are fine.' And she gestured for the phone and spoke to them herself.

Talking to their grandmother, Laura could hear her daughters laughing now, as if without a care in the world.

'Listen,' Venetia whispered to Laura, 'they're incredibly happy.'

'Great,' murmured Laura, not letting herself be riled by her mother's air of triumph, and she wandered down the steps into the garden.

She and her mother were getting on well enough. The smooth luxury of the expensive hotel certainly helped. Conversation was pleasant, if sometimes hard work. But they never touched on anything more intimate than whether the other had slept well, which suited Laura perfectly.

A young couple in hefty boots, their arms locked, passed her on the gravel path down to the woods. 'Beautiful afternoon,' said the man to Laura.

'Yes,' Laura agreed, watching them amble on, banging into each other, then separating, then knocking into one another and laughing.

Laura had not known romantic happiness – what it was simply to walk in the countryside with a man she adored, just to go away for a weekend, the two of them. Yet the hotel felt full of couples doing exactly that.

Beyond the hotel's parklands stretched salt marshes and, in the distance, on the glittering slope of the horizon, she caught the gleam of the North Sea. She stood still a moment. In this part of the world it was the sky that filled the landscape, the entire sweep of the earth diminished by the enormity overhead so you could almost feel the turning of the earth. Her breath quickened.

'Phillip,' she murmured, casting her eyes down.

Thoughts of him were always with her. It was as if she had acquired a familiar, a secret internal lover, never to be shown to the world. She would be washing up and picture him chatting to her at the kitchen sink. Or she would imagine him next to her driving, walking, sitting on the sofa, in her bed, waking next to her with his arms about her in the early morning. She knew only too well this had never happened. But this dream world was the one place where she could give her longings some shape and form.

'Honestly, Laura,' said Venetia, joining her in the garden, 'the girls just wind you up and know exactly how to play you.'

'Of course they do.'

'But they tell you all their woes and leave you in a dreadful state, then they swan off, absolutely fine, without giving you another thought.' Venetia leaned on her arm as they went back into the warm hotel. 'Really, they don't need you half as much as you think they do.'

At least, thought Laura, catching a waiter's attention to order some tea, this dreadful cancer has not diminished my mother's bluntness.

'I'm hungry,' said Venetia, settling her thin frame on an antique wing chair. She was eating once more. That debilitating pain had eased and she would have hot buttered teacakes. 'And the scones and jam, please,' Venetia added to the waiter, glancing at her daughter as a child might – aren't I good, eating it all up?

Laura smiled.

But, thought Venetia, she looks at me with the distraction of someone whose mind is elsewhere. 'What about you? Laura?'

'Oh, er . . .' Laura had no appetite for anything. 'The teacake, please.'

Which she will pick at, thought Venetia, as Laura rested her head back on the sofa. There were shadows of exhaustion under her eyes and Venetia followed Laura's gaze out of the tall shuttered windows and wondered what her daughter was actually seeing. Not, she thought, the clouds buffeted by the wind and the shifting light, but something quite different in her own mind.

Venetia was at a loss to know how to ask outright what was troubling her daughter. It was not the girls, she felt pretty sure of that. But what? A man? She could understand Laura being lonely. But there was a new sadness about her now that reached to her core. But if it was a man, who? And when had Laura made time for one?

'The first of March,' Laura was saying conversationally.

'The days feel longer,' went on Venetia. 'I really noticed it this morning.'

'You are sleeping all right?'

'Oh yes, yes,' said Venetia. 'And you?'

'Wonderfully.'

Venetia doubted it. Certainly Laura played the part of the loving daughter to perfection, constantly kind. But what she was concealing was a mystery. Venetia kept coming back to the obvious. A man? Maybe a woman? It had to be a lover. She could not think what else was causing Laura such grief.

'Have you spoken to Isabel?' Venetia asked, unable to pose the question she really wanted and because Isabel was the only subject on which Laura gave signs of genuine life.

'Yes, she's all set for moving. And her mother keeps telling me how well it's all turning out.' Laura grimaced. 'I hate the way she's so grateful.'

'I know,' said Venetia, 'but let her think life can be kind sometimes, and that it will be kind to her daughter. I think that . . . oh, what's his name? I've gone blank. What's he called?' Venetia asked, suddenly frightened. She, who once had such brilliant recall and never lost her way in an argument, kept having lapses in memory. 'Laura, you know. You liked him. He would have been pleased. The chair of the governors.'

'Phillip,' murmured Laura.

'Of course,' Venetia snapped briskly, as if to prove she was as mentally energetic as ever. She was told it was the drugs, but this loss of control terrified her. 'Phillip . . . Snowe, wasn't it? And now at least Isabel's being given a chance to . . . well, recreate herself, for want of a better word.'

'I know,' said Laura, tracing her finger around the primroses in the tiny china jug on the table.

That's another change in Laura, thought Venetia. She can't sit still any more, as if she always wants to be elsewhere.

'Isabel worries about the money you're spending,' said Laura.

'We can afford it.'

'Yes, but . . . anyway, I hope Dad won't throw too many of his tantrums around her.'

'You know I can't guarantee that,' said Venetia. If she had learned to control Patrick's tantrums, her life might have been very different. 'But he thinks she's got a real gift. And she'll give him something to think about.' Apart from himself, she wanted to add. Or am I being unfair? she wondered. She could not fault her husband these days, so very attentive, so overly caring. But this love heaped upon her too late added to her sense of loss over what might have been.

To Laura she said, 'Isabel will have a home, a second chance. And her mother . . . you can see her relief. And mine too. I need to be busy, you know that. For as long as I'm able, I can look after her. Then you'll have to. You're very good, Laura, to take on this responsibility. Anyway, I'm sure Phillip Snowe would have been pleased.'

Laura said nothing, her face quite empty.

'He was passionate about that school.'

Then the waiter arrived with a great silver tray. And as Laura poured the tea, Venetia watched her closely for some clue as to what she was thinking. But Laura was too accomplished at concealment and Venetia gave up once more, casting her eyes around the elegant white room, at the vases of spring flowers, the soft, milky lighting. From the corner, a quartet began playing Mozart and she noticed an elderly couple take each other's hands, their fingers intertwining. I would like to do that, thought Venetia, to stroke another's hand with my thumb, to curl it around another's. A picture of her parents flashed into her mind, her mother washing up at the kitchen sink, ground down by the demands of a low income and six children, then the transfiguring smile as her father wrapped his arms around her waist and whispered in her ear, 'The warmth of your neck, my angel, the gold in your hair. Oh sweetheart, I was thinking of it at work, the way it catches the light, the way you . . .'

Venetia smoothed down her slim-fitting tweed skirt. Patrick had said she looked 'nice' in this tweed, though she had worn it for years and he had never noticed before. But this was the new Patrick, doing his best to be a good husband. 'You look nice,' he had said. *Nice*, she thought, wincing. *Nice*, such a paltry little word. But, she supposed, it was the best he could do. She sagged into the chair. At the back of her mind was the suspicion that it was not really love, but fear, the acts of a scared man forced into a corner.

'I can't quite believe I'm here,' ventured Venetia. 'How lucky I've been. Why should I be so fortunate – the one to live? I think,' Venetia went on, 'about Phillip Snowe sometimes. You must too. I got the impression you two got on rather well.'

Laura remained silent.

'I mean, I was the one expected to die, yet his was the life cut down. My children have all grown up, but his are only in their teens. And he had a wife who clearly adored him, and he her. The injustice of it seems so wrong. Me getting this new chance when his were all taken.'

Laura exerted herself and managed, 'You know life doesn't work like that.'

'Yes, but . . .' Venetia trailed off.

Laura's eyes were fixed on the vase of primroses.

'Did he buy those pictures of yours in the end?'

Laura shook her head.

'I'm sorry, I thought he liked them.'

Laura's expression remained impassive, her eyes dry. All her tears had been shed. But as she contrived to put a smile upon her face and ask the waiter for more hot water, to divert her mother from Phillip, her vision began to blur. She had not cried her last, after all.

Not now, she begged. It was just one stray tear. Don't let it fall. She tried to blink it away. But it was too late. Venetia saw and, slowly, she began to wonder.

She remembered her suspicion the morning she had turned up unexpectedly at Laura's house. Laura had been unusually excited because Phillip was due to call round. Also, the day she announced her own illness Laura kept asking about Phillip, saying it couldn't be true and how had he died? And now it began falling into place, explaining how distracted and disconnected Laura had been ever since.

Laura put her hand to her neck, and that bewildered, fretful gesture made Venetia's heart reach out to her.

'Laura, please, what's wrong? For once in your life, talk to me. For my sake, if not yours. Was there something . . .? I don't want to pry . . . but you and . . .' Venetia felt clumsy and intrusive, forcing an unwanted intimacy. 'Did you . . .' she ventured, 'did you *like* Phillip?'

Laura glanced up warily, expecting, out of habit, to see a frown, but her mother looked uncharacteristically nervous.

Venetia went on, 'I know you're unhappy, but I don't know why. Laura, were you and Phillip . . .?'

At the sound of Phillip's name linked with hers, more tears came into Laura's eyes. I must lie, she thought. Again. Quash this suspicion. There's no need to admit anything. But to deny Phillip out loud seemed to taint him, and now the tears were falling so fast she could not stop them.

Venetia had never seen her daughter like this, staring down at her hands, barely moving, crying so silently, as if to warn her to keep away.

'You were more than friends . . .?' she began warily. Then she asked outright. 'You weren't having an affair with him, were you?'

Laura said nothing.

'Oh Laura, did you love him?'

And this question was too much for Laura.

She nodded. 'Yes, and I still do.'

For a moment, Venetia was at a loss. How little you ever know of anyone. Phillip, the family man. Her own daughter.

'Did he feel the same?'

Laura's eyes glanced up and met her mother's. 'Yes. I think so. I don't know any more.'

'But . . .' ventured Venetia, terrified Laura might shut her out again. 'You two . . . how long had it been going on? I mean, who knows? Does his wife, his widow –?'

'No,' said Laura, her eyes on the floor. 'I don't see how. No one knows.'

'But your friends?'

'I've not told anyone – except you, now.'

Venetia hesitated, unsure whether to view her daughter with pity or respect. To be on her own with such sadness. I know how hard that is, thought Venetia, how it drains the life out of you. And the realization of the depth of Laura's loneliness made her grab her hand. 'My darling.'

Then sympathy from such an unexpected source was too much for Laura. 'Oh Mum,' she whispered, 'I miss him. I miss him so much. I think about him . . . not an hour goes by when I don't long for him. But we had almost nothing. And it seems absurd to be feeling like this. We only met a few times, really. A dozen, maybe –'

Laura stopped as suddenly as she had begun. She had said too much. Articulating her feelings already seemed to trivialize and demean them. Yet part of her longed to talk and talk, to give Phillip back a reality he had begun to lose. And it was so sweet to hold on to that, such a relief to speak the truth, she said, 'He promised he loved me. And I still believe him. But we never got the chance to find out. And that's what hurts most of all. It was the possibility . . . for the first time I seemed to have a chance of another life, of sharing it, of love. And now it's gone. I've no idea if he'd have left his wife, his family. Any of that. And I'll never know. But what we had . . . it was beautiful.'

Then Laura was lost in weeping.

Dear God, what do I say? pleaded Venetia. How can I make it better? 'But you had that time together, however little. No one can take that from you.' I wish I had known such joy, thought Venetia. I wish I had done the same, had a lover. But no one asked me. And if they had, would I have had the courage to say yes?

'But was it what I thought?' said Laura, barely audible. Phillip had made love to her and then, within one day, he was dead. The melodrama appalled her. 'I keep thinking I got it wrong.'

'Listen to me,' Venetia insisted fiercely. Suddenly it was the most important thing in the world that her daughter had known what she had not. 'You know what love is. And you have had it. And you should thank God for that. Even if the love was doomed.'

Venetia felt crushingly old. She would not confide in her daughter and say, not once did I ever feel like this for your father.

But she could give her daughter this. 'For a man like Phillip to have compromised himself and risked his family, it must have meant something. Trust yourself. He loved you.' Then she reached out to stroke her daughter's hair from her face.

Laura took her mother's hand and pressed it to her cheek. 'Thank you,' she said, not quite sure whether to trust this openness with her mother. Would she end up hating Venetia for having exposed herself like this? 'Thank you.'

But then, any intimacy between them was interrupted as a great voice boomed across the room, 'Venetia! Laura!' Patrick was striding towards them, all eyes in the room upon him.

## 52

At once Laura leaped up. What had happened for her father to turn up so unexpectedly? The girls!

'Now don't panic!' he announced, as if to the entire hotel. 'Laura, don't look so worried. There's no drama!'

Just you arriving, thought Laura, noticing teacups suspended mid-air, a frisson of recognition among the hotel guests. He couldn't have made more of an entrance if he had arrived in a painter's smock with brushes behind his ear.

'I thought you'd like a surprise,' he said, drawing up a chair, screeching it along the floor, then plonking himself down, the great showman who'd got his audience's attention. 'Because I got fed up on my own. You two getting on all right? Good, good. Pleased to see me?'

'Of course, darling,' said Venetia, all smiles.

Laura doubted she meant it.

'Now, Venetia, I'm sorry, I know we agreed to wait until you got home. But I thought it would be fun if I came here myself and told Laura our plan.'

'But Patrick . . .' Now there was no mistaking the annoyance on her mother's face. 'We agreed. We discussed it all.'

'I know, I know. But I . . . I've been dying to tell her.'

'Tell me what?' Laura felt a fearful premonition. What was going on?

'Do you remember,' said Patrick, signalling to the waiter, 'how I said a while back that we could help each other? You and me. At that poor man's funeral. I mentioned it then.'

'Yes,' began Laura, 'but . . .' But with the improvement in her mother's health she had assumed the idea had been dropped.

'Now your mother and I have been working out exactly what you can do.'

Do? What were they up to? Was this little mother–daughter tête-à-tête, this new intimacy, really all about softening her up to become her father's carer, his amanuensis, his dogsbody, his slave?

'We've got it all sorted,' Patrick was saying.

No! No! She would not listen. She would not have anything to do with them.

'Now I know what you're like . . . Tea, please,' he ordered the waiter. 'Really strong. None of this scented stuff my wife likes. Now Laura, no arguing. You're good –'

'You're so good,' her mother was emphasizing. 'So good.'

So good, echoed Laura, as it all became clear. Don't you mean, such a pushover, so malleable? She clenched her fists. She would not accept this role. She would not be a sacrificial lamb. She would draw the line. And fast.

'Was this the idea all along?' she said, looking her mother in the eye. 'Sweeten me up and then land me with *him*?' You, thought Laura, may have spent your life tiptoeing round him. But I won't. Just because Phillip has gone. Just because I have no man to love.

She got to her feet. Her knees felt like water. She could hear her voice, far too loud. 'I am not like you,' she was saying to her mother. 'I do not want to be you. I'm not going to take your place.'

Then she ran from the room, as if she might flee the future that seemed more bleak than ever. She lurched past the waiters, the startled guests, and out into the darkening evening, with Patrick hard on her heels.

'What the bloody hell are you on about?' he yelled, following her into the garden. 'You *are* good, very good, and I want to help you with your painting. You should have been concentrating on it all along. But with the twins, I know, you put them first. But it seems a waste if you don't start painting properly.'

'What are you saying?'

'That I can help you. But if you're going to be so damned difficult . . . though I warned your mother you would be.'

'What do you mean? What sort of help?'

'With your work, for God's sake. And I know what you're like and how you hate the idea of using my name, but you're hopeless at promoting yourself – now don't get all huffy – but you know what this business is like. And I'm only doing it because I rate you as an artist.'

'Do you mean,' she interrupted, not quite able to believe it, 'that you'll make time to help me?'

'Yes.'

'With painting?'

'Of course.'

'But you said "help each other".'

'Yes. Hold on, I need to sit a minute.'

Laura was aware of her father's laboured breathing and instinctively she gave him her arm as they walked over to a bench.

'I've not done any work since your mother got ill. I don't know why exactly. I just can't. And it's driving me mad. And I've always sought your opinion, haven't I? I've always said that. No one else's. And you might help me get started again.'

'You don't want me to look after you?' Laura needed it spelled out. 'Cook for you? Organize your diary? All that stuff Mum did.'

'Of course not. What on earth made you think that?'

Because, she thought, you have spent your entire adult life believing you had the right to be fussed over.

'Don't you see?' he was pressing on. 'You're the only one of my children who has real talent. Mark had something – but never in your league. I always thought you'd do it when the time was right. Professionally. I mean, the thing about you, Laura, is that you have such a . . . well, instinctive gift. You're a natural.'

'No, I'm not,' she snapped, suspicious of all this flattery. Since when did she have all this talent? He had never mentioned it before. 'And if I was so brilliant, I wouldn't have spent my life feeling like some second-rate dilettante. Fitting my painting in between looking after the girls. Mum making me feel guilty if I wasn't saving the world.'

'I never knew why you let your mother persuade you to take on all that charity work,' he said with a dismissive wave of his hand.

'Because,' she hissed, 'what else are we alive for? Aren't we here to love one another? Isn't that, ultimately, what matters? And because I had so much, I had to give so much back.'

'But you hate it. Admit it, you do,' he said with an air of triumph. 'Just as I would. Every second. Because you know what, Laura? You are much more like me than you realize –'

'No, Dad,' she interrupted fiercely, 'I most certainly am not like you.'

'You are, because what you were given is talent – like me – and the point is you need to use it. Because you could be not just good but very good, maybe great.'

She could not believe he had no ulterior motive for these compliments. Or was it his vanity speaking? He needed to think he had passed his great art on to one of his children. 'Don't delude yourself, Dad.'

'And don't you put yourself down. Or me for that matter.'

'Well, how come no one's noticed this great talent of mine? Couldn't *you*, at least, have mentioned it, instead of treating everything I do like some pretty little flowery knick-knack?'

'That's not fair. I don't. And anyway, I thought you could see for yourself, you've such a good eye.'

'But why . . .?' she began, wondering whether he was, in fact, speaking the truth. Did he really think she was that good? Because if he was right, it gave a whole new dimension to her life. But she still did not trust him or that animating glimmer of hope. 'Why didn't you say something before?' she demanded.

'I thought it was obvious. And you know, I was working.'

'Working?' she repeated with as much scorn as she could muster. It was easier to revert to a slanging match with her father than confront the possibility that her painting had potential and she might take her life to a completely different plane.

'Yes, I was busy. And I know you're thinking what a feeble excuse –'

'Too right.'

'And I thought you didn't care about your work,' he said, accepting her vehemence unflinchingly.

'Didn't care? I cared more than you could ever know. But what was more important? Tell me, Dad. What should have come first these last eight years? My art or my children?'

'My art or my children?' he echoed, now as sarcastic as her. 'Work or family? Don't try and trick me with that old chestnut.'

She looked at him combatively. It was a relief to have her selfish, irritable father back. She knew where she was with him.

'Come off it, Laura! I can't answer that. Of course the girls are important – but not all those people your mother and Father Eoghan rope you into doing good turns for. Just tell them you've got too much work – that's what I'd do. Just forget about them for a bit.'

'Forget about them?' she echoed.

'Don't look at me like that. I know you think I'm a selfish old sod. And I am. But I'd like to see you really getting stuck into your art, Laura. See what you can really do, when you give it your all.'

She eyed him with a mixture of scepticism and derision, then she sighed heavily. 'For that,' she said, 'I need money. For the childcare. That's what it boils down to. If you even want to have that choice you need to have, or be making, lots of money. Lots.'

'And that's what I'm going to give you. Money. So you can work as much as you want. You can pay me back – I know how up yourself you can be. But your stuff could sell, once you get established. So, here you are, Laura, here's your chance to paint – no excuses – just paint.' And he stood before her as if throwing down a gauntlet.

To paint all day, all night, whenever she liked. To lose herself in work. It was like a prayer being answered. She could mitigate the oppression of grief and loneliness. She could find rapture in the concentration, that elusive joy of forgetting everything in the capturing of an image, a colour, a shape. She might not be the great painter her father thought, or that she wanted to be. But so what? She was being offered a future, and the idea was intoxicating.

Possibilities – fulfilment in work – hovered about her, ready to alight if she just embraced this opportunity. But it was not as simple as that.

'Oh dammit, Dad.' She drew in her breath fiercely.

'Go on,' he said, almost taunting her. 'You know you want to.'

'What about Eliza and Alice? Okay, I get a full-time – no, a live-in – nanny and I do nothing but paint. Then what? The girls will miss me – the way I missed you. The way Robert and Mark missed you. The way Mum –'

'That's a choice you have to make,' he interrupted. 'And you don't need to tell me it comes at a cost. Of course I've lost out. Don't you think I know that? I've been a bad husband – and I didn't need your filthy looks these last few weeks to tell me that. And I've been a bad father. But the truth is – however much you might hate to know this – those moments when I'm painting, when it's just me and my work, are more important to me than anything – than you, even, and, I hate to say this, your mother. They have been the very best moments of my life, better than anything I've ever, ever known. And if I had not admitted that, I would have been some frustrated . . . I don't know . . . failure, like . . .'

'Like what?'

'Oh, never mind.'

'Like me?' she said, in clipped tones. 'Is that what you're trying to say?'

'Whether you admit it or not, Laura, you've much more of me in you than you dare to acknowledge.'

'No Dad, I don't,' she cried, backing away from him. 'And I never want to be so work-obsessed, art-obsessed, self-obsessed. You think that your talent lets you off every other responsibility. That you've a right always to put your needs first. All the love that people say goes into your painting . . . and it does, I can see that . . .' She fixed him with a furious stare. 'But the price of that humanity in your work was your inhumanity to us, to your family, to those who loved you and needed you. And that's the trouble with brilliant people like you – you think you're entitled to be careless with people who in your eyes are ordinary, mundane, average.'

The first argument she had had with Phillip – about Isabel West – came flashing back to her. What about the ordinary children, he had said, the ones with no special talent? It's my job to protect the ordinary child too.

'There's nothing ordinary about your talent,' shrugged her father.

'That's not the point,' she cried. 'Look at . . .'

She hesitated. Look at your children, she wanted to say. What misfits we've turned into. Mark, a control freak marrying another. Robert, flitting from woman to woman, job to job – and jobs that reflected none of his abilities. And me. What was she? Drained and depleted, grieving for a married man she loved so pathetically briefly that the smallness of their time together, compared with the magnitude of her feelings, was enough to tear the life out of her.

But then, she thought, who did have it right? Once she might have looked at the likes of Phillip and Julia and thought they had cracked the art of living. Perhaps, for a while, they had – with their interesting work, lovely daughters, beautiful home. But, given Phillip's unhappiness, that had not lasted. It was not what it seemed.

'Laura, please,' said her father, reaching once more for her hand, but she stuck it in her pocket. She knew she was being petulant but she had not courted this unprecedented intimacy with her father, his sudden outpouring of feelings. She wanted him to be what he always was. She wanted her mother to be what she always was. She wanted Phillip. If only he had not been on that street at that time. If only. . .

'Laura, listen to me,' her father was saying. 'Yes, I've been a dreadful father. But I'm trying to make up for it. I'm offering you the opportunity to make the choice. You can neglect your children the way you accuse me of neglecting you, but that will be your decision, and you'll have to live with the consequences, as I do. But what else are you going to do with the rest of your life?'

Laura averted her eyes. She felt cornered, scared by the directness of his question.

'I can't think of anything better than expressing your God-given talent,' her father pressed on. 'Just, for God's sake, Laura, don't bury it.'

On this cold spring day, Laura recognized she was being offered a new life, salvation – redemption, even. Such a gift – utterly unexpected and, in her eyes, totally undeserved – meant the despair, binding her fast, could loosen and she might find all manner of doors opening.

'You know,' he continued, 'I always envied you.'

She eyed him warily. 'Me? Why on earth?'

'Because I always had to work at being good. I had to put in all that donkey work to get it right. I spent hours and hours at the National Gallery, just staring and staring, trying to work out how it was done. Though in the early days part of me was glad to sit in the warmth rather than go back to my cold digs.'

'Come off it, Dad. You were twenty-three when you met Mum, who immediately took you under her wing. Your days as the starving artist were thankfully very brief. I'm not some journalist you're trying to win over with a sob story.' And despite herself, Laura softened. This was the father she knew, inventing his own myth. 'Knowing you,' she said, 'you went to the National Gallery and took a cab home.'

'Maybe,' he smiled conspiratorially. 'But the thing is that I knew my limitations, even then. Technically I had the ability. That came easily. But to turn that into flair was slog – sheer slog. But you – and this is a terrible thing to admit to your own daughter – I am envious of you. Because to be as good as you are without all the work I had to put in makes you very special.' He turned away, as if embarrassed by this confession.

And Laura, in her turn, was embarrassed for him. She and her father had never once talked like this and she was utterly unprepared for his apologies, his compliments, his confusion of feelings. And part of her did not want them. But she took his crabbed hand.

'I'm sorry,' he went on, clasping her fingers tightly, 'that it's taken your mother's illness to get me to tell you all this. But I've had a lot of hard truths to swallow lately and it's all a bit humbling. So I'm not going to plead any more. Just give it a go. Paint what you want and see what happens, because your mother wants to see you happy before she dies.'

'So was this her idea? You helping me?'

'I wish I could say it was mine. It should have been. Your mother loves you very dearly, you know.'

Laura recognized her parents' help for the blessing it was, the tide of life urging her forward once again. But this was not how her life was supposed to be. I should not, she thought, be assuaging my lovelessness in work. I know what I am missing. How I know . . .

A life with Phillip was what she craved.

But that was impossible. So she could choose. She could live as she had done for so long now, compensating for her loneliness by doing good turns for others and finding comfort in reliving every moment with Phillip, remembering every inch of his loving body, recalling his every sweet word and turning him into a dream figure, picturing the ideal life with him she might have had, inventing imaginary scenarios of blissful union with a man she had been denied the opportunity to get to know.

Or she could accept her parents' offer. And her life would either be narrowed or broadened by the choice she made.

## 53

Anna stood in the rain on the Strand. People rushed by on their way home to happy and unhappy families, others off to the theatre, on dates, charging about with umbrellas and phones to busy and empty evenings. But Anna ignored the crowds and the drizzle soaking through her old coat. She was conscious only of Phoebe's father, right by her side.

It was not even three months since her father's death and she was fully aware that the manner in which she had just spent the afternoon – in bed with a man even older than him – would set a psychologist nodding knowingly. But what she had done had nothing to do with her father. Possibly bereavement had hammered it home that time was short, and patience and caution could be thrown to the wind. But that was all.

'Are you all right?' asked Phoebe's father, placing a solicitous hand on her shoulder, but with a quick glance about to make sure, observed Anna, that no one he knew was around. He's used to these sorts of assignations, she reminded herself.

Not that theirs had been a prearranged rendezvous. They had met earlier in the day, seemingly by accident. Though there was nothing accidental on Anna's side. She had been in this part of town by design, knowing this was his territory and the chances of 'bumping' into him were high. She wanted him. She was determined to find him. And she did, making her intentions so clear he took her to a hotel and they spent the afternoon together.

Now they stood in the gloomy early-evening light trying to find a cab. He was insisting she went home in a taxi, handling her so attentively, thought Anna, unable to contain her self-mockery, as if she had had a bad fall.

'Here we are,' said Phoebe's father, his fingers lightly brushing hers, as a cab pulled up. He brought his face close. She could smell cigarettes and an astringent cologne. 'You're so beautiful,' he whispered, his breath warm in her ear. The oldest line in the world, Anna reminded herself. 'Don't you ever, ever forget it.'

And taking her by the arm, he opened the cab door and helped her in, giving the instructions to the driver himself. Then he kissed her goodbye, for a long time. She kissed him back. Even she could tell he was extremely skilled. And she was young and naive enough to be overwhelmed.

Finally, he let her go and Anna put her fingers to her bruised lips as the cab pulled away.

When she saw her friends with their boyfriends she thought of their love in terms of a gorgeous little Cupid, rather sweet and cuddly. But she was not interested in that milky-skinned cherub. She wanted more of a grizzled Pan, with an artful tongue and knowing hands and glinting eyes. And now she had had him.

She stretched out her legs in the back of the cab, twirling her ankles which she had never thought to admire before. So very slender, so very lovely, he had said between kisses.

He was artful with words too. Extremely so. She did not think there was an inch of her he had not described with a lyricism not normally associated with a mathematician. In all varieties of ways he told her she was beautiful. And for all her brilliance Anna chose to be uncritical with this information.

Not that the afternoon had been perfect. Far from it. But no doubt, she thought, closing her eyes and letting a slow, half-triumphant, half-regretful smile spread across her face, it was the first of many compromises she would have to make with men. Because – and now tears came to her eyes – the afternoon had only put the slightest dent in her loneliness. She yearned to be comforted with the closeness of love. But love had not been on offer that afternoon.

Yet the practical, realistic side of her nature recognized it had certainly not been without its blessings.

One thing she had learned this afternoon was that she could be attractive to a man who was comfortable with women and not some social misfit who needed her help with his maths A-level.

Moreover, she could talk to Phoebe's father – and that made him unique. And although some of their conversation had been about as romantic as a discussion on mortgage rates, for part of the afternoon they had lain in bed mulling over a problem that had been tormenting her since before her father's death.

How was she going to tell her mother that she had turned down her place at Cambridge?

Instead of going to her parents' university – that great, lustrous institution that her mother, in particular, revered and worshipped for giving her so many wonderful, wonderful opportunities – she had accepted a job offer at a new investment company from a business contact of Phoebe's father.

In the back of the cab, she shuddered, imagining all too well her mother's outrage and disappointment.

'Get it over with,' Phoebe's father had advised.

'But my mum . . . she's changed since my dad died. She barely eats. Just picks at things at odd times. And I've heard her being sick. And when I ask if she's okay she just says she's fine and tries to ask about me. But I don't want her to know, as I don't want to upset her even more. And she's not working, which for my mum is plain weird. She just says she's on compassionate leave but those lawyers don't do compassion.'

Then he had told her something which she thought ridiculous. 'Use that brain of yours, sweetheart, and win her round. Ask for her advice. She'll like that. Say you need her help – in buying some clothes for work. Get her to take you shopping.'

She had scoffed, 'She hates shopping. Once a year she just goes to her personal shopper and stocks up in one fell swoop so as not to waste time.'

'It's not about shopping, you daft thing. It's about her needing you to need her. Trust me. I know what I'm talking about.'

## 54

As Anna made her way home, Julia was in her bedroom, feeling a little less dreadful. Come the evenings, the awful nausea which went on all day, and which she had never experienced with Anna and Rose, eased a fraction. When she was pregnant with them she had spent her spare time making plans. Now all she did was throw up. But that was just a measure of how very different having this baby would be. Which was why she was not going to have it.

It was not until yesterday that she at last came to a decision. She had made list after list of pros and cons because, in the past, this process had given her clarity. But it wasn't until late last night, when the call came from her boss in New York, that she knew what she had to do.

She was fired. In losing the Clifford James case, she had lost the firm's biggest contract. Julia knew there would be no mercy, no allowances for grief or accidents. But although she had been expecting this call, the reality brought with it the stamp of certain defeat.

She would never work at this level again. In losing such an important client she was tainted. By now, everyone in her office would know what had happened, and yet no one but Kate, her loyal assistant, had rung to commiserate or ask how she was. Even those she had helped in their careers wanted nothing to do with her now. Also, Julia was in no doubt that a fair number of her fellow partners would be downright delighted to be shot of her. Too successful too quickly. Too sure of herself. She had seen it happen to others – indeed, she had been in the office and avoided the eyes of those suddenly struck down – and now it had happened to her.

But that she could endure. Just.

What was worse was that at the back of her more articulate fears was the sense that she was responsible for Phillip's death. For this reason she was not fit to be a mother to this new baby. She felt she had stumbled at every step, that she no longer had any idea how to behave. And with the loss of her job all her old codes of conduct had gone, and she did not see how that could change. So she had booked an appointment at the clinic for tomorrow afternoon. No one but Angela knew. She had deliberately kept her pregnancy secret from the girls. She could not bear to burden them with this horrendous decision. And after tomorrow she would feel . . . She had no idea how she would feel. She certainly did not expect to feel better. She did not believe she deserved that. But at least, she thought, slumping on her bed, she would not be sick.

'Mum?'

Julia opened her eyes in surprise and propped herself up on her elbow. 'Anna!' Normally Anna deliberately avoided her, certainly did not seek her out. 'I didn't hear you come in, darling. You look lovely,' she said, trying to be inviting. But Anna did look rather pretty, flushed and fresh with pearls of raindrops on her cheeks.

'Mum, I need to talk to you. It's important.'

Anna had intended coming straight out with her news. But it was so unlike her mother to take to her bed during the day, she was knocked off course and instead asked anxiously, 'Are you all right?'

'Of course,' lied Julia, forcing herself upright. 'What is it, sweetheart?' She sipped her ginger tea in the vain hope she would not feel so dreadful. She needed to concentrate. For weeks she had had a sense of danger approaching her eldest child – that the magazine might prosecute her thieving daughter – but whenever she tried to ask, Anna just brushed the matter aside.

'Mum . . .' began Anna, sitting down on the bed by her side.

Anna noticed lines around her mother's mouth that had not been there before. Her eyes were bloodshot too, as if she had not slept. Anna did not want to inflict yet more pain on her grieving mother and for a moment she hesitated. Should she add to her all too evident distress? But was she going to spend three years of her life just pleasing her mother?

Anna took a deep breath. 'I'm sorry, you're not going to like this but . . . .'

'They're taking you to court, aren't they?' cried Julia. 'I knew . . . I kept hoping they wouldn't prosecute because they wouldn't want the publicity. I'll get the best criminal lawyer, I promise –'

'What are you talking about?' interrupted Anna, now as frightened as her mother. 'The magazine isn't prosecuting. I mean . . . not as far as I know. They don't have any idea what I did. I covered my tracks.'

'But you said you told them the truth,' said Julia, in confusion. 'That you'd stolen the stuff.'

'Of course I didn't.'

'But your text. That evening in the hospital. With Dad. You said you'd been fired – for telling the truth.'

'But that wasn't about taking the clothes. I'd never tell them that! That could mean . . . I could go to prison, never get a job. Oh Mum, I'm so sorry.' And suddenly Anna hugged her impulsively, the way Rose might. 'I should have thought. I'm so sorry. The text was nothing to do with the stealing.'

'What was it, then? Anna, tell me,' said Julia, holding her daughter tightly. She could not remember the last time Anna had allowed her so close.

'It's all right,' said Anna, gently disentangling herself and then taking her mother's hand. 'You will be proud of me because I was honest, which – understandably, I know – you don't think I am any more. But you see, I was at one of the editor's posh breakfasts and the guests were talking such bollocks I got to thinking how much I hate your generation – and I do. Not you, Mum. You're not like that. But I look at so many people your age and all the greed, the arrogance, the hypocrisy . . .' Anna choked back a sob. 'Dad wasn't a hypocrite, was he?'

'No, never.'

'Dad never went around claiming he was some man of the people who understood others' suffering. He just got on with making money and then he gave all his time and energy to helping other people. Oh, but I can't talk about Dad without . . .' She wiped tears from her eyes.

'Darling,' said Julia, her tired face broken with tenderness and relief that at last Anna was not shutting her out.

'I was getting so angry and when the editor put me on the spot in front of all those people and asked what I thought I told them they were the most spoilt generation ever. And I said that had turned them into the most narcissistic, self-serving bunch of hypocrites.'

'Oh God!' Despite herself, Julia smiled, not sure whether she was appalled or impressed. 'So what happened?'

'I was ordered to leave the breakfast, then five minutes later the editor's secretary told me I was fired.'

Julia gave a faint laugh. 'Sweetheart, I've spent the last twenty years holding my tongue and listening to those whose hearts bleed for the working classes yet never go near them if they can help it.'

Tears swam in Anna's eyes. 'But I keep thinking of Dad and how he never made any pretence that he was like these trendy thinkers. And sometimes I miss Dad so much I just don't think I can bear it. And I want to tell him all this – about what I said. But I can't. Once I said to him – oh Mum, I was so horrid – I said I thought hell was full of do-gooders. Why did I say such awful things? And I can never take them back. It's too late. And I will have to live with that for the rest of my life.'

'But we all say the wrong things,' said Julia, as much to herself as her daughter. 'We all do the wrong things. None of us gets through life without wishing we had acted differently.'

'But knowing that other people fail as well is no comfort,' said Anna, echoing Julia's own thoughts.

'But why should we think we're any better?'

But Anna was not listening. 'I worry Dad used to think I didn't care – care about anything. That he felt he was on his own. He used to try and get me to read the papers, take an interest in the world, and I ignored him. But I do care. I do. But he'll never know. And I hate this world I live in, run by people like those fuckwits at that awful breakfast. There's an intellectual lethargy about them. They just do what they damn well please and cloak it in nauseatingly well-meaning words that in reality don't mean a thing. And people will suffer. They will, Mum. And I wish I could tell Dad what I said, as he might have been proud of me. Wouldn't he?'

'Oh yes, he would have been so very, very proud, though he might . . .' and for a moment Julia smiled, 'he might have suggested you moderate your language. But of course he would have been proud of you. But he was so proud anyway. How could he not be? And the thought of you now, going to Clare, to his old college. He was so thrilled for you.'

Anna put her face in her hands. 'What I was going to say to you . . . what I came in to tell you' – Anna blurted it out – 'I'm not going to Cambridge. I don't want to go to university at all. I've got a job. A friend of Phoebe's father has started up this new investment company and wants me to join them and I've said yes.'

The earth might just as well have given way under Julia's feet. 'But doing what?' she cried.

'Doing . . . well, doing . . .' Anna looked at her mother warily. 'I'll be a PA, but –'

'A secretary, in other words,' interrupted Julia, but trying to temper her feelings. This intimacy with Anna was so wonderful, so unexpected, she was terrified of jeopardizing it. But the waste, she wanted to cry, of your extraordinary gifts, the deliberate throwing away of the sort of opportunity she herself had worked so incredibly hard for. It was appalling, and she had an acute sense of herself as a single mother. She and Phillip would have handled this together. He was equally passionate about education. 'You must think about this,' she began. But that was an absurd argument. Of course Anna would have been thinking non-stop. 'You'll just be photocopying,' Julia tried again, 'and making coffee for some man.'

'Actually, Mum,' said Anna, 'it's not a man, it's a woman. Charlotte O'Neill – she's heard of you. And to begin with, yes, I'll be doing some of that boring office stuff. But I don't care because I'll be in the office of one of the top people. And she promises me I can learn so much.'

'But what did you think you'd be doing at Cambridge?'

'Learning something, of course. And I could have three very nice years having a good time and doing some maths, which would be quite interesting, I'm sure – though Phoebe's father tells me he barely gives any tutorials these days, which I always assumed were the best thing about university. Or, Mum, I can be out in the real world, learning to make my own way, which is what I really want.'

'But . . . get your degree and then do that. Or you'll have no qualifications, nothing.'

'So? Qualifications don't mean much these days.'

'Of course they do. People are obsessed with qualifications. And you'd get a first.'

'Firsts are handed out like confetti now – you know that.'

'But what happens in three years' time when all those who've been to university come to the bank on graduate trainee schemes? You'll be left behind,' pressed Julia, trying not to sound nagging and priggish. She wanted to make a case for the excitement and joy of university, but all she could do was warn her daughter of the dangers in the world.

'Half of those graduate trainees lose their job after six months,' said Anna. 'Besides, Charlotte says it would be a waste me getting hidebound by one of those recruitment systems, that if I'm as good as she thinks I am, as Phoebe's father says I am, then the sky's the limit. Forget that trainee scheme, she says. Learn on the job. Watch how decisions are made, follow her about. Even you must see what an opportunity that is.'

'Yes,' conceded Julia. 'It is. But do it in three years' time. There are no guarantees with this.'

'There are no guarantees – full stop. And the only thing I'll be guaranteed at Cambridge is debt. Look, it's up to me to make this work. And if I'm still running the photocopier three years down the line, then I'll have blown it. It'll show I'm not as clever as you all think I am. As I think I am. But maybe I could earn a fortune and take on Dad's legacy and give it away and do good things like that.'

Julia saw the passion in Anna's young face. And she was lost for words because she knew her daughter well enough to be in no doubt that argument was pointless.

'But,' she said in one last-ditch attempt, 'the education you will receive. And I don't just mean the maths. Just being there. The whole experience, the people you will meet, the beauty and history of the place. I loved all that. Education is what made me. I mean, without it I can't bear to think what I'd have become.'

'But the world's different now. Don't you see? For a lot of us, university seems an expensive waste of time, for those who haven't got the gumption to try it on their own. I don't want endless paper qualifications. I want to be out there, doing things with my brain. And maybe I don't need to go to university in the way you did because of all you gave me. All the things you longed for, I had right from the start, thanks to you. Music, books, travel . . . all that. You gave me so much.'

At this Julia squeezed Anna's hand.

'And maybe,' said Anna, the thought just occurring to her and wanting to say whatever might stop her mother looking so distressed, 'maybe I was able to speak my mind the way I did at that breakfast because I already had so much. I didn't need their rotten magazine job the way you might have done at my age. All that was thanks to you and Dad and your hard work. I'm sorry it pains you,' went on Anna, desperate for her mother to understand. Then, taking Phoebe's father advice, she said, 'But please, Mum, I need your advice. I need some work clothes. I can't wear what I normally wear, can I?'

At last, Julia smiled. 'No, you can't.'

'Perhaps we might go shopping or something?'

'Together?'

'Yes. They want me to start on Monday. So I've got to sort out what to wear.'

'Monday?'

'Eight o'clock.'

'But –'

'Should I get a suit?' interrupted Anna.

And Julia knew she might as usefully rail against the wind.

'That would be a start,' she said. The spirit had completely gone from her. 'If there are any of my clothes you'd like . . . That grey suit with the boat neckline would be good on you.'

'But don't you want it?'

'If you like it, you can have it.' Have the lot, she wanted to say, I won't be needing them. But instead she suggested, 'The colour might be nice on you – a bit softer than black. And try it with those new shoes of mine. They're higher than you normally wear, I know. But walk about in them for a bit,' she said, hearing the front door slam and Rose racing up the stairs.

'Anna?' shrieked Rose, sticking her head round the door. 'What on earth are you doing in those shoes? They're gorgeous.'

'Hello, Rose,' said Julia. 'Haven't you got homework to do?'

Julia did not want Rose here now. She wanted her elder daughter to herself. This was too precious a moment to jeopardize with Rose's forceful presence. And if they were discussing what to wear – one of Rose's favourite subjects – Rose would take over, knowing best.

'I wouldn't recognize you,' said Rose.

'I've got a job,' said Anna bluntly, 'in an investment company. I'm not going to Cambridge. And Mum's helping me sort out what to wear for the office,' went on Anna, as though that was the end of the matter.

'I see,' said Rose, not seeing at all and longing to know how Anna had won her mother round with such news. But, with a maturity beyond her years, she realized that sometimes it is wiser not to ask certain questions. Or at least bide your time.

'So what do you think?' asked Anna, quickly slipping on the grey suit to keep off the subject of Cambridge.

'Something's not quite right,' said Julia, fully aware that Anna was trying to keep her diverted. 'But Rose, your homework?'

'The skirt's too long,' said Rose, ignoring her mother. 'Particularly with those shoes – which I love – you must never, ever take them off. But the skirt needs to go up.'

'I think she's right,' said Anna, hesitantly.

'Of course I am. Just see,' smiled Rose, lifting the hem. 'Oh, I've wanted to do this for so long, Anna. All my friends let me give them make-overs.'

'Rose, don't hassle her,' said Julia, protective of Anna being upstaged by her little sister. 'Last night you were complaining you had masses of homework.'

'This is far more important,' said Rose, 'because if Anna listens to me she could have some really sexy clout in that office. And she'll need it.'

'It's not just about how you look,' murmured Julia, sitting down again. She felt so sick.

'Oh, get real, Mum. Have you any pins? No, of course you haven't. Now don't move, Anna, while I get some.'

'There,' said Rose. 'That's better. You see, Mum needs her skirts long and dowdy for her work – just kidding, Mum – but you need to lighten it up a bit. And you've got nice ankles and you should make the most of them. Really, Anna, you should. They're slim, elegant . . .'

Rose noticed a faint blush spread across her sister's pale face. Had someone complimented her ankles before? Some man? Her sister never blushed, but now her cheeks were a rosy hue.

Could it . . .? Could it possibly be love? wondered Rose. She looked at her sister's pink face in astonishment. Let it be sex at least, she thought. We need some happiness. And her elder sister's life seemed nothing but maths and more maths. But if she's giving up on university, thought Rose, something – or someone – has altered her vision. She glanced at her mother to see if Julia had noticed the strangely hopeful smile on Anna's lips. But her mother was oblivious, sitting on the window sill, gripping and ungripping her wrists, staring out at the rain pelting down outside.

Julia's eyes were drawn to the patch of sodden ground at the front of the house. Under the street light, she could see that the frail narcissi Phillip loved had forced themselves up through the muddy grass. Tulip leaves and hyacinths were piercing their way out of the waterlogged soil. Soon all the chaos of oncoming spring would be there, even in a tiny London garden.

'Mum,' pressed Rose, 'Mum, please, what do you think?'

Julia turned away from the rain and looked at her elder daughter. 'It's perfect,' she said. 'Try it on with one of my white shirts.'

But then, the wave of sickness that had been threatening for the past half-hour overwhelmed her, and she raced to the bathroom.

Julia tried to avoid her daughters' anxious faces.

'Mum, you've got to tell us,' begged Rose, when her mother emerged from the bathroom. 'What's wrong?'

'Nothing, just a bug. I'll be all right in a couple of days.'

'Don't lie to us,' said Anna. 'We hear you being sick all the time and never eating. And Angela is so worried.'

Then Rose burst into tears. 'I've been too scared to ask, but I keep thinking you've got cancer and –'

'Sweetheart, no! No! It's nothing.'

'How can it be nothing,' cried Rose, 'if you die . . .' Sobs choked her.

'My darling,' said Julia, putting her arms around her daughter. 'It's nothing terrible. Really.' Julia could not admit to her daughters, I'm pregnant and am going to have an abortion. 'It's just . . .'

'Just what?' demanded Anna.

'Just still in shock,' said Julia. 'About Dad.'

'I don't believe you,' whimpered Rose. 'All my friends reckon you've got cancer and that I should know the worst. But Rose B wondered if you might be pregnant.'

Julia winced. Anna saw it. 'Oh Mum, are you? You're not . . .?'

Julia recognized the understanding in Anna's eyes. Even as accomplished an actor as Julia could not lie to her daughters when they were looking at her with such concern and love. She gave a weak nod, then steeled herself.

But to her eternal surprise, Anna cried out, 'Oh Mum! This is wonderful news.'

Then Rose was hugging her tightly, saying, 'I'm so happy, I'm so happy. I can't believe it! Part of Dad, living on.'

No! No! thought Julia. This will be a new life with its own gifts and demons. Not your father.

'This is the best possible news,' cried Anna. 'I was so worried. But now, oh thank God. And I'll help, I promise. Don't you see? Not going to Cambridge, I'll be around.'

But I don't need your help, Julia was about to insist. Besides, you'll be working. And I'm not going to have the baby. I can't.

'And I can help too,' said Rose.

'Thank you, thank you,' said Julia. 'But . . .'

But what? Was she going to say she was having an abortion?

When she had been debating whether to have the baby, she had wondered over and over how her daughters would react if she did. Not for a minute had she expected such excitement and love.

'To watch a new life unfold after all we've been through,' Anna was saying, uncharacteristically sentimental.

'Why didn't you tell us before?' demanded Rose. 'We needed something good to happen.'

Because, Julia wanted to say, you need such superfluous energy in bringing up a child, which I don't have.

'Don't you see how lucky we are?' Anna was saying. 'A baby to hold, to cuddle, to help grow up.'

Julia said nothing. It occurred to her that, if she did not act fast, the decision would be taken out of her hands.

'I love the idea of a baby in the house,' said Rose, stroking her mother's hand. 'I didn't think . . . well, it never occurred to me before.'

Then Anna asked, 'When's it due?'

I must speak now, thought Julia. I have to stop this outpouring of love, this minute. Her mind raced hither and thither, searching for what to say. But she sat absolutely passive.

She contemplated her future as she had thought it would be, as she had planned it, with Phillip. But she might just as well be reliving a dream. The last few weeks had brought her widowhood. And motherhood. But motherhood without Phillip brought no thoughts of happiness. The idea of little feet, soft baby curls, a tiny, trusting hand taking hers, gave her no pleasure. Yet she realized she could not destroy her daughters' joy. She would have to have this baby now. Whatever the consequences.

'When?' declared Anna.

Julia breathed. 'August.'

'I'm even more glad I'm not going away,' said Anna. 'Imagine if I'd had to leave a new baby brother or sister.'

'But you mustn't,' Julia said, choosing her words carefully, 'let this stop you getting on with your lives –'

'This *is* our life,' interrupted Anna.

'You might feel differently when you're kept awake all night by crying,' said Julia, as much to herself as the girls.

'I don't sleep much, anyway,' said Anna. 'It can sleep with me.'

'And me,' said Rose.

'No, no. None of that bed-hopping. It'll have to get into a routine.'

'Stop, Mum!' cried Anna. 'Before you start organizing it, let's see who the baby is.'

'But you don't understand,' said Julia. 'Some women let their babies ruin . . . well, not ruin their lives, but dominate them in a way that's not good for anyone – the mother, the baby, the rest of the family.'

'Meet that problem when the time comes,' insisted Anna. 'Really, Mum, if you stop running things, the world won't collapse into chaos. Nor will you. Or us.'

'And maybe, with a baby in the house,' said Rose, 'you'll be a bit more indulgent towards us.'

'You speak as if you're kept under lock and key.'

'Well, maybe I am. Because the thing is,' said Rose, 'please can we talk about this baby in a minute. Though I am pleased. Truly. But since this is confession day, I've got one too.'

For one ghastly moment Julia thought Rose too was going to announce that she was pregnant.

'Now, I know you've not got so much work . . .'

That was an understatement, thought Julia, but she felt there had been enough news for one afternoon without letting her daughters know she was also out of a job.

'And what with the baby, even you will have to take some time off. So I want to help. To make money.'

'But we're lucky,' said Julia. 'We're all right. Your father was a wealthy man. And there's insurance money. At least in the short term, nothing's going to change –'

'But I want to make it for *myself*. Can't you understand? You, of all people, should know that.'

'Is this about modelling again?'

'Yes.'

Julia recalled the dreadful last day with Phillip. That morning – that morning when she would have first been pregnant – Phillip had asked her to reconsider letting Rose model.

'Please,' her daughter was saying.

Julia was learning in a hard school how little power she had. She could not stop her children making mistakes. She could not stop them making their own choices. She could not, as she would have loved in the past, give her daughters her own hard-won experience. Because where had that experience led her?

'Will you just think about it?' asked Rose. 'Instead of writing the idea off?'

'Okay, I'll think,' said Julia. The fight had gone out of her. 'But no promises.'

'Of course,' said Rose, a picture of restraint, but Julia noticed the triumphant glint in her eyes.

'But now, Anna,' went on Rose, hurriedly changing the subject in case her mother snatched away this victory, 'you're going to need lots of clothes. There's this great website which has the sort of clothes just perfect for you. That honorary boy look that you like.'

Julia watched Anna leave the room to fetch her iPad. Even at eighteen, she thought, Anna seems too slight and vulnerable to be embracing the world. Yet what option do I have but to let her make her own way? None. She no longer felt qualified to offer advice. She lay back on the bed. Outside she could hear the rain, beating down with real passion now, working its way into the earth, endlessly renewing that eternal stream of birth. And, thanks to her daughters, she had found herself caught up in it once more, forced to continue, whether she wanted to or not.

'Mum,' said Rose, whispering to be sure Anna could not hear. 'I know you're worried about Anna not going to Cambridge. But you really mustn't,' she insisted. 'I promise you. I think she's got a boyfriend.'

'Really?' How many more surprises would the day bring? 'But who?'

'Don't know,' shrugged Rose. 'And she certainly wouldn't tell me. You know what she's like. But she looks happy. Doesn't she? Sort of pleased with herself.'

'Well, yes, she does,' agreed Julia, thinking, oh please, let her have found some man to pour all that affection into.

'And she's found fashion,' Rose went on. 'Fashion and love.'

Despite herself, Julia smiled. 'Fashion and love?'

'So she'll be fine. They'll get her through.'

'But seriously –'

'I am serious,' said Rose, riffling through Julia's wardrobe once more. 'Now this tweed of yours,' she said, trying on a shapely, narrow skirt. 'I've always loved it. May I have it? I mean, let's face it, you'll soon be too fat.'

# Epilogue

Isabel West was tired, her eyes hurt, her thin legs felt heavy, but she ran up the three flights of stairs to what was now her own room at the top of Patrick Cusack's home. All day she had washed brushes for Patrick, sorted and stacked the new consignment of paints, mixed oils for Laura, answered phones, filed letters. She had also spent two hours drawing, with Patrick looking over her shoulder, criticizing her relentlessly, edging her forward, making her do better.

It was almost eighteen months since she had met Laura in the churchyard at Phillip Snowe's funeral and now her life was better in ways she could never have imagined. And she had Laura to thank. Laura had arranged everything. Laura, from the moment of the meeting that had changed Isabel's life, had taken charge.

Isabel had not wanted to go to the funeral. But her mother had said Phillip had been so kind to her. So she had gone and she had been in bits afterwards because her mother was right, he had been kind but she had been ungrateful and rude to him. And there had been so much kindness since – more than she ever thought possible. If she had not gone to the funeral . . . It did not bear thinking about. But life turns on a sixpence, her mother said. And this time it had turned in her favour.

She lay down a moment on the bed and touched the picture by her side, of her mother's face. Patrick had painted it for her and it was her mother exactly, but he had seen beyond her illness and given her, thought Isabel, the beauty she had been robbed of.

Isabel rubbed away a tear. Just weeks after Phillip's funeral, her mother had moved into a residential home nearby, and that hour-by-hour anxiety which her mother's illness had placed upon her young shoulders had lifted.

She looked around the light airy room, the May sunshine filtering through large windows. Still, Isabel could not quite believe she was living in the famous Patrick Cusack's house with his wife, like part of the family. She was doing what she loved – what her mother had longed for her to experience – learning to paint. That strange joy she had known – even in the midst of the Hartley Estate – that wonderful vitality when she was drawing had not been an illusion. She was good at art. It was not a lie. She truly was. More than that, Patrick Cusack, a man with work in the National Portrait Gallery, no less – and Isabel had to keep pinching herself – told her she was an artist.

*An artist.* She kept repeating the words to herself. Though she had overheard Laura telling Patrick to ease up, to stop pressurizing her, saying that Isabel was also a teenager who had experienced more than her fair share of the darkness, and she needed to discover some lightness too.

But Laura does not understand, thought Isabel. I want to be pushed to the limit. I'm too hungry to mess about. I need to learn. Come the autumn, she was going to start at art school, even though Patrick kept trumpeting on that she would learn more with him and Laura. But Laura insisted Isabel needed to meet people her own age and have her own friends. So Laura had made Patrick exert some influence at the art school where he was honorary chair and get her a place, even though she did not have any A-levels.

But I will work from now on, Isabel repeated like a mantra, getting up from the bed. Because I will never, ever go back to the Hartley Estate, she promised herself for the millionth time, fetching a sequinned jacket from her wardrobe.

The jacket was a present from Laura, and Isabel hesitated a moment in front of the mirror, admiring herself – a novel experience.

Laura had said the jacket suited her, that it gave her a magical, silvery look. Laura was right, realized Isabel. She had never looked so pretty in anything, and Isabel had said she would save the jacket for best. But Laura suggested Isabel try and make something 'best' about every day, even if it was only for those moments of catching sight of herself in the beautiful jacket. So now she was putting it on just to fetch the twins from school, as their nanny was at the dentist and Laura was busy painting.

She brushed her hair – Laura had taken her to a decent hairdresser's – admired the way it framed her face, then ran down the stairs quietly so as not to wake Venetia, who slept in the afternoons, and out to the studio to let Laura know she was leaving.

Isabel had expected Laura to be working. But Laura was standing by the window, her forehead leaning against the pane. Laura's features, Isabel noticed, were very strained, her cheeks drawn, her brow creased. This was what Patrick was always telling her to do. To 'look'. But she had no idea what Laura's 'look' actually revealed.

She could not understand Laura. She adored the woman. That went without saying. Laura had solved problems Isabel had believed beyond the wit of anyone. But she had no idea what Laura was thinking half the time.

Was Laura happy? At first glance you would think so. And how could she not be? was a question Isabel asked herself. Certainly, in Laura's shoes, Isabel would be on top of the world because one of the most prestigious London galleries wanted to put on an exhibition of her flower paintings. It would do well, Isabel was convinced. Patrick said so too when he had discussed it with Isabel. He thought Laura's work was very special – and Patrick, Isabel had discovered herself, rarely paid compliments. Isabel liked that about him. She thought it great the way he ranted and raged if something wasn't good enough. She knew where she was then. She could learn. And she was improving, so much and so fast, she could feel that power in her. And it was intoxicating and wonderful because it told her that life could be good.

'Laura,' she called, putting her head round the studio door. 'I'm just off to get the girls.'

'You're early,' said Laura, turning round hurriedly and glancing at the clock. 'They don't need collecting till four.'

'I know, but I want to sit on the heath and watch people. Patrick tells me I need to look at faces. Just look and look, he says.'

'Does he now?' murmured Laura, who was concerned that Isabel was taking every word her father said as gospel truth.

'He also says,' went on Isabel, 'that beauty can take time to reveal itself.'

At this, Laura smiled. Her father was writing his autobiography – or rather, yelling an inventive work of fiction to his secretary – and she wondered whether this was a line he was going to use. 'Well, it's a gorgeous day,' said Laura. 'Enjoy it.'

'I thought I'd take the girls to the park, if you want. Give you another hour or so to work,' she said.

Isabel saw the hesitation on Laura's face and knew exactly what it meant – Laura felt guilty that she had not seen much of the twins lately.

Though God knows why, thought Isabel. They were perfectly fine. In fact, they were more than fine. Isabel wished they could be a bit quieter and go to bed a lot earlier but on the whole they were pretty good, as far as children went, amenable and cheeky in a pleasant enough way.

'You can finish that,' went on Isabel, nodding at Laura's painting.

'Well, yes . . . thank you. It's taking longer than I thought.'

'You always say that,' said Isabel.

'Before you rush off, tell me what you think of it.'

Laura was painting a series of oils of white blossom against white clouds. Technically, Patrick had told Isabel, his daughter was brilliant. And Isabel could see that. But what Laura's also done in these pictures, Patrick had told Isabel in private, was capture the bliss and freedom of silence. And that's great, he said, because that's the sort of picture people like to have on their sitting-room walls, so that would make Laura's work really commercial and pots of money would cheer Laura up no end. But, Patrick had gone on, silence can also be pretty damned melancholy, so there's only a very fine line between silence being heaven or hell. And if Laura wants to make money, she needs to make sure she doesn't cross it.

'I think . . .' ventured Isabel. Although she was pleased and flattered to be asked her opinion, she found it almost impossible to put what she felt into words. 'I just want to keep looking at it,' she said.

'High praise,' smiled Laura, 'thank you.'

'And . . .'

'And what?' Laura nudged gently, inordinately protective of this skinny, troubled girl.

All Laura's instincts made her want to shield Isabel, standing there with her new eagerness for life in her sequinned jacket. If she could just guard Isabel for a few years, give Isabel faith in herself and a taste of the goodness of life, it would be like money in the bank, something for Isabel to draw upon over the coming years so she could turn her considerable powers into something creative rather than destructive. Then, at least, some good might have come from Phillip's death.

'It's beautiful but sad at the same time,' said Isabel, wishing she could explain herself in more impressive words.

Laura sat down for a moment. She was fighting the sadness the whole time, summoning all her formidable creativity as the cure for forgetfulness. Because she thought she could drown her grief in work and the sense of success her painting was giving her. She knew there could be no quick fix, that in the relentless, mindless tasks of daily life – making tea, putting the girls to bed, glancing at the papers – Phillip would be on her mind. She would try to recall his every word. But they were fading. He had said he loved her. But how? She could hear the sound of the radiator ticking in her room, the bus pulling up outside, those mundane irrelevancies. But what was the exact inflexion of his voice? Was it the 'I love you' of a fleeting moment of passion? Or the 'I love you' of commitment?

There was no answer, but her yearning for Phillip, and the life she had hoped she might share with him, invaded her painting. A hint of despair touched these white flowers on white.

She should have known herself better. Work, however exhilarating, was not enough. At least, not for her. Even when she thought she was concentrating with every ounce of her being, she remembered. And in remembering, her sadness resurrected itself, as potent as ever.

If poets talked of love being like sickness, they were wrong. When she was ill she wanted to be better, to be free of whatever was ailing her. But she was frightened to be free of Phillip because, if she ever forgot him, something within her might die as well.

The last year had proved she was not an artist like her father. His art was where he found the meaning of life. He had such a singularity of vision and need, his work satisfied on all fronts. But it was different for her. She had thrown herself into her painting with as much passion as she could muster, but it could not fill this abyss inside her.

Her work was good. She could see the power there, but she wanted to reach out with that power and share that intensity with a similar soul. Then her mind would return to Phillip and her fear that, for the rest of her life, this sadness would remain.

The sadness would dim, of course. And consolations would come her way. Yet her need for that other human being remained unrequited. And she would find herself with her head against the window pane, longing for what she could not have.

'Laura?'

'Oh, sorry,' said Laura, returning her attention to Isabel.

'Your dad says they won't make so much money if they're too sad. Some wistfulness is good, but don't overdo it.'

Laura laughed. 'Well, when it comes to money, he certainly knows what he's talking about. Not that I'm knocking it. Far from it,' she added. 'But here.' She found her purse. 'Go and have a coffee, take the girls to that new cake shop – but don't let them have anything too sugary.'

Isabel hesitated. Laura had told her that she more than earned her keep, that all her help with the painting, the children, around the house, was invaluable. But Isabel knew Laura just said that to make her feel good. Laura gave her far too much.

'Go on,' said Laura, 'you can sit and look at the people in the café. You love all that.'

'Well, thank you, thank you.'

I'll pay her back one day, Isabel told herself, going out into the spring sunshine. She would. She knew it. She would be a success and make a lot of money, and the spring day, all blossom and soft new leaf, seemed to be agreeing with her. Even the calm, cloudless sky felt on her side and, enjoying the sun sweet on her shoulders, she walked over to the heath and sat on a bench near one of the children's parks.

It was busier than usual today and Isabel cast around, looking at the new faces brought out by the spring warmth. On the bench opposite sat a woman with a baby asleep beside her in a pushchair.

The woman's long dark hair was pulled back from her pale face. There were lines of sorrow about her eyes, a foreboding in the cast of her mouth. Yet, thought Isabel, watching the woman's concentration upon her child, there is still a suggestion of loveliness about her. To Isabel, the older woman's anxiety and age were of purely academic interest. Such pain and loss did not frighten her. This woman was simply an unusual subject. And Isabel sat quietly and viewed the woman with an artist's eye.

Julia had pushed her nine-month-old son across the heath thinking, not for the first time, how she loved this boy more than her daughters. It was wrong, of course, to have favourites, but this little boy's inauspicious start to life, the fact that he would never know his father, the sense that the odds were not as stacked in his favour as they might have been, made her even fonder and all the more protective of him.

From the moment her newborn baby was placed in her arms she was bowled over by her feelings, because they were so very unexpected. During her pregnancy, she had feared that her ambivalence towards this new life might continue once he was born. Or worse, that she would want nothing to do with him.

At best, she had hoped she would react as she had with the girls.

With them, when a nurse placed the red, yelling infant in her arms her first thought had been, can't you take it? Haven't I done enough? Yet with Phillip by her side, she had loved these helpless creatures. But she had also been mightily relieved to be able to afford to pay others to endure some of the slavery of looking after them.

But something changed with this boy. It was not that she had suddenly discovered new joys of motherhood. The last eighteen months had been the toughest she had ever known. When, as a teenager, life had been hard, her difficulties had always been leavened by a sense of hope that she would set herself free and take command of her destiny. But not now.

Julia had not whinged or railed against the unfairness of life – that she had lost her husband, that her children had no father. Not once had she blamed anyone else, nor deceived herself to assuage her own sense of responsibility. *He was wounded for our transgressions; He was bruised for our iniquities.* That Easter lesson hounded her, because she knew she had transgressed. Phillip had tried to be good, to serve. But she had wounded, she had bruised. Phillip had been acquainted with grief, yet she had been blind to his sorrows. She wished she might pray, as Phillip had done, to some God who might help her. But she had no faith there was a God who could help her understand the world she now lived in.

Her rational, organized mind had been flung from its familiar channels. Her rather narrow vision had been forced to expand, to accept she had problems she could never solve. She had caused hurt and could never make amends. The life she believed she held in her grip had been taken away from her as easily as sweets from a child.

After the collapse of the Clifford James case she, who had once been so in demand, so respected, had been cold-shouldered and had only recently found work as a part-time support lawyer in what she had once derided as 'Mummy Valley', on a fraction of her old salary and with not a jot of the prestige.

But out of all the chaos of loss, violence and death, by some awesome serendipity, had come this child, unplanned, unwanted. He defied all Julia had believed in. Right from the start, she found it hard to tear herself away from this new life. Her amazing genius of a boy taught himself to smile! Then to sit! And now he could crawl! Why she found such utterly ordinary behaviour so absorbing she could not explain. Because it was so primal? So vital? She was not quite sure. But, as she sat under the budding horse chestnuts in the spring sunshine, she had the sense not to question too closely.

Julia never used to sit like this, but then her shoulders never ached like this, her legs never felt so heavy. She was conscious of every one of her forty-six years, that she had lost the exuberance and energy she once had and this child demanded. He was a burden. That fact was inescapable. But she did not battle any longer against the servitude. Her boy stirred in his sleep and she looked on him with love. But she begged him not to wake so she could have a moment's more peace.

When Anna and Rose were born, they had slotted easily into a routine of her making. But this boy would not conform to her timetable.

He slept when he wanted, woke when it suited him and just yelled his head off if the mood took him. It drove Julia to distraction and she worried that the girls would resent the endless intrusion and interruption. But they had surprised her, and they had delighted her.

'You'll have to put me in handcuffs to stop me picking him up if he's crying,' Rose had told her.

Anna had said, 'So often when someone needs help there's not much you can do for them. But a crying child, you can transform their world with a cuddle. There's none of that helplessness,' she had gone on in a rather embarrassed tone, 'that you feel in the face of other people's helplessness.'

Other people's helplessness had become a mission for Anna. In her spare time from her job, she was searching for causes and trying to create a better world in a way that worried Julia. Anna seemed to have set herself an impossible task, working for justice when her father had been killed by random violence. And violence that had gone unpunished because the police, with almost nothing to go on, had never tracked down the mugger who shoved Phillip to the ground.

'Dad would be proud of me, wouldn't he?' Anna kept asking, in a way that wrung Julia's heart.

Yet Anna was happy. To Julia the sight of her awkward, brilliant child having friends she genuinely seemed to enjoy, having work she loved, was a miracle. The director who had given her the job was taking her to a conference in Tokyo next week and the company was paying for her to learn Japanese. Also, in what Rose called Anna's 'saving the world' mission, she gave maths tuition at Hartley High in a special Saturday-morning class. Plus, Julia learned, she was giving away 15 per cent of her income to the hospice Phillip had worked for.

Phillip . . .

Julia closed her eyes for a moment.

Phillip, with all his visions of a better world, had been killed trying to do good. But had all his good works made the slightest difference? She had told the girls they had. But had they really? He had enriched her life immeasurably. And their daughters' lives. He would have good reason to be proud of them. But my darling boy, she thought, stroking his hand as he lashed out in his sleep. Her son would grow up never knowing his father. And some day she would have to explain why, to describe the man his father had been.

Phillip was 'a good man'. That is what she would tell her son. Julia had always thought that to sleep easy in her bed she simply needed to work hard and use her intelligence. But I was wrong, she berated herself in the middle of long, wakeful nights. I should have been kind. In my arrogance and stupidity, I should have realized. I should have been kind, like Phillip.

Her baby began stirring, opening his eyes. Don't wake, thought Julia, stroking him gently. She was going out tonight and did not want to be tired. It was Rose's birthday and Rose was taking her and Anna, Angela and Angela's new husband, James, and Mirela out to dinner. Rose was paying, using her first cheque from her modelling.

A few months ago, Rose had taken her aside. 'Some of my

friends,' Rose had explained, 'think they have years and years before they grow up. I don't mean have sex, drink and so on. I mean properly grow up – take responsibility for themselves. But I don't want to be like that. And the modelling – I know it seems shallow to you – but it's something I might be able to do, to make some money for myself. And if you think I'm being irresponsible, letting it go to my head in some stupid way, or not eating, say – I know Dad always worried about that – I'll stop, I promise. But let me prove to you I can be sensible. Please, Mum.'

And so far, Rose had proved herself. And tonight she was so proud to be taking them all out to dinner. 'This is my treat,' she kept saying.

Both her daughters had found their own way forward. And it was not her way. The world, she had to tell herself, was different and they were different from her. But through no planning of hers – through its opposite, in fact – she was now close to them in a way she had never thought possible.

Julia looked apprehensively at her son, his eyes still closed. Heaven knew what lay ahead for him.

This little boy had opened new doors for her, shown her worlds she had never before encountered. One minute he reduced her universe to the size of a baby's cot and she would watch the way he kicked for joy, murmured in his sleep, his fierce concentration when he grabbed her finger, and she would find herself carried away by love, her entire vision concentrated on this small being, not wanting to miss a second.

But at the next moment, she would feel herself swept up in a colossal, chaotic current of humanity, all belting headlong for better or for worse, to some unsuspected destination. Just driving to the heath that afternoon she had seen the newspaper billboards about another dreadful massacre in the Middle East. In the corner shop where she had stopped to buy some water she heard the two o'clock news – an eighteen-year-old soldier shot dead. It took so little for kindness to turn to hatred, for confidence to become fear, for the familiar security of home to be terrorized in a world where men and women were cruel.

She looked anxiously at her son.

Would he know pain and fear? Or wealth and ease, she thought, as he chuckled in his sleep. However passionately she worked to cherish him, how on earth could she keep him safe?

Once she might have had answers. But not now.

She looked at the children charging around her, and the thought of them being threatened by ignorance and poverty and brutality made her stomach lurch. I know, she thought, what it is to grow up without a father. I know what it is to live day in, day out with the sickness of someone you love. I know what it is when death splinters your family. But these silly, screaming, smiling children, knowing the joy in the flowers on a sunlit day, dear God, protect them.

What had happened to her to make her so frightened? She felt no wiser from her experience. No better able to advise, to bring up her child. Her own mother used to say that you learn wisdom in the school of hard knocks. Julia always found the cliché maddening and would tell her mother so. Besides, Julia had spent her life doing her best to avoid those hard knocks. But now she had had them. And she felt more foolish than ever. All she had discovered was her own frailty, how little control she had, however hard she tried.

But her beautiful boy was awake now, well and truly, and she forced herself to concentrate on him. She picked him up, kissing his velvety face. At once he stopped crying and fixed her with his enormous smile.

She sat still for a moment, clutching him. The delight he could bring her was among the most profound she had ever known. She held him tighter but his feet and fists pounded into her. He hated to stay still. Anna and Rose had not been like this. She could picture them both sitting quietly in Phillip's lap. Oh Phillip. She stifled a cry. Phillip.

But this little boy's legs were kicking her, as if to say, get walking, get moving to wherever, happiness or tragedy. You must keep moving.

She stood up, feeling her age pressing upon her, and glanced across at a young woman opposite, wearing a pretty sequinned jacket that made her look, thought Julia, both fragile and fearless, as I once was. But I have to quash my fears, Julia told herself, for the sake of this new life, this new life Phillip will never know. I must.

Because this young boy is the life after death.

She buried her face in his soft neck, breathed in his warmth and sweetness and whispered his name. 'Alexander.' This had been Anna's suggestion, after Alexander the Great, son of Philip of Macedon. All the potential was there in his little body, eager and questing. She looked into his blue eyes, Phillip's eyes, she thought, he will have Phillip's eyes. And he will know Phillip's kindness. I can pass that gift on to him. I can give him that certainty.

He smiled at her and Julia smiled back, her magnificent, confident, beautiful smile. Then, holding her strong, hearty boy close, his eyes everywhere, alert and hungry, she wandered back to her car, through the children fighting and playing, crying and laughing, past the swings and roundabouts. She had things to do. Feed Alexander, put him to bed, get ready for tonight. And for a brief moment her world fell into place and she was buoyed up on that release when the fragments fall into place and life makes a fleeting sort of sense.